"MEISELMAN" IS A TRI
COMIC ESCALATION.
— SAM LIPSYTE, AUTHOR OF
"HARK" AND "THE ASK"

AUTHOR
Landes, Avner

TITLE
Meiselman: The Lean Years

DATE LOANED	BORROWER'S NAME	DATE RETURNED

DO YOURSELF A BIG FAVOR AND READ THIS BOOK.
— BINNIE KIRSHENBAUM, AUTHOR OF "RABBITS FOR FOOD"

Praise for *Meiselman*

"*Meiselman: The Lean Years* is a triumph of comic escalation, as well as a rich, witty exploration of the major elements of life, including family, community, love, work, ambition, faith, and ritual, not to mention the unforgettable power-hitting of the legendary Frank Thomas, AKA 'The Big Hurt.' Meiselman is a compelling figure, trapped between a craving for the validation of his world and a desire to somehow escape it, and Landes charts his unraveling with deadpan precision and a deep commitment to capturing both the horror and hilarity of living inside certain American and Jewish and Jewish-American paradoxes. While reminiscent of past astonishers like Stanley Elkin and Bruce Jay Friedman, Landes comes to the plate with a stance and a style all his own."

— Sam Lipsyte, author of *Hark* and *The Ask*

"Avner Landes's debut novel echoes the later work of Isaac Singer set in the modern Orthodox community in Chicago. Equally, it calls to mind the contemporary novels and stories of Sam Lipsyte. Here you have the Channukah gift to end all Channukah gifts. Seriously funny—*painfully* serious and hilariously funny—*Meiselman: The Lean Years* is the literary equivalent of Charlie Chaplin slipping on a banana peel. Do yourself a big favor and read this book."

— Binnie Kirshenbaum, author of *Rabbits for Food*

"*Meiselman: The Lean Years* is a rich buffet of novelistic pleasures, including vivid characters, a finely textured portrait of the Jewish suburbs of Chicago, and a series of tragic-hilarious set pieces that simultaneously make you smile and cringe in recognition. Avner Landes delves into the head and heart of his comic hero with dexterous and supple prose that thrills and surprises on every page."

— Aaron Hamburger, author of *Nirvana Is Here*

"Landes's darkly funny debut chronicles a suburban schlemiel's endless capacity for self-sabotage....Meiselman's delusions of grandeur repeatedly collide with reality, to tragic and hilarious effect."

—***Publishers Weekly***

"Meiselman is miserable: under-sexed, overworked, a human receptacle for small humiliations. Thankfully, Avner Landes is a superlative chronicler of American Jewish middle-aged male misery, bringing to mind the Bruce Jay Friedman of *Stern* and the Saul Bellow of *Herzog* in this funny, lively, rendering of one man's *tsuris*."

— **Adam Wilson, author of *Sensation Machines***

"If Saul Bellow wrote a comedy of manners set in the Bush years, it would resemble Avner Landes's very funny and ribald *Meiselman: The Lean Years*. Combining the workplace comedy and a portrait of a marriage, this rollicking tour through Meiselman's agitations and mortifications is both a treat and a trick of Landes's sharp and fluid prose."

— **Leland Cheuk, author of *No Good Very Bad Asian***

"If you like Nikolai Gogol's comic stories about put-upon underdogs, or John Kennedy O'Toole's *Confederacy of Dunces*, about the life of a misshapen man, or if you like Sam Lipsyte's insane comedy of a feckless antihero, *The Ask*, or even if you like Saul Bellow's ebullient novel of middle-aged collapse, *Seize the Day*, then you will love Avner Landes's comic novel *Meiselman*, a novel that belongs on the same shelf as these books."

— **Joseph G. Peterson, author of *The Rumphulus***

Meiselman

Avner Landes

Meiselman

The Lean Years

Avner Landes

Tortoise Books

Chicago, IL

FIRST EDITION, MARCH, 2021

Published in the United States by Tortoise Books.
www.tortoisebooks.com

ISBN-13: 978-1-948954-14-3

Cover design by Gerald Brennan. Shutterstock images 403810543, 646825078, 85434244, and 1339970315 used per standard license agreement.

For Dalia

I’ll show them. They—they can’t make small of me. – *McTeague*, Frank Norris

In baseball, you can't kill the clock. You've got to give the other man his chance. That's why this is the greatest game. – Earl Weaver

The Day Before

Unable to tuck away recent humiliations, Meiselman rocked listlessly in his oldfangled swivel chair. Skeletal and thinly cushioned, it squealed like a distressed baby seal. He grabbed a number two pencil off his desk, drew out his thumbs, and, teeth gritting, pressed against the implement's midsection. On the brink of the snap, he pulled back.

The second humiliation, the one after Shenkenberg's slight over the phone, was proving too much for Meiselman to bear. How his boss Ethel had yelled at him. Barked across the hallway through her open office door. "Are you kidding me, Meiselman? Can you not follow a simple instruction?" Loud enough for the other administrators in the back offices to hear, the underlings' faces surely twitchy with smirks and mock horror over the number two's apparent comeuppance. Rarely did she yell like this. Never before had she directed such fury at him.

He did not blame Ethel for the humiliation. "Meiselman, you are not to talk to him," she had repeatedly instructed him since finalizing the Shenkenberg appearance over a month ago. What logical reason could she have for placing such a restriction on her Events and Programs Coordinator, her number two? Shenkenberg must have put her in this intolerable position. In the past, speakers had issued irrational demands regarding specific sound systems, guarantees over minimum and maximum crowds, and food—they all expected to be fed—and in each case Meiselman, through Ethel's direction, had rejected the demands. "We are not running a soup kitchen," Ethel liked to say.

Shenkenberg, however, was different. Shenkenberg was a draw, a major one at a time when Ethel was selling an expansion to the village, so Meiselman had no choice but to comply with the author's most unreasonable demand that he speak to no one except Ethel, the library's director and number one.

Helpless to hush the sulky whistle jetting from his nostrils, his deadeye stare out his office door fixed on his boss across the hall, who stood in front of her desk, achy back to Meiselman, arms spread, hands clutching the desk's edges, a poring-over-battle-maps posture. The arms and shoulders of a swimmer. Not a dasher, but a long-distancer or butterfly specialist. Immense, yet elegantly hewn from hours spent kickboxing. Meiselman, who stood several inches taller, always felt shorter next to Ethel. He liked that at any time of the day he could lean left and take in one of her exciting pairs of heels and the fat rose tattoo above her ankle, its red petals and green leaves thick and rich like birthday cake frosting. Get too close and the thorns would slice, a sting he would feel only later in the shower.

Ethel finally called him into her office, and as he crossed the hallway from his office to hers, Meiselman determined he was willing to apologize for violating her instruction to not contact Shenkenberg directly, but would reiterate the absurdity of trying to plan a gala event with such a restriction in place. He might also mention how he did not appreciate the dismissive, annoyed tone Shenkenberg took with him, or the way Ethel dressed him down in front of his subordinates.

Stepping into her office, he spotted her hands underneath her white blouse, clutching at her back. She cried, "It's really radiating today. Grab my coat will you? And the bag," by which she meant her purse, which was the size of a gym bag and the color of split pea soup. Its cumbersome buckles on the flap pockets were purposeless. Magnetic snaps kept the pockets closed. When Ethel showed up with it last month, she'd joked to Ada, the only other marginally fashionable woman in the office, that the bag cost as much as a baby from the Far East. Its color matched Ethel's fingernails, down to the shade.

Escorting his boss to the car, Meiselman shuffled down the hallway half a step behind, trying to come up with a manly, or less womanly, way of handling the purse. He tried clutching it by its handles, as if holding a satchel of money, but he feared he was creating crippling stretch marks in the purse's leather. He settled for a forearm cradling.

In the middle of the hallway, Ethel stopped them at the alcove, where her secretary, Betsy Ross, sat behind her L-shaped desk eating macaroni and cheese from a Tupperware, a gossip rag flat on her keyboard. Ethel tapped the desk's edge and inquired about a letter. Betsy Ross responded with a nod and wink. Meiselman was unsure whether he understood the understanding. As Ethel and Meiselman stepped away, Betsy Ross called after him.

"Meiselman," she said. "The purse suits you."

Not everything about being the number two is glamorous, he wanted to answer the secretary, who every day paired tan pants that tugged on her crotch with a white blouse whose short sleeves exposed pale, rashy triceps. But he stayed quiet, and they continued down the hallway, Meiselman still a half-step behind his boss.

Mitchell was waiting for Ethel and Meiselman outside his office, which was next to the exit door. Shoulder leaned against his office doorjamb, hands resting on the handle of his umbrella, its tip digging the hallway's linoleum, the library's IT specialist updated Ethel on his outlandish plans for the expansion. "You're the boss," she said, nothing more than perfunctory encouragement so she could continue on her way.

Ethel winced in pain as she pressed her hip into the door's metal bar. Meiselman swung his arm around to assist, and right as the door to the parking lot cracked open, the stormy gray sunlight framing the door, Mitchell halted their departure once again, this time with a bellow of Meiselman's name.

"Something you want to tell us, mate?" he added.

Meiselman mustered a sullen stare Mitchell's way, but the IT specialist read Meiselman's glowering as incomprehension and lifted his umbrella to stab the purse's body. He bounced his hip off the doorway, leaned forward, and, flashing his crooked, coffee-stained teeth, cackled in Meiselman's face. Mitchell accentuated the laugh with a brotherly cuff of Meiselman's neck, glancing at Ethel for recognition. Ethel feigned mild amusement.

The hairy-knuckled, shiny-fingernailed hand of Mitchell relaxed on Meiselman's shoulder, and he resumed discussing with Ethel his plans for the library's digital future. If this man who spent his days fixing printers and disassembling motherboards was not spoiling Meiselman's new lavender dress shirt with his touching, he was, at the very least, putting a wrinkle in it, and Meiselman was fed up, literally and figuratively, with everyone putting their dirty paws on him. This would be the moment when he would stop taking it from the Shenkenbergs, the Betsy Rosses, and the Mitchells of the world. After thirty-six years, Meiselman had reached a limit, a breaking point. Eyes bugging, forehead flushing, Meiselman grabbed the purse by its handles, and using his free hand, he grabbed Mitchell by the forearm and pressed his thumb against the wrist's jutting bone. "Never put your hands on me uninvited," Meiselman said, coolly. Mitchell drew his hand back, arms raised in surrender.

"No need to get all huffy," the IT specialist said. "Just joking, mate."

"No touching in the workplace, guys," an exhausted Ethel said, pushing through the door. "A good general rule."

Why did Meiselman not keep squeezing until the underling was down on his knees pleading? Where had thirty-six years of letting up and standing down gotten him?

Ethel eased herself into the driver's seat of her silver Mercedes and asked Meiselman to fasten her seatbelt. "Certain movements are unbearable," she said. By this hour of the day, her nostril-tickling perfume had worn off. What he smelled now was raw. The sweat that dampened the folds of her chubby neck mixed with the powder she used to whiten her face to a ghostly complexion. What more could he do for her? he wanted to ask. Did she need help carrying her purse into the condominium? Did she need help undressing and getting into bed? He would promise to turn away. Could he throw the comforter over her hurting body? Instead, he said, "That Mitchell is always touching people."

But all she said was: "You're not going to call Shenkenberg again. Right?"

Saturday

Pre-dawn and that nasty Mrs. Woolf is mowing. Yesterday, it was the screen door whipping open and slamming shut, the bent base of her ratty beach chair clacking the pavement with every lean forward to water the overgrown grass and dandelion clusters bordering her stoop. The day before yesterday it was what seemed like the never-ending whorl of a discharging garden hose.

Staring down at his neighbor from his bedroom window, Meiselman thinks he perceives a grin in her mess of wrinkles, as if she knows her behavior is nasty, as if her terror is deliberate. Sadie, her dog, bleats over the mower. The dog's curly white chin hairs remind Meiselman of the ladies at the nursing home where his mother volunteers. Patches of shaved pelt suggest disease. A triumphant, complicit bleat, possibly. The neighborhood will not sleep as long as my mistress is alive. Or the dog is Meiselman's ally and the cry is a plea: Save me from this old lady's derangement. Yesterday, she was watering weeds. Today, she is mowing an aimless trail. There is a limit to my obedience.

The front lawn's ankle-high grass jams the mower, stalling the old lady's progress.

Whenever conversation turns to the neighbor's chaotic lawn, Meiselman's mother recalls Mr. Woolf's stately stone trail that extended from the front of the house to the sidewalk. After her husband's death, Mrs. Woolf stopped spraying and, over time, the bursting weeds split the stone slabs into shards.

The growl of the mower strengthens as it jerks free.

Violations and abuses must be nipped in the bud, lest they accumulate and strengthen. But what type of neighborly response do these intrusions warrant, and why should it fall on Meiselman to ask others to behave decently? He can call the police with an anonymous complaint. Neighbors will then watch from behind closed curtains as this woman, who is no longer fit to live amongst the citizenry of New Niles, is carted away to an institution for the elderly. Nothing, however, is straightforward anymore. State specialists will conduct surveys and interviews. The violator will execute her right to face the complainant. Victimhood will be questioned and reversed. In the end, it will be Meiselman who is carted off.

Meanwhile, Deena sleeps soundly through this crisis. Typical Deena. Pogroms could be breaking out in the street, and this woman who does not compare prices at the grocery store, dumps change into a jar every couple of weeks never to be used, drives with the gas gauge pointing red, and refuses to shut the front door in the summer when the air conditioner is blowing (or in the winter when the furnace is firing), would stay sleeping. Deena, his wife of four years, lacks foresight. Worries, decisions, the long term, it all falls on Meiselman.

Three flicks of the window, three dull hums of rattling glass do not disturb her sleep. Thirty years old, six years younger than the boyish Meiselman, and wrinkles are already developing off the corners of her mouth, a product of the way she sleeps, meatless lips pressed together, deep concentration in this one area of life. A body half his size, the build of a scrappy utility infielder, a player brought off the bench late in the game to sacrifice a runner over, who then stays in the game as a defensive replacement. Every championship team needs one. "Quirky," is how his mother once described her. "She looks so quirky in those little jeans." Yet her body requires great amounts of sleep. Could it have something to do with her breathing, and the enormous energy expended to push air through such flat nostrils? Or her body needs long periods of rest to grow all that hair. A head of hair larger than her actual head. Curls like Meiselman's, although not as tightly wound, more like a spider plant, the tendrils bending downward at their ends.

His knuckles drum the window, triggering a stretch of her long neck. How will a body this size carry a baby? How will the doctors extract the child without having to slice her belly? Two bangs of his fist rouse her from the mattress.

"What's that noise?" Deena grumbles.

"Mrs. Woolf testing our resolve. She's mowing, today."

Staggering to the window to join her husband, she says, "We can turn on the air and close the window, so you won't be so bothered."

"Perfectly cool evenings. For this we have screens," he says. "Make me make sacrifices? Make me alter my lifestyle?"

"Getting old is frightening," Deena says. "She shouldn't be mowing at all with that leg."

"Don't feel sorry for her. Prosthetics these days are bionic. She chooses a pegleg. Everything she does is queer. And she moves fine. A barely noticeable limp. Meanwhile, I'm going to be a mess if I don't get any sleep."

"She could, at her age, be losing all sense of time."

"I've read articles about victims mimicking the behavior of their aggressors."

"That's vicious, Meisie. And you sound like your mother."

Convinced his wife will not join in his outrage, Meiselman returns to bed sore, Deena following behind.

"Not my mother. This is me talking," he says before turning his back on her and pulling the comforter over his body. "I've lived on the same street as that woman my entire life. I can tell you stories. Yelling at me when my ball would roll onto her lawn. Letting her dog defecate on the sidewalk. Never a neighborly word."

"'Never a neighborly word' is your mother," Deena says, slithering across the bed, her hand worming its way toward his body. Her fingers crawl up his undershirt and settle on his stomach. "You are cold." Two fingers slip underneath the waistband of his white underwear and immediately find the puffy mole above the hairline. She begins digging at it with her nail as if it were a speckle of mud. "Yesterday it was Shenkenberg and Ethel. Today it's Mrs. Woolf. You have to learn to turn the other cheek," she says, now twisting the mole.

Deena's touching does not feel particularly good. Her hands are cold, a dry hangnail scratches, and her preoccupation with the mole is making him feel bad about his body. On the other hand, he's finding a degree of pleasure from her lips, which graze the side of his shoulder as she speaks. Saturday morning, however, is not the right time. Sunday night is when they now have sex.

Soon after they got serious about trying, sex was timed to her cycle, but after months of failure, Deena decided that too much planning, too much timing, was an invitation to the evil eye. A new approach had them having sex on Friday nights, a time of blessing, a time when prayers are answered, the optimal time for procreation. Superstitious remedies were pursued, as well. Deena ate mandrakes, drank willow water blessed by an Israeli seer, recited Psalm 145 daily, and visited the graves of rabbis. Deena's barrenness, though, could not be cured, and frustration ended this routine.

Sunday night has become the unspoken, official time. There are spontaneous moments, yes, but not after nights when he has barely slept. Even soldiers, he has read, are guaranteed six hours. Also, predawn light is filtering into the room, and maybe early on in the marriage Meiselman had a fondness for daytime sex, confident that whenever Deena looked at him she saw only his prime qualities, namely, his mop of curls tightly clustered like a cauliflower floret, dimples distinguishable even underneath his fastidiously manicured beard, and teeth white and straight like the keys of a piano: no chips, no cracks, no cavities. An earnest, conscientious man. Now, however, he suspects, the daylight draws attention to his marks of decay, blemishes that make him look rigid, fusty, and humorless: caving cheeks, clipped hairs poking out of a pyramid-sloped nose, wild hairs curling out from the eyebrows and earlobes, a hunching back that causes a barely perceptible face lunge, breasts that have turned puffy around the areoles, and hands that at rest resemble claws, the hands of a stalker, a beast on the prowl. Lately, he has become increasingly self-conscious about crumbs and snot collecting in his beard.

Deena may have him pinned, but she is a lightweight, and he can easily turn the tables and end her shenanigans. A crudity breathed into his ear suddenly has him reconsidering. Something about her knowing what can help him fall back asleep. A screechy giggle tacked on. Even the pain from how she pulls on the mole now feels good. His body is starting to transition, and it may be a fine diversion until the newspapers arrive, and he should be able to finish quickly. Most importantly, it will relieve the pressure of making sure it happens tomorrow night. Therefore, he conveys his appetite with an eager, forceful kiss, to which she responds in kind.

"One second." She pushes herself off his body. "I need to brush my teeth. I need to make myself nice."

He pulls her down by the bicep.

"You taste fine. I smell nothing, good or bad."

"For me. I am revolting myself."

The door to the master bathroom closed, he works at keeping himself primed, but the unhealthy sound of her unsteady urine flow—tinkle, gush, tinkle, gush—as if there may be a granular blockage—dispirits him. This, along with the other sounds of her preparation—lathering, spraying, brushing, spitting, swishing, more spitting, more spraying, slapping—leads to a further waning of desire. Sounds that establish expectations. I'm clean, I'm spotless, I'm yours. Minutes ago, they were transitioning smoothly. Now they run the risk of being out of synch, one body primed while the other needs prodding. There have been times when both bodies were unable to transition in unison. He sensed she went along hurting and burning.

Outside, a car bounces into the driveway, squealing to a brake and sending Meiselman running from bed to window right in time to watch the black bandana-ed delivery woman heaving the newspapers out her minivan window. Thump, thump, thump. The *Chicago Tribune, The New York Times,* and the *Wall Street Journal*, all gift subscriptions from his father, landing on the driveway.

"I better go get the papers," Meiselman yells through the bathroom door. "We'll finish later."

* * *

Some rules gleaned from his father through the years: Grown men should never wear sweatpants or sneakers unless they are playing sports. Sweaters are appropriate only when worn with a jacket. A jacket does not require a tie, but a tie always requires a jacket. Every man should own a blue blazer and gray slacks. Every man should own a pair of brown *and* black dress shoes. Jews do not wear black to funerals. There is a rule about herringbone whose exact wording he cannot remember, but its gist is that it is a pattern to be pursued.

Meiselman has rules of his own. On brutal summer days, even on weekends, he never rolls the sleeves of his collared dress shirts higher than the elbows. The summer after they married, Deena pressed him to wear sandals. He agreed on condition he be allowed to wear socks. When he swims in a public body of water, he covers himself with an undershirt and swim trunks manufactured from an old pair of khakis cut at the knees. Even in front of his wife he refrains from casual nudity, slipping on his white underwear underneath his towel after a shower. This is irrespective of you, he answers his wife's teases. Would you parade naked in the king's court? The entire world is God's court. This is how a teacher Rav Fruman explained it. (The exception to this rigidity is after sex. Meiselman, feeling free on his naked walks to the shower, basks in his largeness and sinewy build. Once washed, he returns to screening himself.) Meiselman has spoken to his boss, Ethel, about a dress code for the library administrators, but his arguments do not move her. People need to be sensible, she argues. People are not sensible, he argues back.

Standing at the front door of his house in a tank top and white underwear, Meiselman considers the rush of sprinting down the driveway in such an outfit. What a *vilde chayah*, spying neighbors would surely chatter. In that man's house dishes are stacked in the sink, cats run wild, fruit rots in wooden bowls, and the couch upholstery has unidentifiable brown stains. They would assume he lacks a steady job. Humiliations should be avoided, not pursued. Therefore, Meiselman pulls a trench coat from the closet. In the mirror, he catches his reflection. The beltless coat has left his shins exposed, the look of a flasher. Silly, maybe. Improper, no.

His house slippers are missing from the doormat. Deena is constantly moving them. The slippers smell. Their insides hemorrhage yellow batting. They will be chucked, she threatens. Why spend money on something only worn in the house? It's not enough that *I* have to see you in them, she counters, dryly, always dryly. This argument may end in a tease, with Meiselman cuffing Deena's neck and shoving her face into the slipper. He may cover her mouth, only a matter of time until she is forced to inhale the stink. Deena may giggle wildly, attempting to break free, playfully slapping away the slipper. Playing offense, she may flick his nipples, his Achilles heel. Someone eventually gets hurt. He bangs her nose against the slipper. She smacks the temple of his glasses. Annoyed, angry, they walk away. A chronic need to have the final word, she often steals the slippers and stashes them deep under their marital bed.

(Admittedly, the slippers are starting to revolt Meiselman. Each time he wears them it is as if he can feel the organisms responsible for the putrid smell creeping across his feet and nesting in the spaces between his toes, latching onto his calloused heels, yellowing his skin, mutating the texture of his nails.)

Slinking into the bedroom to snag the slippers from underneath his bed is not an option. A freshened Deena may think his priorities have changed, and he has come to finish the job. His priorities have not changed. Confirming that the world has not endured any cataclysmic events during the nighttime and reading the recap of yesterday's White Sox game are his only priorities.

There is a chance she has fallen back asleep, but rummaging for his slippers risks waking her and ruining his morning reading of the newspaper. The moment he sinks into his recliner, Deena might shuffle into the living room, stretch herself across the couch, prop pillows under her head and comment groggily about her dreams, as if he is her therapist. It was like your father and I were married. You and your mom were quite upset when we broke the news. Your brother was happy. Your father was poking my ribs, teasing, It won't work if both of us don't emote.

The thought of stepping onto the driveway barefoot and blackening the soles of his feet, sidestepping puddles, which attract birds and mosquitoes—both renowned transmitters of disease—repels Meiselman. On the closet floor he finds a suitable pair of galoshes, a type of footwear that, according to his father, all men should own.

The growling of Mrs. Woolf's mower has ceased, and save for chirping birds and spewing sprinklers, it is quiet outside, as it should be at daybreak on a weekend in an idyllic suburb like New Niles. Some look up at the open Midwest sky and see grim monotony. Meiselman keeps his gaze straight ahead and soaks up the sight of his paradisiacal suburban street, a never-stale source of gratification. Lots are clearly delineated by thin cement walkways, driveways, and hedges. Encroachment will not be tolerated. Split-levels, like the one Meiselman's parents occupy, spacious four-bedroom houses that appear from the street as modest bungalows, are the most common style of house in this section of New Niles. Increasingly, people from Meisleman's community—specifically the Orthodox Jewish community—have been buying up two adjoining lots and knocking down the existing structures in order to build McMansions. Six, seven bedrooms. Three-car garages. Pools and basketball courts, sometimes indoors. Like the monstrosity at the corner that now blocks Meiselman's sun.

Lawns are slowly rebounding from the harsh winter, except for next door. Mrs. Woolf's jungled lot is verdant and healthy, covered with lush weeds, a bevy of planters, gnomes, and other sculptures, as if untouched by months of snow and freezing temperatures. Separating Meiselman's home, a three-bedroom, two-story colonial—supposedly a gift from his parents—from the property of his terrorizing neighbor is a tall hedge of bushes, whose branches are bare except for a smattering of pink and green buds.

Moving down his driveway, Meiselman does not see or hear any sign of Mrs. Woolf, meaning he will not have the opportunity to finally confront her about the early morning disturbances. He veers right, crossing his front lawn diagonally in order to gather the blue newspaper bags at the end of his parents' driveway, his galoshes squelching as they pad the dewy grass, whose blades tickle his ankles.

Because he lacks the kind of job that requires him to beat the morning traffic downtown, Meiselman assumes his father must think of him as indolent. To prove his industriousness, Meiselman has been delivering the newspapers to his father's front door every morning for the last several years, although his father has yet to acknowledge the gesture.

Looping back to the end of his driveway, Meiselman suddenly hears new noises coming from Mrs. Woolf's lot. The hollowed sound of stone dinging metal, light grunting accompanying the banging. Whatever his neighbor is doing will surely outrage him. Yet, he does not feel he has the energy for a confrontation. He wants his papers. He wants to find out the score from last night. So he keeps his eyes on the blue-bagged newspapers several feet ahead, instructing himself to stay focused, but right as he crouches for the bags, his eyes lift.

Through a gap in the hedge, Meiselman spots Mrs. Woolf sitting in the middle of her front yard, sundress hiked, the idle lawnmower in the space between her legs, which are spread in a v, good leg bent at the knee, pegleg flat. Behind the mower, a jerky trail of trimmed lawn. She is hammering a rock against the mower's wheel. Purposeful work would have demanded proper tools.

"The Meiselman boy," she calls out. "Care to give an old lady a hand?"

The ones parading as self-sufficient always end up being the most burdensome.

"Some weather," he responds.

"Don't know why you're in a trench coat and galoshes," she says. "That rain from yesterday is in Pittsburgh by now. Now how about helping me get this mower back to the shed. Jammed rudder."

"'Lingering clouds with a chance of precipitation,' says here." He has pulled the *Tribune* from its bag.

"Should only take a minute," she says.

"Have a good day," he answers.

Hugging the three newspapers, he charges up the driveway, pleased at not having involved himself in her nuttiness, yet also displeased by his impotence. Night after night of disturbed sleep, and all he could muster was a neighborly word.

Shabbat is the only day of the week he and Deena sit in the more formal living room at the front of the house. With the *Tribune* in his lap, Meiselman settles into his recliner—nailhead-trimmed, chestnut hide—part of the three-piece couch set his brother Gershon gifted them for their wedding. The most luxurious furniture in the entire house.

Today's headlines are dull. More stories questioning whether the country has found itself in a protracted conflict, everyone suddenly a general. Meiselman can safely move to Sports. Leaning forward to set the other sections down on the coffee table, he notices a steaming mug of coffee on the side table. Only now does he spot Deena across the foyer, on the other side of the house, sitting at the dining room table reading *Love is Just Another Way to Feel Sorry for Yourself*, the book she had asked him to bring home from the library on Friday. She had to ask only once. The coffee suggests she is not annoyed about what happened upstairs. Small gestures like the book, for her, outweigh.

"Thanks for the coffee," he calls out to her.

"Whatever," she says.

Or the gestures do not outweigh. Maybe they merely neutralize, and the coffee is her attempt to prove a larger point about him taking her for granted.

Meiselman, hoping to remind his wife of his attentiveness, asks, "How's that book I picked up for you?"

"Inspirational. Did you know there is no Hebrew word for romance?"

"He talks about Hebrew in the book?"

"No, learned that in my Judaism for Beginners class years ago. I'm making connections. Love," Deena explains, "is helping another person grow spiritually."

"Like how I helped you become religious?"

"Not that kind of spiritual," she answers. "More like...here it is: 'Helping the other person control obsessions and destructive emotions. Saving the other person by liberating him or her from volatile and dispiriting patterns.' Let me finish reading."

"Sounds Christian to me," Meiselman says. "Jews don't believe in controlling emotions. Jews believe in controlling actions."

"Two minutes, I promise."

Twenty minutes later, she enters the room wearing her white-trimmed pink soccer shorts, which hug her vagina and fail to cover her cheek bottoms. Standing in front of Meiselman, she pulls back her curls, her skimpy white t-shirt lifting, exposing her cupped stomach and its trail of faint black fuzz. She rubber bands her ponytail, which flops off the side of her head like a tassel. Her way of showing him what he sacrificed for the newspapers.

He says, "That mowing was something else."

"Don't let it ruin our weekend," Deena says. "Besides, she's not half as bad as our other neighbors."

It is ruining my weekend, he wants to answer, but she wants to move on, move back to the dining room and her book, and she is almost out the door, and even if this is what he originally wanted, to be alone with his newspapers, now that she is the one rejecting him, he wants her back.

"That new family whose kids ride on our lawn?" he says, playing dumb.

"No, our other neighbors." She turns back to him and shuffles forward, slightly hunched, index fingers discharged. "Your parents, Meisie," she says, poking his side.

"My parents? They are asleep by ten and we rarely—"

"I'm joking, Meisie." Another poke under the ribs.

"I know," he answers, pulling at the hairs of his moustache, forcing out a chuckle.

"You thought that was funny, Meisie?"

Standing over him, she grabs his sides, a sometimes-ticklish area. He catches the molesting fingers of her hand and bends them back until she collapses onto his lap, right on top of the sports section, its pages crinkling underneath. The thought of the unnatural fold she is creating in this unread section aggravates him. She rests her head against his breast and puts her hand on his neck, the tips of her fingers skimming his beard line. Using the hand of the arm hooked around her skimpily covered backside, he jerks at the newspaper, trying to wrestle it out from under her. Ends up lifting her off his lap. She grabs his wrist and with her eyes and a tilt of the head implies an interest in returning upstairs. He runs his free hand over the newspaper's crease.

"It's been almost two weeks," she says, releasing her grip.

"That's not fair," he answers. "Last Sunday, on our usual day, you ran out on me. You ran out on me to check on your father."

"I just don't want two weeks to turn into a month," she says, her pinkie digging her bellybutton.

"I share the same fear, trust me. Just now is not good. Tomorrow, no matter what. Besides, we have to leave soon for shul." Glumness sags her face and body. To shift her focus, he shows her the front of the sports page. "Look at this picture of Frank. Look how strong he looks. This is the year it will all come together."

* * *

How his son can degrade himself by sitting in the back of the men's section with the riffraff, the scoffers, the proudly tardy, the new members with no standing, men who will never be asked to be officers, who do not pay full dues, and who step out after the Torah reading to drink whiskey in the kitchen, his father does not understand. The people in the front rows—the officers, the board members, men who have been coming since the shul's founding, men who post plaques commemorating the deceased—talk just as much as the men in the back rows, he argues to his father. Not as much, and it's about business. And maybe, sometimes, politics, Israel. It would not hurt to engage in meaningful conversation, every now and then, something other than sports, for crying out loud. Should one not sit with one's contemporaries? Goofballs who talk *narishkayt*? Can one not be a positive influence, an island of piety? Besides, it's not the back back. It's more the middle. Harvey, leave him alone. Let him sit with his friends if he wants to.

Another example of his father not having steered him wrong. Meiselman should have heeded his father's advice and taken a seat closer to the front. Now, for as long as the two men attend the same shul, or until Meiselman has a son to use as a buffer, he will be stuck every Shabbat morning feeling squeezed by Ben Davis's hulking body. The shoulders of the two men rub, their knees knock, yet only Meiselman shrinks in his seat. Today, this inability to own his space is frustrating Meiselman more than usual. The wooly smell of Ben Davis's pilly sweater, which he wears even during the summer, sticks in Meiselman's nose, its stray fibers tickling his neck.

In spite of a main sanctuary that seats seven hundred, the shul is neither august nor awesome. Its gray industrial carpeting, fluorescent lighting, walls painted a simple white, and rows constructed out of stackable chairs—gray fabric, gold trimming—give it the feel of a convention center. At the front of the room is an unadorned stage with an ark whose curtains are a spiritless brown. To the side of it sits the rabbi. A frosted glass partition divides the men from the women.

"It's usually so freezing in here," Ben Davis says, the same complaint he utters every week before pushing up his sweater sleeves.

Spring is here. Time to take off the sweater, Meiselman wants to encourage his seatmate. Wear a blue blazer. Do you not see that every other man is either in a suit or jacket? But they do not have this type of relationship. When Ben Davis wipes his nostrils raw on one of the bathroom paper towels, Meiselman never offers him a tissue from his travel pack. Likewise, Meiselman does not suggest to Ben Davis that he excise the skin tag hanging off his eye, and never has he uttered a word of concern or curiosity about the withering, black thumbnail or the black spots dotting his eyeballs.

"Good week?" Meiselman asks.

"Eh. You?"

A greeting that has become a formality, a way for the two men to segue into their weekly review of the White Sox.

“Four hits, no runs,” Meiselman says.

“Runs, shmuns,” Ben Davis responds. “The problem is this guy Wright; a below average fastball that he consistently leaves over the plate.”

“A team is only as good as its fifth starter,” Meiselman says. “That’s what worries me about this year’s squad.”

Light physical contact with other men does not generally bother Meiselman. At times, he even finds it pleasurable; the tickle of a barber’s infinitesimal snipping, the comb’s lifting of the hair, or the tailor running chalk across the rear, or the hair of a woman in a crowd grazing Meiselman’s neck. Men, contact with other men is the subject of this meditation. With Ben Davis, Meiselman feels as if his shoulder is sliding off a brick wall. Ben Davis, meanwhile, sits unaware of the touching.

Trying to talk his way through this discomfort, Meiselman says, “Did you see that picture of Frank in the paper this morning? Did you see how strong he looks?”

“Strong, shmong.”

Meiselman shushes Ben Davis as the usher comes down the aisle. A ticket for talking during services—fifty dollars, all proceeds going to charity—would be a hardship for a man like Ben Davis, presumably, although Meiselman cannot not be positive, seeing as how he does not know what the man does for a living. Work is another matter the men do not discuss. Why his lips are always chapped, why his hands have sores on the knuckles, why the president of the shul comes to him in the middle of services when there is a leak, a decomposing rodent behind the fridge, or a bird trapped in the vent are some of the questions Meiselman would like to ask Ben Davis. The ushers circulate near the back rows, reluctant to ticket the members in the front. Services finish without any fines.

At Kiddush in the social hall, Deena is in a corner with her two new friends, women who wear skirts above the knees and high heels sloped like playground slides. Deena met Molly, the more bejeweled of the two, at a JCC class she took when she was becoming religious for Meiselman. Several feet away, Meiselman stands in a circle with the husbands of Molly and the other woman. Owing to Deena's friendships, Meiselman was thrown into this weekly gathering of men. One of the first conversations was about beer. The other men compared German and Japanese brews. Over and over, Jeremy, Molly's husband, used the word *reinheitsgebot*. Meiselman asked for a definition. Jeremy told Meiselman it was a concept beyond definition, something either known or not known. They asked Meiselman what he drinks, and he answered, "I buy American whenever I can." "I hear you," Scott said. "I'm into this good imperial stout called Catbird."

For the next several months, the conversation moved to bike riding, and then grilling. Today, the men are talking waters.

"New Mexico Springs is an acidic water I like," Scott says.

"Those acidic waters are beyond me," Jeremy says. Jeremy, Molly's husband, is a pediatrician. "Mississippi Pure anyone? Wonderfully sweet."

Ben Davis is lurking behind the circle of men, his shaky thumb and index finger delivering a cracker with creamed herring on top to his mouth. Does decency call for Meiselman to step aside and invite Ben Davis into the circle? Does he even have the pull to introduce new members?

"In the newspapers," Meiselman says, "there was something about high levels of lead in the Dale County water system."

"Who'd drink from the tap?" Scott asks. "You," he stabs his finger into Meiselman's chest, "should try Almond Grove." Nipping at the buttons of Meiselman's blue dress shirt, as if checking the shirt's quality, he adds, "Medium minerality, a neutral orientation. And it's great for virility." Everyone in the circle laughs. Meiselman spots Ben Davis sucking herring cream off his fingers and wiping his hands on the bottom of his Styrofoam plate.

On the way home from shul, Meiselman tells Deena about his seating issue.

"Check my neck. Is it red from the scratching?"

"Two, three stitches should do the job."

She suggests moving seats.

"You make jokes and impractical suggestions," Meiselman says. "My own wife and you can't sympathize. First Shenkenberg and Ethel, then Mrs. Woolf, and now Ben Davis? I'm sick of it. Sick of always being the one left feeling disturbed."

Sunday

Meiselman's fingers fidget and twice he jumbles the access code. On his third attempt the tiny bulb glows green, and he is through the door and off down the empty hallway, the absence of buzzing fluorescents making his movements and actions innocuous, a spirit passing through. Just the tiny yelps from his rubber-soled shoes striking the waxed floor. The lights will stay off, for now. No need to worry about other administrators. They do not share his work ethic. They will not come into work on a Sunday. Without a second to spare, he shucks his coat as he walks. At the entrance to his office, he sets his briefcase down at the entrance. His tossed coat falls short of the chair in front of his desk, but he leaves it heaped on the floor. Standing in the middle of the hallway, he is pulled in two directions. A vigorous debate on the ride over. Does he pursue the morning's main objective without delay, or does he detour to Betsy Ross's desk and satisfy his hankering for something sweet that has been harassing him since his Sunday breakfast of a whole-wheat bagel sprayed with Not Butter? Amazing!

Last week the underlings stood around Betsy Ross's L-shaped desk in the hallway alcove. Eyes glazed, throats wobbling, they'd stood silently as the chocolate mounds melted in their mouths. In the breakroom afterward, they'd analyzed the filling. Not hazelnut. Not almond. Walnut, maybe? Meiselman had not eaten Betsy Ross's chocolates then because they were not kosher. But now...are the chocolates *treyf treyf*? Are we talking pig, or an animal not ritually slaughtered? After all, what goes into homemade chocolates? Eggs, butter, sugar. Not lard. The utensils are problematic, but surely the oven's heat burned off any *treyf* impurities.

The chocolate melts on his tongue as he fights the urge to chew. How often does something end up being better than imagined? Before pursuing his other task he grabs a second chocolate from the earthenware bowl. This time he cannot fight the urge and the sickening sweetness of the additional chocolate offsets any enjoyment accrued from the first piece.

His body is tingling. From the sugar or from the excitement of what is to come? Slats of sunlight slice his boss Ethel's desk, motes hovering in the trails of natural light, which is sufficient, even perfect, for Meiselman's objective. The underlings gossip about Ethel using her own money to furnish her office with an antique desk, leather guest chairs, and framed lithographs of famous dead writers. Only Meiselman discerns the message the library's director hopes to convey to the underlings through such opulence. I am not you.

And the message Meiselman attempts to convey by keeping the walls of his office across the hall bare, his library-issued desk free of tchotchkes, family photographs, and White Sox paraphernalia? That this office is not a last stop, but rather an anteroom for the great role that awaits, the job that will leave everyone in the community gossiping about the Meiselman boy having finally made it. Not *him*. *Him*, I know. Everyone knows *him*, but now the younger son, too.

No question Friday was a setback. He is still sore from the rapid series of humiliations suffered as the workweek came to a close, particularly Shenkenberg's slight over the phone, which had triggered Ethel's public upbraiding. There is ground to be made up on this Sunday morning, just as soon as he finishes his second task, which starts with wheeling Ethel's high back, brown leather desk chair to the framed photographs massed at the desk's end.

His interest is a specific photograph in the back row. Pulling the sleeve of his purple button-down over his hand to prevent smudging, Meiselman lifts the frame by its edges and rests it on his lap.

What about this picture excites Meiselman? There are prettier women. Deena is a far prettier type. In this fifteen-year-old photograph, college-aged Ethel is thirty pounds thinner. Not too skinny, healthy. Her arm is around the shoulder of a friend, who is wrapped in a large beach towel, a concealing too total to excite Meiselman's imagination. Ethel, whose body is coyly angled, heel off the ground, toes digging the sand, chin dipped, is the focus. She playfully grabs a buttock, her ass, which juts and is plastered by a wet green bathing suit bottom that sticks like rubber. Her white t-shirt has been cut short, and her exposed midsection is pleasing. Just the right amount of flesh hugs the suit's waistband. Everything about this picture is pleasing. The shirt's neckline is also cut out and the day in the sun has marked her pale shoulders with blurry freckles. He cannot exactly see the freckles, but he certainly can imagine them. Her brown hair, stringy from the water, bumps over her clavicles. This is before she cut her hair mannishly short and colored it black, a haircut Meiselman surprisingly finds agreeable. Is the photograph pleasing because she has lost control of her smile? A big black hole that will swallow him up. Ethel hardly smiles anymore. Always something pressing to do. Some weeks, Meiselman removes the photograph from the office and brings it into his own office or the bathroom. Now on Sundays he saves himself for his wife. In the past, even with instructions to save himself, Meiselman was never able to. Saving himself, in recent months, has become easier, evidence of either improved discipline or aging.

Before leaving the office, he filches a stick of Ethel's cinnamon gum from the top drawer. Two chews are all it takes to access the pleasurable burn, to taste what she tastes. He grabs Ethel's bottle of perfume from the second drawer, pumps away from his body and whiffs. After shutting the drawer, he checks that he has left no evidence of his molestation, and makes an effort to remember his checking.

Able to finally sit down to work, he sees more letters have arrived. The handwritten addresses and excessive postage make them easily identifiable. One letter is typed on hotel stationary, another on paper ripped from a spiral. The offended patrons use biblical verses and apocalyptic language in designating the library a disgrace for hosting Shenkenberg. It does not appear these letter writers are demanding a response, so he files them away and moves to the final one, which is typed on the official stationary of the Rabbinical Association of Chicago. The sender has even made the effort to identify Meiselman by his proper title.

Dear Events and Programs Coordinator,

It is with great modesty and trepidation that I write this letter. To our dismay, in recent years, a war of propaganda has been initiated against the Torah-abiding Orthodox community, a war that has now reached levels not seen since the attack of the "Reforms." Here in the Chicagoland community a battle in this war has been waged with the recent publication of a "book" by a "writer" raised in the aforementioned community. Although I have been fortunate to have not come into contact with this "book" and have been vigilant about discouraging others from allowing this "book" to fall into their laps, I have been briefed by those less fortunate people who have come into accidental contact with this "book" and were not able to turn away in time. These readers have testified that this so-called "book" transgresses the severe sins of evil speech, scoffing, gossip, slander, and demeaning Torah scholars, and is a potential stumbling block to the members of our Chicagoland Torah community.

Specifically, its heresies are aimed at ridiculing and misrepresenting the life of a great teacher who served the community for over half a century. This great teacher, a Survivor, found refuge, following the Destruction of Europe, in the village of New Niles. Jews and non-Jews celebrated this Rabbi for his modesty and pleasant ways. To involve this beloved Rabbi in scenes of a lustful nature, to present him as boxing enthusiast and someone given to imbibing at unsanctified times is the greatest of disrespects. Through consultations it has come to my attention that a difficult relationship with his father has left the "author" of this "book" bitter and starved for love and attention. Instead of turning to Scholars for professional counseling, this "writer" chose the childish response of lashing out.

The granting of a public platform to this heretic presents a spiritual danger to those who do not have the ability to discern truth from lies. The people who allow heresies to multiply are worse than the heretics because they allow the cancer to grow, the infection to spread, the fever to elevate. The American right of free speech, a value our institution has fought for since the battle to save Soviet Jewry, does not give one the right to yell fire in a place of worship. If there is not a "rescheduling" of this "speaker" I will be forced to galvanize the community. May G-d have mercy on our community, pour forth a spirit of purity, and grant us insight.

Signed with a pained heart,

Rabbi Avraham Baruch Fruman

President, Rabbinical Association of Chicago

This is not another crank letter Meiselman can file away and forget. If anyone can galvanize, it is Rav Fruman. When he warned the community of cauliflower thrips, decreeing that the vegetable must be soaked in saltwater for at least an hour before cooking, they listened. When he issued the outright ban on eating fresh broccoli and Brussels sprouts because of bedding microorganisms, they listened, too. They followed his call for smoke-free shuls and yeshivas. They adhere to his ban on organizations fundraising through bingo, raffles, and other games of chance. (The only decision of the Rav's largely ignored is the one calling on parents to limit spending on bar-mitzvahs and weddings.)

A rabbi of Rav Fruman's stature can mobilize minions, and Orthodox Jews do not circle hooting childish rhymes, homemade signs in hand. One can expect a throng of bearded men chanting Psalms in unison, a responsive reading, Rav Fruman wailing the lead. The women, prohibited from reading out loud, will gather across the street, peering deeply into miniature books of Psalms.

Besides, does the rabbi not perfectly capture the problem with Shenkenberg? Does he not perfectly articulate how Shenkenberg's slanderous book about Rabbi J- connects to a graver threat, which is the younger generation's eagerness to pummel traditions, question authority, and erase old certainties? Society, with increasing gusto, marginalizes the old. Why else does the family ignore PopPop's stories about growing up Jewish in South Carolina, preferring to gossip about which cousins are marrying *shiksas* and which *schleppy* relatives still rely on parental handouts. (Everyone except for Meiselman, who leans into PopPop and asks, "Did you have kosher meat in South Carolina? What about kosher candy? Tell me again about your friend Dewey Schwartz.") Dismissiveness is Shenkenberg's bread and butter, as Meiselman painfully learned from their call on Friday.

If Rav Fruman galvanizes, any fuss over this book—minor until now—risks spiraling into a quagmire, putting Meiselman on the defensive and tasking him with defending Ethel and the library's mission. Or will Meiselman feel compelled to switch sides, to support his Orthodox community and become the protestors' inside man?

And where is Ethel when the city's leading rabbi is threatening to galvanize? Shrugging at Meiselman's concern.

"The anger of the religious community is palpable," Meiselman warned last week after receiving the first calls and letters in protest of Shenkenberg's appearance.

"Outrage nourishes these people," Ethel answered. "Controversy will help us. Set up an extra ten seats for every complaint. Meiselman, you can't satisfy everyone."

Short of calling in a bomb scare the night of the event, or pulling the fire alarm as the attendees takes their seats, what can Meiselman do to stand up to Shenkenberg and protect the memory of Rabbi J-? Maybe he can slip an embarrassing question into Ethel's notes. Question one: You say this is a work of fiction, yet you don't bother changing Rabbi J-'s name. Like Shenkenberg, Meiselman sat in Rabbi J-'s class his senior year of high school and experienced the rabbi's righteousness. A dented timepiece hanging off his suit vest, the rabbi would shuffle around the room pulling naked candies and apricots from his pants pocket, placing the lint-covered treats on the desks of his students. Gently cupping the students' cheeks, he would urge them to taste something sweet. On the last day of senior year, Rabbi J- handed Meiselman and each of his classmates a micro-sized kabalistic book that would protect them from bodily and spiritual harm. For twenty years, Meiselman has kept the book tucked inside his wallet, and it is on his person at this very moment. Part two to question one: Did you not experience Rabbi J'-s kindness?

Perhaps this is Meiselman's moment to finally reverse a lifetime of letting everyone put their dirty paws on him. But first, he must learn what he is up against. Meiselman scours Shenkenberg's publisher-provided press packet. An unidentified interviewer asks Shenkenberg about significant childhood events and how they may have influenced his decision to become a writer. Sports never interested the writer. Spent his time alone reading in his bedroom. A children's edition of Josephus's *The Wars of the Jews*, a Hanukkah present from an uncle who had abandoned his religious upbringing, was a favorite. At twelve, he stole a copy of *A Tale of Two Cities* from the local library—presumably, the New Niles Public Library—and read it until the pages fell out. *Sadly, sadly, the sun rose; it rose upon no sadder sight than the man of good abilities and good emotions, incapable of their directed exercise, incapable of his own help and his own happiness, sensible of the blight on him, and resigning himself to let it eat him away.* Did Shenkenberg deliver that quote from memory? All Meiselman can remember from age twelve is reading the 1979 White Sox yearbook by flashlight. A horrible White Sox team, but the yearbook had fabulous black and white photos of braless bell-bottomed girls and wide-collared men rushing the field on Disco Demolition Night, mustachioed cops on the chase, batons swinging. Steve Dahl in a helmet, and a bonfire raging in center field.

How Meiselman struggled to produce consequential childhood memories at his sessions with Dr. Lin. After the unfortunate discovery of the photographs in his bedroom, Meiselman's mother had demanded he see a psychiatrist. This was during the transition years, his late twenties, still living at home, having never left, not even for university. An account of his father letting him puff his cigar at a baseball game and stories about Gershon's practical joke of luring Meiselman into a dark bedroom and slapping a hanger against his testicles, were cut off by Dr. Lin with irrelevant questions like, “Do you masturbate?”

“Not really,” he would answer.

“Any dreams?”

“Nothing I remember.”

Dr. Lin told Meiselman he could call her Sam, although he thought it disrespectful to call a doctor by her first name, even though Dr. Lin disrespected her profession by sitting with bare feet, her legs draped over the arm of the chair, a posture that shifted noticeably sometime after he told her he was a twenty-eight-year-old virgin. From then on she wore shoes, crossed her legs tightly, and sat forward, elbows on her knees. She rejected the explanation that his abstinence was legalistic, he being an unmarried Orthodox Jew.

One week, between sessions, a memory surfaced. The thought of sharing it embarrassed him, but he grasped its potential in helping the doctor understand his fascination with the bathing suit photograph his mother had found under the mattress.

Not knowing how to start, he uttered banalities about his week. Finally, “My mother takes me to the pool.”

“Recently?” the doctor asked.

“Seven years old, the summer I started wearing glasses. For some reason we go all the way out to Des Plaines. Not nearly as nice as the New Niles pool. The clientele. Lots of ponytails. The men. It’s also the first time I’ve ever seen my mother in a two-piece bathing suit.”

“A bikini?” Dr. Lin asked.

“Yes, a two-piece.”

“Is this noteworthy, her wearing a bikini?”

“Like I said, she usually wore a one-piece.”

“Well, that’s all the time we have. Let’s pick up from here next time.”

“We face each other in the shallow end,” Meiselman continued at the start of the next session. “Her back is up against the pool’s wall, elbows relaxed on its edge.” New details resurfaced as he talked. “The suit’s straps are pulled down to her biceps. Freckles cover her browning shoulders. She faces the sun, eyes closed. I’m staring at her and, impulsively, I loop my finger under one of the straps and pull. Down. My mother slaps away my hand and stares down at me, and I guess I imagine we’re playing a game because the second she turns back to the sun, I go for the other strap. She doesn’t stop me in time, and I pull the strap down below her elbow and her, you know, pops out.” Hand to his chest, he demonstrated for the doctor the breast falling out of the suit. “She slaps her fingers against the center area.”

“The nipple?”

“It was horribly brown.”

“What happened next?”

“She wasn’t happy. She ordered me out of the pool, and we went home.”

“The attraction to bathing suits was there at an early age,” Dr. Lin said. “Why bathing suits is the pivotal question. Why you didn’t go to your local pool, why you wanted it off her, and why your mother wore a different bathing suit for this out-of-town adventure are also questions worth exploring.”

Questions leading to more questions. For the money his parents were spending, the doctor should have offered hypotheses. This is why, looking back, his time with the doctor frustrated him, as if it was nothing more than an exercise in dignity trashing. At that same appointment, for example, he shared, to little interest, another recovered memory.

He had trouble starting. He always had trouble starting.

"Just whatever is on your mind," Dr. Lin urged.

"I'm eleven. Sitting on my bedroom floor. Pink carpeting. Pink walls."

"Pink?" Dr. Lin asked.

"It came with the house."

"And your parents never replaced it?"

"Years later, when I was in high school."

"But for a long period you slept in a pink bedroom?"

"It was more of a peach color."

"Go on."

"Anyway, I'm on the floor assessing my stamp collection, thinking about how I'm going to change the focus of my collection from foreign to American stamps."

"What prompted this decision?"

"Something has always intrigued me about the lives of our forefathers. Imagining how they lived, the stamps they used."

"Your forefathers?"

"Founding fathers, but this is not crucial to the story. I mention it because I am waiting to leave for a stamp show at the Holiday Inn, so I go downstairs to tell my mother I'm ready, and she shoos me out of the kitchen, which she often did. Meanwhile, I overhear her saying to the person on the phone, 'This is not nice,' and, 'Civilized people don't act like this.' A minute later she stomps upstairs and gently opens the door to my bedroom. Eyes watery, a put-on smile, she speaks excitedly about the big party I have to get ready for. It's the first I'm hearing about Ethel's birthday party."

"So you didn't go to the stamp show?"

"No, I had Ethel Lewinson's party."

"Were you disappointed? After all, this would temporarily derail your bold plans to pursue an American collection."

"I had a schoolboy crush on the birthday girl, so I imagine I was excited."

"Go on."

"Get to the party. Ethel's mother sends me down to the basement where the other boys and girls are sitting in a circle in front of the television playing Truth or Dare. Ethel, the birthday girl, is taking a dare. Kids huddle in the corner and decide Ethel and I will go into the bathroom and kiss. She protests and everyone has a good laugh because maybe they knew I had a thing for her. But rules are rules and off we go. The bathroom is a downstairs kind—windowless, unfinished, lid off the tank, a rust-streaked sink, and a dried-out bar of soap. Ethel stands in front of me, eyes shut, munching on her thumb cuticle with her big front teeth. Briefly, I consider playing the good guy and suggest we lie to the group. But the opportunity is too great, so I put my lips together and inch my face forward. Her face melts right as our lips are about to make contact, and she barrels forward, grabbing her stomach. Then, she starts yanking the back of her pants. Brown drops are leaking from her pants leg. She bolts from the bathroom. Panicked, I pull the roll of toilet paper off the spool, get on my knees and start mopping up the mess, streaking brown across the floor. When I look up, Ethel's father, a big man with a mustache and gold chain—always with the shirt open—is standing in the doorway. Takes me upstairs and has me call my mother to come pick me up. On my way out, her father says, 'You tell her Ethel got sick and *everyone* had to go home.'"

Dr. Lin turned her chair into her desk and jotted notes into a legal pad. After flipping to a clean sheet, she stashed the pad in the top drawer of her desk, turned back to Meiselman and said, "Yes, it's fairly common for adolescents, especially girls, to experience involuntary eliminations during their first sexual encounters. Let's go back to the pink carpeting."

"Like I said, more of a peach color."

Not Josephus, not Dickens. Mother's brown nipple and a girl defecating in her pants. Why would God have selected Meiselman to stand up to this famous writer and his slandering of the great, late Rabbi J-? Maybe this is Meiselman's moment to shine, to stop being an object, to stop thinking that the high road is the only road. It is time to unleash his aggressive capabilities. Time to play ball!

* * *

Reading the dubious novel is crucial if Meiselman stands any chance of taking on Shenkenberg, so he ventures out from the administrative offices and onto the library's main floor, where he hustles past Circulation with his head down. It is Sunday, the library's busiest day, and he cannot chance a librarian detouring him with fatuous concerns, like whether he knows the date of some bestseller hitting the shelves, or what to do about the inebriated mother babbling to herself in Periodicals. Veering left, he proceeds to the Classics and Adult Fiction room in the library's rear. Entering the hall, he disappears into the bookcases and wends his way through the room, cutting over to a different aisle whenever he encounters a patron. It is when he turns the final corner that he practically bowls over a runty teenager in an oversized New York University sweatshirt planted in front of the Sd-Sp section of the shelves, head cocked, her index finger running over the spines of the books. A strand of the girl's blonde hair is colored pink. Hoops spiral the upper rim of one ear. The bottoms of her jeans are frayed and cover her shoes, which are, he speculates, some type of athletic sandal.

As a rule, even on weekdays, Meiselman avoids offering help. Answer one question and soon he is pulling microfilm and magazines for lazy, spiteful school kids or filling out reserve forms for anxious Jewish grandmothers, women like his mother, who couch powerful statements in questions: "Isn't there a way to manually turn down the air?" "Why don't people read *The Shawl* anymore? Or *Sophie's Choice*?" "Do you think a place like New Niles, a place with such a large survivor population, should be hosting a *shmendrik* like this Shenkenberg?" This girl with the pink hair and nubby nose, however, scowls at the books in a way that suggests she is at the library to accomplish the simple task of locating a book. Nothing more. A girl who probably lolled away the school year smoking cigarettes and marijuana with other disappointing teenagers. Saturday nights were spent paying older men to purchase alcoholic beverages from convenience stores and grudgingly revealing to boys with patchy facial hair what is underneath that oversized sweatshirt. The end of this reckless year nearing, a threat of summer school has been issued. They demand the minimum from her. A short paper. No groundbreaking theories, but simple proof the book was read. They review with her the punishment for plagiarism. The book is step one. In this girl's life there is room for only one task at a time, and this task overwhelms her like her sweatshirt. Between her fingers, nails chewed to the stubs and speckled purple, a shade darker than the lettering on her sweatshirt, she holds a scrap of paper with what is presumably the name of the book. A safety pin pierces her eyebrow, he now notices, as she looks up to him for guidance.

"*Julius Caesar* by Shakespeare?" she asks.

A girl given to immediacy, she must have spotted the sign for Adult Fiction and turned right, ignoring the sign for Classics, arrow pointing left. Meiselman did not want to complicate her search by sending her to Denise's desk. One obstacle can derail a fragile flower like the pink-haired girl. They sent me this way, they sent me that way, she will cry to the adults in her life that question why she failed to return home with the book. He motions for her to follow. At the end of the bookcases, he stops, allowing her to lead them across the hall's entrance path separating the sections of Adult Fiction and Classics. Meiselman straggles a step behind because what would they discuss? The bagginess of her blue jeans makes it difficult for him to gauge the sum of her dimensions.

He pulls *Julius Caesar* by Shakespeare from the shelf and hands it to the pink-haired girl. Gripping the book by its sides, she stares down at its cover. Is the drawing of Brutus raising his sword over Caesar's head causing excitement or dread? Chin tucked, she moves her face closer and closer to the cover. Opening the book, she riffles through its pages with her thumb. Before excusing himself, he waits for a thank-you that never arrives. Tell a girl like this to say thank you and she will respond with an eye roll.

Back at his desk, Meiselman is unable to process more than a few sentences of the Shenkenberg book's back cover—"Ely plays caretaker to the revered rabbi....Ultimately, the student becomes the rebbe, the teacher, the master." The book's opening sentences—*On the first day of class, I volunteered to erase the blackboard, which earned me the nickname "The Manager." It stuck and the responsibilities mounted.*—also fail to grab his attention. All he can focus on is the presumed painfulness of the safety pin pinching the pink-haired girl's eyebrow. Did the piercing cause her to bleed? Did her no-good friends even bother soaking its tip in rubbing alcohol, or a flame, like Meiselman's mother used when digging splinters from his palms and fingertips? What was the safety pin holding together? The grief this girl must cause her parents. If in high school he would have sat in English class with such a girl he would have had a staring problem, and when she would show without her copy of *Julius Caesar* by Shakespeare he would gladly have smuggled her his own.

The insouciance of this pink-haired girl troubles him. Does he not have a duty, as her senior, to fix this glitch in her? If not now, when? If not him, who? He must correct the behavior of this wayward pink-haired girl. Otherwise, she risks becoming a sour, contemptuous adult like Shenkenberg, who slights former schoolmates over the phone.

Back out on the library's main floor, he sees that the line at Circulation extends outside the roped lanes. The pink-haired girl would sooner flee than wait in a line like this. As the senior ranking administrator present in the library he is tempted to reassign a librarian to Circulation, but not wanting to get bogged down, he trudges across the open floor, past Information and the DVD carousels and a short bookcase featuring staff picks, dodging into the James Winfield Reading Room.

The reading room's ceiling rises to a magisterial height. The patrons are silent for fear of the echo, which reverberates sounds of squealing pencils, snapping binders, paper torn from spirals, and slamming textbooks, none of which rouse the students, mostly Asian and Indian, crammed at the rows of tables. "Where have all the Jewish students gone?" his mother often asks after visits to the library. Eyes scanning far and wide, the swish of his brown corduroys joining the chorus of sounds, Meiselman does not spot the girl's distinguishable head of hair. The room's bright whiteness is an infertile environment for a misanthropic teen like the pink-haired girl.

In the windowless Computer Lab, a mildew smell permeates. Oily-haired, acne-faced gamers in black t-shirts occupy most of the terminals, unmindful of the anxious students waiting patiently on the side for a vacancy, colossal textbooks and overstuffed notebooks slipping from their arms. The naïve students do not understand that the gamers will stay on until closing time, confident the students lack the courage to remind them of the one-hour limit on the blue computers and the half-hour limit on the red ones. In the back row, Jackson and Alvin, two middle-aged regulars, are using the computers, no doubt, for nefarious purposes. Last year, Betsy Ross circulated a petition to ban inappropriate websites and oblige all users to register. Meiselman signed the petition in a rare moment of disagreement with Ethel, who, predictably, opposed the ban. His boss takes pride in her flexible morals. A civil liberties group marched into the village hearing arguing that anonymity is an inviolable right, censorship a slippery slope. Slippery for the smooth-soled masses, maybe. Meiselman, he wears cleats. The measure failed. There is only one girl in this room and her hair is orange and chopped short.

What came first, the pink hair or the safety pin, the stain or the scar?

Meiselman takes the staircase up to the second floor two steps at a time. In the green-carpeted Kids Area, Linda, a middle-aged volunteer, whose bony joints move with the stiffness of an action figure, reads to a group of children sprawled across giant beanbags. The children wait an eternity for her to lick the tip of her finger and turn one of the book's giant pages. Parents wait in the back, stacks of books in their arms. Off to the side, a mother is standing up to her child, who is insisting they stay until the end of the story. The mother tugs the child's forearm. The child pulls back. There is no time to see who will emerge victorious, but Meiselman would bet on the child. Parents of this generation lack resolve. They refer to their children as friends.

Science is empty of people.

Girls no older than ten choke the aisles of Young Adult.

Every corner of the library searched and no sign of the pink-haired girl. Journeying through the bookcases of History, he reaches the last aisle and through the spaces between the shelves he spots a flash of pink. Taking cover behind the bookcase, Meiselman pulls a dense biography of Abraham Lincoln—*The Lincoln Enigma*—and observes his pink-haired misanthrope sitting in front of a windowless wall at a lone desk in the corner of the library's second floor. Act I, scene I and out cold, the upper part of her body slumped over the table, head resting on an outstretched arm, the copy of *Julius Caesar* by Shakespeare closed and slipping from her palm. Her immense sweatshirt surges through the slits in the chair's back, the glossy pink strand of hair bunched on her collar like a tuft of cotton candy. Meiselman wants to put his hands in it and pull it apart, take bites, not stopping until she lets out a giggly thank you.

Meiselman emerges from behind the bookcase, hands in his pocket, intent on dealing with her as if she were a vagabond, a runaway teen treating the public library as a shelter. Approaching, he lets out several abrupt commands—"Excuse me!" "Young lady!"—not nearly loud enough to rouse her because he may have already decided he wants to use her non-responsiveness as an excuse to put a hand on her. Although he anticipates giving her only a pat, maybe a shake, and his hand becomes uncertain after it pillows against the sweatshirt's shoulder, the softness of the cotton stunning his hand into submission, his forearm and bicep turning heavy. Chills break out across his back. He skims the edge of his thumb along her shoulder blade, jerking it away, and resting it on the chair's back, the moment the pink-haired girl languidly lifts her head and looks up at him over her shoulder, the safety pin side of her face droopy and red from sleep.

"What?" she asks.

The safety pin is tarnished, and, suddenly, Meiselman is overcome with compassion for this vulnerable teenager. An image of him massaging disinfectant into her eyebrow enters his mind.

"Et tu, Brute?" he says.

Pulling his hand away from the chair's back will draw attention to the touching, so he stays put. She runs her hand through her hair and the ends brush the top of his hand and come to a rest on his fingers. She does not readjust. Neither does he. Either she does not know or she does not want to know.

"Huh?" she asks.

"Book is working out?"

"Working out fine."

He steps away, leans back against the desk's edge and faces the girl. She straightens and stares into the book, flipping past the introduction. Her lips, the color of a cherry lozenge, glossy with ointment, move as she reads.

"Well, if you need anything don't hesitate to ask for me, Meiselman. I'm in charge here today." Knocks on the desk and takes his leave.

Again, not a thank-you.

Only God knows where the morning has gone. Already time to return home for Sunday lunch with Deena. Afterward, he will head to his father's house for the White Sox game, another Sunday ritual. Periodically, throughout the game, he will anticipate how tonight's sex will unfold and who will initiate. When one of them does not take the lead, they end up childishly arguing over who will strip first. Meiselman's father, sitting behind him on the couch, will interrupt these thoughts by asking if his son went into the office earlier today. Yes, I did, Meiselman will answer proudly, because if he has learned one thing from his father it is that men with serious jobs, men who are serious about their jobs, go into the office on Sundays. His mother would say, "Sharon invited us for lunch this Sunday," or "We must look for new drapes on Sunday," or "The newspapers. You must. This Sunday." And every time his father would answer, "Got to go into the office, Pooch. Big deposition." By the time Meiselman was nine or ten, Sundays were like every other day of the week in that his father was out of the house before he was awake. Gershon, his innately independent brother, would also depart early, leaving Meiselman to accompany his mother to Aunt Sharon's for breakfast and to drive from store to store comparing drapes. His father insisted only he knew which papers could be chucked, so those were left untouched.

✶ ✶ ✶

Her car is gone and the desolateness of the two-car garage, its oil stained concrete, a rusty rake hanging on a nail—who rakes? not Meiselman—and the two ten-speeds up against the wall, tires punctured, an unmet resolution from the first year of marriage, spawns a fear in Meiselman that Deena has abandoned him. At breakfast, she may have mentioned an errand. She talked and talked while he raced through the recap of the White Sox 4-1 victory last night over Tampa. Because he is positive that Sunday lunch is as important to her as it is to him, he knows she will return home shortly.

Taking advantage of his time alone, Meiselman elopes to the master bathroom, Sports in hand. Unclench, undisturbed, without Deena's questions booming through the door. To drink? Orange juice is fine, but please remember to shake before you pour. Chips? Only if they have salt. Cannot stand the baldies you've been buying. How was work? Major developments on the Shenkenberg front. Even though he brings reading material into the bathroom, Meiselman is not one to loaf.

For months, Meiselman and Deena have argued the advantages and disadvantages of cell phones. She could purchase one, but he would not. Was this not one of the advantages she claimed? Yet, it is turned off.

In the kitchen, he pulls Deena's brown bread from the freezer and breaks off four slices. He tidies the newspapers and stacks them on a chair at the end of the table, then sets the glasses, napkins, and cutlery. Deciding on a next step is tricky because what if Deena is not merely tardy? What if her abandonment is permanent?

After separating from their goodbye kiss this morning—bodies and hands not touching, just two lurched faces, lips puckered—she said to him, "Big surprise coming your way today, Meisie." Eager to get to the library, to get to the chocolates and photograph, he did not ask questions. Replaying the scene, he detects not a playful tone but one that is sinister and mocking. Big surprise for you when you get home, Meisie. I will be gone, gone for good with the maniac motorcyclist Randy, the patient I spend our dinners and nights discussing. Spilled from a motorcycle without a helmet. "Thank God nothing happened to that face," she says over and over. Meisie, you would never ride a motorcycle, even around an empty parking lot. Last week, she asked Meiselman to stop at the Center, so he could celebrate with his wife and the other therapists as Randy, two shattered legs but an intact spirit, took his first unassisted baby steps. "He will inspire you. Those goals you talk about will become paper tigers." Deena bought cupcakes and streamers and made signs using the color printer at home. He knew then. She falls asleep thinking about Randy. She dreams about Randy. Running up the stairs, Meiselman imagines finding her nightstand's bottom drawer empty. But the two pictures of Deena's mother—a high school graduation photo and another one from her wedding day—are inside the shoebox along with her mother's worthless silver-plated necklace. Deena would never leave these items behind, even for the motorcycle maniac Randy.

Back downstairs, peeking through the front curtains, he considers a different meaning behind her parting comment. At breakfast, he passed her Real Estate, finger pressed to a listing that caught his eye. She read it once before taking it from his hands and reading it again. He thought, at the very least, he would get the usual teasing threat about him living as a bachelor in the Upper Peninsula of Michigan. But she stayed quiet, and instead of handing him back the section, she folded it into quarters and set it down next to her table setting because perhaps Deena does have foresight, and while standing over the kitchen sink she anticipated her husband receiving more letters and immediately appreciated the hopelessness of his situation. If her husband respects the library's mission and allows Shenkenberg to speak unopposed they, the community, will stigmatize Meiselman as a cancer spreader, infection grower, fever elevator. On the other hand, is he willing to go up on the stake to defend fundamental beliefs? To expect martyrdom in this day and age is archaic, barbaric. This is New Niles in the new millennium. Protests are futile, intransigence slows nothing down. Everyone is replaceable with a click of a mouse. Skipping town and starting anew must have seemed the perfect solution to Deena. So his ever-impulsive wife dialed the listed broker, and while on hold, she may have fantasized about the four-bedroom country house in the UP Meiselman showed her earlier at breakfast. Four hundred miles north of Chicago, I will start a new life with Meisie. Cradling our morning mugs of coffee on the bedroom balcony, we spot deer darting across our land. Right there, Meisie, behind the pond. Are those wild turkeys? Quick kiss because we are living a dream. Oh, Meisie, I call to him, the great room's cathedral ceiling carrying my voice to the kitchen where he is spreading mayonnaise on our roast beef sandwiches, high-cholesterol no longer a concern in this rural existence. Later that night, the window shades open, not a neighbor in sight, we wrestle on the couch, each trying to strip the clothes off the other. To the hot tub. Knock flutes of champagne because we are in love. Randy lifts his leg out of the water, showing off his lateral movement. Meiselman tries forcing Randy out of Deena's fantasy, but all he can do to knock Deena's fantasy dead is to think of the pink-haired girl's hair touching his hand.

Deena's middling reaction to the real estate section was most probably her finally having tired of his weekly joke of moving to one of the coldest parts of the country. Do White Sox games even transmit that far north?

If Deena returns home in the next fifteen minutes, which he is confident she will because these lunches must mean the world to her as well, they will still have enough time to eat before the first pitch. But he will have to have the meal prepared, not only to save time, but so that when Deena comes through the front door, winded and tripping over her shopping bags and excuses, she will set her eyes on the table set for two, cut sandwiches on each plate, glasses filled to the brim with orange juice and will coo, What do I do to deserve you? Leave *her* fretting over her tardiness, leave *her* questioning whether she reciprocates equally.

Meiselman, therefore, must floor her. Tuna melts it is, and he will not cheapen the sandwich by using individually wrapped slices of American. The circumstance calls for Swiss! Topped with rings of red onion! No side of greasy Jays potato chips, either. On the counter, a perfectly soft avocado. In the refrigerator, a package of cherry tomatoes whose sweetness will leave her squealing. Purple-tinged lettuce will make a sumptuous bed. Spreading butter across the frozen bread, Meiselman now worries whether Deena will arrive home by the time the sandwiches are ready.

Does Sunday lunch mean nothing to her? Sunday lunch is not weekday breakfast, newspapers held up like dividers, coffee swigged and oatmeal spooned at a frantic pace. Sunday lunch is not weekday dinner, usually leftovers, Deena frustrated over a patient unwilling to do her exercises, incomprehensible to her how someone could choose to spend the rest of life in a chair. "She will be dependent on the charity of loved ones," she cries. "This should not be your concern," Meiselman answers. "If you've followed protocol, given her the proper recommendations, you are not liable." Sunday lunch is not Shabbat dinner at his parents, his mother recounting how she was wronged that morning in the bakery, Meiselman's father nodding off at the other end of the table, the tines of his fork plunged into a chicken thigh. "Harvey, if you are so tired, then go up to bed." Sunday lunch is a sandwich from scratch and naturally evolving conversation, starting with the mundane and progressing to intimate matters, the only time all week they have such discussions.

Last week at Sunday lunch, Deena raised the issue of the second test. Meiselman had ingested the supplements, consumed great quantities of limes and leafy vegetables, and taken only cold showers for weeks, and Deena felt it was time.

"To do it in a cup again?" he asked. "Shouldn't that humiliation be a last resort?"

"Humiliation? Have you ever seen what one of my examinations looks like? I hate, hate saying this, but I want that old man to die already so I can start seeing a woman."

"You told me you like looking in the mirror," Meiselman said. "All I'm saying is we should wait until the doctor has tried everything on your end. I'm talking statistics. Think I read that only forty percent, less than half—"

She slid his plate to the side, leaned forward and nipped him under the chin to get his attention. "But, Meisie," she said, covering his hands, "they have done everything on my end and it's a go. We are waiting on your little guys to wake up." Deena then added, "The doctor said I can go into the room with you, so you don't have to do it to a strange woman."

Devouring delectable sandwiches, musing on the nature of love, this is what will set the mood for an easy, natural transition later tonight, but if she brings up the second test again, there is no certainty over how she will take the confession that he went in for it early last week and has already received the dismal results. Such news will alter her opinion of him as an object of affection. Maybe it is better that she has not showed for Sunday lunch. The cheese is rubbery, the bread is damp with tuna juice, and the guilt she will feel when she encounters her spoiled sandwich on the table might be enough to get him out of tonight's lovemaking, if he so chooses. Your disregard for our special lunches, he will tell her, has taken me out of the mood. Or her apology will facilitate a more natural transition, a more passionate session. The latter option is preferable because he does enjoy the act, just not the anticipation.

Arriving at his parents' house, he finds his father sitting stiffly in an open stance on the couch's edge, a newspaper open in front of him, hiked grey trousers advertising his twiggy legs, which are shorn of fat and muscle, like two baseball bats whose handles are dipped into chunky black shoes with therapeutically thick rubber soles. His father is constantly recommending the shoes to Meiselman, arguing that one can never have too much support. His old man is always trying to sell his son on therapies. "In one hour, the dentist will have your teeth looking like you brushed them with Elmer's." Or, "Sitz baths make all the difference." Or, "Embrace the gray early." No denying the plushness of his father's hair, like the satin pillow of a ring box.

They do not greet one another as Meiselman takes a seat in the barrel-backed swivel chair between his father and the television. "Dad, Dad," he turns to his father as the leadoff hitter Harris steps into the batter's box. His father peers over the top of the newspaper as the first pitch, a strike down the middle, crosses the plate. Between pitches, he lifts the newspaper eye-level, lowering it in time for each pitch. For the most part, this is how he will watch the entire game.

Harris singles to center, steals a base, and moves over to third on the inning's second out. Frank keeps the inning going with a walk. A wild pitch brings a runner home, and Meiselman and his father stand up to slap each other five. His father's slap is timid, hesitating at the moment of contact, as if afraid his son will take his hand off.

"Looking good," his father says.

"Just the first inning," Meiselman answers.

"I've got a feeling. I've watched enough games to know."

Top of the fifth, with the White Sox leading 3-0, Meiselman says to his father, "What a day, so far."

His father responds with a finger up in the air, as though telling his son to hold the thought. Closing the newspaper and setting it down on a second pile of newspapers on the other side of his legs, he sinks back into the couch's corner, crosses his legs and says, "You know, the '59 Sox." Here goes. The same spiel Meiselman endures every Sunday. The great Go-Go Sox team of '59. Ted Kluszewski, "Big Klu." Biceps so big they had to cut off his uniform sleeves. Jim Landis. Couldn't hit a grapefruit, but could stop a grape from getting past him in the field. Early Wynn. A real headhunter. A sportswriter once asked if he'd throw at his own mother, and he answered—Meiselman can hear his father's wheezy laugh—You don't know my mother. She could really hit a curveball. Won the Cy Young that year. Sherm Lollar, Nellie Fox, "Jungle" Jim Rivera, the headfirst slider. Al Smith, Bob Shaw, Earl Torgeson. The team's first pennant in forty years. Lost the Series to the Dodgers. 1917 is the last time the Sox have won it all.

“I know, I know,” an exasperated Meiselman answers. “You’ve been telling me since I was a boy. But this year’s team is the one I’m going to tell my boys about. Frank Thomas, ‘The Big Hurt.’”

Stunned by Meiselman’s dissent, his father stares at his son for several seconds, his jowly cheeks shaking, before throwing a hand at his son and returning to the sorting, transferring sections from one pile to the other without stopping to read. His father’s finger comes back up, and he says, “The point I’m trying to make in all of this is that the ’59 team had real character. Does this year’s team have the character to win? That’s all I’m asking.”

Meiselman feels bad. Yes, he pledged he would stop taking it. But from his own father?

The same commercials air every game. Spots targeting people who lack credit and cannot put money down, offers for car insurance and same-day carpet installation, ballplayers hawking used cars, and lawyers who are experts in creating victims and victimhood. They sit casually on the edges of desks and implore people to find ways they were wronged. Finally, a commercial for an everyday product comes on. A blonde in a blue one-piece challenges her man, and she is off running down a white sandy beach, but as Meisleman’s father sets down a section and sits up straighter, the clink of the front door’s deadbolt throws him off the couch.

“Nothing about the shirts,” he breathes into Meisleman’s ear.

“What shirts?”

“Hey, Pooch,” his father greets his wife.

Meiselman’s mother enters the living room in her tan trench coat, a gray sweatsuit underneath, keys clutched in her palm, her purse hanging off her shoulder.

“What did they say about the stain?” she asks his father.

The newspaper is back up and from behind it his father answers, “Theresa said you were smart to have me bring it in before it settled any further.”

“Your nicest shirt,” she mutters, exiting the room.

Seconds later, they hear his mother tramping upstairs, his father’s eyes on the ceiling as he fishes the car key from his pocket. Dangling it in front of his son, he says, “Move the shirt to the trunk.” Rolls his eyes and wipes his forehead with the back of his hand. Crisis averted.

The shirt secure in the car’s trunk, Meiselman steps to the sidewalk for a better view of his driveway. Still no sign of Deena. Should he not be home in case the hospital calls looking for consent? Out carousing with motorcycle maniac Randy, therapist and patient sang along to the car radio, a song they shared during sessions in the Center’s workout room. Deena began mocking Randy’s falsetto sound. Horseplay ensued, fingers tussling in front of the radio’s tuner. Deena rammed the car into a blue U.S. mailbox, the front of the car crumpling like a balled sheet of paper. Consent for surgery, a no brainer. Consent to keep her plugged in? Quality of life issues for Deena, quality of life issues for Meiselman, too. At first, the community will hail Meiselman’s devotion to his vegetable wife, gossiping to one another about his daily visits and willingness to change bedpans. The gossiping, however, will take a perverse turn, and soon rumors will start spreading about Meiselman’s involvement with an older woman, nobody giving him the benefit of the doubt, nobody wanting to hear about a friendship struck up in the hospital waiting room, the mother of Deena’s companion, who sadly did not make it out alive. He fell for her simplicity, the toothpick-thin cross, peach cardigans, and dirty blonde ponytail. In consideration of Deena, just hands, no mouths.

If the doctor comes out and says, I’m sorry, your wife did not pull through, Meiselman can expect the generosity of the community to overwhelm him. For the week of mourning he will feast on chicken, salads, candy platters, and kugels, lots of kugels. How fortunate there are no children, community members will whisper to one another. Ethel will pay a condolence call, offering classy air kisses at her arrival and departure. He will want to collapse his head into her beefy chest for a good cry. The mourning period over, Ethel will suggest getting lost in work is the best way to cope. She will compare it to when she lost her dog. Unable to lose himself in the work, he will pack up and drive north. Won't stop driving until he reaches the UP. He will rent, at first. Wheel-less tricycles, cracked wiffle bats, and a sit-and-spin, all belonging to the neglected children next door, will litter his front lawn. The mother of the children will get in the habit of dropping the kids off at Meiselman's house unannounced before disappearing for days. He will help them with homework and teach them to brush and floss. Scouting an exceptional talent in the oldest Ty, Meiselman will cultivate his math skills. In the meantime, he will revive the springless trampoline in their backyard, dumping the pooled water from its center. The lumberyard job he takes will be too much for his callus-free hands. Fortunately, the owner notices Meiselman's other skills. At the local bar, he will establish a reputation for ordering seltzer with lime and asking the bartender Wally to turn to the Tigers' games. Eventually, he will fall for the next-door neighbor, a peppery redhead with hair down to her jean-busting, globular backside. An ice fishing trip with the future brother-in-laws. A scuffle with an alcoholic ex. Experience the exhilaration of getting a fist to the face, as well as the thrill of knocking another man to the ground. He will discover his fiancé has Jewish ancestry. How can she be Jewish with a name like Thompson, his mother will grumble at the wedding. His parents will leave word that they sold Meiselman's old house to a lovely Indian couple.

The White Sox are not putting runners on base, denying the Meiselman men another opportunity to sit on a pitch together or slap five. Looking to infuse energy into the room, Meiselman asks his father the question he wants asked of him.

"Did you go to the office today?"

"Of course, sure, why not? Your mother wanted to go to some store, or something somewhere, but, boy, do I have a ton of work."

"Also went in today," Meiselman says. "Just buried with this Shenkenberg."

"What is wrong with Frank? Should have *shmeised* that pitch."

"Fastballs are no good, I keep telling you. Ethel expects over two hundred people."

"Loaiza is mowing them down. If he can have a big season that would be huge, just huge."

"Gives up too many long balls and he's beating the weak teams. With the kinds of letters I'm getting, I need to start thinking about security."

"How they allow Astroturf is beyond me."

Meiselman is done trying. He thinks about cutting out early to watch the last innings alone at home, spending the commercial breaks preparing a dessert to spoil alongside Deena's sandwich and salad. Compound the guilt. Ice cream melts quickly. Whipped cream collapses. Cake dries out. Jell-O is impossible to swallow at room temperature. Bananas turn mushy and brown. Attract flies, he can hope.

"Whoa," his father belts. "How about that?" His father bounces up from the couch and thrusts a newspaper in front of Meiselman's face. "Izzy Shenkenberg is speaking at your library? Says it right here in the *Chicago Jewish Chronicle*."

“Yes, yes, he’s speaking at our library. That’s me. I’m in charge of him speaking at the library.”

“Here’s an ad for it. Do you know about this?”

“Yes, I wrote it, designed it, got the quote, faxed it over. I do all the marketing. It looks good, no? Got *your* attention.”

The Jewish weekly rag in his hands, his father walks over to the room’s doorway and calls, “Pooch, Pooch? Better come see this.”

“What’s wrong?” she asks, running down the stairs. “Did they call about the shirt?

He puts the ad in his wife’s hands. Looking over to Meiselman, he asks, “You’re responsible for this?”

“It looks wonderful,” his mother says. “The font is gorgeous. Letters big and legible. Lately with ads, I find I’m just straining.”

“Izzy Shenkenberg the writer is coming to your library,” disbelief filling his father’s voice. “Boy, that’s big.”

“Yes, and I’m in charge.”

“Is he the one who wrote that book about the boy in the concentration camp with the talking pigeon?” his mother asks.

“No, he’s the one who took care of Rabbi J- at the end of his life and then wrote a book airing all of Rabbi J-’s dirty underwear. How he likes to gamble on boxing and goes drinking at bars or something. Bunch of lies meant to make religious Jews look bad. Like we don’t have enough people making fun and calling us goofy. A New Niles boy. Bum.”

“I’m going to hang this on the refrigerator,” Meiselman’s mother says.

“I’ve been corresponding with Rav Fruman on the matter,” Meiselman says. “He’s just livid we are hosting him. But the library’s mission has to be respected. Shenkenberg is not that nice of a guy. The other day on the phone—”

"Fruman? What does Fruman want? Fruman is a *nudnik*. Everything is objectionable to Fruman. A total Neanderthal."

"If Shenkenberg is a bum and Fruman is a *nudnik*, what do I do, Dad?"

"Take him deep. Show him what you've got."

Take him deep. Yes, yes, he will take Shenkenberg deep. And he will show everyone what he's got.

"Take him deep, Konerko," his father repeats, eyes back on the game.

"I'm going to highlight the name of the library," his mother says, "so people know why I hung it up."

Act hurt, jilted, abandoned, Meiselman reminds himself as he spots Deena's car in the driveway. And add forgetting to close the door to his list of her sins.

"You are the most thoughtful husband," she says, racing downstairs and throwing her arms around him, kissing him furiously on his beardline. He tucks his neck, forcing her to back off. "My sandwich," she says. "I loved it."

"Come on, Deena. The bread must have been soggy, the cheese hard, the avocado, surely, black."

"Perfect. It was all perfect. And those tomatoes, wow."

"I tried to wait."

"You had your game. You look disappointed. Did they lose?"

"No, a White Sox winner, but Frank did something to his hamstring. Took him out of the game. Not good. We need him."

Heels off the ground, she wraps her arms around his neck and rests her head against his chest. Stooping for kisses and hugs makes him feel predatory. Now may be an ideal time to make his move. Removing the burden will allow him to enjoy the rest of the night without worrying over the when and how of the transition. If he kisses her and she reacts, he will move his hand under her shirt and get close to her pits, counting on a giggling fit to hasten the process. So, he kisses her on the lips lightly, and then follows it up with a more forceful one. She pulls back and clamps a hand over her lips.

"We can't touch, I don't think," she says. "I'm spotting."

"Spotting how much?"

"A couple of spots. Not sure about the color. More brown than red, more yellow than brown."

"Larger than the size of a quarter. If it's not larger than the size of a quarter we're good. We can take the lenient view. We don't have to be so rigid."

"Combined, the spots seem larger than a quarter. Usually, I know, but this time I don't, and I want to play it safe. Maybe take it to a rabbi to have it checked?"

He was ready, he was willing, a smooth transition was afoot. What if this is the moment where the seed will finally stick, and now a rabbi might rule that they have to separate for twelve days, or fifteen, seeing that Deena is a bleeder? The pressure of a smooth transition after not having done it for a month will be great. He does like it, but not when it turns into an onus, an unmet husbandly duty.

Deena runs upstairs to retrieve her underwear, leaving Meiselman to study her purchases, which are lined up next to the door. Groceries, mostly. A black shiny bag with rope handles catches his attention. Inside, a white cardboard box. Puts his hands into the bag and stealthily lifts the tissue paper. Deena calls down to tell him she will be another second, giving him time to pull the garment from the bag and hold it for a closer look. Is this the surprise? Does she not know that white does little for him? Black is his color. But pink, he is learning, will also do. At least, she did not pick an asexual color like tan.

Spotted underwear in hand, Deena trots down the stairs and says, "Please don't take it to our rabbi. Took it to him that one time a couple months back, and I can barely look at him anymore. Molly says her husband takes it to Rav Fruman, the guy from the yeshiva."

"'The guy from the yeshiva?' He's the head of the yeshiva, the Rosh Yeshiva, and President of the RAC, and you call him 'the guy' like he's the man who comes to fix the air conditioner."

The coincidence of this predicament must be a sign. On Friday, Shenkenberg reveals his disrespectful, dismissive nature to Meiselman. Earlier today, Meiselman receives a threatening letter from Rav Fruman highlighting the threat posed by Shenkenberg's disrespectful, dismissive behavior. Now, Meiselman returns home to his wife telling him that he needs to see Rav Fruman because of a questionable discharge. Fate, destiny, he has always thought of such ideas as heretical, the beliefs of people who want to see God as a personal benefactor, a pal. But maybe God does, every now and then move away from big picture matters to involve himself—itself—in more minor matters like the life of his humble servant Meiselman.

* * *

Stopped at New Niles's longest red, Meiselman marvels at the strip mall up ahead to the right. Well-crafted, well-enforced village code has prevented this structure from becoming a hodgepodge of clashing storefronts. All of the stores, from the mom and pop shops to the brand name retailers and restaurants, share the same burnt orange brick façade, the color of the clay of Arizona, a state Meiselman has yet to visit. Meiselman has never been west of the Mississippi. For signage, the stores are restricted to using blue and green. Lush ivy borders the façade. Spring is barely here and the grounds are already green. Flowerbeds fill the parking lot medians.

Bushy bald cypresses conceal the utility chambers off to the side. How fortunate Meiselman is to live in an ascending village like New Niles. His parents at his age—Gershon recently conceived—sensed the decline of the South Side neighborhood where they were born and raised, and fled north to the ripening village of New Niles, just outside the Chicago city limits. Migration, one can assume, will not be forced on this generation of Meiselmans. His brother left because he is innately curious and independent and not because his dreams outpaced and outmatched the opportunities afforded by his hometown, as his mother claims.

Abutting this edifice of prosperity and cleanliness is a professional-grade Little League field. This ball field, with its dirt base paths, grass infield, elevated pitcher's mound, towering yellow foul poles and distances to home plate marked on the outfield walls, surpasses the one at the Jewish Community Center where Meiselman played his year of Little League. Try fielding a grounder after it has rolled through a divot-and-gravel-filled infield. Try finding a ball in knee-high weeds. Despite these obstacles, Meiselman held his own and was not counted among the nebbishes who induced moved-in infields every time they came to the plate, roomy batting helmets falling over their eyes on late whiffs.

The light changes and Meiselman drives through the intersection, but instead of turning right to head to the baseball diamond to cheer on the local New Niles Boars, he slows into the left hand turn lane and faces the blight situated across the street from the strip mall and field. The drabness of the yeshiva's main building, a three-story box, reminds Meiselman of the pictures teachers showed him whenever highlighting the miserable lives of refuseniks in the Soviet Union. Who can tell whether the building's original color is gray or white? The bricks of the monumental chimney—rebuilt after its collapse five years ago—are a shade whiter than the rest of the building. It punches fists of black smog into the air, the building laboring to warm itself as dusk encroaches on this mild afternoon of sun and temperatures in the low 50s. Rust from window grates stain streak the facade. Many of the windows' aluminum blinds are bent in the center, permanent damage from someone peering out for too long. Some blinds resemble an open hand fan. Some windows are missing blinds altogether and instead have bedsheets for privacy. Bedsheets! The brick walls of the church on Jaworski Drive are hose-washed on a biannual basis. A silver cross the size of a human body caps its wondrous spire to an intrusive height. And the yeshiva has bedsheets in its windows!

A younger, naïve Meiselman may have been fooled into believing that the yeshiva's disrepair is a form of asceticism, but he has seen how Rav Fruman, the yeshiva's head, dresses. Like the Godfather, a homburg hat—no feather—thick band tied into a fat bow on the hat's side. Like Gandhi, black-framed, round eyeglasses. An Abe Lincoln topcoat worn over a buttoned-up vest, no tie. Underneath, a dress shirt, buttoned to the top, white as the chalk on a baseball diamond. The Rav is no *schlep*, yet, he tolerates unkempt grass, creepers climbing his buildings, a potholed parking lot, weedy walkways, and bedsheets!

Most objectionable is the yeshiva's study hall. A short walk from the main building, the squat structure is shaped like the Star of David and sits prominently at the front of the grounds. Was there a time when its dome shimmered like a freshly minted dime? What do drivers think now as they spy this moldering edifice when crossing into the village? Most of these drivers will never step inside the study hall and discover that the dome is a sham. Instead, the high ceiling is flat and marred by reparative patches of white plaster. There is no great rotunda with renderings of fatherly Abraham holding a knife over the man-child Isaac, or one of Joseph the Dreamer in Pharaoh's court, seven scorched stalks devouring seven healthy stalks, seven lean cows feasting on seven fat cows, the favored son explaining to the Egyptian king that the party never lasts and lean years are surely to follow. Or does Meiselman have the story backward, and it is the lean years that precede the party? The dome's lack of functionality suggests it exists solely for aesthetic purposes. Does this mean there was a time when the yeshiva felt an obligation to enhance the public sphere? If so, what explains this inward turn?

The study hall is empty. Evening services do not commence for several hours. Strolling through the hall's adjoining corridor, its light the hazy yellow of used cooking oil, Meiselman is struck by the smell. Is this the musty smell his mother complained about whenever he returned home? Claimed it was stuck in his hair and clothes. The building's smell and interior lighting are the most distinct memories of his brief time at the yeshiva. He transferred out after freshman year.

More disrepair as he steps down the hallway. A black garbage bag covers the water fountain. Trashcans overflow. Inside the classrooms, *gemaras* are tossed onto desks, some open. The desks are jumbled as if students were using them for a game of bumper cars. Turning the corner at the end of the hallway, Meiselman spots a lanky rabbinical student sitting on a folding chair, his legs in a tight feminine cross, body folded forward, fingers twirling and untwirling a sidelock.

"The Rav?" the rabbinical student asks Meiselman, not making eye contact. He says, "Me too. If he has time. The Rav is busy. We are the least of his concerns."

Inside the office, Rav Fruman sits behind a desk. He is talking on the phone and briefly glances across the room at Meiselman, who stands at the open door. The moment Meiselman tightens his fist for a knock, a beardless fortysomething in a starchy white shirt, black pants, and tinted glasses rushes the door, finger up in the air.

This man, whom one presumes is the Rav's secretary, smiles while gently closing the door in Meiselman's face.

Meiselman takes a seat across from the beardless student, who has a ridge of acne simmering across his forehead. His fingers move to underneath his black velvet kippa, and he begins scratching at his crown with four fingers as if using his head as an emery board, eyes cinching as his pace quickens, flakes of dandruff falling onto the shoulders of his black sport jacket, which clashes a shade darker than his pants. Out of gas, he stops, opens his eyes, and takes a breather. He wipes both hands up and down his pants legs before resuming. Finishing another round of itching, the man sweeps the scalp shavings off his shoulder. Several flakes cling. With his tongue he dampens his pinkie and lifts them off one-by-one. He holds the flake-speckled finger in front of his nose, and then up to the light before taking a whiff of it. His tongue inches out. He shrugs at its taste. Looking at Meiselman, he says, "The Rav's too busy to see you, right? My third time in the last week. Come back later, every time. He's in charge of it all, the Rav."

The door opens a crack and both men straighten in their seats. "Psst," the secretary hisses through the opening, and the beardless student jumps from his seat. The secretary whispers, "Not you," and then nods in Meiselman's direction.

"And what do you come here to see the Rav for?" the secretary asks Meiselman.

A good question. Does he come to see the Rav for the underwear or Shenkenberg? For a personal matter like the underwear, the Rav may have him wait even longer. Opening with the underwear, however, will prove to the Rav that Meiselman is Torah-abiding, earning him much needed respect for any potential Shenkenberg negotiations.

"Tell him Meiselman from the public library. He'll know what it's about."

"From the public library here in New Niles? Oh, yes, yes, the book." He looks back at the Rav, who is still on the phone. "A minute, please, and then I come get you." The door again closes in his face.

Quickly realizing the secretary's return is not imminent, Meiselman returns to his seat. The beardless rabbinical student is now pinching a pimple bubbling at the end of his eyebrow.

"What is this book you are here to talk to the Rav about?" he asks Meiselman.

"The Izzy Shenkenberg lecture at the New Niles Public Library," Meiselman answers, eliciting the same impassive shrug as the dandruff tasting. "Wrote that defamatory book about Rabbi J-?" Meiselman adds.

"Maybe it's better you don't tell me about any controversy," he says. "I can't get involved in nonsense."

The pimple pops. The man sits up, uncrosses his legs, and gets to the task of wiping the blood and puss with his pinkie.

Out steps the secretary to tell Meiselman it will be just another minute. He says nothing to the man on the folding chair, simply glances down at him, revulsion covering his face. Just as the door is about to shut again, Meiselman springs from his chair and catches the secretary's attention. He says, "Actually, I'm here to ask, as well, about a stain on my wife's undergarment." Returning to his seat, Meiselman begins to suspect that his brief history with Rav Fruman may be the reason for the long wait.

It starts when his brother, Gershon, was a student in the Rav's class freshman year of high school. Every week, Gershon came home with rumored tales of Rav Fruman's past. An Arkansan commune child shipped off to Vietnam. Returned home decorated and maimed from jumping on a grenade to save a platoon leader's life. A scarred hand that, to this day, he keeps balled and pressed against the bottom of his ribcage, a man ready to self-administer the Heimlich. At anti-war rallies, the Rav, before he was the Rav, played guitar for Dylan. One drunken night, in one of New York City's bohemian neighborhoods, the Rav, looking for a bathroom, an innate sense of modesty preventing him from public urination, stumbled into a synagogue and the prayers of grizzled men stimulated a memory of a childhood lullaby. Boarded a plane for Israel the next day. Eventually cut the blonde hair that hung to his shoulders. There was adult circumcision. Years later he learned that, no, he was Jewish only on his father's side and, therefore, not Jewish at all. The decision to convert, he supposedly told Gershon's class, was not even a decision.

Five years later, Meiselman was a student in Rav Fruman's freshman *shiur*. In the dormitory, Meiselman and his classmates discussed Rav Fruman's conversion conundrum. Of course I'd go through with it again. It's everything and everyone I know, Meiselman answered himself, none of his classmates asking to hear his thoughts.

At last, the secretary calls Meiselman and has him wait in the doorway as he announces him. "Here to talk about the matter with an additional question about a garment."

Particleboard abounds in the office of this man who tolerates bedsheets in his building's windows. The shelves of the bookcases sag. A majority of the books' bindings are stripped or shredded. The window on the opposite side of the room looks out onto an endless, muddy field. Fluorescents flicker overhead, and the legs of the Rav's metal desk are rusted. Are the nicks in the gray linoleum tiles part of the design or is Meiselman staring at more disrepair? Over the Rav's shoulder is an army-green filing cabinet, perhaps where Meiselman's brief history at the yeshiva is filed away, including notes on the lone interaction between Rav Fruman and the student Meiselman?

Day 1: During roll call Rav Fruman informs students that classmate Meiselman is an *eynikl* of the great Rav F- of Eretz Yisrael, may the memory of the righteous be for a blessing. Rav Fruman asks student Meiselman to explain the relationship. Student explains that the great Rav F-, may the memory of the righteous be for a blessing, is his father's mother's mother's father. Rav Fruman explains to the class that since it is through mothers and he is not a direct descendant through fathers, the connection is not as significant as previously thought. Classmates express disappointment, although there is clear relief that they can continue ignoring their fellow student. Rav Fruman is convinced student Meiselman, who comes from the more modern part of the community, will ultimately follow the path of his brother, Gershon, and transfer after freshman year to the *tumahdika* high school across town where the boys and girls learn together. No need to engage student Meiselman for duration of year.

Does the file note how Meiselman passed his time in class studying the Rav's face, looking for features that betrayed the rabbi's former identity, like the ruddy cheeks, the bulbous nose, and blueberry eyes? Does it mention how in his daydreams he would shear the Rav's beard and grow his hair—yellow as the corn he munched on in Arkansas—until it was down to the shoulders of his tattered army fatigues, loose threads from torn off medals hanging from the shirt's breasts? In Meiselman's daydreams he would strip the wig off the Rav's wife, dirty her blonde hair, dangle a braid to her tailbone, and stick a dandelion behind her ear. Shoes were never considered for this woman. He parked their camper on a beach in California. They made love in front of a crackling fire.

Does the file comment on Meiselman's jealousy every time the Rav dug his puffy knuckles into the spines of the other students whenever dissatisfied with the phrasing of a question or answer? Does it elucidate why the Rav never snagged a hunk of Meiselman's cheek between his knuckles, pinching until the skin turned a purplish red, or why he never tested the elasticity of Meiselman's fingers? Why did he exclude Meiselman from this exercise in pleasurable pain, an exercise meant to teach that at the end of the day pain is temporary and fleeting? "Knowing the *daf* cold," Rav Fruman used to say. "That will never leave your body." Did he believe Meiselman was uneducable?

Meiselman waits in the doorway as the secretary hands the Rav documents to be signed. When they finish, the Rav orders the secretary to make "the call." After dialing the number, the secretary hands the receiver to the Rav. While the phone rings, the Rav rotates his balled fist, signaling to Meiselman that he should approach, keeping it turning as Meiselman advances. Right as Meiselman reaches the desk the Rav punches his balled fist forward, as if Meiselman needed halting, as if without it Meiselman would have continued, climbing over the desk until his hands were around the Rav's throat demanding to know how he can be expected to stand up to Shenkenberg, stand up for himself and the memory of Rabbi J-, while pleasing Ethel and honoring the library's mission.

Rav Fruman is not speaking to anyone on the phone. He nods steadily, scornful eyes lifting to Meiselman every couple of seconds. Is he checking the weather, the time, the scores? Is he receiving instructions from a higher power? Eventually, he places the receiver down on the desk and says to the secretary, "Disconnect the call, will you."

"You are a Meiselman?" the Rav asks.

"Yes, Harvey and Linda's son."

The redness has been drained from his withered cheeks, and only a drizzle of yellow remains in his white beard. The sidelocks wind around his ears more times than Meiselman remembers. Tattered jeans, fatigues, and sex on a beach in front of a crackling fire are hardly imaginable. The fingernails of the Rav's pruned fingers, however, shine.

"Gershon is your brother." Not a question. "Good, sharp head." Taps his temple.

"Thank you," Meiselman answers.

"Terrible what your parents did to him, transferring him to that *tumahdika* school. But it's not my place to say. God had plans for him. God plans, man laughs. You understand?"

"He ended up being very happy with the change. He was fortunate to have Rabbi J- as a rebbe like my father and uncles before him. Became a National Merit finalist, accepted early to Columbia, so all in all, the right decision for him."

Here is an opportunity to segue into the Shenkenberg conversation, but before he can pivot, the Rav turns to his secretary and says, "His brother makes a good *parnasa* working for that big company. What's the name?"

"Aqualeben," Meiselman answers. "Water."

"Big *ba'al tzedakah,*" the Rav explains to the secretary. "Gives money to yeshivas and mikvas all over the country and *Eretz Yisrael.*" Leans over to the secretary who is at his side, lowers his voice and says, "Write this down. Tomorrow we put in a call to Gershon Meiselman. Tell him we saw his brother and ask if he is interested in that project we discussed earlier with Grossberg." The secretary pulls a small electronic device from the breast pocket of his white shirt and starts tapping away with a pen-like device.

"I'm sure he would love to hear from the Rav," Meiselman says.

Rav Fruman sits back, massaging the knuckles of his bad hand.

"Your father is a lawyer, no?"

"Yes."

"Let me see the garment."

Why today out of all days did Deena have to wear her childish, yellow underwear with the words "Hey You" on the back, a pair that barely covers the minimum?

"Nu, nu," the Rav says. "The garment. I have people waiting."

To be lumped in with the repellent man in the hallway stings.

Meiselman turns the pair inside out and folds it in half so the stain is on top. The Rav stands and snatches it from Meiselman's hand. Holding it between his fingers, the Rav considers the stain from different angles, before dropping the underwear on the desk. He steps out from behind the desk and walks over to the blind-free window. Without being asked, the secretary takes over like a sous-chef or scrub nurse and collects the underwear off the desk, bringing it to the window and draping it over the Rav's bad hand. Then, the secretary tears off a sheet of white perforated paper from a stack in the tray of an out-of-commission printer that sits on top of the filing cabinet. Meanwhile, the Rav is pumping his lips in and out, a sloshing noise coming from inside his mouth getting louder and louder and, with the secretary back at the side of his boss, the Rav's lips part and a glob of saliva, thick as sap, dribbles down from his mouth onto Meiselman's wife's underwear. Using the back of his good hand, the Rav wipes at a stubborn strand of saliva hanging from his lips.

The two men get to work. The Rav ejects an index finger and begins mixing the saliva into the brown stain before pulling it back for a quick examination of the underwear. Dissatisfied, he lowers his finger and mixes some more. He examines it again. Satisfied with how he has reconstituted the discharge, he motions to the secretary, who presents the paper and, in a well-rehearsed movement, the Rav flips the underwear onto the paper and presses down hard, the secretary sliding his hand underneath so he is supporting the paper at the point of pressure. One final push, the

Rav gritting his teeth, an eye closed. The secretary lifts the underwear off the paper. It has left a brownish red mark.

The underwear is returned to Meiselman. Not wanting to stand in front of the Rav and secretary with the yellow underwear in his hands, Meiselman stuffs it into his front pocket. He will not return the underwear to Deena. Too many men have touched it.

The Rav is holding the paper up to the window. Daylight is fading.

"When did this happen?" the Rav asks.

"Earlier today."

"Earlier today seven hours ago or earlier today three hours ago?"

"Five."

"Too long. Next time you need to get it here as quickly as possible."

The Rav points out to the secretary an area of the brown mark that is of interest. The men mumble to one another and nod as if impressed, as if they have discovered evidence of Deena's eggs being of a particularly high quality.

"Is your wife on any of those pills?"

"God forbid, no. We are desperately trying to start a family."

"Never the pills. They permanently harm the essence of the woman's biology. Leading doctors have told me I'm right about this."

"Remind the Rav," the secretary says, "to give you a *bracha* before you leave. After we discuss the other matter."

"We need to let it dry," the Rav says. "To be safe."

Nobody speaks. The secretary is reading something off his device, smiling. The Rav moves the finger he used to reconstitute the discharge along his lower lip as if applying lip balm. To taste or to cleanse?

"I was a student of the Rav's as well," Meiselman says.

"Does your wife have infections?" the Rav asks.

"Not that I know of."

"You don't know this of your own wife?" The Rav and secretary share a laugh. "Well, does she complain of burning, or a smell?"

"Years ago, I know, she had some. But she's very clean now."

"What year?"

"Right after we got married, so four years ago."

"What year were you a student of mine, I'm asking."

"I think it was '83-'84."

"5747? I don't know your calendar. Your brother, I remember. You, not so much."

The Rav holds the paper up to the window again. Knocks his head from side-to-side.

"To be safe," the Rav says, "tonight, you should separate from your wife. Tomorrow, if she's clean, then she is permitted to you. From what I see, though, it should not be a surprise if her time comes soon."

The ruling should have relieved Meiselman of the anxiety that had been building, all day, all week. Told he is forbidden to his wife, however, he now feels deprived. The thought of not being allowed to touch his wife's little body, brushing her jawbone with a pinkie, tickling the underside of her foot, pains him. He wants what he cannot have. It is that elementary.

Besides, he could hear in the Rav's tone that the ruling could have gone either way, yet he chose to restrict, to deny Meiselman and Deena. Who is Rav Fruman to make decisions about the state of Deena's body? Does Rav Fruman not bleed the same blood as

Deena? Does the Rav's saliva not foam like other men? Meiselman went voluntarily to the Rav because they always tell you to ask. Who tells you to ask? Rabbis like Rav Fruman tell you. There are straightforward questions one asks a rabbi, the gaps in knowledge that only a rabbi can traverse. But where is the system of checks and balances, the system that guarantees Rav Fruman is acting objectively and not out of malice, because maybe the Rav is harboring resentment over his parents taking Gershon from him twenty-five years ago, or maybe he is striking at Meiselman over the Shenkenberg affair, or maybe he looked at Deena's devilish underwear, considered the ease at which his wife can pull them to the side with as little as a hooked pinkie, and teemed with jealousy, questioning how a man like Meiselman, a man who is only the number two at his job, is blessed to have such an untamable wife? A medical doctor, a man or woman charged with safeguarding physical, not spiritual, safety, passes along the facts and a recommendation, but the patient still must make the final decision, must consent. In twenty-first century America we ask individuals to take responsibility. Meiselman's mother asked Dr. Lin if there were pills her son could take. "There are pills to control compulsions, but I'm not convinced that a man in his twenties looking at revealing photographs is a compulsion, or at least an unhealthy one. Furthermore, this is a conversation that should be between doctor and patient," Dr. Lin answered, pointing to Meiselman, who stood behind his mother. "Even though I'm paying the bills?" his mother asked when telling over the story to Meiselman's father later that evening. Would life have turned out differently if he had demanded those pills? Would he have become the director of the New Niles Public Library instead of the number two? Would he have taken a different path, like moving out of New Niles and getting an executive position with the largest water company in the world?

"Don't just nod. Tell me you understand," the Rav says to Meiselman.

Why is Meiselman always following the rules of other men? Why does he see such behavior as a requirement for decent living? When does he get to establish the arbitrary rules other men must follow?

"Yes, I understand," Meiselman grumbles.

A lost battle, but the war is far from over, especially with a card left to play, one that will prove to the Rav that he, Meiselman, is a decision-maker, too.

"Earlier today I received your letter," Meiselman says. "I'm sorry to tell you—"

"Wait, what?" The Rav waves him off with his balled fist and looks over to the secretary. "A letter?" The secretary whispers into the Rav's ear. "I told you," the Rav growls at the secretary. "This is your affair." Composing himself, the Rav turns to Meiselman and says, "I'm sorry. Some people from your modern Orthodox community, some who maybe had a relationship with this Rabbi J- who was talked about in this book or magazine article, whatever it was, expressed displeasure over this writer speaking at the library. I've never been to this library, and I didn't know Rabbi J-. Knew of him, of course, but he taught at the *tumahdika* school across town and our paths never crossed. I'm sure he was a lovely man. This is what I hear. Also had a difficult life, from what I understand."

"Yes," Meiselman says, "and I don't approve of Shenkenberg's style either, but my job—"

"Whatever. It's not here, it's not there, it's not anywhere. People expressed outrage and he," Rav Fruman points to the secretary, "felt it would be smart politically if I wrote a letter since as head of the RAC I represent the entire Orthodox community, not just the yeshiva community. Sometimes I have to play a little politics like everyone else," he says, rubbing his fingers together. "In the end what can we do? It's a public library. You can't go up against the state. This is one rule we've learned."

The Frumans and Shenkenbergs of the world are never pushed into a corner, never forced to play defense. At the doorway, Meiselman stops and says, "One more thing. With all due respect, the appearance of the yeshiva is appalling, just appalling. Ungroomed grass, cracked windows, some of them with bedsheets in them. Bedsheets! Is this the message we want to be sending the greater world? That our finest institutions look like a deserted prison, a crack den, a house of prostitution? After everything the village has done for our community? Where is our *hakares hatov*? They see this disrepair and think we are interlopers."

"And this bothers you?" The Rav sits back in his chair smiling, stroking the chin of his beard with the balled fist. "What you talk about," he says, "is the *klipos*, the shell, the peel. We throw out the peel because it's the inside, the spirit that concerns us. This is precisely the message we send them, the others. The *goyim*."

Meiselman is flushed. He can feel himself stammering as he tries to talk.

"With all due respect, Rav," Meiselman says, "you seem to take quite good care of your shell."

The Rav laughs off Meiselman's attack with a shaggy, villainous gurgle. Four fingers of his good hand to his lips, he says, "Because of who your brother is I will not say anything. You came, you asked a question. Maybe you didn't like the answer. Maybe you are upset because I didn't remember you, but if you did not distinguish yourself this is certainly not my problem. Also, you should tell your wife that this is why we tell women not to wear light-colored undergarments. Unless, unless," here the Rav draws out his words, "she had a reason—and I'm not a psychologist trained in such things—a reason in the subconscious for wanting there to be a questionable stain so she could begin early her time of separation from you. But what happens between you and your wife is not my concern. Now, goodbye."

How could Meiselman think winning is something one simply decides to do? One does not go to sleep a wimp and wake up a warrior. Winning has to be practiced, worked into every action, every utterance. Banking on becoming the lucky underdog is a losing proposition.

The man on the folding chair outside the office has his arm down the back of his shirt and is scratching away. Meiselman stares down at him and holding out a hand says, "What kind of woman would want to be with this?"

"You mean the Gelman girl? The Rav told you to tell me she's not interested?"

The rabbinical student takes his arm out of his shirt and puts both hands on his knees. Sad, helpless, he stares up at Meiselman.

On the drive home, Meiselman envisions how the rest of the night will unfold. He will enter the house and refrain from mentioning the front door being left open. Instead, he will stifle his wife's greeting with a kiss, keeping his lips planted. She will pull back and say, Oh, good, we can touch, leaving him to wonder whether she is speaking genuinely, because why does she wear light-colored underwear that risks revealing questionable stains. This concern will fade when she initiates the next kiss, the tip of her tongue pushing for entrance. Something will stop her, and she will say, I can't believe I'm okay, and Meiselman will say, You are great, you are perfect. She will ask, Why was the spot fine? Did he think it was an infection? Not wanting this transition to fall apart, he will have no choice but to turn aggressive, slide a hand up her shirt. They don't feel compelled to give reasons, he will answer. She never wears a bra around the house. No need. She will try leading him from the foyer. Where are we going? he will ask. Here on the mat is fine. With all our shoes? He will sweep away the footwear and force her down while lowering his pants and underpants to his knees. After a minute she will say, This is not comfortable. The floor hurts my back. Besides, don't you want to see what I bought for tonight? He will answer, I saw it and it can wait. White does little for me. Pink is my new color. Soon, her grimaces will signal that the discomfort is overwhelming any pleasure, so he volunteers to go on his back. It will not take long for him to experience the same discomfort, and he will succumb to her suggestion they resume in the bedroom, where they have always had sex in this house except for those two times, two of the greatest times. Her eyes closed, he will wonder whether she is thinking about another man or a previous time or a previous time with another man. Sometimes Meiselman's eyes are open when he is thinking about other women. As always, while in the thick of it, it will feel like one of the better times. To delay the finish he will consider how Rav Fruman doesn't give a fiddle about defending Rabbi J-'s legacy, but other people do care. He must stand up for decency. He must not let the bully get away with it. For once, he will have the final say. Shhh. You are mumbling to yourself, she will say. When he comes out of the shower—she showers before, he showers after—Meiselman, noticing how the spill is fully on his side, will ask that they change the sheets. She will argue she is too tired and get her way.

This is more or less what happens.

Monday

She is not stirring. She is not hovering. She is not concerned about earning a reprimand for a burnt pot. Today it is our oatmeal. Negligible. But what if it were our baby boy's bottle? You'd leave him with a lisp, damage that cannot be undone with elbow grease. Arms spread, fingers grappling the stovetop corners, Deena keeps her eyes closed and tilts her face upward, the pot's spiraling steam hitting her neck. Too much steam, he can tell, but not wanting to interfere with her fine mood, he will not step in to remind her she should have lowered the heat at first bubble. Meiselman, who shuttles through the kitchen preparing their morning coffee—his job—shares her mood, the relief they are not one of those couples who goes long periods without having sex.

A mug in each hand, he sweeps his elbow across her back as he passes, light touching as if she is new to him. His gesture catches her off guard, causing her to flinch. But why should she be surprised? On the mornings after, Meiselman always piles on the gestures, so after setting down the coffee on the table he is back in the kitchen for a spoon and a quick peck on her crown. She pulls her head away. He reaches in and lowers the burner to a simmer.

Not wanting to unsettle the fine mood between them, he refrains from mentioning the noises coming from the old lady's lot at first light, a shovel plunging the ground, the thump of tossed dirt, trickling granules. Over and over.

“After I wash the dishes and make the beds, I’ll run the shirts over to the cleaners before work,” he says.

Every morning he washes the dishes and makes the beds, and every Monday morning on his ride to work, he takes in the shirts, but this announcement is part of smothering Deena with gestures. Most husbands would reserve such gestures for a Monday morning after a sex-free Sunday night. But Deena has a facetious outlook, and if he were to mention the shirts after a sex-free Sunday night she is liable to say, Thanks, exactly what I need from my husband.

At first, he found her facetiousness amusing, an innovative approach to defying others. They were younger. Now there is often difficulty in knowing whether or not she is speaking sincerely. Did she truly enjoy yesterday’s sandwich? Only the crust ended up in the garbage—he checked—and Deena childishly forgoes crust.

Fighting the urge to unfurl the newspapers, he returns to the kitchen to pile on more gestures. Deena never wears her scrubs top to breakfast and her stubby, coffee colored nipples—dark roast with a pinch of creamer—drill her white v-neck undershirt. At the counter, she is dishing out the oatmeal. Pressing up against her back, he hooks his arm around her and grabs a breast over the shirt. With his free hand he reaches forward and twists the blinds closed since his mother is at her sink washing the dishes, just across the way. The breasts are not his favorite part of her body, but they are a source of insecurity for her, so he is mindful to constantly paw at them. Deena lowers the serving spoon and claps the hand that claps her breast. He cannot tell whether this is meant as an unspoken blessing, a plea for more, or gentle admonishment. All this time together, and he still cannot tell. Like when he sticks his fingers inside her. Once, years ago, she complained it burned and, ever since, he has done it apprehensively.

Deena squirms away from Meiselman's grasp and lets out a loud moan of frustration. She begins chiseling the bottom of the pot with the serving spoon.

"Salvage what you can and let the pot soak," Meiselman says, even though he knows that it's not waste that is upsetting the woman. Waste is never a source of distress for her. Spoiled dairy, stained tablecloths, shattered glasses, and cold air leaking in and out through the open front door are acknowledged with facetiousness, if noted at all.

"I'm bleeding," she says. "This time I am sure. We probably weren't allowed to do what we did last night."

Now he understands that her disposition at the stove as the oatmeal cooked was not contentment, a fine mood, the relief they are not one of those couples who goes long periods without having sex. It was guilt. Sin, especially of the unintentional variety, is what rankles Deena. If, by accident, she pops chocolate into her mouth less than five hours after eating meat, or sponges off a meat plate with a dairy sponge, she is hard to console. Meiselman blunders, on occasion. Eating those chocolates yesterday, a possible blunder. Defying Rav Fruman's ruling, not a blunder. Newly observant Deena constantly views herself as still in training, looking to make the team, and she fears her missteps risk making her look amateurish. Upon discovering the sin, she sometimes lets out a shriek or a moan. Then comes the listlessness, fingers twisting her hair. A spell like this can last minutes, and only ends with her saying, "We haven't given *tzedakah* in months. Can we send a check to Teyvah?" Wanting to end her gloom, he agrees. In the morning, however, he does not mail the check as promised, but rips it up and drops it into the garbage. Why is it food pantries and hunger with her? Why does she not strive to help cure disease?

He cannot spend his morning involved in one of her downturns in mood, the rest of breakfast taken up with crafting comforting lines to assuage any guilt she may have over them having had sex while she was bleeding. You know what sacrifice people brought for unintentional sins in the days of the temple? he might ask her. Turtledoves. If God truly cared, he would have demanded livestock. If that fails to pacify her, he might say, Guilt is good. Is there any greater indication of one's devotion?

When perusing the main headline, the words "School," "Education," and "DCFS" jump out at Meiselman, indicating nothing consequential has occurred since hearing the AM670 newscast on his return home last night. He spots the word "Hamas" in a headline below the fold. A story relating to Israel must never be ignored. *Hamas Designates New Leader*, reads the headline. Somewhat interesting, although its placement and font size imply it is only mildly important. Having limited time until Deena starts lamenting over her sin, he swaps the section for Sports.

From the corner of his eye, he notices Deena peering over the Tempo section, perhaps readying to unburden her guilt. If he has any chance of getting through today's newspaper, Meiselman must get started on the White Sox recap at once, but right as he begins studying the box score, Deena's mouth opens, and he braces for her unloading.

"On this date in 1943, the Warsaw Ghetto Uprising began," she says.

"Right," Meiselman says, "*Yom Ha'shoah* is next week, and that's the Hebrew-date anniversary. Last year, for the sixtieth, we hosted an actual ghetto survivor. An Israeli professor who wrote some book about the uprising. I wasn't impressed, if you remember. Not one of my better invites. Nevertheless, an impressive crowd."

"I vaguely remember."

"The event or that I was disappointed with the speaker?"

"Both?"

"Your typical Israeli who puts down Diaspora Jews as weak and passive because they don't know what it means to fight. Which is not true. Take my *zeyde*, World War Two. Or Uncle Sherman, Vietnam."

"Wasn't your *zeyde* a dentist in the army? Wasn't he based somewhere in Texas?"

"He wore the uniform."

"And wasn't Mrs. Woolf in the ghetto?" Deena asks.

"If that were true she might have greater sensitivity to issues of space and privacy. But she was in a camp, never a ghetto."

"The camps were worse than the ghettos, I'm pretty sure."

"Especially for the people stuck with Mrs. Woolf."

Deena reaches across the table and slaps his hand, hard enough that his spoon drops into the bowl.

"We're not allowed to touch, remember," he says.

"I forgot, but that wasn't funny. At all."

"In the privacy of our own home," he says, because what is marriage worth if husband and wife cannot share an indecent joke every now and then?

"So is Shenkenberg this year's *Yom Ha'shoah* event?" she asks.

"God, no! Just a tasteless coincidence. It's the sixty-first anniversary. Calendar is too packed with national holidays and bogus awareness months for us to observe non-rounded anniversaries. Probably won't do anything again until the sixty-fifth."

He puts Sports to the side and looks for the front page section so he can examine that article on Hamas, but Deena seizes on his break in reading to say, "Today is also the anniversary of the Oklahoma City bombing."

"Few people remember, I'm sure," he says. "After 9/11, Oklahoma City is but a footnote."

"A footnote? 'The bombing claimed the lives of a hundred and sixty-eight people,' it says here."

"It's not three thousand. Last month, two hundred died on that train in Madrid. Who even asks where they were when they heard about Oklahoma City? Isn't that the marker? Knowing where you were."

"I do. I remember where I was when I heard about Oklahoma City."

Meiselman is not about to admit that he, too, remembers, with ease, where he was when he heard. At the recording studio. Tim, the sound engineer, called Meiselman into the studio to listen to the report on the radio. The correspondent talked endlessly about the building's daycare center.

"You remember unusual things," he says to her. "You have a memory from when you were barely two years old. The one of your mother when she was sick. Transferring the store-bought cookies onto baking sheets? Not even two, amazing."

"That's called trauma, not an 'unusual memory.' Let's stop talking about this. Everything you're saying today is gross and upsetting me."

Is she angry with him for not showing adequate excitement over meaningless anniversaries? Daily, she plies him with this trivia. Does he usually act more enthused? Is this collateral damage from his new aggressive approach? He can guarantee that the Shenkenbergs, Frumans, and Gershons of the world do not sip their morning coffee while asking to be bombarded with frivolities. Read my horoscope, please. *Capricorn: You are feeling unrestrained. Efforts to shake your excess humility are starting to pay dividends. Now is not the time to avoid serious discussions with loved ones.*

This week is ideal for seizing on that newfound bold, take-no-prisoner, take-them-deep, refuse-to-be-the-schlepper energy. A chance meeting will lead to the resolution of a brewing conflict. A true player in the housing market does not sit on a piece of land but is always trading up.

Deena pushes her bowl forward, even though it has more than a few spoonfuls of oatmeal at the bottom. Standing, she turns her back on him and faces the hanging cabinets dividing the breakfast area from the kitchen. From the bottom shelf, she takes a bag of chocolates, unwraps a piece, and tosses it into her mouth. While chewing, she plucks a second piece.

"Chocolate for breakfast?" he asks.

"I need it to empty my system."

"Chocolate does the opposite, no?"

"These are specially designed to do the opposite."

"Then toss one my way."

"I don't think you need it."

Is this frustration with him tied to his continued failure to provide her with a family? Before they knew for certain that doctors would have to intervene to create a child, the coming of her period was a mournful moment, the mark of another failed attempt. She would announce through the entire house, "I'm bleeding. We can't touch." The floorboards would creak above as Deena moved from bedroom to bathroom washing and stanching. Downstairs, Meiselman would sit in his chair visualizing a bulb-headed baby floating on the toilet surface, shards of bloody shell on its forehead, although he knew biologically this was not the case, that they had not even made it that far.

Needing to reorient her possible frustration with him, he says to Deena, who is chewing the chocolate like it is tobacco, "That spot on your underwear yesterday. Surely it was blood."

"We know now don't we?" She shrugs, the second chocolate clasped between her front teeth. "We asked, didn't we?"

"Technically it was unintentional, but you thought it was blood and you still sent me to that Rav Fruman. As if you, we, were fishing for a more favorable answer."

With his accusation, guilt slowly sprouts across her face, desolating her eyes and crossing them inward as she stumbles back into her seat. She reaches for the business section—Business?—but he can see she is not reading, and after a minute she lays the newspaper flat on the table, grabs her napkin, and spits out the chocolate. "Tastes like carob." Balling the napkin, she says, "I don't want to be upset about last night. It was nice."

"Upsetting you wasn't my intention. My point, I guess, is that you thought it was blood and you should have been more trusting of your intuition. You know your body better than some rabbi. Don't you?" Meiselman says. "Maybe I'm angry about the whole system. They don't want us to trust ourselves, so they set it up that we have to ask. It's how they establish power. Restrict, restrict, restrict. That's all they know how to do. People controlling other people. Why do we have to live by other people's restrictions? We are educated. You are practically a doctor, but somehow they know better?"

"I've lost you. I'm confused. Who is 'they'?"

"'They' are the Frumans and Shenkenbergs of the world. With their arbitrary rules. What if I were to have refused Shenkenberg's demand to be transferred and instead issued a demand of my own that he stay on the line so we could review the schedule, like I do with every other speaker that comes to the library? But I acceded. Why? Why do I constantly accede to everyone's arbitrary rules?"

"Again about Shenkenberg and that call? Listen, I have to go to work. I'm sorry, but can't we finish talking about this later?"

"Yes, but I think we should give money to charity," Meiselman says. "There is a fallen soldiers fund I read about in the newspaper. A hundred sounds good?"

"That sounds like a lot."

With no intention of ever writing a check, he says, "It's only charity if you feel the hurt."

Dirty shirts heaped in his arms, Meiselman waddles along the edge of his lot snooping for the source of Mrs. Woolf's most recent early morning disturbance. Squeezing through the narrow passageway between his garage wall and the hedge that borders their two properties, he emerges into his backyard and immediately has his answer. On his neighbor's side of the chain link fence, molehills surround a pit the size of a kiddie pool. Leaned against the fence is a shovel. Is the old lady softening up the land for seeding, or is the point merely to terrorize, and tonight he will wake to the sound of her filling the hole?

* * *

Six of the twelve spots in the employee lot have reserved signs tacked to the building's brick wall and on one of them is written the name Meiselman. The New Niles Public Library, the Village of New Niles, cannot afford to have Meiselman circling the block, and the other employees are reminded of his indispensability every time they pull into a full lot and are forced to reverse and hunt the side streets for parking.

"Dad," he one time asked. "Do you have a parking spot at the office?" "Downtown we have garages. I purchase a yearly pass. Boy, do they kill you on that." "Gershon," he one time asked his brother. "Do you have a parking spot at the office?" "It's New York City, nobody drives. I have a guy. Door-to-door." Others can snidely estimate the salary of a civil servant, but what dollar amount do they place on an employee knowing his employer has cordoned off real estate for him? A prime spot, in fact, at the end of the lot, away from the other cars, the branches of a thick-trunked tree providing shade. At the end of those hot summer days, the underlings bake for minutes before the air kicks in, but not Meiselman.

To be hailed by his colleagues for a sensational work ethic. This is why Meiselman arrives at the library an hour before the doors open. A desire to inspire, not self-promote. Circulation will clock in shortly to empty the return bins. The librarian scanning the returns might ask the colleague loading them onto the carts if they are the first to arrive.

Meiselman is already at his desk, the colleague might answer.

Meiselman does not count. Meiselman is a machine.

Not a machine, the colleague might say. An everyman like you and me.

More like a yes man, the other worker, a bitter man, might grumble. This is how he became Ethel's number two. He's not difficult like those other loud-mouthed administrators in the back. Betsy Ross complaining she cannot type because of some mysterious ailment with a Nazi-sounding name, or Mitchell whining about the library descending into irrelevance if it fails to adopt his digital plans. June is a nice enough lady, but her self-muttering disconcerts her colleagues. Ada is pleasant, but does she not sense how uncomfortable she makes everyone by constantly having her bra strap showing? Does she never tire of continuously pulling at the collar of her shirt? These administrators don't realize how good they have it, the bitter employee might continue. They get to sit. Try spending the day on your feet gunning barcodes. Red lines go through all of my dreams. That laser can't be healthy. My thumb aches when it's humid. Twisting the top off a pop bottle has become torture. A cancerous thumb is all I will have to show for forty years of service. Thinking he has a sympathetic audience, the worker turns his lament into outright disparagement. Nepotism and cronyism is how Meiselman rose to become the number two. The rumor is he and Ethel were high school lovers, and that, even now, there is the occasional Sunday morning fling.

The viciousness of this rant's final turn sets off the, until now, silent coworker. Hey, Meiselman is a married man, a decent man.

Meiselman is not the typical worker who looks to retard the start of his workday by fixing himself a cup of coffee. He would happily head straight to his office without a stop at the breakroom, but the next administrator to arrive—usually Mitchell—would curse Meiselman for not making a fresh pot, call him selfish and grumble to the others about him not being a team player. In this day and age, everyone is expected to be a team player.

Today, and, maybe this is part of his new approach, part of acting less restrained, part of unleashing his aggressive capabilities, Meiselman determines he has had enough of being bullied every morning into clearing the soggy filter from the machine's basket, washing out the half-full pot left souring overnight, scrounging the cabinets for the measuring spoon, and then spending the rest of the day fishing for compliments from any underling he spots with a mug. Today, he tops off the pot, which was left half-full over the weekend, and turns on the burner, and he can already hear the underlings raising a ruckus over this new light roast's superiority.

Back in his office, the voicemail woman speaks through Meiselman's office phone in a nasal drone, as if annoyed he was not in his office at 3:42 a.m. to answer Ethel's call.

Why was Ethel up at such an hour? Why was she not tucked under her comforter—foot sticking out the bottom, the woman cannot be restrained—deep in a dream about one of the clean-shaven, Italian-shoe-wearing men she favors? Moving into her new condominium, one of her effeminate men struggling to haul a box packed with shoes from the elevator, knee bobbing up and down, trying to keep the box from falling. Finally, Ethel grabs the box from his hands and barks, Where is my number two? leaving the boyfriend to wipe his brow with a monogrammed handkerchief, although since it is a dream he might use something unusual like a slice of Swiss cheese. Meiselman, in blue jeans and work boots, enters the frame, a couch balanced on his back. Next, Ethel and Meiselman are picnicking on the grounds of the Taj Mahal. Turkey wraps. A dollop of mayonnaise hangs off her lips. He goes to clean it with a finger. She tells him to use his mouth. Right at the moment of contact, his boss wakes up in a panic, suddenly remembering she has not yet reviewed with him the catering for the Shenkenberg event.

"We will use Cracowaia," the voicemail message continues, her voice meandering as if she is thinking out loud to her sounding board Meiselman. "Stanislaw is such a doll. King Solomon's is out of the question, sorry. Dry, pricey pastries heaped on cheap plastic trays will not cut it for Izzy Shenkenberg." He cannot tell if this is sincere or a subtle knock on the writer's prima donna behavior. "I know there will be a lot of kosher people in attendance, but it's not our job to feed people. They can drink pop and pick at grapes for all I care. Cheesecake and baklava, watermelon and berries. We'll order for a hundred. We'll get two hundred plus, but order for one. Proper tablecloths and those glass platters they used last time. The works, Meiselman. You know what to do."

Even after listening to the message a second time, Meiselman remains unsure whether it should flatter him. Her confidence in him is unquestionable, and he appreciates her using the words "we" and "our," but why does it not bother her that by ordering from the Polish bakery down the street, and not King Solomon's, he will be one of the "kosher people" left drinking pop and picking at grapes? Nursing a cup of pop, he will sidle up to Ethel and troll for a compliment. Does the cheesecake have that fresh citrus kick you like? You know I can't eat any of this? She might turn to Shenkenberg and repeat, Can't? Chooses not to. Shenkenberg will pluck a crumb off his plate and place it on Ethel's tongue. Can this be walnut, he might ask. I'm going to say pecan, she might answer. Meiselman off to the side, not a part of their guessing games.

Can it be he has managed to penetrate her dreams twice in one night? The next message—time-stamped 5:14 a.m. by the joyless voicemail woman—leaves no question over how Ethel views her number two. "And, one more thing," she says. "This back of mine is still acting up. I'm not sure I'll be able to moderate the conversation portion of the event. You're going to have to do it. Going to need you to do the introduction, as well, I imagine. Right now, I can't even stand. Definitely not making it into the office today. Tell people I'm working off-site. I'll let Shenkenberg know about the change of plans. I, not you, Meiselman. I."

It would be indecent to gloat over this development, Ethel tabbing him, Meiselman, to replace her as the face of the library for her special night. The number two acting as the number one. She deserves a pause of concern, an acknowledgment of the suffering that has set his elevation in motion. She is a woman who lives for the center stage, so the pain must be severe. Backaches are the new ulcers, he recently read. Dr. Lin championed this theory of a mind-body connection, of unconscious conflicts manifesting as physical ailments. Voiced these ideas to him when he told her the story of his father leaving him off the family relay team for the firm picnic in favor of Meiselman's cousin Jeremy, an actual inbred... There is no time to reminisce, to explain the marriage of cousins or ponder the value of Dr. Lin's analysis. All the pieces are falling into place for a refurbished Meiselman to challenge his nemesis Shenkenberg. Yes, nemesis. Now that he is introducing the writer and moderating the debate portion of the event, reading the book is crucial. Pause of concern over.

Maybe there is time for a quick summary. Meiselman, thirteen, woke up with his left leg numb from the knee down. Mr. Woolf came over to help carry Meiselman downstairs to the car. In his thick European accent he asked, "This is adequate how I carry you?" In the background, his father was telling anyone who would listen about his doctor's order to not even move a chair on account of his back. The doctor gave Meiselman pills, and he was better by the end of the day.

Meiselman, playing the compliant patient for the first time under Dr. Lin's care, offered, "If I could not physically run the race then my father could not reject me."

"That's a bit obvious. Let's dig deeper. Thirteen, becoming a man? Through this mysterious ailment you found a way to announce your father's weakness. He humiliated you and you found a way to humiliate him back, replacing him as the man of the house with this neighbor." Then, the doctor asked, "And what about the contradiction? Your father was fit enough to run a race but unable to carry you, his ailing son?"

"It was his back, not his legs. Earlier that year, we were playing catch in the park when his back gave out. My mother had to drive onto the field and load him into the car."

"Your mother carries your father. Your father is unable to carry you."

"Is that a question?"

"You tell me."

He could go on and on, but he must begin preparing for his upcoming duel with Rabbi J-'s slanderer. Hoping to immerse himself into the heart of the book's action, he skips to chapter three of *The Sad Rebbe*, but:

Chapter 3; Or, The Japanese Woman Who Tired of Me

That we would never rid the tweed couch of the dog smell occupied my phlegm-filled head that afternoon. The couch was our first find as a living-together couple, discovered while driving around the neighborhood looking for a landscaper to clear the choke weeds overtaking our front lawn. Jenn maintained the discovery was serendipitous. The word serendipity, I insisted, should be reserved for scientific finds.

"I'm going to make you some tea," Jenn said.

"I don't think I can stomach any of your Japanese remedies," I answered. "They all taste like hay."

"Is your joke intended as nasty or funny?" Jenn asked. "I need to know how to laugh."

fails to seize his attention. Ethel is entrusting him, Meiselman. There are doubts, at times, about the relationship, like when she takes Mitchell or Betsy Ross into her office and shuts the door, forcing her number two across the hall to bare a jealousy that sharpens with each passing minute. Do not doubt the strength of the connection, the stability of the hierarchy, she is reassuring her anxious lieutenant. The payoff will come when he informs the other underlings of his ascension. Biding his time until their arrival, he takes another stab at Shenkenberg.

The opening passage of chapter six:

Chapter 6; Or, We Try Running Away and Get Lost in the Back Alleys

One student raised his hand and asked if goldfish are kosher. To be kosher a fish has to have scales and fins. Or is it that they can have one and not the other? My mind was rid of even the basics. In an effort to brush off the kid, whose name I'd still not bothered to learn, I told him we were running out of time and proceeded to read to the fifth-graders from the library book that featured the experiment. "'The fish in the warm water, in the higher temperatures, were more active than the fish in the cooler water. The regularity of these breathing movements provides a measure of the ventilation rate. Genotypic and environmental variables both affect ventilation rates.' Did everyone get that? Let me repeat, 'Genotypic and environmental variables both affect ventilation rates.'"

The fifth-graders stared back at me blankly.

The same kid interrupted again. "Are Jews warm-blooded or cold-blooded?" he asked, his wet finger hanging over the lip of a beaker.

"Jews and all people are warm-blooded."

does not hold Meiselman's interest. Besides, where are the outrageous passages about Rabbi J-? Ready to slog ahead, Meiselman lowers his eyes, but before attempting another immersion, the side door to the administrative offices clinks open. A second later the door slams shut, especially hard this morning with the wind. Anxious to share the development with the underlings, Meiselman has trouble focusing. The squishy sound of rubber-soled shoes slapping the linoleum means it is one of the male underlings. Mitchell or Numbers. Meiselman does not care to share this information with Numbers. Meiselman is not convinced the man even knows his name. Meiselman has always enjoyed having a nickname of sorts, so when he started at the library over a year and a half ago, he decided he was going to build morale and show his good nature by handing out nicknames to his fellow workers. It may appear unimaginative to christen the library's financial officer Numbers, but the name has more to do with the way the man talks, how the intermittent, brief conversations he has with his coworkers are built around him slinging questions crammed with figures. Twenty-two fifty an hour for eleven weeks for Skimple minus the two mandatory vacations and C3 volunteer status, he may ask Meiselman. The name never took off, and his coworkers call him Jerry. As he does every morning on his way to his office, Numbers, in his blue windbreaker, the same one he wears even in the dead of winter, stops at Meiselman's door, knocks the doorpost, tips the bill of his New Niles Country Club baseball cap and waits for Meiselman to respond with a two-finger salute before continuing to his office at the end of the hallway. He will stay in the office until the end of the workday. Meiselman is not one to make crass jokes about the work ethic of any ethnic group, but the man's industriousness is impressive. Jokes do circulate about the man's bladder.

To fill the time until the arrival of an underling worthy of hearing about Ethel's back and Meiselman's elevation, he returns to the day-to-day.

"Yes, yes, Mr. Meiselman, the best," Stanislaw Paprocki tells Meiselman over the phone. "Only the best, as Madam Ethel have us always give to her." The man's accent and English are not inspiring confidence. Where are the pauses, the repeating back of the order, some indication it is being recorded? An in-person follow-up at the end of the week, Meiselman notes to himself, is crucial.

The side door opens and closes several more times. He hears Mitchell, June, and Ada exchanging morning pleasantries and insipid details of their weekends. Does Mitchell think his colleagues care to hear stories about shopping for seeds? Does Ada think they want to picture her lounging with her dogs and husband on the couch while nibbling on microwave popcorn? When he becomes the number one, they will have no choice but to ask about his weekend. Pretty ho-hum, Ada. Endured my father's worn stories of the '59 Sox while fantasizing about my wife's death freeing me up for a move to the UP. Um, your bra strap is showing. Foxy shade of red.

Reviewing his work calendar, he is reminded that at this week's Book Club, in commemoration of Earth Day, Professor Michael Westbound will discuss his book, *Shallow Ends: The Swimming Pool and the American Dream*. Because this man is not a radical academic or agitator, like Shenkenberg, Meiselman does not anticipate a crowd larger than twenty. Using the standard ratio of one question for every seven attendees, Meiselman can expect two to three questions, meaning he should prepare two questions of his own to prevent an uncomfortable silence. *Question: What does America's performance in international swimming competitions say about us as a nation, particularly our poor results in the long distance, diving, and synchronized swimming disciplines? (A joke about whether s.s. can be considered a sport?)*

Ethel was unenthusiastic about hosting this speaker and thought a gardening workshop would be a better event for Earth Day, but Meiselman believes swimming and swimming pools have the ability to capture the public's imagination, because who as a child did not hold jealous feelings for the classmate whose parents built a pool in the backyard, refusing to take the gloomy view held by Meiselman's mother. "A pool in Chicago? Use it for three months? And the insurance? Neighborhood hooligan jumps the fence and drowns? But Sam's father has always been a big show-off. Your father and I knew him as a kid. Asshole." On a hot Shabbat afternoon, the bottoms of his dress shoes sticky against the repaved street, Meiselman walked up and back past Sam Kippleman's house, hearing his schoolmates pleading with one another to watch each other's dives. Up and back, up and back because maybe a classmate would spot him lingering and call him to join. Years later, the same walk on an even hotter day, boys, and now girls, calling out the score of a water basketball game. With his long reach, Meiselman would have dominated. A knock on his office door pulls him from this gloomy daydream.

Mitchell taps the tip of his umbrella against Meiselman's office door. He waits for Meiselman to acknowledge him, relaxing the weight of his body on the handle of his umbrella, its tip digging the linoleum floor. Mitchell, the library's IT specialist, uses the umbrella—massive dome, wooden handle fashioned like a swan's neck—as a walking stick, even though he has no disability and there is nothing particularly proper about this man who walks around beltless, blind to how his pompous stomach creases the waistband of his filthy olive tweeds. Is he also blind to the plaque clogging the spaces between his teeth, and the frizzy ball of white hair that pops from his hairline like a dust ball? Perhaps, given the smudges on his lenses.

As part of his ongoing effort to curry favor with the number two Meiselman, the Brit underling opens their conversations with generic comments about the White Sox. Nothing from the way he discusses baseball indicates he is a true fan.

"The pitcher really carried the team yesterday," he says.

"Yes, Loaiza had a nice game," Meiselman answers briskly.

"The men that relieved him did a fine job, as well."

"Yes. Sorry for my curtness, just have a lot on my plate this morning."

"Oh?"

"Maybe you've heard the news?" Meiselman asks, even though he knows Mitchell has not.

"Do tell, do tell, I'm working on some exciting stuff, as well. Sure you've heard about my Capsule project." He points the umbrella at Meiselman and says, "If you'll indulge me. Imagine Shenkenberg as a young patron archiving every writing, drawing, and scribble. Copies of report cards, love letters to childhood sweethearts..."

"I knew Shenkenberg when he was younger," Meiselman says. "A sheep. Followed the older kids, the ones in my class. Their pet."

"Now you're thinking, Meiselman! A photo of Shenkenberg with his pals. We do encourage photography and video. One can enter into the Capsule whatever he or she would like. Remember, the first rule about the Capsule is that there are no rules. One does not even need to keep his or her entries clean. Racism, violence, and misogyny are the only things we will not tolerate."

While Mitchell drones on about his latest vanity project, Meiselman wheels up and back between his desk and the file cabinet in the corner of his office, pulling random files, making superfluous checks on pages, and throwing out the occasional "Uh, huh." At one point, Meiselman says, "Between you and me, I don't even understand the interest in Shenkenberg's adult offerings." But Mitchell forges ahead.

"Well, you seem to be in the thick of things, so I'll leave you to it," Mitchell says. "Must tell me about your exciting plans when you get the chance."

Mitchell retreats from Meiselman's office humming a bouncy tune before Meiselman has an opportunity to share his news.

Are June and Ada ideal recipients of the major development? With June's constant muttering it is never clear if she is listening, and Ada always seems more focused on adjusting her shirt collar. Betsy Ross, on the other hand, loves gossip. She is generally half an hour late on the dot. Until then, more Shenkenberg.

Meiselman's approach until now has been misguided. To expect he can finish an entire book and compose a forceful introduction and provoking debate questions in less than a week is unrealistic. The book's last chapter, where resolutions are reached, should be the focus of his reading. From this he will be able to reconstruct conflicts and themes presented in earlier chapters.

The book's final chapter opens with the book's protagonist, Ely, visiting a concentration camp in Poland while suffering a flare-up of raging hemorrhoids. Meiselman does not even share such information with his wife out of fear it will repulse her, although she has no problem telling him about the occasional flare-up, even sticking a finger back there and giving it a long itch in front of him. This attack of hemorrhoids in a crematorium surely is not the integral part of the book, the passage feeding the controversy, the part that needs countering. Moreover, the reading is making his lids heavy, and Betsy Ross has yet to arrive.

Meiselman pulls at his chin hairs as he struggles to stay awake through a particularly mocking—and boring—passage about Ely crawling across the crematorium floor trying to retrieve loose change that has fallen from his pocket. Suddenly, family and friends are surrounding a mud pit and cheering on Meiselman as he pins Ethel to the ground. He has her arms over her head, his knees forcing down her tree-trunk thighs. The referee falls to his stomach and slaps the mat for a three count, and Meiselman's head snaps back against his office swivel chair, eyes popping open. Betsy Ross knocks again and says, "Sweet dreams, I hope." She is fastening a missed button in the middle of her blouse.

"This book is killing me," he says. "Up to page 283. Should be done by tomorrow."

"I read courtroom thrillers only," Betsy Ross says. "My mother was a stenographer, you know. But I'm going to try to read this one. Not every day you get to meet a celebrity author like Izzy."

"Not worth the hype, if you ask me. Very crude."

"Don't tell Ethel that."

"She knows my opinion."

Meiselman's father hated Ron Kittle. Every time he came to the plate, his father would yell at the television, "Why, why, why does everyone think this guy is the savior? Talk about not earning your praise. A guy that strikes out a hundred fifty times a year, a guy who swings at everything. He would swing at his own mother! Love him, why? Because he hits home runs that land on the roof? And if there were no roof would they still love him?" "I think he looks cute in his glasses?" his mother would always answer. "And those blonde curls." "See?" his father yelled at Meiselman, looking to his son as either an ally or a medium to reach his wife. "The things that distinguish him are meaningless. Rooftop home runs, glasses, blonde curls, and teeth that look like a mouth full of caps."

Ron Kittle's famous quote: "Fans appreciate home runs. I mean, they don't stand up for singles."

"Betsy," Meiselman says, "some people demand we pay attention to them, and intimidate us into following them by making us feel like we are behind the times if we don't. When all they are doing is leading us down a road of shallowness."

The secretary nods through Meiselman's sandbagging of Shenkenberg, and the moment he finishes she jumps in with, "Just like my son-in-law. One of the most successful loan officers the bank's ever seen. Sent him all over the Midwest to do training. What happens? His manager leaves and everyone thinks he is a shoo-in for the job. Instead, they give it to some Mexican because she's a poor immigrant. Single mother. People want to make nice stories out of everything. This woman barely speaks English and refuses to learn how to use a computer."

"Maybe we should talk about this later," Meiselman suggests, eager to move away from this inappropriate chatter and segue into the essential news of his new duties.

She steps toward his desk and lowers her voice, "Look, I admire the lady's work ethic, and I'm sure she's a fine person. But my son is even better at the job, and that's all that should matter. Not that she brings in homemade breakfast burritos for birthdays or a piñata to the Christmas party. And I'm no racist, for the record. My cousin married a Guatemalan girl."

"Would love to chat, Betsy, but I must get back to Shenkenberg. See, Ethel—"

"I'm not here to chat, FYI. Ethel wants to know what is happening with the catering."

"Complicated. I will call her later with the details."

"Doesn't sound like she's going to be available later."

"That's right," Meiselman says. "I remember her telling me when we spoke earlier this morning. You would not believe what time she called. Anyway, tell her that all the food has been ordered and Stanislaw said, 'Only the best.' And send her my best."

"Thought you said it was complicated."

"Ethel has enough to worry about without the complications of my job."

"She sure does," Betsy Ross says, her voice trailing and her eyes giving Meiselman a knowing look. The secretary plays with the gold chain of the modest cross hanging around her neck before grasping it in her palm and saying, "I will pass along the message and your prayers."

'Prayers' is too grave a word to use in connection to a creaky back. Should he fish around for more information regarding Ethel's condition, or should he update her on his new responsibilities? Or try to do both at the same time?

"Well, keep me in your prayers, also, will you?"

A hint of sarcasm in his voice, maybe. Why else would she let go of the cross and drop the corner of her mouth in a sardonic grin, before lunging across at him with a raised hand, fingers pinched together in front of his face, holding it for a moment before dropping it straight down, tapping it against the desk, bringing it up diagonally before sweeping her arm across the width of his body?

She has crossed him.

"Happy?" Betsy Ross asks, pulling back. "Mocking me. And I thought you were a fellow believer." She is speaking again in a loud whisper. "I mean I know you're not Christian, but I thought you were a believer," she scoffs before charging out of his office.

As if the secretary's crossing has cast a spell on him, Meiselman no longer feels the thrill of his elevation. What is this quirk of personality that prevents him from parading his successes? He has never been good at selling himself, tooting his own horn. He is not the ballplayer who, upon hearing the stadium roar, walks back up the dugout steps to tip the bill of his cap. His teammates have to push him out of the dugout. When he was a child, his mother, who was always pointing out the piggish behavior of other adults and children, was constantly telling him to not act like a *chazer*. This is a fine message for a child who has a parent fighting on his behalf for a spot at the trough. But too much timidity becomes a retarding force. Nobody is looking to turn anyone else into a winner. Except, maybe, someone's spouse. Hopefully. He is constantly championing Deena, is he not? But is she championing him?

Even though he calls every day, the secretary at Deena's office answers him like he is a stranger, coldly putting him on hold and forcing him to hear about various treatment courses the hospital offers for chronic conditions. "My back does not ache, my heart is not inflamed, and my spine certainly does not bend!" he yells into the phone. "All I want from you people is a child! There must be something more I can do besides consume leafy vegetables and grainy beige pills!"

The recorded message is playing a second time when his wife picks up and answers, "Deena Nussbaum."

"Your office voice is so assertive," he says to her. "'Deena Nussbaum,'" he mimics her. "Borderline abrasive."

"Sorry, just overwhelmed."

"No, I like it. Very sensual. Wish you talked to me like that more often."

"We aren't supposed to talk like that during my...you know..."

"During your what?"

He can tell there are people in the room and this light torture amuses him, but not wanting to jeopardize his chance to share with her the news about his elevation, he stops. He starts by telling her he, too, is overwhelmed at work, and he manages to get out the bit about Ethel's bad back, but right as he reaches the integral part of his news, he hears Deena pulling away from the phone to ask a colleague to set up Mr. Reynolds on the treadmill—"two miles an hour, slight incline, wobblier than he looks"—and when she puts the receiver back to her ear she says, "This is about Shenkenberg again? Look, I promise we will talk about it later. Just not now. I have a patient that's been waiting for half an hour. You just have to get over it, Meisie. Bye."

If I am not for myself, who will be for me? Apparently nobody. Does a wife not have some responsibility to champion her husband? The question feels silly the moment he asks himself, as if he is a needy child asking Deena to play the role formerly played by his mother.

He pops out of his chair, exits his office, and charges toward Betsy Ross's alcove desk in the middle of the hallway with the clear mission of sharing his news. She pauses him with a finger, while stabbing at the keyboard with her other hand. Before hiring her, did anyone bother tallying the words-per-minute of this woman who types like a mechanic? And she makes him wait and wait and wait.

And she makes *him* wait? If only he had the gumption to grab her by the scruff of her neck and force her to take a hard look at the letterhead of the good stationary sitting on her desk, the one with the library's name and logo raised and in color—vermillion—the stationary the secretary extracts from the supply closet when serious matters have been negotiated and hashed out and now need to be set in stone and signed. He would show her the names of the administrators listed on the side and embossed in silver. Second name from the top, underneath Ethel Lewinson, Director of Library Services, is Meiselman, Events and Programs Coordinator. Only once one moves down the list past June and Mitchell, past Ada and Numbers, past, even, Roger, who has not worked here in five months, and Jane, who is officially retired but comes in once a week to sort mail and flip through book catalogues does one find Betsy Ross, Manager of Library Offices. Way at the bottom of the list, where the font gets a size smaller, the second to last name, right above Fyodor "Fred" Galitsky, Head of Library Security. Manages offices but does not have one of her own. Sits out in the hallway. And she makes him wait? I make you wait, he wants to tell her. But the secretary beats him to the punch and, eyes still on the screen, says, "Not now, Meiselman. Must, must finish this for Ethel."

Why *is* the good stationary out? What has been negotiated and hashed out? Have plans for the expansion progressed? Is Ethel awarding Shenkenberg an honorarium? What will be set in stone and signed?

"Oh, working on the letter," Meiselman says. "Yes, that is more important."

Betsy Ross leans over the monitor, turning her head from side to side before cupping her hands over her mouth and whispering, "*You* know about *the letter*?"

He laughs in her face. "Do you think Ethel and I haven't discussed *the letter*? I, in fact, am writing an addendum to *the letter*."

"And Ethel knows you are writing this letter?"

"An addendum," he corrects her. "A formal concurrence with the letter's conclusion. She knows and she doesn't know. Didn't want to bother her with the specifics considering her…" trails off the same way Betsy Ross trailed off in his office earlier. "The addendum should be seen as objective, unbiased, a work of my own volition. Put it on my personal stationary. Carry more heft that way."

His masterful phrasing has not betrayed his ignorance. In fact, Betsy Ross believes they are sharing secrets. She agrees it cannot hurt, and tells him that in fact it may even help. "Although from what I gather," she says, "it's a done deal." The next disclosure compounds Meiselman's confusion. "But still, I'll pray to my god, and you pray to your god, that we don't need these letters," she says.

"Remember," he says. "It's an addendum."

Tuesday

Regimentation of breakfast has been achieved, and Meiselman is no longer saddled every morning with negligible decisions about what to eat. Twenty years ago, advertisers would have begged to photograph Meiselman and Deena at breakfast, mugs of coffee and glasses of orange juice crowning their bowls of oatmeal—bananas in his, brown sugar and milk in hers. (Although they may have decided to replace the room's peeling maroon and gold damask wallpaper, which came with the house and makes the kitchen look like the inside of a mosque, according to Meiselman's mother.) Today, advertisers show families whose members do not have time for one another in the morning, mothers plying kids with jelly-filled cookies that are heated in an unconventional manner, fathers checking watches before filching the same cookies off the table and running away to work, newspapers tucked under their arms.

It happens every few months, a string of *Tribunes* with inconsequential headlines. *Governor Cautioned on State Budget*, the headline today reads. In a smaller font, off to the side, *Tentative Deal in Fallujah.* "Cautioned." "Tentative." Stay tuned, the editor is telling Meiselman. In future editions, we will let you know how everything turns out.

He entertains grabbing Sports, but puff pieces are what the editors offer on the mornings after White Sox off-days. Puff pieces about players returning from career-threatening injuries. Puff pieces about players bucking the spirits of terminally-ill children. Puff pieces about the anonymous men working pedestrian jobs for the ballclub: the man who packs the equipment bags before road trips, the man who sweeps the gum and sunflower shells off the dugout floor. The workers inevitably tell of ballplayers playing pranks. Used to wash the jock straps in a giant tub. One day Wynn hands me the underwear belonging to this kid Hicks we just called up. Massive grandma panties. Kept my mouth shut because asking questions of a veteran like Wynn was above my pay grade. Geez, the roar in the clubhouse when I hung those panties up in the kid's locker. Now, of course, we use industrial machines.

Without a newspaper in hand, Meiselman starts getting nervous Deena will interpret his empty-handedness as a readiness to turn weekday breakfast into Sunday lunch. Not having hashed out the details of his latest plan to give her a child, he is still unprepared to discuss the second test. Better to be the one proposing the solution and pressuring the other person to fall in line. How many times can he say no to her proposals before she mistakes his principled stance as an uncompromising disposition? He will not rear a Chinese child or a statuesque blonde from a former Soviet Republic. If they take that route he will buy only American or Israeli.

The Tempo section is open in front of her, and he risks losing control of the conversation, unless he can preempt her impending sharing. It is clear she does not want to hear any more about Shenkenberg, although if given the chance, he would relay the preposterousness of Shenkenberg's putdown over the phone. "Meiselwho?" Shenkenberg asked. "The only person I know at your library is Ethel."

Of course I know Meiselman, Shenkenberg might have thought after hanging up the phone, but treating him like a cipher is a small dose of revenge for how Meiselman made me feel about myself in high school. How could I forget that day? Meiselman, a year ahead of me, stood off to the side as his classmates egged me on in the lunchroom. Like he was too good or mature to enjoy my shenanigans of scarfing half-eaten hotdogs and soggy fries left on the table from the earlier lunch period. Surely he hurt with envy as Ruben Fishman proclaimed, "Shenkenberg is funny as hell." Only Meiselman refused to laugh when I uttered, "They is some good pickings," followed by a loud belch. Meiselman's voice did not join the chorus of "Iz-zy, Iz-zy, Iz-zy, Iz-zy" as I downed a bottle of Tabasco sauce, a cheer that turned into screeching laughter as I began gagging, Meiselman's classmates ushering me to the table of Russians, right in time for a hurl that would paste their subsidized baskets of food with regurgitated red sauce. Meiselman must think I was too drunk on my popularity to notice how he tried sticking his decency in my face by purchasing a fresh hamburger and fries for Maria Polkovitch, and how he returned moments later with a new hotdog for Yvgeny Switchkova—all so the others would not presume Meiselman's charity had anything to do with his fondness for Maria's purple-colored lips and spiky black hair.

Maybe Meiselman should give up on expecting Deena to sympathize with any of his plights. Tell me you did not notice the bedlam next door when you returned from work last night, he may try arguing. The four-foot spool of plastic sheeting parked in the neighbor's driveway, a hill of dirt fit for sledding in the backyard, a pit suited for a mud wrestling match. I don't notice anything that goes on outside, she would surely answer. At night, I pull straight into the garage and walk the five feet to the front door without looking around for things to get upset about. Read your paper, instead of getting upset over the same things again and again. The suggestion he is somehow implacable will be enough to silence him. Women easily tire of implacable men. His father might not share his mother's outrage, but he is easily placated. Or is he his mother in this equation, and Deena his father?

All he wants to do is touch Deena, now that it is forbidden and he has nothing to offer verbally. Every month after she starts bleeding, he questions why he did not take enough advantage of the weeks she was clean. Every night they should have. He has tried describing the pain of not being able to touch, but she responds to the flattery by relaying what she learned in the family purity classes she took before they married.

"This the holiest period for a married couple. Like angels we are limited to the power of speech."

Confident she will recoil before contact is made, Meiselman reaches for his wife's hand.

"No touching, remember?" she says.

"So hard to remember."

Across the table, an article is getting a careful reading. Deena marks her spot with an index finger and reports to Meiselman about another massive storm that hit the southern parts of the city.

"Heard that on the radio last night on the drive home," he answers.

"Okay smarty-pants," Deena asks, her finger jumping to the opposite page. "Nineteen years ago today, Coca-Cola announced what?"

This is one of those times he cannot read her tone, and though he knows the answer to her question, he is not sure he wants to be right, so he turns up his palms.

"Something you don't know. Amazing. They should put that in the newspaper." She reads, "'Nineteen years ago today, Coca-Cola announced they were changing the formula—'"

"A story still untold," he mumbles, knowing his interruption is a mistake, but unable to stop himself. "There's a theory that the company introduced a new formula they knew would fail in order to prove the singularity of the classic recipe."

"God, is there anything you don't know?" she asks, her chair sliding back as she stands. She clears her bowl and mug and, without discarding the uneaten cereal or pouring the coffee down the drain, drops them into the dishpan.

The hanging cabinets dividing the breakfast table area from the kitchen obscure most of Deena's body, and Meiselman can see only his wife's hands, which linger over the countertop. Deena's fingertips languidly peck the Formica in a way that reminds him of Betsy Ross's inept typing. His wife's fingers drift to a wicker basket packed with two bunches of bananas, one ripening and one overripe. Without consideration, she drops the black speckled bunch into the garbage. Next, Deena turns over the greenish bunch and presses her finger into a gray bruise blemishing the underside of one of the bananas. She cracks that banana off the stem and drops it into the wastebasket, too. Done with her winnowing, she moves over to a lone red apple, picks it up by its stem, and gives it a spin. The stem snaps and the apple crashes to the counter. Another bruise for her to soothe. She moves to the counter in the rear of the kitchen, her face no longer obscured, and sticks her nose to the coffee pot. Eyes closed, she inhales, her shoulders rising. On the exhale, her face sours, tongue falling out of her mouth. The aimless roving continues and takes her to the stove, where her face is once again obscured, although through the gap between the cabinets and counter, Meiselman can see her scraping a serving spoon against the bottom of the oatmeal pot. She is grazing on the flaky dredges.

"You just dumped an entire bowl," he says.

"I like the burnt stuff."

Here he thought they had achieved regimentation, yet Deena is roaming for other options. Oatmeal heavy on the back of his tongue, he, too, can appreciate how the sameness of each bite will eventually take its toll. Of greater concern right now is the jammed line of communication between them.

"Right here is something worth noting," Meiselman calls to his wife, proceeding to tell her about ten more soldiers being "lost" over the weekend.

"Hope someone finds them. Anyway, I knew that. A non-story."

The facetiousness coloring her response is unmistakable.

Meiselman makes a final attempt to get the sharing back on track by meeting Deena on her own turf. "Today," he says, "is the fifth anniversary of Columbine." Deena, her neck stretched as she tilts her head back for a better view of the cabinet's higher shelves, starts reorganizing, dumping boxes and bags of food into the garbage, while Meiselman tells her that if it were not for 9/11 turning what was major into something minor, the newspaper this morning would be full of puff pieces about mourning families and still-coping victims.

Deena shuts the cabinet doors, frustrating his flow, and says, "We never have anything good to eat."

"What about those chocolates from yesterday?" he offers.

"They did the trick," she answers, opening the refrigerator. She pulls a brick of cheese and gives it a smell before bringing it to the table with a knife.

She is failing to secure the brick and is using her napkin as a cutting board. An accident waiting to happen. He walks to the other side of the table and reaches over her back with both arms to secure the cheese. She slices off two ramp-shaped pieces. Bringing his arms back to his body, he gives her shoulder a squeeze. She tilts her head to the side. He slides his finger down the collar of her v-neck. When he reaches the base of the v, he dips his finger into her shirt and slips his two fingers into the pathway between her breasts, her skin still sticky and damp from the shower. Deena grabs Meiselman's forearm with both hands and throws him off.

"Enough," she says.

Let us not care just this one time, he wants to say to her.

"How frustrating that we can never seem to remember in the beginning," he says instead.

Nibbling at the cheese with her abnormally pointy incisor, she grabs the front page. Whenever immersed in a book or article, she has the habit of following along with two index fingers pressed together, eyes nearly crossed. What has her attention? She substitutes the section for Sports and starts on the second slice of cheese. Sports? Not once has he ever seen her pick up Sports. The thumb and forefinger of her free hand mince the remaining cheese into crumbs. She nods in understanding before putting down the section.

"I have work."

She does not fold the section or clean up the mess of cheese.

"What were you reading in the sports section?"

"An article."

"About?"

"Something you already know about, I'm sure," she says, exiting the kitchen and heading straight for the foyer closet. Door scrapes open. Hangers slide. Scrub top. More sliding. Silver trench coat. Door closes with a bang.

Sports now in front of him, Meiselman spots a distressing headline that may or may have not been the one that caught Deena's attention. An opinion column off to the side: *Frank Sours Optimistic Clubhouse Mood with Contract Grumbling*. There is nothing puff about the disgruntled star player poisoning the clubhouse mood three weeks into a promising season.

Two paragraphs are all Meiselman can stomach. How Frank can exhibit such selfishness at this time is incomprehensible. Does Frank not feel the whip of history on his backside? A country fighting two wars, the enemy parading the burnt corpses of fellow Americans through the streets of their crap towns while our citizens are still unable to unite behind the cause. Nobody has asked Meiselman to hang a yellow ribbon in front of the house, pay a war tax, or ration his supplies. The President has stopped golfing, but Meiselman passes the thawing links of the New Niles Country Club and sees that his countrymen are not making the same sacrifice. They hung the bodies from a bridge over the Euphrates, the same river God promised Abraham. Haphazard knots around a leg, the rest of the body flailing like a spent piñata. Meiselman's father charges that the other party is cheering for defeat on the battlefield because it will enhance their electoral chances. The newspaper has not carried this claim. Says he saw it on cable news. This is a moment of fracture, and not hairline disagreements, quibbles about taxes and education funding. The fracture is compound, a ripe moment for the Shenkenbergs and Frumans of the world who make their bread feeding such fracture.

Eventually he finds the article that caught Deena's attention. A piece suggesting steroids are to blame for the increase in sports injuries. Human growth hormones create more muscle than a person's bones are able to support.

Deena marches back into the kitchen, grabs the brick of cheese off the table, and says, "Lunch."

While she wraps it in a napkin, he asks about the article, specifically about the age at which a man reaches his physical prime. "Around my age?" he looks to clarify.

"No," she answers. "After thirty men produce less testosterone, which, by the way, can lead to moodiness. Like menopause for men. By forty, men are losing five pounds of muscle every ten years. Read the article yourself, Mr. Know-it-all."

Washing the dishes, he catches his reflection in the window over the sink. He lifts his arm and flexes. Reaching across his body, his sudsy hand gives his bicep a squeeze. Lean, and not much more room for growth.

* * *

Ethel's arrival brings with it the fun challenge of trying to guess the fineness of the day's heels from the deepness of the toll when they strike the corridor's linoleum. A hollowed pecking may indicate a pair of heeled slingbacks, ones with wondrous spikes that, given Ethel's weight and proportions, defy rules of balance: the heels he enjoys most. A weighty doorknocker sound indicates a more practical and sturdy pair. But still heels. Always heels. But a less glamorous pair will mean she is probably rushed and will be wearing glasses instead of her ocean-blue contact lenses. The style of the straps is always a surprise. Meager strapping, say, a single buckle across the ankle, is a preference. Too many straps, too intricate the weaving, and she looks unattractively biblical. Not wanting to miss the arrival, most of Meiselman's morning is spent fighting the need to urinate.

Ethel is a natural in heels. No awkward half steps, no curled toes gripping the insole. The longest strides the skirts allow. The workday already underway, Ethel's entrance will be harried. Betsy Ross will hand her any messages on the go, shouting directions behind her, and Ethel will not look Meiselman's way as she turns into her office and hangs her coat on the back of the door. Given the warnings over the storm due to pummel the south of the city later today it will be her black trench, the one that hits right in the middle of her thighs. After setting her purse down on the desk, folded sunglasses on top, she will sit at one of the guest chairs in front of her desk and, while shuffling through the messages, will call for Meiselman, and what if he is off urinating? Even if he tends to be briefer, and more frequent, than most men. He could have been back by now, he repeatedly tells himself.

For distraction, Meiselman reads Shenkenberg with his chair turned to the side, a signal to the underlings that he does not want to be disturbed. Also, in case he falls asleep again. Who decided it is unacceptable for everyone except the boss to close his or her office door?

It takes a moment for Meiselman to remember he left off with the acclaimed author Shenkenberg sitting in the pews of one of Europe's great yeshivas lusting after a blonde, teenage Russian in boots and a miniskirt. Was there a pierced nose, a tattooed wrist, pink-colored hair?

People see a grown man reading fiction, and they see a loafer, especially during the workday. So every time he hears footsteps or voices outside his office, he puts down the book, twirls the curls covering his forehead and starts nibbling the end of his pencil, occasionally tapping it against the notebook left open on the desk. Here and there, he writes notes like, "Still no mention of Rabbi J-." He sighs the sigh of a spent man and pulls random folders from the file cabinet and scatters them across the desk. He rests the phone in the crook of his neck, the dial tone eventually falling into the rapid ring of an off-the-hook receiver. This is the scene he wants Ethel or any of the underlings to witness when they pass his office.

Impatient to arrive at something useful, he skims in search of Rabbi J-'s name, and he finally spots it, but he cannot hold off urinating much longer. He has waited three hours, trying every known trick, sitting with an open stance, periodically standing with his legs crossed. But a pinch in his side sticks, as if he is doing damage to a kidney. With his luck, Ethel will hustle through the door the minute he makes a dash for it. What kind of luck does he have? He does not consider himself particularly lucky or unlucky. His luck tends to break even.

Reading is impossible with his mind obsessing over his need to urinate. He cannot wait much longer, but right as he stands from his desk, Mitchell puts the upper half of his body through the doorway.

"Hope our players used the off-day to rest their tired—"

"Not now, Mitchell."

Meiselman brushes past Mitchell, bumping stomachs with the man, his knee knocking loose the umbrella. The bathroom in the break room is a clear shot down the hallway with Betsy Ross his only obstacle. She is sitting behind her L-shaped desk eating macaroni and cheese from a Tupperware while reproaching June and Ada for crowing that they will miss the storm. Do they not know that the secretary has a sister and brother-in-law south of the city that own a shop with a leaky roof?

There is great relief when he turns the bathroom door's knob and it rotates. Too great, perhaps, because the moment he flicks on the light and his eyes lock on the white bowl, whose lid is down, all of the pain that had been stitching his side surges to the tip of his penis and before he can get his zipper down a spritz of urine sprays the inside of his underpants. He slides onto the bowl and empties his bladder, eyes closed in ethereal bliss, heart pumping hard, a smile creeping across his face. Finished, he assesses the damage of his premature release. The bespattering is significant. His hair is moist, and he is worried about it trapping a smell, so he brings his penis up to the sink and using his cupped hands gives his scrotum a good rinsing. He mops it up with a wad of toilet paper, the cheap paper turning pulpy and sticking in his hairs. Nothing can be done to dry or rinse the soiled underpants.

The fertility specialist had recommended this step months ago. Cool the testes, he said. But the thought of it rubbing against the material of his pants revolted him. Would he not have to start laundering his pants after every wear? Stepping out of the bathroom, Meiselman feels there is something aggressive, perhaps predatory about having shed that extra layer, of letting it all hang freely, so to speak. That it is not put away. Like everyone in the office will be able to see it pressing up against the underside of his fly and think he is about to take it out and use it. Although, he cannot recall the last time he felt this gallant. Someone to be feared. Addition by subtraction. Is this why Gershon left his boxers at home when he went off to college?

Back in the hallway, Betsy Ross is talking traffic with Ada. Despite constantly showing her bra strap, Ada is decent and cannot conjure a scenario where she would ride the shoulder. "It's a no-brainer," Betsy Ross stresses, "The city is at fault for not handling the traffic problem." Betsy Ross tries roping him into the conversation, but Meiselman brushes her off.

"Must finish the addendum," he says. "Ethel called and asked for it."

"You spoke with her today? She's a fighter, I swear," Betsy Ross says. "She said she'd be out of touch for the next couple of days."

* * *

The last minutes before lunch pass achingly slow, the open book resting face down on his lap, the stiffness of its spine stimulating his unsheathed penis. He is only pretending to read. He is too distracted. There is the mysterious letter Betsy Ross is drafting, plus Deena's sour mood this morning, and constant memories of the pink-haired woman's hair swaying against his hand.

The telephone's digital ring realigns Meiselman's roving mind. A patron with a nutty complaint? You call it a workshop, but not once did Mr. Arnold ask if anyone had questions. Or Deena ringing to apologize for the unpleasantries she lobbed his way at breakfast. Or Shenkenberg ringing to apologize. Or Ethel blaming her absence on the balky back. Tell the team I'm working off-site. And, remember: Do not call Shenkenberg!

No, no, no, and no.

His mother, voice rickety, asking, "Where are you? We've been trying to get a hold of you for the last hour!"

"I am at work."

"I know you are at work, I'm calling you at work! But what are you doing at work when that neighbor of yours is making a mess of your property? Isn't that more important than work? Water is just everywhere. Everywhere!"

"Mrs. Woolf is doing this?"

"Yes, Mrs. Woolf! It's certainly not your father and I flooding your land."

Meiselman spins around, so the back of his chair is facing the door, the phone cord wrapping his neck. Bending forward, he plugs his finger into his other ear.

"Can you maybe ask her to turn it off?" he loudly whispers. "Can't leave work. Ethel's out. I'm in charge."

"I'm not decent." Deep breaths come at him through the phone's receiver. "I guess I can call out to her," she says. The phone tumbles to the bed. Meiselman, assuming this will resolve the matter, turns back to his desk and moves his brown lunch bag from drawer to blotter. Unfurling the bag, he hears his mother in the background muttering, "I don't even know if this window opens. Will I be able to close it? And there is a screen. Then what? Stick my head out and holler across two yards? I'll end up with a broken neck." Loud thumping as his mother returns.

"You're just going to have to do it yourself."

"Can you go over there?"

"She's not my neighbor. You wanted to be a homeowner. This is part of the deal, mister."

"Tonight I will go over there and give her a talking to. The time has come," he says, thinking a show of solidarity will calm her.

"Tonight will be too late! By tonight your entire house will be underwater. Now! The library will survive without you."

Will it, he wants to ask, but his mother beats him to it with a question of her own.

"Why you and your father excuse this woman's boorish behavior—"

"Not me! Deena. Deena is the one. Deena and Daddy. On this one, I am with you."

"Tell your wife she's always been like this. Her husband was also a survivor, and he was the kindest, gentlest man. Suffered greatly living with her."

Meiselman stuffs his paper lunch bag and the Shenkenberg book into the front pockets of his trench coat and exits his office. Betsy Ross is not at her desk. Under the guise of pulling a tissue from the box on her desk, he nudges the computer mouse, which lights up the monitor. She has not left open any documents that may shed light on the letter's content.

Upon returning home, he heads straight to the backyard. Staring at his neighbor's pool of water from his side of the fence, he immediately questions whether his mother was speaking hyperbolically. The pool of water is shallow, with plastic sheeting lining the bottom, and a foot-high retaining wall made of small rocks surrounding it. The threat, in other words, is difficult to decipher.

He digs for a memory to prove there is a tendency for his mother to overreact. Entering his mind is the time his father gallantly strode downstairs, stomach sticking out, wearing an old pair of blue jeans that were snug in the crotch and short in the legs, his argyle socks and cordovan penny loafers on display. He announced to the family that he was off to the hardware store, the first step in complying with his doctor's order. Gardening was the better of the two options. "Needlework?" Meiselman remembers his father asking. "Sounds a little..." Did that thing of tilting his hand from side to side. An hour later, he came home with a watering can stuffed with seeds, a spade, and a short-handled rake. "You going to grow me roses?" his mother asked, dismayed over what her husband spent for the thorn-proof, sheepskin gardening gloves. From a window upstairs, Meiselman spied his father timidly pressing the tip of his loafer into the recently thawed ground. Fingertips to the mud, disgust overtook his face. He rubbed his soiled fingers clean with his thumb before throwing a dismissive wave at the ground and walking away. By the time Meiselman came downstairs, his father had already plopped himself on the couch, a pile of newspapers at his feet. Without prompting, his father said, "Too muddy. Scared I'll make a mess of everything. I'll get my guy to do it. With needlework, I can at least, enjoy the television."

In no way does this memory resolve the question of his mother's apparent overreaction to the mess in Mrs. Woolf's backyard. Incidentally, when Meiselman shared this memory with Dr. Lin, the doctor asked if he knew the kind of doctor that made this recommendation to his father, and whether it related to a problem with the head or heart. Meiselman did not know.

All the memory does is highlight his father's general unwillingness to dirty his hands, although plenty of memories underline this aversion. Some weeks when returning from shul, his father would turn severe when they hit their block, directing the Meiselman boys to change course and step into the street so as to avoid the dog droppings. "Your mother will kill me if you step in it." Gershon defied his father, plowing ahead, sidestepping the shit, while Meiselman followed his father down into the street, his father grabbing Meiselman's bicep as if his son were too daft to avoid getting hit by a car. Or was his father using Meiselman for protection? PopPop used to tell stories of black people in South Carolina stepping out of the way for white people. Different, of course. If Meiselman's mother heard pogroms breaking out in the street, his insomnious father would duck behind an open newspaper. Pooch, what's the use of us getting involved?

It would be unwise to assume his mother is overreacting, especially since she has a knack for foreseeing how barely perceptible transgressions can easily evolve into greater injustices. A short while ago, upstairs in her bedroom, his mother was tightening the bedsheets—no, she said she was not decent, so she must have been in her towel, having just stepped out of the shower—when she'd sensed disorder outside. All she could see from her second-story bedroom window—two lots over—was the hose leading into the pool of water, and the fear of calamity surely brewed at the sight of the frothy backwash bubbling above the water's surface.

* * *

The old lady Mrs. Woolf, keen on seizing the attention of her neighbors at every opportunity, has painted her front door fire engine red, the optimistic red of the mid-1980s, when Meiselman was a high school student and his mother was painting her nails and lips the same color. This was the same period when his mother's hairstyle was a scrum of curls like Meiselman's is now. People ask if his are natural, and he wants to ask what kind of man would *patshke* with his hair like this. They are passed down on his mother's side. Not PopPop, but MaMa. This should have been the first clue that the woman in the black and white bathing suit photograph, the one his mother found under his mattress, was his grandmother and not some random woman friend of PopPop. In the 90s, Meiselman's mother changed her polish and lipstick to a more elegant, brownish red.

The freshness of the door's paint job surprises him, not a speck of rust munching the brass knocker or mail slot. Above the peephole a glinting gold sign tacked to the door reads in cursive, "The Woolfs," an audacious sign for a woman who has been living alone for twenty years.

The white knuckles of his clenched fist thump the door. Impatience is key to displaying outrage, so he hammers the knocker thrice. Waits several beats, and then rings the doorbell, which is the sound of a howling coyote. Sadie charges the door, panting. Paws scratching the wood, she emits sickly bleats. Meiselman tries backing her off by kicking the door's bottom, but the dog's cries only grow louder. From behind the door, deep in the house, a grouchy Mrs. Woolf yells at Sadie to shut up and move away from the door.

For thirty-six years he has lived a pitch's distance from Mrs. Woolf and not once has he stepped foot in her house, so he is reluctant to comply when she instructs him to enter on his own.

"It must be a pit in there, with that dog running wild and crapping it up with its hair," his mother, who boasts of owning a longer streak, often speculates. "Your father tells me I'm wrong. When has he been inside?"

How will he, someone who does not know woods, describe to his mother the refinement of the foyer's flooring? I doubt it was maple, he can already hear his mother saying. The color of maple syrup, I said. How will he convey the heaviness of the shine? Like you, mother, she must get on all fours, pillow padding the knees, scooping goop from a canister and working the wood with her hand's heel. I'm sure Mrs. Woolf doesn't do it like me. The walls of the foyer are the same pistachio green of the first Meiselman family car he remembers, a station wagon whose backseat faced the traveled road, seats Meiselman and Gershon occupied because his mother believed it should be her kids and not someone else's who *brekh*. Straight ahead, a mirror with a rust-colored frame hangs on the wall. Beneath it a table with a top that looks as if it were sliced straight off the trunk of a tree. A white doily covers the wood. Filling an oval, silver dish on the table are those classic, red-swirled, peppermint suckers, a candy Meiselman has not seen or sucked in years.

"Yoo-hoo, in here," Mrs. Woolf calls out.

The living room is to his immediate left. It has the same pistachio green walls and heavily shined wood flooring as the foyer. In front of the bay window is a piano, keys facing outside, a dust cover pulled over the instrument and its bench. Drapes drawn, the anemic sunlight filtering through the fabric is the only light, and it dies well before the couches—also pistachio—which are set farther back in this deep room. Sitting on the floor in front of the larger section of the L-shaped couch, on a shadow-streaked rug of that famous painting of the American farmer holding a pitchfork and standing next to his wife, is Mrs. Woolf. A glass coffee table, clean of books or knickknacks, separates Meiselman from his neighbor, who is heaving, her back up against the couch's base, legs flat on the floor. Her jeans are rolled to the knees, exposing both legs, the wood one, which is also the color of maple syrup, and the real leg, which has a trail of crusty scabs, like minor Hawaiian islands, running up her bumpy, purplish shin. The sleeves of her lumberjack flannel are rolled to the elbow, its top two buttons undone, wrinkled, bronzed cleavage on display. Her arms hang at her sides.

"A Meiselman here to rescue a damsel in distress," she says over a light gurgle. "Usually when I'm out back, Sadie is sunning herself on the patio. Came inside looking for her and she's in here soothing her back against the rug. Can't blame her." Mrs. Woolf gives the rug a pat. "She knows better. Turning into an old stubborn bitch like her owner, I guess. Anyway, next thing I know, I'm on all fours picking up her hairs, not even considering how I'd get myself back up. Got short hamstrings like my pa. Then, you show up, like heavenly manna." She adds, "Catch your breath first. You look unhealthy. Face like the inside of a watermelon."

He needs her to tell him his face is reddening? Feels like it's up against a space heater. Wants to rip off his coat and purple button-down and claw at his tingling chest hair. Is this the "rush" seasoned aggressors talk about? He needs to air his grievances at once and tame this pumping blood.

Mrs. Woolf, thinking she can calm things down with small talk, slaps the thigh of her real leg and says, "Doesn't help that this girl is getting more and more fed up with working for two. Cramps up on me. This isn't what she signed up for."

Other than the leg, she is sturdy. Her neck does not loll. Her voice is smooth for someone her age. She is not leaking unsavory fluids or gases, and her eyeballs are clear. Her skin is not as liver-spotted as PopPop's was at the end of his life. Although, she does not have him fooled into thinking those chalk white teeth stuffing her mouth are originals.

"You look just like your father," she says. "Two skinny men."

Looks more like his mother, but he is not about to correct her.

Bending the knee of her good leg, she straightens her back against the couch and, hands flat on the carpet, she tries hoisting herself from the ground. Face tightening, her bottom lifts momentarily before falling and thumping the rug.

"Your father's sweet. Every Monday and Thursday night returns my can and recycling bin to the side of the house. Like how you bring him the newspapers in the morning sometimes."

"Every day. Every day, I bring him the newspapers."

"Truth is, I'm outside a bulk of the day, and I'm perfectly capable of retrieving my own bins. Just look old. Don't feel a day over eighty-five. But it makes him feel good, and I don't want to be ungracious. Too many people are these days."

He sees what she is trying to do. She is trying to undercut him with basic civility. He, a thirty-six-year-old man with a backyard on the verge of flooding, is not interested in turning this encounter into an uplifting story about forgiveness. Nothing, at this point, will succeed in dialing down his aggression. He knows she is a survivor. One of the lucky ones who got a proper job. After coming to America and completing all sorts of degrees she worked for the government. Sent on dangerous missions to teach third-worlders how to grow food. Every couple of months Meiselman's father would retell a conversation he had with the neighbor, his voice dipping as if he were letting his family in on some state secret. "They are plenty nervous about an increase in soy prices." "Who eats soy? Only queer people like her," his mother would shout back. How she lost the leg Meiselman does now know, but she used to sit in shorts in the front of her house, outstretched legs crossed at the ankles, unconcerned with how the prosthetic and its big bolt through the knee might scare a child like Meiselman and send him running back into the house. Gershon, from an early age, waved to the old lady, and as he got older he began saying hello and asking about her travels. Meiselman also knows there is a question about the spelling of her last name. “What Jew spells Woolf that way,” his mother asks on occasion. “She probably got the spelling at immigration,” his father reasons. “You’re always defending her,” his mother yells back. His father walks away mumbling, “It’s not her. It’s her husband with the name Woolf.”

Not a story of forgiveness, and not a story about finding himself in the lair of an ageless oracle who will dispense cryptic wisdom on how Meiselman might oppose Shenkenberg. Thirty-six year old men are not ripe for lesson learning. Grabbing a corner of the coffee table to steady herself, she says, “Just give me a second.”

This rambling, this stalling, has gone on long enough. Meiselman steps to the side so the coffee table is no longer between them. Five feet of rug—the full length of the farmer’s wife’s body—separate Meiselman from his neighbor. If he steps closer to loom over her, she might hold up her hand like a felled ballplayer and ask Meiselman outright for help getting up off the floor.

“Your hose,” he begins. “You’ve left it on and water is everywhere. I’m not interested in having my backyard flooded. I have drainage issues. Seepage, in the past, has been a problem.”

“That hose in the pit? No, no. That’s not going to be an issue. The water is contained.”

“Just barely. In minutes, the water will breach that slapdash wall you built.”

She turns the wrist of the arm connected to the corner of the table and asks, “Now, what time is it?”

Unable to manipulate him verbally, she has resorted to flashing him her arm, hoping to dull his outrage with the blurry, blue-inked numbers tattooing her skin. It does, he must admit, dim his resolve. He is not impenetrable. He is not an animal. But he directs himself to stay the course. “It’s time for us to sort out this matter regarding the hose,” he says, pleased with how he cleverly turned the words of her question against her. “One needs a permit before digging trenches on private property.”

“A trench? That’s a little thick. Just a bored, retired woman doing some final experiments before they plant me in the ground. Rice paddies. Testing their viability in a suburban-slash-urban setting. Bored planting vegetables and herbs. And fed up of squirrels acting like squirrels. I’ll have a look as soon as I catch my breath.” Mrs. Woolf brings her elbows back and rests them on the edge of the couch cushion.

“We are not in the country! Sitting water is a breeding ground for mosquitoes and other virus-carrying insects. And this project is highly disruptive. My wife hasn’t gotten a full night of sleep in weeks, and we are trying to start a family. Sleep, the doctor said, is integral.”

“Standing water, you mean.” Her aloof veneer is cracking. She can no longer contain her nastiness. “And if sleep is what you are worried about,” she continues, “you might not be going about it the right way.”

Exiting the living room, unsure of whether he has done an adequate job of conveying his outrage, he stops at the table in the foyer and dips a finger and thumb into the silver dish to pinch a classic peppermint candy, but soon his middle finger is climbing over the bowl’s lip to help secure a second candy, and then his naked ring finger and pinkie have also climbed into the dish to assist in drawing an entire fistful. He tightens his claw around the loot, the twisted ends of the wrappers sticking through the slits between his fingers. He transfers the candies into the front pocket of his pants.

Only once he is outside does he hear the heft of Mrs. Woolf’s parting comment, how she effectively grabbed the final word and spoiled what was an otherwise fine display of aggression. Wanting to take back the last word, he circles around the house and stands in front of the pool of water, which is even shallower than it appears from the other side of the fence. Through the purplish blue surface he can see the plastic-sheeted bottom. He grabs a hold of the hose, whose end is still plunged into the water, and follows it to a faucet fixed to the house's rear wall, next to the patio door, behind a row of unkempt bushes. Reaching his arm through the prickly branches, he shuts off the water, unscrews the end of the hose, and drags it back to the pit. Then he throws the entire hose into the water, before crossing back over to his property.

* * *

Not wanting to draw attention to the fact that he has been away from the library for most of the afternoon, Meiselman parks his car on the street adjacent to the main lot. He leaves his coat in the car, rolls up his purple shirtsleeves, and slips a broken-pointed pencil behind his ear. Rather than following the sidewalk to the front entrance of the library, he cuts into the lot's back rows.

After depositing Mrs. Woolf's hose in the pit, he'd returned home and spent the next hour surveying his neighbor's lot from his bedroom window, waiting for her to emerge and discover how he had indeed grabbed the final word. Eventually, he'd grown hungry, pulled his brown paper lunch bag from his coat, and set it on the windowsill. The jelly in his peanut butter sandwich was warm, and after three disagreeable chews, he spit the masticated bread into his paper napkin. The potato chips had been crushed to breadcrumbs and could not be eaten. He rarely eats the tomatoes, carrot sticks, or other raw vegetables Deena prepares for his lunch, and today was no exception. Room temperature apple juice is vile; that, too, was dumped.

With no sign of Mrs. Woolf, he'd bounded downstairs to forage for food. All he'd found in the refrigerator were the three jumbo salmon patties Deena fried on Sunday for tonight's dinner. Her signature dish. What she ate with her father. Now, she subjects him. He loves the patties in spite of the dish being food of the wealthy modified for the poor. Not wanting to leave behind evidence of his midday invasion, he'd eaten the two patties over the sink. Too many questions would be raised if he'd left only the third patty in the refrigerator, so he'd stashed it in the brown paper bag with the rest of his lunch, which he is now chucking in the library's dumpster off to the side of the parking lot.

He is through the first set of doors, and right as his hand smacks the brass plate of the second set of doors, his eyes lift and through the door's glass he spots the pink-haired girl standing in the circulation line straight ahead. She, in the same bulky sweatshirt from the other day, is fanning herself with a slim paperback. Third in line with two librarians at the desk, it should take her no more than two minutes to check out. Not wanting to encounter the pink-haired girl in the presence of other patrons and librarians—because who knows what turns the encounter may take?—he reverses, backpedaling through the first set of doors until he is on the sidewalk, ten feet from the entrance.

The buildup of bacteria in his mouth from the nap he took after eating the jumbo patties is significant, but a problem he can easily counter with one of Mrs. Woolf's peppermint candies. Sucking away, he counts down from thirty. Fearful that he is counting too fast on account of his excitement, he initiates a do-over from ten, and right when the library's outer door opens, Meiselman grabs its handle and steps around, hoping it will lead to what will seem like accidental contact. A stroller rams his shins, a mother stiff-arming the door and pushing him out of the way. He retreats to his previous starting line, but forgoes the countdown. When the doors open again a balding woman cradling a tote bag full of books emerges. Finally, on his fourth try, after he is through the first doors and is standing back in the vestibule, biding more time by fussing with the Shenkenberg flier on the bulletin board, he sees, out of the corner of his eye, the door swinging open. He lunges for it, and his timing could not be more perfect as the crown of her bowed head crashes into his chest. He steps back to hold open the door for her, hand to his heart, apologizing for the collision.

"Oh, you," he says. Pointing to the book, he asks, "Didn't I help you find that the other day?"

The pink-haired girl stares at the cover. "Yeah, bit the bullet. Got a card and checked it out."

"Great story," he says. "Reading it for a class?"

"Yep."

What more can he ask her? The way she slides her eyebrow's safety pin from side to side tells him she wants out of the conversation. The girl is a sloucher, her shoulders practically higher than her chin.

"Now that you're a card-carrying member you should think about taking advantage of our wonderful programming. The name Izzy Shenkenberg ring a bell?" he asks, handing her the flier in his hand. When she does not reply, he continues, "Controversial writer. I'll be hosting him for a reading this coming Sunday. Then we will have a debate-slash-dialogue. Fireworks expected."

She plumps her lower lip as if mildly interested, snags the flier from his hand, and begins walking away. Palm pressed against the door, ready to exit, she stops and, staring down at the publisher-provided photograph of Shenkenberg, asks, "What makes him so controversial?"

A little girl and her mother entering the library force the pink-haired girl away from the door and closer to Meiselman. He stays planted, his chin inches from her hair.

“Well, he writes against religion, and is, uh, very lewd. A firebrand. The type of irreverence your generation seems to value. Personally, between us, I don’t care for him.”

“Some way to sell someone on a program. Whatever, I don’t care about religion one way or the other, no offense. Parents are Jewish, barely practicing, but I’m an atheist.”

“Well, could be worthwhile for someone in your position.”

She does not take the bait, does not teasingly ask: And what is my position? Instead, the pink-haired girl crosses her eyebrows at him like he is just another doltish adult in her life, and exits without a thank-you or a proper goodbye.

Will she let the flier fall from her fingers and flutter to the ground as she walks to her car? Will she get in the seedy convertible of an older man, or has she arranged a time with her mother? Certainly, she is too indolent to ride a bike or walk any great distance. These are the questions that make Meiselman discreetly trail her through the parking lot. She keeps walking and walking, past the first row of back-to-back cars, past the second row, with Meiselman dodging behind vans. She is reaching the back of the parking lot, or what is the front of the parking lot for Village Hall, which faces the library at the other end, when, suddenly, she veers left toward the alleyway. She walks around the dumpster and gets into a haphazardly parked red convertible that is a newer and sportier car than the one Meiselman drives. The overcast sky does not deter her from putting on a pair of pink-framed sunglasses. After she starts the car, he spots her folding the flier and tucking it under the visor. Meiselman does not think he has ever met an atheist.

* * *

"What a day!" He preempts Betsy Ross as he enters the back offices. Mitchell is sitting on the front edge of her desk, leg dangling, the handle of the umbrella hanging off his wrist. Meiselman continues, "A woman wanted her five-year old to sit in on the ten-to-twelve reading group because she had errands to run. We are not running a day care. Then I have a reporter from the *Tribune* hounding me to do a story about Shen—"

Mitchell cuts off Meiselman's ramble and says to Betsy Ross, "Ask Meiselman. He seems to know what's going on."

But they do not ask his opinion. They simply resume the argument they were having when he interrupted. Something about the veracity of a memorandum detailing an agreement with the Crown Prince of Saudi Arabia to lower oil prices before the election. One of them dismisses it as the lies of a press that hates the President. "Naïve, naïve, naïve," the other one answers. "Their party has always harped on the incompetence and dishonesty of government, and they are doing a fine job of making the case." "War is not easy. Hiccups are inevitable." Then one of them lobs that same charge Meiselman heard from his father, the one about certain Americans rooting for defeat in order to buttress their party's electoral chances.

Because he wants no part of a discussion he knows nothing about, Meiselman turns his back on them, opens the supply closet doors and asks, "Staples, where are you?" He seems to have missed this story about the memorandum. If forced to voice an opinion, it seems more important for him to find common ground with Betsy Ross, given the outstanding question of the letter. What advantage is there to being in synch with Mitchell? "Jumbo is my size," Meiselman says, locating the staples.

"Grade-a liars," Mitchell says. "Tell her, Meiselman."

Turning away from the supply closet, Meiselman yanks two peppermint candies from his overly stuffed pants pocket and asks, "Anyone?"

Mitchell accepts one, seeming to get a genuine kick out of the candy's distinctiveness, but Betsy Ross declines by saying, "If you aren't going to eat my chocolates, then I'm not going to eat your candies. Now, boys, if you'll excuse me, I must get back to this letter. Hopefully, it's the final draft."

Why is the good stationary out again, and why does Mitchell say, "Thank you for making those changes, dear," before saying goodnight, cockily swinging his umbrella as he walks back to his office?

Betsy Ross says to Meiselman, "Ethel's going to be very excited to hear that news about the *Tribune*. I'll leave word with her. Could be a real spirit-raiser, I pray."

"Better not," he says. "Nothing is official from what I gather, and I certainly don't want it to turn into, God forbid, something spirit-crushing."

* * *

Stepping through the front door of his house, which Deena has left open, he is not his usual haggard self. His stomach still full from his late lunch, he could go without dinner, and use the extra time before tonight's game to learn how the irascible Shenkenberg spent his free day in Poland away from the group. The bathroom, is Meiselman's guess. Everything with that man is the bathroom.

It is only when he is standing inside the house that he begins wondering what happened after Deena discovered the jumbo salmon patties missing. Confessing to being home and eating the jumbo salmon patties is not an option. Discovery of shifty behavior can swiftly spiral into outright distrust. Besides, she will not appreciate his need to confront Mrs. Woolf.

Preemption is always the best option, so he infuses his usual, "Hello, love," with less energy than normal, and makes a racket by throwing coat hangers to the floor and banging the closet door shut. The commotion does not cause her to come out and greet him, or even return the call. Instead, he is forced to bellow from the hallway, "What a day! Poor Ethel and her back. Poor me, stuck working for two."

"If there is anything I can do, let me know," she says, her voice carrying down the hallway from the kitchen.

One day he will share with Deena the offensiveness of this frequent offer. Would his mother ask his father if she could litigate on his behalf? Would Gershon's wife propose traveling to some South American village to broker a deal for water rights? Would Deena appreciate Meiselman dictating a patient's course of treatment? Nobody offered to help him file the studio's returns when he worked as an accountant. Only now when he lacks a job title tied to a specific trade do people assume he does nothing more than push papers for a living.

He does not need to see her sitting on the kitchen floor in front of an open refrigerator, squeeze bottles of mustard and ketchup, glass jars of pickles and horseradish sauce and a carton of eggs surrounding her, to know the source of her preoccupation. She paddles through the shelves, pulling a yellowed stalk of celery and yellowing florets of broccoli, which she dumps into the garbage can behind her.

"Want to read this Shenkenberg book for me?" he asks.

"You make it sound so terrible," she answers. "Hey, have you seen the jumbo salmon patties? Did I stick them in the freezer?"

She stands and opens the freezer door.

"Terribly crude," Meiselman answers. "Still, this is no journeyman I'm debating. Most people think he's young and inexperienced." Sticking his head in the freezer alongside hers, he plows ahead. "Mid-thirties is not young. His other book—some stories—was a hit. And today I find out he's published in national magazines and has won awards. Went to Princeton, which doesn't necessarily bow me, but it bows them."

Has his rambling not made clear his demand that she forget about the patties, at once? What he needs from her is to sit him down at the table, cover his hands, and say, My man is just as smart. Then again, no: such banal words of encouragement will not suffice. She should face him standing up, poke him in the chest, and with fire in her eyes say, The man I married is no slouch! The man I married hasn't won awards, but he can rattle off the batting averages, home runs, and runs-batted-in of any White Sox player from the past twenty years. Encyclopedic! You think most men can do that? Besides, you have home field advantage. You are playing for a tie; he is playing for a win. Or maybe she will use her sarcasm to boost him. He's nothing more than a glorified storyteller. Three hundred years ago, he'd be travelling village-to-village by horse and buggy, working for soup and lodging.

"The patties I made Sunday night," she says.

"Wasn't there something about being short a can?" he asks.

"Short a can? What? No, I remember making them."

"Your memory is probably of making them a different week."

"When you took my underwear to Rav Fruman. I can see it, I swear! This is crazy."

"Like a feeling of déjà vu? Is that the feeling?"

"I can see myself turning down the burner. I can hear the sizzle."

“Sounds like déjà vu.”

“I know déjà vu. This is not déjà vu. Nothing like déjà vu.”

He steps over to the kitchen window and lifts a blind with his finger.

“My parents are eating leftover chicken from Friday night,” he says.

“It’s Tuesday. After three days, things start to grow.”

“Nothing that can’t be killed in the oven.”

“Besides, I could barely get it down Friday night, why would I want it now?”

“My mother’s orange chicken, seriously? Delicious.”

“Plus, I don’t need your mother thinking I’m a bad wife who doesn’t have time to make dinner. You’ve heard her speeches about working mothers.”

“My mother,” he begins, but is unable to finish the sentence because how does his mother think of his wife? He assumes she is impressed, like Meiselman, by her professional success. Anyway, why should he reassure Deena that his mother thinks highly of her when, moments ago, his appeal for reassurance went unanswered?

“But you’re not a working mother,” he says.

She decides to boil eggs. Mourners’ food. Abstaining from making a joke about taking his with ash and salt, he says, “Funny, I’ve been craving eggs.”

After sitting down to a dinner of hard-boiled eggs, Israeli salad, and whole-wheat couscous, Meiselman repeats his Shenkenberg speech from before, but when he arrives at the point about the writer winning awards, Deena pops the entire yolk into her mouth, pushes it against her inner cheek and says, “Remember, they’re coming to hear Shenkenberg, not you.”

The stakes are obviously not clear to her.

"He was so rude. If only you would have heard the sighing as he waited for me to transfer him to Ethel. Like I'm the help."

"Maybe, but they are still coming to hear him."

He heard her fine the first time. He adds salt to his couscous.

"It doesn't have enough salt?" she asks.

He shrugs apologetically, adding salt to all three dishes.

"Take Molly," Deena says. "You wouldn't believe how excited she is to see him. Says it's one of the funniest books she's ever read. Made her book club read it."

"What does Molly understand? She's been Jewish for ten minutes and suddenly she's an expert on our literature?"

"Molly reads everything. Molly is amazing."

"The last thing I need is a bunch of Mollies at the event."

Single, single, single, pop out go the first four batters for the visiting Yankees in the top of the first inning. Then, walk, single, hit batter, single, and double before the White Sox finally get a second out on a ground ball by Jeter. Another walk before a fly out ends the top of the first inning. Seven runs is the damage. Between innings Meiselman checks the newspaper for an article on the memorandum Betsy Ross and Mitchell were squabbling over earlier. From the heatedness of the argument he presumes he will find the article on the front page, surely, in the first five. Finally, on page fifteen, he locates the story, a two-column article sandwiched between a story about the buffoon Nader calling for a troop pullout and a five-paragraph filler about the Secretary of State reiterating his support for the President. Its placement does not correspond to the argument's intensity.

The Yankees score another run in the top of the second to extend the lead back to seven. Frank is not playing again. This morning's article questioning his commitment did not motivate him to try and play through the pain. Meiselman, losing interest, flips to the higher channels, settling for an action movie on one of the two free movie channels they receive as part of the basic cable package.

Deena enters the family room, hugging a laundry basket. She says, “The hot oil splashed my thumb. Look.”

Meiselman grabs the finger.

“No touching,” Deena says.

“Don’t see anything.”

Meiselman fishes a candy from his pocket, even though he is running low. Deena’s tongue falls from her mouth.

“But these are a novelty,” Meiselman says.

“Not really, they have them everywhere.”

“Guess they aren’t too good for my teeth anyway,” he says, setting her up for a joke, their joke, about her marrying him because of his teeth and dimples. Instead, she grapples an armful of laundered whites from the basket and drops them into his lap.

“I’m so tired,” she says. “Fold them yourself, please.”

Not the right time to tell her he will not be needing the underwear anymore.

Wednesday

"Explain something to me," she calls out to him from the kitchen.

Meiselman—purple shirt, no underwear—slows to a shuffle. If he learned one thing from living with his mother it is that the demand to "explain" is rarely a simple request to elucidate.

"Explain to me why I found a photo of your grandmother in a bathing suit under your mattress?" His mother had accosted him one night at the front door upon his return home from the recording studio. This was during the transition years. She did not wave the photo in his face, demanding an explanation. In her mind, the question of his depravity had already been settled. Why else would she have come to the door armed with Dr. Lin's phone number? Not only because of the photograph, but also the Saturday nights spent watching the White Sox instead of taking out any of the girls recruited through friends and relatives. Still, she'd pressed for an explanation, something to feed her husband, a man who could be mollified by the flimsiest excuse. Something about the way these women subtly flaunt their immodesty, he claims. Batting eyelashes. Dipped chins. Perfectly angled backsides. I know what your son is talking about? He's sick, clearly.

If Deena ambushes Meiselman with Mrs. Woolf's coiled hose, a picture of a pink-haired woman torn from one of her magazines, or a crumb from a jumbo salmon patty pinched between the tips of her tweezers, the ones she uses to clear unsavory hairs from above the lip, jawline, and brow, he will counter by asking her to explain why she was out of bed, showered, and dressed thirty minutes before the alarm sounded, and why, as he stepped into the bathroom, he heard the screen door slamming shut and, moments later, the peeling of the newspapers' plastic sleeves. Did she even remember to retrieve his father's papers? And why did she leave the front door open? She has proven incapable of providing a satisfactory answer to this last question, leading him to theorize that the more he questions a habit, the more, in a childish protest, it becomes entrenched. He may ask why she served only herself a bowl of oatmeal, and how she could be so presumptuous to grab the front page before he has had a look, not even offering it to him as he stands in front of the table, Shenkenberg book in hand. Obviously, he does not have exclusive rights to the front section, but has he not, after all these years, merited the right to first look? Open newspaper angled toward him, she directs his attention to Opinion, asking again for an explanation.

Having not yet read the day's headlines, and not wanting to appear clueless or ignorant (a real fear after yesterday's sidelining during Mitchell and Betsy's argument over what turned out to be a back page story), Meiselman, in an attempt to shift the conversation, mentions the relief of finally having a night free of disturbances.

"It doesn't bother me like it bothers you," she says, setting the newspaper flat on the table. She points to a side column and says, "Not sure if I have enough of the history. But I keep seeing and hearing things."

Maybe he should begin by explaining the difference between news and opinion. Questioning Deena's ability to manage the newspaper should not be interpreted as belittlement. Casual readers increasingly confuse opinion for fact. Furthermore, Deena's intelligence charms him. Others may surreptitiously scoff when he compares her to a doctor, but he overhears her phone consultations, how she effortlessly rattles off the names of negligible nerves and minor bones. In certain times, in certain cultures, such knowledge would have made her the village doctor. Or witch doctor. A joke. Recently, at the Green Grove Mall, Deena and Meiselman bumped into an orthopedic surgeon from the hospital who told Meiselman he calls Deena the Magician from Montreal. Why the doctor was under the impression Deena hailed from Montreal puzzled Meiselman. As to why she refused to correct this misconception, Deena, at the time, said, "Montreal sounds romantic. Isn't French mandatory there? Also, he's very senior."

Tapping the column, Deena says, "I know how much you like him."

Political discussions with Deena often turn maddening because his wife, like most people, effortlessly vacillates between opinions. Sadly, in these times, vacillators and ditherers are trumpeted as moderates, when all they are is irresolute and ill-informed. He is better off answering from the other side of the kitchen, so before opening his mouth, he fills the coffee maker and begins brewing.

"I admire him, not 'like him.' And what is there to explain? It's a hatchet job."

"What's a hatchet job?" Deena asks, turning in her seat, eyeing him through the space between the hanging cabinets and counter. He keeps his eyes on the coffee maker. "Start from the beginning," she says. "I know nothing."

Give Deena credit. Most people do not know what they do not know. The coffee maker burbles before settling into a steady stream.

"Everyone was fine with the plan until they weren't," Meiselman explains. "Nobody, if you remember, was protesting."

"Is that true?" Deena asks. "I remember seeing stuff on the news."

"Nothing significant. Nobody serious. No soldiers burning uniforms in front of the Washington Monument. Not like the fifties or sixties or seventies or whenever that was. The point I'm making is that it's becoming increasingly fashionable to be against the war. General Powell is a convenient scapegoat for the fickle middle, the ditherers. If only he would have protested, if only he would have acted on his supposed opposition in a more resounding manner, they argue. The world heard him loud and clear when he made the case. Are they saying he did not believe his own words, that he was a puppet, a mere mouthpiece? That's exactly what they are saying. Playing the good soldier, the same role he had played his entire life. Understand?"

"Maybe?"

Back to a trickle, he pulls the pot, the last drops sizzling dry on the burner. He fills the mugs and brings them to the table. Taking his seat across from Deena, he says, "Can I ask you a question?"

"Sure, ask."

"Do you think these same columnists would have celebrated him had he resigned in protest? They would have called him disloyal. The loneliness of a man in the General's predicament is intense. Take me, for example. If I were to resign over Shenkenberg, move away, buy a house in the UP, Ethel would lose sleep for a night, maybe two, or a week, a month, whatever. But then she'd find a replacement, a yes man, and Shenkenberg's indecency toward me—and Rabbi J-—would go unnoticed, unpunished. The world has an abundance of yes men. You know why?"

"I've got it, I think. I'll just reread the article."

"Because everyone has a family to feed," he answers. "You think my father likes that his job is crafting ways for corporations to avoid taxes, or that Gershon enjoys paying pennies on the dollar for water rights, or—"

"It doesn't take much to feed me."

"A soldier does not walk off the battlefield because he disagrees with the plan."

"Okay, yeah. I'll just reread the article and let you know if I have any other questions."

Can she, who for the second time called an editorial an article, be trusted to go at it alone, or will she overlook the slander implicit in the headline *Did Loyalty Finally Trip Up Colin Powell?* That the General's entire career can be ascribed to a willingness to click heels and toss off salutes on command, discounting attributes like bravery, acumen, and service. An apt time for Meiselman to reiterate his recommendation that she read the General's autobiography.

After his time with Dr. Lin came to an end, Meiselman, looking to strengthen his character and steel his mental state, had binged on the autobiographies of great Americans. Favorites included: *Iacocca* by Lee Iacocca; *Sam Walton: Made in America* by Sam Walton; *Grinding it Out: The Making of McDonald's* by Ray Kroc; *Dave's Way* by R. David Thomas; *Be My Guest* by Conrad N. Hilton; *Arnold: The Education of a Bodybuilder* by Arnold Schwarzenegger; *Bo Knows Bo* by Bo Jackson. The wisdom in those books continues to guide him: "The ability to concentrate and to use time well is everything," Lee Iacocca; "I've always played with kids that were five, six, seven years older than me," Bo Jackson; "I think the harder you work, the more luck you have," R. David Thomas. None of the books, however, had impacted him as profoundly as *My American Journey*, by Colin Powell. To such an extent that on many occasions he has considered rereading it.

Since Deena will, once again, ignore his recommendation, he feels the best course is to relay one great anecdote that will put her in the General's boots and convey the man's unimpeachable essence.

One story is quickly recalled, but it is not worth sharing since it does not illuminate the man in any meaningful way. Nonetheless, Meiselman cannot prevent it from playing in his mind. First year of college, the future General Powell signed up for engineering classes, and on the first day of class, the professor asked the students to draw a cone intersecting a plane. Drawing a cone was simple, but he found himself clueless as how to proceed. Cluelessness led to boredom, and he ended up doodling a scoop of ice cream on top of the cone. He did not stop there. Jutting from the cone's sides were the wings and nose of an airplane. Despite his aunties' concern about the type of pension available for geologists, the future general switched his major. Definitely not the story he wants to share with Deena, regardless of the similarities to Meiselman's own college experience, his father convincing his son to enroll in accounting classes at the start of sophomore year, even after Meiselman demonstrated aptitude and love for the audio production classes he took in his first year, his meticulousness and obsessive attention to detail major assets. His father scoffed at the idea that it could possibly lead to a career in broadcasting.

Meiselman says, "Your coffee."

She lowers the front page, which is shrouding her head, and briefly regards the mug before shifting her focus back to the newspaper.

"It's an editorial you are reading," he says, "not an article. Just one man's opinion."

"Skimmed it and moved on. But thanks," she adds, thick with sarcasm.

Distracted with trying to recall a Colin Powell story worth sharing, Meiselman marks his page in the Shenkenberg book and begins studying the back cover, specifically the author photo, which has the raccoon-eyed author leaning against a brick wall, an unsmiling face tight with misplaced anger, scuffed black work boots, the author wanting to fool the reader into thinking he is a working man, which is why he conceals his soft hands deep in the pockets of his wool coat.

Meiselman says to Deena, "I can picture how Shenkenberg must have looked when we had our call last week. Sitting at an antique desk that probably weighs a thousand pounds. Every person who drops by has to hear about the desk's provenance, its wood, its age. Meanwhile, he probably puts his boots up on it. No respect even for the things he respects. Had me on speaker. Did I mention that?" Deena is not showing any sign of listening. In fact, she exchanges the front page for Tempo. "As a simple courtesy, tell the person," Meiselman says. "Deena?"

Deena snaps the paper closed. With dead eyes she looks across the table at him.

"Someone like him has a dog, I bet," Meiselman continues. "Something small and furry. Keeps it on his lap. Sits stroking it all day."

"Or a pit bull because he's such a meanie," Deena offers. "Or maybe he is more of a cat person. Or he likes fish and has a wall aquarium. Maybe he never changes the water and it's so cloudy you can only see the fish when they dart close to the glass. Honestly, who cares?" A turn from playful to exasperation. "Maybe he is an asshole. Or maybe he just has other things going on in his life, like a sick parent. Maybe he couldn't hear you because his phone line is broken and he's too damn lazy to find time to call the phone company."

"Maybe he heard me fine."

"I have work," she says, tossing the paper into the middle of the table before standing without bothering to clear her mug or bowl.

Picking at her cuticles, Deena steps hesitantly toward the doorway, as if weighing whether to tell him something. When she moves into the hallway and is out of view, Meiselman decides to share with her one of the General's Rules of Leadership. He used to know all thirteen by heart. Now he knows, maybe, six. "You are right about Shenkenberg," he bellows. "As the General is fond of saying, 'Get mad, then get over it.'" It breaks her stride, and he hurries to think of a follow-up. Something reparative. The result of the second test is a possibility, but better he waits until after meeting with his brother tonight, which should clarify their options and the feasibility of his new plan. Instead, he calls out to her, "Your coffee. You didn't drink it."

Her hand grips the doorframe, and she pulls herself into the kitchen.

"I didn't?" she asks, mouth forming into a sarcastic o, hands cradling her cheeks. "Have you ever seen me drink it?"

"You never finish it, but you like to sip."

"The warmth of the cup is what I like."

She exits again. Seconds later, the screeching of hangers sliding across the closet's metal rack as she searches for her scrubs top and coat.

The front page's bland headline, *Divided Senate OKs Property Tax Relief,* vindicates his initial disregard of today's paper. Light footsteps out in the hallway seize his attention. Is Deena spying on him and, if so, what are her suspicions?

"I'm sorry." Deena speaks softly from the hallway. "Just exhausted, I guess. That's the reason for that."

He plays the victim, staying silent and looking straight into the newspaper.

* * *

Betsy Ross. Every day the same tan pants and wrinkled blouse. Heavy bags under the eyes. Arid lips. No makeup. Frizzy hair. The mug on her desk—"World's Best Grandmother"—has a chipped lip, a crack running up its side, and is stuffed with capless pens and tipless pencils. Pictures of naked, bathing grandchildren are taped to her library-issued monitor. Occasionally a prescription pill bottle out on her desk. Takes pride in showing she has nothing to hide. Betsyross1, Meiselman's first attempt at cracking the secretary's computer password, fails.

Much of her conversation centers on the oldest grandchild, "the bitty genius," "the math whiz," whatever such things mean in her world. Last year, the secretary forced on every passing administrator a story about the grandchild asking the father's obese boss why he had "big tingies on his chest like a mommy." Could Ada have found this cute? Could Ethel agree it was evidence of the boy's precocity? Last month, Betsy Ross brought this grandson to work. Feeling pressured into acting tickled by the boy's presence, Meiselman had kneeled to pat the kid's shoulder. Touching the hands of this child, who had still not learned to wipe his nose, was out of the question. The boy turned to his grandmother and asked why Meiselman had curly hair like a girl. Guffawing, Grandma Betsy whacked the boy's backside. Calling men girls, the boy is a one-trick pony, Meiselman wanted to scream every time he heard the secretary telling the underlings of the humiliation Meiselman had suffered at the hands of this child. The boy is five, which means he was probably born in 1998. Lucas1998, Meiselman's second attempt, fails.

Three terse whistles carry from down the hallway. Two thumps follow. The series of sounds repeats before segueing into a coiling whistle that finally commences with three thumps, two brief whistles, and one final thump. Military marching music. A triumphant ditty. The whistles and thumps are heckling Meiselman's thought process. Such an audacious raid of an underling's computer would not have been attempted if he'd thought he'd have company. As the tune's volume increases, so does the pressure to come up with a third and final attempt. Blocking out the background noise, Meiselman focuses on other features of the secretary. A propensity to talk race, usually not even bothering to whisper, although careful to insert disclaimers. "A Mexican said this to me about his own people." The floor under his feet trembles with every crescendoing thud from this background score, and when Meiselman looks up, the tip of the trumpeter's umbrella comes into view. A rousing whistle brings the tune to a final close. Americangirl1, Meiselman's third attempt, fails.

"Someone got a promotion, I see," Mitchell says, tapping the edge of Betsy Ross's desk with his umbrella.

Right as Meiselman stands, Mitchell moves to the end of the side desk, sits on the edge, and lowers his umbrella like a tollbooth gate, blocking the entryway and leaving Meiselman pegged behind the desk fumbling for a response. Forcibly moving the umbrella would make Meiselman look petulant. Crawling under the gate would look childish. To show he is unperturbed by Mitchell's posturing, Meiselman sits back down in Betsy Ross's chair and puts his feet up on her desk.

"Looking for an address," Meiselman answers the underling. "Ethel has me working on an addendum for an important letter."

"Yes, yes. Betsy mentioned an addendum to the letter."

"You know about the letter?"

"Quite obviously. They informed me some time ago. It's all good, no worries," Mitchell responds ruefully. Or is it dreamily?

"So let me ask you: What message should come across in the addendum?"

Mitchell stares up at the ceiling tiles. Lowering his eyes, he trains them on Meiselman. In a deliberate, somewhat conspiratorial tone, he says, "Obviously, it would be bad form for me to tell you specifically what to write, but general support, I imagine, would be most beneficial."

"Support for the Capsule?"

"You are a decent, sincere chap, Meiselman. To be yourself is all I can ask."

Mitchell shows no signs of drawing the confrontation to a close. The umbrella stays put. He rocks his leg, his heel clubbing the side of Betsy Ross's aluminum-sided desk. "Quite a barnburner last night," he says. "Almost a comeback for the ages. Heartbreaking to claw back like that and fall short. I'm sure the Meiselman clan were on the edges of their seats."

A barnburner? A comeback for the ages? What did Meiselman miss when he turned to the movie? He is not about to ask, and befoul his reputation as a man who watches every inning of every game.

Forced to improvise, Meiselman says, "Thrilling. At one point, I said to my wife, 'This is why we watch all nine innings.' Had our rally caps on. We, you know, have a strict rule in our home. If a rally starts then everyone is to stay seated in the same position. Crossed legs stay crossed. Nobody puts down a bowl or a glass. Likewise, if a person is out of the room, he or she is to stay out until the rally dies." Meiselman stands and puts his hand on Mitchell's shoulder, and in an unintentionally threatening tone says, "Narrow defeats inevitably turn into narrow victories." On cue, the umbrella drops and Meiselman steps out from behind the desk, keeping his shoulders stiff as he brushes past Mitchell. Their elbows knock and

Meiselman is proud that he, for once, has made the other person feel the jolt.

"Don't let them back in the room?" Mitchell calls back to Meiselman, who is halfway down the hallway. "You are a rigid man, Meiselman. A rigid man who runs a severe household. Keep the wife and kids on a tight leash, I bet."

They have worked together too long for Mitchell not to know.

"We cannot have children," Meiselman answers. "My wife—"

"Yes, of course. Foot in the mouth, foot in the mouth." He bites the umbrella's handle. "Not the first time, not the last."

Meiselman is ready to score this latest encounter a draw, but added to the unsettling breakfast it is clear he is barely playing .500 ball today, or for that matter, the week. Even after adopting this new aggressive approach. Spotting the flashing message indicator on his telephone when he steps into the office, he anticipates a further lowering of the winning percentage. Possibly Rav Fruman's assistant calling to tell Meiselman that the politics of the Shenkenberg situation have changed. Or a message that will bump up the winning percentage, like his mother congratulating him on passing yesterday's test. You do not shy away from injustices, unlike other men in the family. Still, I would've thrown it in the garbage. Or the winning percentage remains unchanged and it is just his mother calling to remind him they are to visit Gershon tonight at his hotel. As if Meiselman needs reminding. For Meiselman, everything with Deena hinges on the meeting with his brother.

"Meiselman, you are the best," chimes Ethel on the voicemail. Why, oh why, does he constantly anticipate ruin? He rewinds to the beginning so he can hear it one more time. "Meiselman, you are the best!" The message continues: "Betsy told me about the reporter from the *Tribune*. I've been meaning to suggest we contact some media. The *New Niles News* and *The Reader*. Small fry, but assembling a pool, turning it into an event, could really boost the library and Shenkenberg. A wunderkind's homecoming is the angle to play. We should call Izzy to make sure he is okay with press. I will take care of that, not you. Ugh. Can't kick this back thing. Probably won't be in contact until Thursday. You're—"

The best? In charge? The only thing that brings me relief? Even after replaying the message several more times he cannot make out her final thought.

"We" this, "we" that, yet it is Meiselman tasked with assembling a pool. An inconsequential fib has backfired. Journalists jump at the opportunity to write puff pieces about abandoners of faith like Shenkenberg, but glorification of the writer will come at the steep price of complicating the defense of Rabbi J-'s legacy, and dash Meiselman's hope of breaking the status quo in his own life. From the beginning, he could see how this would be a dicey balancing act of respecting the library's mission while discrediting Shenkenberg and his message. (What is the message? He must get back to the book.) What would Colin Powell do? The General would not dare spend a second crafting ways to sabotage the plans of his superiors. Rule Number 1: "It ain't as bad as you think. It will look better in the morning." Germane, but can Meiselman afford to wait until tomorrow morning? Rule Number 4:"It can be done!"

The outgoing message on the *Tribune's* assignment editor's tip line is welcoming, but Meiselman, who has yet to craft a message that will separate him from the cranks who call about misplaced commas, unfilled potholes, and stripper-obsessed politicians, panics at the beep and begins to ramble, "I'm calling as a concerned citizen of New Niles. I'm also a daily reader. We've had some real bores this week, no offense, like that desperate editorial this morning about General Powell. As the war and campaign slog, why not look for news here at home? In New Niles, the public library is preparing to welcome prize-winning author Izzy Shenkenberg, a native who wrote a book disparaging a local rabbi. A survivor, no less! Now, I'm not a Jew. Roman Catholic. Also, not much of a fiction reader. Biographies of great Americans are more my speed. But this is a rabbi who was loved by Jews and non-Jews alike. The one catching flack for the invite is the interim director, a man named Meiselman."

For the *Sun-Times*, he leaves the same message, but adds, "The considerable survivor community of New Niles is up in arms. The Israel Philharmonic performing Wagner is one comparison I've overheard."

For the *Chicago Reader*, after he is transferred by a reporter who insists it sounds like an article more appropriate for the monthly Religion column, whose columnist works remotely but calls periodically to retrieve voicemail, Meiselman leaves the standard message, but adds, "There was a letter writing campaign. Threats to galvanize were made."

The reporter at the *New Niles Village Voice* is unfamiliar with the names Rabbi J-, Shenkenberg, and Meiselman, yet Meiselman interprets her silence as interest and suspects she is taking notes, so he sells it hard, juicing it with additional theories. "We live in a period ripe for historical revisionism." Dead air. "Look at how people question the sexuality of historical icons. Lincoln, gay?" Dead air. "Doesn't calling a thirty-five–year-old man a wunderkind cheapen the distinction?"

Finally, she says, "I don't think we're interested. Someone says we did a story on this guy last year."

"With all due respect, he's not some 'guy.' Jews and non-Jews revered him. A great torah scholar, believed by many to have been one of the 36 hidden righteous ones."

"Sorry, I totally did not mean to disrespect this righteous rabbi individual. By 'guy,' I meant the writer, Ingrid Shankstein?"

Meiselman does not correct her.

The secretary at the Jewish Academy informs Meiselman that outsiders are prohibited from directly contacting students and any communication regarding the school newspaper must go through the faculty advisor.

His last call is to Ethel.

"The assignment editors were, for the most part, receptive," he reports to her voicemail. "A pool is assembling."

* * *

Muddled thoughts, backfiring fibs, off-the-mark anticipations, and meandering conversations have bedeviled Meiselman since waking up to Deena's mysterious movements. Even reading, which is supposedly an effective form of escapism, fails to calm him. He can barely focus long enough to get through a passage about Shenkenberg's hero Ely spending the night drinking in the hotel bar with one of the hotel's maintenance workers, and then being too hungover the next day to join the group for a visit to a cemetery and another concentration camp.

To prevent the second half of the day from slogging like the first half, he decides on a stroll to clear his mind before returning to work. But he manages fewer than five steps before he is stopped by the mess of bumper stickers plastered to the rear of Mitchell's hatchback. "Stop this!" "End that!" "Elect" some no-name bozo! Above the moth-colored muffler, a particularly clever one that plays on the words "oil," "soil," and "spoils." This is not some campaign poster pitched into the front yard, a poster board that can be rolled up and stored in the attic post-rally. Stuck to the body of this expensive piece of machinery, only a paint job or the automobile's junking will erase these declarations. Where does this interloping Brit get off with broadcasting such firm opinions?

The upper corner of the sticker curls off the bumper. With his fingernail, Meiselman digs at it until it lifts further and he can clamp down on it with a thumb and index finger. He gives the sticker a yank, but he all he manages to remove is a thin strip. He digs and lifts the corners on the other side, and a second yank gets off a larger swath. Soon all that remains in the sticker's place is a tongue-shaped patch of white fuzz.

Moving on to Betsy Ross's reserved spot at the end of the employee lot, Meiselman expects to encounter more aggravating stickers, perhaps one about an honor roll grandson, but the body of her cobalt blue sedan is spotless. Everyone with a new car, everyone except Meiselman.

Exiting the employee lot, the brown paper bag of his uneaten lunch in hand, he crosses the fire lane into the main lot, which is half-full owing to the after-daycare rush. Human chains of stroller-commandeering mothers—sleeve-tugging children at their sides—push toward the entrance with mulish determination. And some fathers. Fathers, more and more.

Indecency is everywhere he looks today. A jeep the size of something the soldiers in Iraq drive is unscrupulously parked. Its tires edge into the adjoining spot, and this has thrown the entire row of cars into disarray. The other drivers hew as close to the lines as possible, but this driver has made it difficult. If Meiselman were to wait around to confront the mother, he would undoubtedly have to suffer through a speech about how this is the only car that can sufficiently protect the brood, other drivers be damned. Similar to the speech his sister-in-law gave him when he questioned her about immunizations. Squeezing through the narrow space between the jeep and the minivan parked next to it, Meiselman surveys the lot, his hand in his pocket rummaging past Deena's underwear and the peppermint suckers in search of his car key. The tip of his finger bumps along the key's blade. Tapping the key's point, he scrutinizes the jeep's buffed black doors, which gleam from some protective glaze. One final look around as he curls the key into his palm and removes it from his pocket, inching it out from the slit between his index and middle fingers. Continue forward and he will teach this mother a good lesson.

Does his key even make contact with the car before his elbow tightens and his heart cinches? He winces, bows his head, and drops the key back into his pocket. How sad a realization that the only damage he is capable of inflicting is the kind that can be undone with soap and water.

His heart beats faster as he flees from the car. Soon he is tramping up the alleyway along the parking lot's perimeter. Reaching the dumpsters, he chucks his lunch and steps to the other side of the blue containers. Behind the two dumpsters, parked in the misanthropic makeshift spot, is her car. Taking the peacefulness of the village for granted, the pink-haired girl has left the convertible's top down, not appreciating how easy it would be for a library administrator making the rounds to tuck a flier and peppermint candy in the windshield, and then using this nearness, and the screen provided by the dumpsters, to rifle through the car's glove compartment, not to steal or deface, but for this, a name: Madeline Fineman. The pink-haired girl does not strike him as a Madeline. Named after a grandmother, now a Maddy, perhaps. He did not have a car registered under his name until last year. Insurance purposes, his father argued. The compact discs, ones with waifish women strumming guitars on the covers, surely belong to the pink-haired girl.

If he knows where to find her car, he knows where to find her.

Today, he daringly observes her from behind a bookcase in History, tenderly extracting the slender volume *Oregon or Bust:*

The Presidency of James K. Polk for a better view. She sits at the lone desk pushed up against the windowless wall, one leg folded underneath the other leg. Only now does he notice the teenager's habit of winding the pink lock of hair around her ear. She is sporting the same torn jeans and oversized NYU sweatshirt she had on the first two times they met. Deena, whose work requires a uniform, is mindful to alternate daily between the v-neck and crew-neck scrubs tops. The undershirt is changed every day, but not the bra, which needs washing, she claims, only once a month. Whenever he whiffs the bra, he is surprised by how the undergarment absorbs only her body's pleasant smells, just as she argues. By the time Ethel returns to a previously not-to-be-forgotten outfit, for example, the black blouse that sags in the back like an unhoisted sail, exposing her moled and red-tagged shoulder blades, Meiselman is already waiting for the return of a more recent not-to-be-forgotten outfit, say the sheer white button down that fails to conceal her undergarment, whose color never clashes too starkly.

And the pink-haired girl is still working her way through *Julius Caesar*. In front of her is an open notebook, pages clean between the margins, blocky letters and numbers doodled down the sides. The amount of pages left in the play divided by the amount of days remaining to turn in her degree-saving paper? The name of the boy who went burrowing under that sweatshirt—the one who promised to stop there but pushed her into allowing him to stick his fingers inside her?

She steadies her head as if she thinks she hears something. He must strike soon.

In search of verse that will exhibit his charming side and smarts, he flips through the play, which he snagged from Classics on his way upstairs. "Brutus is wise, and were he not in health he would embrace the means to come by it." This is not a line to enchant. Clunky and wordy, it lacks poetry. The line should be easy to memorize, fewer than ten words. "Render me worthy of this noble wife!" Sounds amorous, but he is unsure of its meaning, and the younger generation has an inability to delay gratification. If she surmises he has no information to bestow, she will quickly tune him out. "Vouchsafe good morrows from a feeble tongue." Eloquent sounding, but comprehension is again a problem. Besides, he is asking for a tongue twisting. They may share a laugh, but he would be the butt. "When beggars die there are no comets seen." Succinct, and there is a footnote to explain the archaic English. The next line, however, "Cowards die many times before their deaths," is one he has no trouble understanding. He emerges from the bookcase, his throat lumping with boyish shyness, the line stark in his mind as if painted on a banner tacked to the tail of a plane passing over a stadium.

Marriage is bliss. His wife is his best friend. A match made in heaven. Sex with his wife is so much more than a physical act. Yet there's the lingering regret that unless Deena leaves him a widower, he will never again experience the thrill of the chase, whether as pursued or pursuer. Deena will have been his last chase, his last woo.

Perched on a treadmill at one end of the workout area, hidden behind rows of ellipticals, stairmasters, and stationary bikes, Meiselman had spotted Deena on the opposite end of the room dancing behind the fitness studio's glass wall. Second thing he'd noticed about her, after the similarity of hairstyles, was that she was a sweater. Still is. The back of her banana yellow shirt was a damp rag. In the front, a darkened collar crept downward toward a spot of sweat in the shirt's center, bringing to mind the inkblot test he took on his first visit to Dr. Lin's office. Warshock? Rawshock? The doctor chastised him for taking too long to answer. "An old lady with a large nose beating a baby with her cane?" he guessed. There were no right or wrong answers, the doctor reminded him, over and over again.

The woman in the yellow t-shirt wore camouflage shorts with large Velcro pockets, and he could have declared her a misfit and moved on to another one of the barefooted women in the class, like the nubby-nosed blonde in pink spandex, whose ponytail wagged across her shoulder blades in crisp rhythm to the music, or the woman in the back row with dangling turquoise earrings and unnaturally yellow hair shaved to a crew cut. Run your hand over your glistening scalp, and spray me with your sweat! But these women were scared of the stomp, their feet curling at impact.

The yellow t-shirted woman, however, moved with an abandon absent in her classmates. On her half-turn stomps, her toes splayed and gripped the hardwood floor as if war paint lined her face and she was performing a rain dance, arms windmilling with such fury that Meiselman feared she would gouge an eye or cleanly slice off a classmate's arm or—heaven forbid—dislocate a limb, which would lead to the torturous scene of the teacher—and not Meiselman—searchingly pressing his fingertips into her flesh. Here, no? What about here?

Week after week, instead of heading downstairs to the gym for pickup basketball, Meiselman stayed on the treadmill, watching and plotting a next move. Too winded to continue running, Meiselman would slow to a walk, inclining the machine several degrees so as not to appear feeble. Every week, the woman wore the same yellow t-shirt and camouflage shorts. The dance routine was intricate, but the beat of the music was simple, and Meiselman considered asking the black drummer in braids who slapped the hide of the drum gripped between the knees of his baggy rainbow-patterned pants to keep Meiselman in mind if he ever needed a substitute. Or pay him to take the week off. Double, triple pay. Any amount for the opportunity to get closer to the yellow t-shirted woman's red cheeks and moist upper lip, to reach out and flick at the stubborn drop hanging off the tip of her flat, bony nose. Sneak peeks at her slick, stubbly pits through the sleeves of her shirt. Get his hands tangled in her uncontrollable curls.

At the conclusion of class one week, after a stop at the water fountain, the woman in the yellow t-shirt drifted through the workout area, tearing open and closed the Velcro pockets of her shorts, stopping at various weights machines and sitting down for a press or two before moving on to a different apparatus. Meiselman moved to the area. Each time he finished with a machine, he removed the pin in case his grunting piqued her curiosity. It did not, and then, as if nothing in the room caught her interest, she was off to the staircase leading to the lower level, still futzing with the pockets of her shorts as she descended, the slow tearing of the separating Velcro audible only to the watchful Meiselman. Bunching her curly hair into a ponytail, her yellow t-shirt lifting, she stood in the gym's doorway watching the men play while Meiselman observed her from a balcony above. Sauntering downstairs, he prepared to excuse himself as he brushed past her into the gym, ready to sneak a peek at her bellybutton and the darkened line of skin descending into her shorts. However, just as he stepped off the staircase, she turned from the doorway. She was heading toward him, and he was without a plan. He could stop and ask a question—Do you know what time the gym closes?—but he did not want to sound like a man in need of direction. He settled for a smile. It was before the beard, and his dimples were at the apex of their power. Flashed her a good portion of his teeth, too. Her mind and focus clearly elsewhere, she did not acknowledge him. Not a total waste, since he was afforded a clearer shot of her yellow t-shirt, which on the front had a sketching of a gaunt, grizzled, longhaired man dressed like an Indian. Turning around to behold her as she walked away, Meiselman caught the name "Willie Nelson" on the shirt's back, a list of cities and dates underneath.

"But what if I have only a week to capture his essence?" Meiselman had asked Steve, his boss at the recording studio.

"Willie Nelson is not on my radar right now. Was, like, twenty years ago. But it's all jazz all the time for me now. You know that."

"I just do the books."

"Is that what you do? Thought you were in charge of ordering lunch for sessions."

"We were feasting ourselves toward bankruptcy before I took on that task."

"Touché, my man."

"What about a greatest hits CD?"

"You said you want the artist's essence. All a greatest hits disc will give you are the songs that registered with the public's addled ears. Essence is core, and we get the clearest shot of that with the artist's first work, his first reaction to all the trauma and shit that's been slugging him year after year until he finally had the cojones to stand up to the world and say 'Enough. Take notice. I, too, am a man.' It's like, nobody wants to hear the story of the tenth or hundredth time you boned. The first time is what they want to hear. Right?"

Meiselman, still a virgin, nodded, even though his boss's reasoning sounded convoluted. They only want to hear the story of the first time because of the fumbling and mistaken holes. One does not prefer the doctor straight out of medical school, the lawyer who recently passed the bar, the presidential candidate without executive experience.

Unlike most people, Meiselman does not ask advice simply to hear the answer he wants to hear, so he followed Steve's suggestion and snagged *Red Headed Stranger* from the bin at Record

Rendezvous. Waiting in line to pay, Meiselman decided it could not hurt to grab *Essential Willie Nelson* as well.

The torture of listening to those discs. Could this Willie Nelson not afford more instruments and a better microphone? Thirty seconds was the most Meiselman could take of any song, every one sounding like a drunken lament over a child's strumming. Song after song about the singer's deceitful behavior driving away an honest, decent woman. Not one song easily retrievable if the woman in the yellow t-shirt would ask for a favorite, not one hummable chorus in case she did not wear the shirt and he was forced to execute a more daring approach. Meiselman has a nice voice.

How much easier it all could have been if only he'd had cojones? Could have confronted the woman as she sat vulnerable at a leg-crunching machine and confessed to her, I've been watching you dance for the last month. Your fervor is striking. Tell me who that Indian chief is on your shirt, and I will tell you that through you I've discovered an attraction to sweaty women. Given their differences in age and size, others would hear the story of the courtship and conclude that predation is the essence of the relationship, Meiselman a man constantly on the prowl.

How much easier it could have been had fate done him the favor of hatching a story where he brings water to a yellow-shirted woman passed out on the floor of the dance studio, or one where Meiselman bumps chests with men who were harassing a woman at the gym's entrance, dispensing crude comments about her overly hairy body. If this had been the case, the essence and, therefore, the dynamic of the relationship would have been clear and unassailable. Meiselman as rescuer and protector. In line with what she has confided to him on many occasions. "You saved me," she often says, although from what he is still unsure, although he has theories.

Now, when others ask to hear Meiselman and Deena's story, he omits the weeks spent watching her dancing to African beats, and it becomes a conventional narrative of fate that opens with Deena's, nee Daisy's, walk to the water fountain after class, the first time, according to this version, Meiselman had ever laid eyes on his future wife. Also omitted: Deena's heels lifting off the ground as she slurped at the water, her elbows jutting like a child, a desire swelling in Meiselman to step forward, hook his arm around her waist and hoist her closer to the fountain's spout.

To this day, even Deena does not know the truth of how they became entwined. When they make love he cannot come clean about his love of sweaty, hairy women. Instead, he claims chilliness on account of his low blood pressure and insists on starting under the comforter, fighting her as she tries to kick it off, holding the bedding down until he can feel the muggy heat trapped between their chests.

For Deena, and everyone else, a story of fate, Meiselman stepping forward at the exact moment she'd turned away from the fountain. Knocking elbows, he'd excused himself and delivered a spontaneous quip. "Can it be? Another Northerner who appreciates the country legend?"

The confusion stitching her brow ebbed after he pointed to the shirt.

"This? No, it's my father's. Nabbed it from his drawer."

He showed her the Willie Nelson disc in his portable player. She found the coincidence exciting and told him about her father's devotion to the singer, the concerts attended, the time he'd met the legend in an amphitheater bathroom. Finally, she declared, "George would love you."

"George is your father?" he asked, prepared to walk away if this George was a boyfriend, because he was not interested in another woman friend like Ethel, a friend that picked up the phone only between boyfriends, spilling exaggerated miseries without ever asking after his welfare. (And when he did share, Ethel would sigh and say, "You're so queer, Meiselman.")

"Yes, a washed-up hippie. For the first fifteen years of my childhood he refused to answer to Dad or Daddy. One day, he got a job as a salesman, and when he came home, he proposed I start calling him Father. He picks, of course, the most formal name. I couldn't. I wouldn't. So, it's George."

She could, she would, soon after they married, but only to Meiselman. Off to shop for Father, to cook for Father, to clean for Father, to help Father buy loafers, she announces on what seems like a daily basis.

Together, Meiselman and the woman in the yellow t-shirt had drifted over to the weight machines.

"People like to modify the manufacturer's safety instructions," Meiselman said, taking the initiative to direct her. "Like, what is the harm in clipping the safety clip to your shorts when running on the treadmill? It's not there because it never happens."

She laughed, even though it was not intended as a joke.

Then she went to work on a stomach-crunching machine, fulfilling a fantasy of his that had been brewing for weeks. With her body curled forward in a fetal position, Meiselman fulminated against men who add muscle at the expense of circulatory health. She agreed and told him about her job, and the grotesque gym injuries she'd treated over the years.

"Why do men think a stiff neck is attractive?" she asked. "But the other end of the spectrum is just as scary," she continued. "Boys who think self-deprecating humor is charming. Are you self-deprecating?"

This frankness.

"Why would I deprecate myself?" he responded.

"We should go to a movie sometime," she said.

He found it scary.

"Aren't I supposed to ask you?" Meiselman asked. "Not that I'm old-fashioned. I believe a woman can pay for a date. But not the first one. On this I am firm."

"Then ask me out for Friday night."

And thrilling.

To outsiders, the religious orthodox can seem rigid and joyless, so he hesitated telling her Friday night was undoable because of Shabbat. But withholding this from the woman in the yellow t-shirt—whose name he still did not know—seemed senseless, since he was already envisioning a future together.

"You're like that?" she responded to his disclosure.

"Not too orthodox, don't worry."

"That came out wrong."

"Shouldn't we exchange names?" he asked, after they made plans.

How would he explain the name Daisy to his parents?

If he had still been seeing Dr. Lin at the time of the courtship, she too would have questioned the relationship's foundation. The doctor, after all, relished in undermining foundations. Why would Meiselman's father despise his son? Why would his mother want him all to herself?

Meiselman's chase of the pink-haired girl is a different type of pursuit. He is intrigued, not enticed, by the pink-haired girl. Mentoring is the goal, extracting her story an added objective. Do the safety pin and pink strands of hair suggest a passing phase, or is she on course to deepen her deviances?

"And?" the pink-haired girl asks after Meiselman flawlessly delivers the line from the play. Is she asking him to repeat the already forgotten line? "The line has a second part," she says.

She furiously turns the pages of the play before stopping midway through the book. She runs her fingers through the lines. When she gets to the bottom of the page she shakes her head and stares up at the ceiling, before turning to an earlier section.

"Chapter two," he says.

"Act two?" she corrects him.

"Act two. Read the play twenty years ago, but I remember," he says, tapping his temple. "Caesar, I believe," Meiselman says, "is speaking."

The glint in her eyes is no longer that of a grazing animal being led to slaughter, but of a squirrel measuring the leap from one branch to the next, as if in Meiselman she has found an elder worth impressing.

"Down to the line number, my professor can tell you."

Professor? Is he dealing with a college student? Not a pink-haired girl, but a pink-haired woman? Even better? Even worse?

"Aha, got it. 'The valiant never taste of death but once,'" she reads.

"Also a fine line," Meiselman says. "But the passage *I* read has real force. Read it again."

Diligent to prevent more accidental touching, he maintains his distance, pacing behind her chair, an arm behind his back, his other hand reverentially sweeping the spines of the books in History, because she may have dismissed what happened on Sunday as an accident, but twice and it becomes a trend, a tendency.

After the pink-haired girl rereads the line about cowards dying many deaths, Meiselman says, "Life, Shakespeare is saying, is about killing the inner coward. We are born, literally, in a cowering position, and we are tasked with stiffening our spines. For example, my brother. At three months, he refused my mother's milk, demanding a bottle." What he does not share is that because of this trauma—biting, vomiting—his mother had abstained from offering her breast to Meiselman. "History's greatest bullies, and I've read many articles on this, were at one time cowards, products of bullying." Knee up on the chair, the pink-haired girl is twisting her index finger into the threads of her ripped jeans. Its tip is purpling as he throws out observations about cowardice, unsure of how, or if, they coalesce into a guiding message. He is most definitely losing the pink-haired girl. He sits on the edge of her desk, faces her, and delivers what he hopes sounds like the crux of a message. "It comes down to this. 'Don't always be an automatic vote.'"

She releases her finger from the threads and holds the flushed finger up to her face. Together they watch purple recede to red recede to white. She repeats, "'Don't be an automatic vote,' I like that."

"'Don't always be,' I said. Not never. Not absolute. My father gave the advice years ago. I was a boy. We were sitting around the breakfast table reading the newspapers when, suddenly, he blurted it out."

"Everything about my parents is automatic." She puts out her hand, as if to pat his forearm, as if they are friends and she has something to share. He disregards the impulse to recoil or stand and move out of her reach. She nips his purple shirt at the elbow. "Like last year, I wanted to attend the rally in D.C. with my history teacher, Mr. Belevaqua, and my parents were not having it," she continues. "They don't shout ultimatums, mind you. They like to have discussions, 'Take the emotion out of it,' 'Weigh the pros and cons,' as my father says. So he—my father—explains why it would be a bad idea to attend the rally, saying I can't appreciate potential ramifications, as if it's some type of high-end logic. Keeps using the word 'branded.' 'You don't want to be branded an outcast, branded a radical, branded as part of the fringe.' Isn't 'branded' a term for cattle? Just lay down the law and forbid me from going, instead of pretending it's a discussion." Very briefly, the pink-haired girl stops, her vacant eyes locking on him, forcing him to lift his chin and scratch the jawline of his beard. "My parents' little parlor game of getting me to no ended with me running upstairs crying. My father sitting on the edge of my bed, clearing my bangs to the side, probably deriving some sadistic pleasure from seeing my eyes red and puffy. But that's a different story for a different day."

Purging from his mind the image of her in bed wiping tears away with the sleeve of one of her father's old, blue Oxfords she wears for pajamas, its tails skimpily dressing the tops of her pale thighs, he reflects on how the pink-haired girl's striking openness and articulateness accord with articles he has read on the younger generation's propensity to indiscriminately share. Or there is something about him that invites openness in others. Many misinterpret his taciturn nature as non-judgmental. He does judge, although he keeps most verdicts to himself.

"Can I share with you a story about Colin Powell?" Meiselman asks.

"Wait, listen, I didn't finish my story. I sat and listened to your speech."

To show her muffling of Meiselman was intended as playful, she sticks out her tongue, whose underside is brownish purple and not the youthful pink he imagined it to be. Then she scrunches her nose and out comes her hand to check his forearm, chills breaking out across his upper back even though he is unsure whether there was even contact. He is ready to listen, hoping her story provides a clue as to why she has made reading *Julius Caesar* at the public library part of her routine. Did her parents' prohibition regarding the rally set her on a course of radicalism? Soon she was coloring her hair and liberally piercing herself and marking her flesh with Latin passages. The NYU sweatshirt and jeans do not comport with such a scenario. If radicalized, he would expect, at the very least, some leather.

"On the one-year anniversary, without telling anyone, I went down to Daley Plaza for the rally. Argh. So pathetic. Two-hundred protestors, tops."

With this overexcited, almost manic, style of speaking, the pink-haired girl cuts a savvy, mature figure. To reaffirm his predominance over her he lets out a patronizing laugh, as if her childish thoughts charm him. He says, "Listen, I'm sure it wasn't your parents' intention to make you feel cowardly. They are your parents."

"Let me finish, let me finish," she says. This time, no question, there is contact. He feels it radiating up and down his spine, a chill that gives way to a dazzling numbness in his upper arm like the feeling when bumping his sharp elbow against a doorpost. She has his attention. Then the excessively pierced girl with torn jeans and pink hair says, "Not one person looking the least bit respectable. The men either had shaved heads or hair down to their butts. Some covered their faces with bandanas, although most of them had beards ten times longer than yours, which was fine, because how many unfunny, punny t-shirts could I read? Grandfathers with earrings and goatees. The women were either butches yelling about gay rights, or grandmothers in beach chairs waiving puny American flags. Until they bring out the big flags, they're never going to convince the rest of the country that their intentions are patriotic. Chanting in unison was too difficult for this crowd. Some people were yelling about the McDonald's on the corner. One guy kept trying to hurl a garbage can through a Starbucks window, but every time he lifted it over his head his knee buckled and it rolled down his body and crashed to the ground. Dork."

While he is willing to sit until closing time and listen to her prattle endlessly about this rally business and the sad state of leftist politics, biding his time by studying her idiosyncratic style—for example, just now, for the first time, he notices a diamond affixed to an inner valley of her earlobe, a diamond of refinement, not one picked up at a kiddie store in the Green Grove Mall, but, possibly an heirloom from a dead grandmother—is the partnering diamond affixed to a concealed body part—he must stop her at once if he has any chance of tilting the conversation to a territory that can secure his role as mentor.

"...pouring rain, homemade signs collapsing, colors running."

"So Shakespeare," Meiselman says, grabbing the book from her hand and opening it to the bookmarked page. "Glad to see you are making some progress." Snorts a patronizing laugh. "At this rate you'll finish by the start of the next school year." He nudges her shoulder with the corner of the book.

"Finish? Please. Three times I've read it, mister." She grabs the book. "That's how I knew there was a second part to that line you like. I'm a damn savant when it comes to memorizing lines. It's this stupid paper that's wrecking me. Can't even come up with a topic," she says, bending forward and banging her head against the desk.

Here the pink-haired girl, who more and more he thinks must be a pink-haired woman, is handing him an opportunity to mentor. Placing his hand over the book's cover, he says, "Relax, together."

"Okay, so I'm focused on the words, 'dumb mouths,'" she says. "Shakespeare means wounds, obviously,"—Meiselman nods—"and I was hoping to connect it to the play's theme of oration. How speeches are a vehicle to manipulate others. Antony passing himself off as a blunt simpleton in order to sell himself to the public. I don't know. Sounds stupid when I say it. Not enough to fill an entire paper, right?"

"Yes, there is certainly a focus on speeches and oration and the oratory in this play. The spoken word, so to speak." Because he cannot provide her with direction or add anything to the discussion, he lowers his voice to a dry register hoping the seemingly irrelevant comment he is about to deliver, one of the few facts he remembers from studying this Shakespeare play in college, will be received as wisdom. “During the performances of his plays, Shakespeare would stand off to the side of the stage and edit the play based on the crowd’s reaction.”

She briefly contemplates Meiselman’s comment.

“Interesting, but our professor is not into the historical stuff.”

A heavy lull follows. Finally, she says, “I really have to get back to my paper, but thanks for the help.”

She finds her place in the book, holds it open next to her notebook, and hunches forward, pen in hand, to start writing. She pauses to look up at him, a closed-mouth smile, as if wondering why he has not already excused himself. He strokes his beard, pretending he is lost in thought. Generally when his mind churns it produces nothing but memories or eventualities, the past or future, and this time it does both at the same time. His mind coughs up a scene from the past that will hopefully provide an elixir to the torturous possibility that if he takes his leave from the pink-haired girl, it will be for good.

Last fall, Meiselman and Deena were invited to Jeremy and Molly’s house for Shabbat lunch. Deena had not only insisted Meiselman wear his new suit but she’d also put out a new undershirt, socks, and a dry-cleaned dress shirt for him. She ambushed him with a new tie from Nordstrom right before they were out the door.

“We are a good looking couple,” he said as they exited the house.

“Having a beard doesn’t bother you?” she responded.

The other guests at this meal were a newlywed couple new to the community. There is always a newlywed couple new to the community at these meals. Courtship is a common topic at meals with newlyweds, every couple believing their story unique, and evidence of a relationship established by fate.

Molly and Jeremy sat cater-corner from one another with the doctor husband at the head. Deena sat next to Molly with the newlyweds directly across the table. Meiselman, on Deena's right, sat opposite the hosts' three-year-old boy, who had spilled a glass of pop at the start of the meal. Over the course of the meal, the brown liquid steadily streamed across the plastic tablecloth liner toward Meiselman's table setting, eventually steeping his dessert spoon and wine glass.

"It was the December before the Millennium," Molly said, introducing the story of how she met Jeremy. She was standing, resting a knee on her chair and hugging a crystal serving bowl of cabbage salad.

"I love hearing this story," Deena announced to the table.

Molly and "a boyfriend at the time" had hosted a holiday party at her apartment in Lakeview, and Jeremy had attended as one of Molly's colleague's plus one. "My fiancée," Jeremy interjected. "And I think you had one as well." This detail excited the table, everyone except for Meiselman, who waited for a pause so he could ask for more of the cabbage salad.

It was not a straight cabbage salad. It was not a slaw. The cabbage was red and the dish had exotic greens and a creamy dressing. Who knew toasted sesame seeds delivered such flavor? What Meiselman particularly liked about the salad was Molly's gluttonous touch of using strips of steak for garnish. Serving oneself as much beef as possible without looking piggish was the challenge. Molly, not noticing Meiselman's finger in the air, pushed ahead with the story.

"Coincidentally, a week before meeting Jeremy, I'd enrolled in an Intro to Judaism class at the JCC, which is where we met," she says, nodding in Deena's direction. "Out of the blue, a week later there is this Jewish, religious doctor, a pediatrician, just the yummiest kind of doctor in my living room, telling me about how he doesn't eat pork but hated not having Christmas as a child. And me, the pork-eater who grew up with a Christmas tree, is arguing with him about the superiority of Hanukkah. Is that not *bashert*?" Then the hostess Molly put down the bowl on the table, leaned forward, and rested her hand on Deena's shoulder, so everyone at the table would know the following comment was for her benefit. Lowering her voice to a loud whisper, Molly said to Deena, "*Bashert* means, like 'meant to be,' 'from on high,' 'decreed by *Hashem,* God.'"

Even though Meiselman's wife surely knew the word's meaning and did not need a public explanation, Deena graciously nodded in understanding. Apparently, only Meiselman caught the slight implicit in Molly's aside, her insinuation that there was something authentic about her own transformation to religious Jew, a purity of motives that was absent in Deena.

"The morning after the party I get a call from Jeremy. He misplaced his umbrella, and would I check my apartment? Sure enough, it was under the bed where we had stacked the coats, so we made up to meet on a street corner later that morning and, lo and behold, we, again, got into this incredible conversation about the power of shared belief. Mind-blowing stuff. He recommended I read Heschel." Again, Molly pauses for another aside directed at Deena. "Let me give it to you later. You'll so benefit from it." Molly continues, "Meanwhile, I get home and realize I never gave him back his umbrella. So there we are the next day, same street corner, more conversation. Total *bashert*. And now we have this beautiful boy, with another on the way."

The faces of Deena and the newlyweds radiated as if blessed to hear this providential episode.

"Just the cutest," Meiselman said, taking a wad of tissues from his pocket to mop up the spilled pop. "But, come on, really? Forgot to take his umbrella, twice?"

"What?" Molly barked, hugging the bowl even tighter, closer to her hip, as if she was protecting it from Meiselman.

"Color me a skeptic whenever the coincidences pile too high." He waited for someone to ask why he felt it was strange, but nobody asked, so he elaborated. "This is something out of the movies."

"Uh, oh. Sounds like you aren't too original, Jeremy," the newlywed husband joshed his host.

"We are lying?" Molly yelled back at him, picking up the bowl of cabbage, asking if anyone wanted more because it had mayonnaise and needed to be refrigerated at once. Meiselman raised his hand. The hostess dumped the bowl on the table. Exiting the room, she shouted, "I'm pretty sure I remember how my husband and I met!"

"Nobody is calling anyone a liar," Meiselman calmly explained, while serving himself more cabbage salad. With all eyes on him, he was forced to take more cabbage and less steak than he would have liked. "I'm merely suggesting the story is not as innocent as you want us, or yourselves, to believe. You both, after all, had fiancées, correct?" Under the table, Deena patted his leg. Only later would he understand it was intended as a reprimand. At the time, he interpreted it as encouragement, Deena pleased that her husband was standing up to Molly's public ridicule of her. "What I'm suggesting is that maybe it was not all that *bashert,* maybe it did not come from on high."

"This conversation is ludicrous!" Molly yelled from the kitchen.

Deena, this time, pinched his thigh.

"Listen, my fiancée and I were having problems," Jeremy said. "By the way, Deena. I have this sharp pain in the arch of my foot when I bike long distances. The doctor said—one second—Molly, babe? You need help with dessert? We are talking about my foot. Deena's going to tell me about my foot."

Deena removed her heels for the walk home, ignoring her husband's concern about tearing her pantyhose. Several blocks of silence passed. At one point, she mumbled, "They already have a run, and I have blisters." More silence until they hit the home stretch. Turning into the driveway, she said, "It's not charming."

"Your blisters?" he asked.

"Your dissections of other people's business. Sharing all your theories and psychology."

"I wasn't trying to be charming. I was being honest."

"Then next time try to be less honest and more charming."

"She was trying to cheapen your commitment to Judaism."

"She was just telling the couple some stupid story of how they met."

If only Meiselman could now locate an umbrella to leave behind for the pink-haired girl.

"I'll tell you what," Meiselman says to the pink-haired girl. "I'm the number two here, the interim director, but I relish the opportunity to assist the occasional student. Like a McDonald's executive spending time on the line flipping burgers."

"Like it keeps you grounded? Sound like my father and his reason for sitting with his office staff of thirty-year-old blondes."

He does not want to sound like her father. Or does he?

"Elevates me," he corrects her. "Meet back here tomorrow at, say, four, and I'll have three paper topics for you."

She taps her pen against table. Then, she looks up at him, eyes squinting, as if searching for a motive. She pulls an appointment book from her bag. Leather cover, snap closures, cloth placemark. The appointment book of a woman, not a girl.

"Sure, why not? With rehearsal tonight and class tomorrow morning, I'm not getting much done before four," she says. "A dumb community college class, and I'm stressed out beyond belief. Half the people in the class still haven't finished reading the play. To be fair, the group has several illiterates and borderline retards."

She pens him in.

A satisfactory encounter. Many questions answered, many new questions generated. Like what is a talented, precocious woman doing at a community college? Also, what is she rehearsing for? The umbrella expertly placed, it is only a matter of time until he learns the answers to these questions.

* * *

Thankfully, he and Deena are not one of those couples that insist on spending every waking moment together. A drive to the store after dinner for the next morning's milk or bananas is a solo job, usually handled by Meiselman because he does not trust Deena to travel the greater distance to the less expensive Jewel instead of the closer and more expensive Lucky's. There was a time he insisted they pay condolence calls together, even when she complained of being unable to put a face to the congregant's name. No, she could not just send a card. Did she want an empty mourner's house when Meiselman's parents' time came, leaving her husband to deliver inspiring stories to an empty living room? Mother took great pride in her appearance. When Dad had his heart thing, she took time to do her makeup before leaving for the emergency room. She said afterward, "I didn't want my drabness to bring down the moods of the other waiting families. Besides, it's not like they were waiting for me to open his chest and get his heart moving." It preoccupied the woman, how decent people behave, he will tell those who come to pay their respects. When driving, she never passed up an opportunity to allow cars to cut in front of her into traffic. "It's what decent people do," she'd grumble behind the wheel. His father plodded ahead, unyielding, as if the cars waiting to turn were obstacles to be avoided. For his father, a different memory. Every birthday, every anniversary remembered. "You should have good strength to get through another year." Even to the grandkids, this was his message. Based on family history, Meiselman has time, at least, for his mother.

(Cancer has been killing the community's young mothers, and whenever Meiselman steps into these houses of mourning and sees the semi-orphaned children, the youngest with his head in the lap of the oldest, the middle child glued to a handheld video game, everyone trying to comfort the boy with a pinch of the cheek, unaware that if he looks up for even a second he will lose a life, he understands Deena's reticence. When it is a dead child, the gloom is even worse. Meiselman sends a platter of pastries from King Solomon's with a note blaming his absence on unalterable travel plans. Book expo in Sacramento, he is prepared to answer if ever asked.)

Tonight, the destination is not local, and the excursion is not about death, but life. Obviously, he does not want Deena accompanying him, because it is not a simple matter of pulling his brother aside at the visit's end and slipping in a request for a donation. If issued too abruptly, without a natural segue, without detailing options entertained and dismissed, the appeal will come out sounding preposterous, possibly deranged.

Around twice a year, Meiselman's mother calls with news of an impending visit. She says, "For an overnight layover it will be just too much for your brother to drive all the way to New Niles." The thirty-five minute drive out to the airport hotel to bring a Lasso Burger from Brad's Burger Barn—extra Lasso onions—to Gershon, which he eats during a visit that lasts no longer than half-an-hour, is worth it to his parents. Meiselman and Deena are encouraged to come along. In the car, Meiselman's father has no ability to silence Meiselman's mother and allow father and son to listen to the White Sox broadcast, so Meiselman usually spends the entire ride with his head craned to the rear speaker. Deena always sleeps both ways. "She's not overdoing it, I hope," his mother inevitably says.

Without pressing him for a reason, his mother accepted his request to drive separately tonight, and to show up at the late end, alone. Fortunate, because he knows he would have ended up spilling his secret about the tests. Until now this problem has been kept from her. Why make her worry? Why spur her into action? She would assume a problem on Deena's end, and he must keep his mother on Deena's side and not have her turn on her the way she has turned on Gershon's wife. Stuck-up. Snobby. New York attitude.

This means he can enjoy the radio broadcast of the game in the car without the guilt of telling his wife to hold a thought until the next commercial break. The suspense of baseball on the radio is intense. Waiting for the one swing that will disturb the announcers' ramblings, which fill the dead air fuzz of the station's delicate tuning. Stories of golf outings and reviews of cannolis and dogs brought to the booth, shout-outs to listeners who live at the far reaches of the station's signal, and tales of barely known old-timers. A long season, they have the luxury of talking slowly, allowing each sentence to sink in. In the silence, the neighboring stations bleed into the signal, forcing Meiselman to hunch closer.

On the foolishness of trying to squeeze his father's Lincoln into a parking spot with cars on both sides, his parents are in agreement, so Meiselman knows to find their car in the lot's emptier back rows. The spot Meiselman takes is in the front, closest to the hotel entrance, in direct line with his parents and Gershon, who sit in front of a window at the back of the hotel's first floor bar-slash-lounge. Separating him from his family is the fire lane, a low wall of bushes bordering the sidewalk, and a craggy branched tree blooming white buds on a thin strip of grass. Through the window, Meiselman can see Gershon eating with his hands, unscrambling the bun and burger and onions onto the foil wrapping, a hesitancy to mix foods since he was a boy. His mother, still in her coat, talks. His father hangs his arms at his sides and stares up at the ceiling, mouth open.

Car beams off, seat tilted back just enough so he can surveil without being noticed, Meiselman lowers the window and eases in for the start of the fourth inning. Cold air streams into the car through the driver side window. In April, the players in the dugout wear batting gloves, and long-sleeved tees under their jerseys. The resting pitchers and coaches are in hooded sweatshirts and knit ski-hats. Only a home run, batters say, can dull the sting that comes from hitting a baseball in such cold. During the next commercial break, Meiselman rehearses his proposal. Calling it a donation is crucial.

Inside the bar-slash-lounge, his mother balls the foil from Gershon's burger and stuffs it into the checkered Brad's Burger Barn bag. She takes a napkin and roughly wipes the tops of her son's fingers. His father is still staring up at the ceiling.

Valentin strikes out on four pitches to start the bottom of the fourth, and the Meiselman party gets up to leave. His mother kisses Gershon on the cheek. His father grips his son's elbow to shake his hand. Gershon is staring down at his shoes, hands on his hips.

Meiselman powers the window to a close and pulls the keys from the ignition. Crossing the fire lane, he takes the circular driveway to the red carpet that extends from the hotel's front, but right as he spots his mother pushing her husband and herself through the revolving door, he has second thoughts about engaging his parents. What if she castigates him for his tardiness, notifying him that visiting hours are over? He steps back onto the sidewalk and jumps the white chain that divides the hotel walkway from a grassy area off to the side. Crouched behind a row of evergreens—or are they pine?—his feet settle into the bushes' soggy woodchip base. The gold light from the canopy's bulbs blast his parents as they walk the red carpet. His father is in a charcoal pinstriped work suit, black wool overcoat, and gray fedora. His mother wears a black skirt suit cut below the knees, black stockings, short black heels, a gray cape over her shoulders. Like movie stars stepping out of a premiere, if only they would smile.

As they reach the end of the red carpet, Meiselman's father steps off the curb and veers left, following the circular driveway to the parking lot, passing the crouched and hidden Meiselman. His father crosses the carpool lane, oblivious to the deceleration of his wife, who breaks from her husband's trail in search of a garbage can for the Brad's Burger Barn bag. All she finds is a tubular cigarette receptacle on the sidewalk, and Meiselman, who can practically reach out from behind the bushes and grab the bag from her hands, sees her growing despair as she searches for a cavity. Finally, the reformed smoker sets the bag down in the butt-studded sand. His father has disappeared into the lot of cars, and Meiselman's mother cries to him, "They don't give you anywhere to put your garbage these days?"

"Terrorism, Pooch. Like my guy told me—" his father's answer echoes back to Meiselman, a screaming plane overhead drowning him out.

The camouflaged Meiselman rotates until he has a solid view of his brother, who is still sitting in front of the window at the back table in the bar-slash-lounge. He, too, is now staring up at the ceiling.

Whenever face-to-face with the reedy Gershon, Meiselman feels vigorous and rugged, possessor of a superior genetic makeup. He feels like a man with a bone-crushing handshake, the type who is forced to stoop when passing through doorways, a man recruited by fellow shoppers to pull jars from higher shelves. Then asked to open the jars. A carver of turkeys and briskets. Without an apron bowed in the back, like his father wears when carving. Meiselman might just tear at the meat with his teeth. The occasional fear that he is developing a hunch feels alarmist when standing next to his brother, whose back and shoulders curve forward like a man recovering from a punch to the gut.

His brother's face has improved. The acne was never dispersed in bite-sized dots. Instead, the pimples banded together into purplish, coin-sized sores that rose off the skin. During his teenage years, a sore the size of an olive mutated on the hinge of his jawbone. His mother and brother whispered to one another about appointments and prescription refills. Gershon's oldest son, who is thirteen, has not shown signs of inheriting this disorder.

Baldness skips a generation, Meiselman has read, meaning Gershon's progeny will be spared. Gershon inherited his baldness from PopPop. He used to mask his follicular shortcoming by growing the black hair long on one side and pulling it across the crown. Employing a generous amount of hair product, the combed-across hair waved lustrously, like the wig of a British lawyer. Its silliness, however, must have become obvious, and now, in a more esteemed look, his brother clips short his few remaining hairs, leaving a tiny island on top.

One more thing, as long as he is dwelling on his brother's physical shortcomings. Can anything other than genes explain Gershon and their father's similar gait? The tentative steps, a hand out at all time to check their balance with periodic taps of tabletops and walls, a steady fear of unsteadiness, even from a young age?

The bar-slash-lounge is empty except for a tourist drinking beer out of a bottle at a cocktail table near the front, and a businessman and businesswoman drinking pink wine at the bar. Traveling coworkers away from the office, away from the hometown. The number one and number two. Have they both tucked away their wedding bands for the night? The bar's walls glow with a campfire-orange light, as if the bar sits in the depths of hell. Other than the large-screen television over the bar showing the Cubs game, the only other light comes from candles in glass casings placed in the middle of the cocktail tables.

His brother is in the back watching the White Sox on a television hanging from the ceiling. In front of him, yellow, orange, and red orbicular candies are scattered across the front half of his table, fenced in by an inward curving row of glass pop bottles, two empty and two half-full. As Meiselman approaches the table, his brother is clustering the candies by color. When finished, he chops his hand down and sweeps the reds off the table. Hands cupping the candies, he shakes them, as if preparing to shoot dice. (This sorting and shaking will continue for the rest of Meiselman's visit.) When his brother finally acknowledges him with a nod, Meiselman considers whether he should reach in for a hug or extend his hand for a shake. Contact between them has always felt awkward. Before he can decide, his brother directs Meiselman to the seat recently vacated by his mother. Meiselman points up to the television and tries skirting around to his father's seat so he will have a better view, but his brother grows impatient, forcing him into the seat with a flap of the hand.

"The flight attendant walks around with a basket of candy," Gershon begins. "In first class they do this."

Here it comes, another Gershon story. Add it to the canon Meiselman and his parents share with family and friends. The food and water of the places he visits would kill any American. The people in some of the countries he visits would kill any American, and this is why he travels with a former Green Beret named—well, Meiselman, for security reasons, cannot share the name, but he has stories about some dicey situations with the former Green Beret, one involving his brother dressing as a prostitute named Olga. The politicians Gershon meets are members of the cruelest regimes. When Gershon visits Israel, they stamp his visa on a separate sheet, so as not to jeopardize future visits to other countries in the region. For every week he is home, he spends three weeks on the road, which is why he keeps a bungalow in Berlin, where the conglomerate is based.

Others, it now occurs to Meiselman, do not see the portrait of ugliness he painted of his brother minutes ago when standing outside the hotel. A stranger meeting Gershon for the first time would surely fixate on his stark blue eyes. Piercing is the only word to describe them. The stranger would focus on the chunkiness of his gold watch and the starchiness of the pink dress shirt he wears with aplomb. They would not notice the hunch, which he hides by keeping his hands on his hips, a man tasked with taking control of situations. Nor would they see the specks of silver in the back of his mouth. They would see the unnaturally white and straight teeth at the front and envy the good teeth of the Meiselman Boys, unaware that only one of the Boys has actually put in the work.

Gershon continues, "There is hardly ever a time when I can find a kosher candy in one of these baskets. Last month, I was coming home from—where was I coming home from? Fuck-it. Yep that's what it's called, Fuck-it. That's a real name of a city. Isn't that totally hilarious? In Thailand. There is nothing to eat there but insects and cats. Fuck-it. Hilarious. I bring small boxes of cereals, but they don't have milk. They use dog's milk in a place like Fuck-it. Can you believe that's the name of a city? So I leave these places starved. When the stewardess came around I picked up one of the candies, examined the ingredients and was like, 'How is this not kosher? It's candy.'"

"Great minds think alike," Meiselman says, hoping a fostering of fellowship will help with the donation request. "Last week, a coworker brought—"

"Right, right, right, one second, one second. Life Savers, Skittles, Nerds. We ate them when we were kids, until one day we didn't. From China, I called my rebbe, Rav Drucker—not my shul rabbi, Rabbi Bergman—that guy is a fool, a hack. Rav Drucker is in Woodmere. Big *gadol.* Gave him a lot of money for his yeshiva's dormitory. When I have a question, I call him. I read Rav Drucker the ingredients and asked him to imagine what it was like finding kosher food in Dupre, Namibia. I didn't tell him about visiting Fuck-it, but that would have been totally hilarious." Gershon is staring up at the television throughout his spiel. Periodically, he pauses, eyes widening at the action, and Meiselman is forced to look up over his shoulder to follow along. "When I finished, he said, 'I am giving you a special dispensation because of your extreme circumstances. But this is not to be brought into the house, and this is not to be eaten in public. Would have been hilarious if I told Rav Drucker about visiting Fuck-it."

"I'll have one," Meiselman says. "A piece, not a bag."

Using the tip of his middle finger, Gershon slides several candies off the table into his palm, but instead of handing his brother a piece, he makes a fist, hangs it over his mouth and dispenses them, one by one.

"Do you remember these?" Meiselman says, taking another stab at fellowship. Dips his hand into his pocket and pulls one of the peppermint candies snagged from Mrs. Woolf's house.

Gershon makes a revolted face. Calls it "Grandma candy." Meiselman drops the sucker into his mouth, pushes it into his cheek, and says, "They use real sugar."

"They've run out ways to enhance first class," Gershon continues. "What comes after seats that recline into beds, private DVD players, and more food than I can eat in a week? The only thing left to do is take away amenities from passengers like you. Heard a rumor about airlines starting to charge passengers for checked baggage."

"That reminds me of an article—"

"Wait, wait, one second, one second. Honestly, I love that feeling of walking down that ratty, red carpet, imagining people like you tallying your measly miles as you look on. Look," Gershon says, nodding up at the television. "A-Rod homer. A-Rod on the Yankees. Pretty good. In New York, fans are pretty excited about A-Rod."

"You're not turning into a Yankees fan on us, are you?" Meiselman asks.

"All joking aside, if you ever need me to donate miles to you, just ask."

Gershon waves both arms over his head. The bartender, who is reading a newspaper at the far end of the bar, notices the motioning and gets the attention of the waiter, who is standing behind a lectern next to the entrance. When they lock eyes, Gershon snaps and flaps his index and middle fingers back and forth, flapping even while the man holds up a finger, flapping even while the waiter sets down his pen and starts walking toward them. Meiselman, in all his life, has never beckoned anyone with such brashness. Careful to not pollute the serene atmosphere with franticness, the waiter walks on the balls of his feet, hands clasped behind his back. A barely perceptible bow when he reaches the table.

"Leo, right?" Gershon says.

The waiter nods.

"Gary," Gershon says, pointing to himself. "Remember?"

Pink splotches on Leo's cheeks and neck suggest a fresh shave. Not at home, but a professional job at a classic barbershop, thrice a week, a towel stuffed between his collar and neck fat, hot gel slathered across his jowly cheeks, and a blade to filch the stubborn grizzle. Slicks back his black hair and holds in his fat with a girdle. Leo will not cheapen himself with a nametag or pad. Poor Leo. His striving is misdirected, misapplied. He is stuck working at an airport hotel. Or he knows his place, which explains the white athletic socks and black Velcro sneakers.

"My brother would like a drink," Gershon says.

"My apologies," Leo says. "Just that the other gentleman you were with had paid and—"

"Listen," Gershon says, "he's going to say he's fine and how he just had dinner and does not like to drink liquids before long drives. Then will come some corny joke about having the bladder of an elderly woman, but I need you to insist, Leo. Insist until you are both red in the face, because I know he wants a drink, especially if I'm paying." Gershon's eyes are on the television overhead. "The Sox can't get a call. I don't hear you insisting, Leo."

Leo breathes deeply, eyes closed. He asks, "Sir, what can I get you?"

Toying this way with people must electrify his brother, and Meiselman wants a taste, so he dismisses any inclination to let the waiter off easy and gives him the speech his brother said he would. "I have the bladder of a misanthropic, college-aged, pink-haired girl," he says, and then when the man insists, Meiselman makes him rattle off the name of every imperial stout on tap, even though he is not a beer drinker.

"I'd go with the Belgian beer," Leo says. "Dark and strong."

"Dark and strong, Leo?" Gershon asks. "Is that how you like it?"

The light from the television reveals a ridge of sweat under Leo's hairline, and Meiselman grows more and more uncomfortable with the waiter's discomfort.

"Seltzer is fine," he says to Leo.

Yellow, according to Gershon, is the worst flavor, which is why he is dropping them into one of the empty bottles. With time running short and Meiselman looking for a question to segue them into the donation request, he asks after Gershon's kids.

"Garland sucks," Gershon says. "By the way, what's with telling Rav Fruman I'd be interested in giving money for some plaza renovation?"

"Tell Rav Fruman? No, he told me. I went to see him about a community matter and he told me."

This launches Gershon into another speech about Rav Fruman telling him on the call that he was one of his smartest students, and that he could have been a major rabbi. God, according to Rav Fruman, had other plans for the other Meiselman boy.

"Understand," Meiselman says, "the man has an agenda—"

"I'm scaling back my commitments, at least until after the election. We're shipping a ton of water to the conflict zones, and if this Frenchie gets elected there's no telling what will happen to business."

Even at the nice kosher restaurants, the waiter does not pour for the customer as Leo is doing now. Gershon lives a life where such service is taken for granted. To not have one's mind tracking dirty clothes from the time they leave the body until they are back in the drawers or closets is a level of comfort Meiselman envies. Leo amazingly twists the bottom half of the straw's wrapper off without his furry fingers touching the plastic.

What concerns Meiselman is that he is not fostering fellowship with his potential donor. Disregarding Leo's discomfort, Meiselman asks, "My lime?"

"I'm sorry, a lime? You asked for a lime, huh? Must not have heard you," Leo says in a tone Meiselman knows well from Deena.

"The Meiselman Boys," read the laundry sticker stitched into the camp clothes of both Meiselman and Gershon. How his mother refers to them still. "The Boys." Meiselman, the wily leadoff hitter, bunts the Meiselman Boys into Leo's head with soft harassments. Beers on tap. Limes. The self-proclaimed veteran waiter thinks he can brush it off, unaware that the power hitter Gershon waits on deck. Gershon does not play small ball. Together, they could have forced Shenkenberg to listen. If only earlier in life Meiselman would have recruited his brother to stand up to the casual, everyday harassers. If only his brother would have offered. This playful harassment of Leo will convince Gershon they are cut from the same cloth, prove he is worthy of a donation.

But Gershon wants to talk about his trip to Michigan the next day, and the lawsuit some small town is filing against his company. "People," he says, "are completely disinterested in local politics until suddenly they are interested, and then it is with a rabidity like no other."

"Sounds like something I'm dealing with at work. Remember Izzy—"

Foiling any chance for a natural segue is Leo, who has returned with lime wedges circling the entire rim of a saucer, an uncut lime in its center. "Let me know if you need any more," Leo says.

From his pocket, Gershon pulls a gold money clip monogrammed with his initials GUM. He flicks through the folded sheaf of crisp bills and pulls a twenty. “This should cover the drink, your tip, and a visit in another ten minutes,” he says to Leo, slapping the bill into the waiter’s palm.

Meiselman, catching the cracking Leo rolling his eyes, prepares to deepen the assault. “One more thing—”

Gershon halts his brother with his hand. “Enough. I want to watch. You’ve been great, Leo. Now go.”

How much easier this would be if Gershon would ask one of the boilerplate questions family members ask one another. Not once, however, has he ever asked Meiselman about his work or wife. Do genetics explain this disinterest? His father, after all, rarely asks. His mother asks, but they always seem to be the wrong questions, or are they the right questions in the way they force Meiselman to hone in on overlooked anxieties. Meiselman must start picking his spots.

“Their offense is lost without Frank,” Meiselman says. “Deena says that the cooler weather will keep him out longer than expected.” Lets out a long, anguished sigh before continuing. “They are so pleased with Deena at work. Don’t know what they would do if she ever has to go on maternity leave.”

Arms folded, Meiselman waits for Gershon to ask the obvious follow-up.

“Why are they not bunting over the runner?” his brother asks.

Before the ten minutes are up Gershon is up waving his hands over his head trying to get the attention of Leo, who is occupied with the couple at the bar.

Gershon mutters, “The worst service in these cheap hotels.”

“Surprised,” Meiselman answers. “It’s a Hilton. In *Be My Guest*, Conrad—”

When Leo arrives at the table Gershon instructs him to ask Meiselman if he wants another drink. Leo stares down at Meiselman glum-faced, almost as if he is waiting for Meiselman to give him the business. The seltzer was flat, the limes lacked tartness. And white athletic socks with dress pants? Meiselman looks the waiter straight in the eye. Is pity preventing Meiselman from launching an assault, or does it suggest a continuing inability to unleash his aggressive capabilities? Gershon watches the game, indifferent to this stalemate. The waiter tilts his head to the side and smirks. A folding Meiselman says, "Delicious seltzer. And limes."

"Guess we're done," Gershon says. "Thanks for putting up with us." Out comes the money clip, and another twenty.

The apology and tip seem to have reenergized the waiter. After sliding the folded money into his apron, Leo clasps his hands behind his back and says, "It's been my pleasure. Have a wonderful evening."

But he has not taken more than two steps before Gershon politely calls him back to the table. The waiter treads tentatively, stopping several feet short.

Gershon asks, "My brother here was wondering, are you homosexual?"

Leo stares at Gershon, his temple veins plumping. Lurching his face across the table at Meiselman, he barks, "Why, you trolling?" Specks of spit hit Meiselman's face.

"Not me, not me," Meiselman argues, waving his arms in front of his face.

One of Leo's eyes, its ball speckled black and green, twitches. The waiter backs off, straightens his shirt, and mutters something indecipherable, which Meiselman, too strung up with fear, surely did not ask him to repeat.

"I said, 'Go fuck yourself,'" Leo repeats before walking away, driving himself straight out of the bar.

Meiselman reaches forward and whacks his brother across the arm. "How? How can you say that to someone?"

"Totally hilarious," Gershon says, slapping his leg. "Wait till I tell people. Your face. So hilarious. I'm great at spotting them," he says. "Kind of obvious. Pretty—" He finishes the thought by tilting his hand from side to side.

"And that word! It's no longer acceptable."

How does one brother know and one does not? Growing up, their father had jokes at the Shabbat table about *fageles* and *shvartzes*, and, on the walk home from shul, they would sometimes pass fellow congregant Alvin Mayer, a middle-aged bachelor who wore a purple beret with a pompom hanging off the top and, after opening up a block of separation, the Boys would snicker in anticipation of their father—always a couple of steps ahead—turning to them with a limped wrist and saying, "Most definitely." But then one week, Meiselman came to the Shabbat table eager to share an overheard joke. Midway through the retelling, his mother shrieked, "Where did you learn such a word?" Shot her husband a glare. She added, "It's ugly, and it's not used by people like us." Immediately, Meiselman absorbed the message. We come from a different generation, but you should know different. They were to evolve. Such words never passed Meiselman's lips again, even if they may flicker in his mind from time to time. On occasion, he has even chastised others for using such ugly language. Is his brother hardwired with an intractable ugliness? How else to explain why, on the night of the aborted joke, Gershon pinned Meiselman to the bedroom floor and poked his anus, demanding to hear the punchline?

"After this half of the inning, I'm off to my room, so finish up your seltzer."

Did his brother not hear the protest lodged by his teammate Meiselman? Light ribbing is fine, but Leo suffered cruelty no person deserves.

"If an underling used that word, or asked someone such a question, I'd have them out on the street," Meiselman says. "It's indecent."

"Don't worry. It's a great story for him, too. He's spazzing about it now, but in another year he'll be telling all his gay friends about it. Laughing like little girls. We would have been forgotten otherwise. In India last week, I got a pie to the face. At the time, it sucked. Had to send my assistant back to the hotel for a clean shirt, but now it's a totally hilarious story."

Meiselman cannot take the chance this behavior is congenital. This reunion, therefore, must end with him not asking for a donation.

After passing along his "warmest regards" to Meiselman's wife, and requesting they not allow so much time to pass between visits, Gershon excuses himself. Wanting to catch the last half of the inning, or maybe not wanting to be seen exiting the bar with his brother, Meiselman takes Gershon's seat. With his last tissue, Meiselman clears the candies off the table, hoping to spare Leo an additional indignity on account of the Meiselman Boys. Is yellow banana or lemon? Right as Meiselman's back molar crushes through the lemon candy, an image of a swelled, purple sore that for years overlay Gershon's Adam's apple flashes in his mind, closing his throat, and forcing him to spit the candy into one of the empty bottles, spitting until every last drop of the taste is out of his mouth.

* * *

On the ride home, Meiselman listens to the postgame show. "Honestly, I don't know if I could've thrown that pitch any better," a dejected Garland says.

Honesty, Meiselman determines, must now be the way forward.

"Some unfortunate news," he says, entering the bedroom. The admission of the failed second test is where he will begin. Conveying the humiliation and inadequacy he felt upon hearing the results will excuse his prior stonewalling, force his wife to demonstrate understanding. She may even feel guilt for any pressure put on him. He may not even ever have to raise his failed idea of depositing his brother's seed inside her.

The overhead is off, but the bedside lamp is on. Deena, in a black tank top and underwear, appears to be asleep in her queen-size bed, her legs and hands wrapping her twisted sheet and blanket as if she is swinging on a rope. Her foot crushes the spine of a turned-over *The Road Less Traveled.* To see how books are treated in the home of the library's number two would horrify people. The pair of boxers she must have been wearing around the house are on the floor next to her bed. Meiselman strips off his purple shirt and pants and leaves them strewn across the bedroom carpeting. On his naked walk to her side of the bed, he whispers her name. She murmurs but does not wake. He takes the book from the bed, slams it shut, and drops it down onto a patch of bare nightstand. It knocks hollow. She does not move. Under the guise of assuming the husbandly duty of turning off her bedside lamp, he sweeps a stack of hardcovers—all library books—off the nightstand. They tumble to the carpeting with nothing louder than the slithering of settling pages.

Kneeling at her bedside, he utters her name again while tugging at her bottom sheet. Her mouth opens and closes as if taking a bite of air, and she clutches the twisted sheet and blanket even tighter, fighting to stay asleep, fighting, perhaps, to keep her husband from intruding on a dream. One about Meiselman? She, after all, features in his dreams during periods of separation. Permitted to touch, he is back to dreaming of other women. "Nobody I really know," is how he always categorized these women to Dr. Lin. How did the doctor know she occasionally featured in them?

He desires Deena tonight, and he is down on his knees, elbows propped on the edge of her bed, eyes on her underwear and flat chest—black is most definitely one of his colors. Nose to her crotch, he does not pick up a scent, ruling out pheromones as the reason for this desire that is rapidly overtaking him and has his midsection pressed against her mattress, hands tugging at the sheet even harder.

His head rests on the mattress, inches from her dimpled, tiny buttocks. He says, "I don't kneel nearly enough. Guess it's taboo in our religion. For anything important, we stand. Down here I feel the confessional urge striking." Every part of his body is slackening and the truths about Mrs. Woolf, the jumbo salmon patties, Rav Fruman's ruling, and who knows what else—the pink-haired woman, perhaps—are on the verge of spilling from his mouth. "The Jewish God does not want us cowering or groveling," Meiselman continues. "He knows we are dreck. God is God. Our sins cannot stun him." The idea that openness and transparency solidifies relationships sounds good in theory, but if Meiselman were to confess something terrible, Deena's opinions will surely shift. She might muss his hair, massage his shoulders, pat him on the back and tell him everything will be fine, but in the back of her mind, things will change. Or not even back. Frontal lobes, right next to an image of herself hopping on Randy's motorcycle and hightailing it out of New Niles.

In a more zealous frame of mind he would know that during this period of separation it is forbidden to rub his fingers against the spiraled sheet and blanket extending from the bottom of her clamped knees, to rub with such intensity that he feels a light burn on the fingertips. But he cannot stop. Stomach pressed against the bed, his groin grazes the mattress's base with each torque of his hips. All he wants is to continue feeding this feeling. A confession, some type of utterance, is needed at once to mask his body's mashing against the mattress. The truth of what happened in Rav Fruman's office is about to come out. An opening, middle, and end to the story are taking shape. Quotes are recalled and embellished—yes, even confessions are full of fibs. All of a sudden, an image of General Powell in his younger years superimposes itself on the scenes from the Rav Fruman encounter. Immediately, Meiselman's mind works on summoning the specific twists and turns of the story, which is indeed the edifying tale of the General he'd wanted to share earlier this morning at breakfast:

Down in Georgia for advanced officers' training. Living on base. Off hours spent fixing up the new house in anticipation of the wife and baby's arrival from New York. On the drive back to the base one night, exhausted from a day of painting in a hundred-plus degree heat, his tank top undershirt brown with sweat, a stop for a burger and shake at a drive-in. Knowing there is no chance of a black man getting served inside, he hopes the waitress will serve him in the lot and let him eat in peace, especially if she spots the officer tags on the car's plates. The waitress approaches after the orders of every other car in the lot have been taken. She, in her late fifties, cherry-red hair shocked silver at the temples, leans in through the driver side window.

Are you a colored, she asks him.

Right when he is ready to deliver his answer, the face of the waitress in Meiselman's mind changes. She is the pink-haired woman and she is nibbling on a pen, and the man in the car is no longer the General but Meiselman. He tries and tries to force himself and his protégé from the movie playing in his head, but they are unmovable and soon, without much choice, the tale proceeds with them fixed in the roles of waitress and patron.

Not colored, Meiselman answers.

Then are you an A-rab?

Because of the beard, you ask? My mother made this comment recently as part of another fruitless attempt to get me to shave it off.

He notices some toothpick-nibbling locals sitting at a picnic bench. One of the men, in a trucker hat with a Confederate flag patch, is fixing for eye contact. When he gets it, he pulls his belt from his pants and jerks it at both ends before whipping it against the ground, his mouth opening in a tarry laugh.

So not an A-rab, right? the waitress coaches him.

No, I'm Jewish. An American and an officer in the United States army.

Meiselman, forever a poor multitasker, can hear how this bastardized memory of the General that is playing in his mind while his body grinds against Deena's mattress is messing with the fluidity of the actual words coming out of his mouth, a riff on an article he read about Buddhists believing that prostration can clear the mind of defilements. If only he could stop his body. But he cannot. Each rotation of the hips is executed with more vigor, his groin striking with more force. The pleasure springs from the crushing of the shaft. Once, more than once, he has done it with his back turned to his sleeping Deena, but this? This is depraved. This harsh self-judgment only further arouses him.

"The moment I looked into the cup after that second test, I could tell it lacked potency," he murmurs to the sleeping Deena. "The color seemed off, yellow tinted. Had the consistency of gefilte fish jelly."

Having successfully refocused his confession, he returns to the story of the General that is playing in his mind.

Look I'm from the suburbs of Chicago, the pink-haired woman playing the role of the waitress answers the General-supplanting Meiselman. I don't understand any of this. But that guy sitting on the bench won't let me serve you. The owner's freeloading brother. How about you go behind the restaurant, and I'll pass you a hamburger out the back window.

Damn hungry, Meiselman as the General kicks the car in reverse and burns rubber to the restaurant's rear, which is pitch black except for an orange light bulb hanging above the back door, moths prancing about. The car's beams shine on dumpsters overflowing with black garbage bags. Behind the dumpsters, an endless forest of towering, spindly evergreens. There is no sign of the pink-haired woman. Was her plan to lure him into a secluded area so the men from the picnic bench could descend on him and belt-whip his butt? Stick his inverted Jew nipples with that toothpick. Milk him for his blood. Better wear gloves, a balding man with a ponytail yells. Don't want to catch no Tay-Sachs.

Unwilling to test whether these scenes of torture, of unconventional pain, can finish the job, Meiselman's state of arousal levels off. He now hears the waitress calling out to him from deep in the forest behind the dumpsters. Following her call, he finds the pink-haired woman flat on her back, a blanket underneath her body, naked except for hamburger bun halves covering each breast, a pickle round on her bellybutton, stripes of mustard and ketchup running up her core, and a machine-pressed patty obscuring the space between her legs.

I know you Jewish don't take cheese on your meat, she says.

All the evidence points to her being a woman, but what if she is a girl? An indecency he is not willing to entertain. Deena's friend Molly, his distant cousin Tamara, and his sister-in-law are all introduced into the dream in her place and, for obvious reasons, summarily dismissed. He cannot find a suitable substitute, and time is running out. He cannot be stuck with any of these women at the point of no return. Back to the pink-haired woman, Meiselman is soon testing the silliness of eating meat off a woman's body. Not silly at all.

How is Deena sleeping through this assault? Her sleep, in fact, has deepened, the creasing around her eyes and in her forehead heavier, her body curled tighter.

"Don't think bad of me for wanting to take a less traditional route after failing the second test," he tells Deena, as he sees himself nibbling the meat patty. "I'm not vain. With pride I would have dropped a blonde-haired Meiselman boy off at school. If it were a black girl I'd even discourage her from straightening her hair. But I cannot control the thoughts of others, and despite what they say, they will never fully accept him or her unless he or she looks like a Meiselman."

He can no longer focus on this speech meant to muffle the sounds of his body, so he goes quiet.

The waitress brings her knees to her chest, and before Meiselman can entertain an even filthier turn in the story, he hits that moment of irreversibility and drops his body flat on the floor, squeezing his legs together for the finish. Embracing the pleasure he grabs a hold of himself at the moment of release as if directing the shot. His eyes tear. "Oh, Ethel," he cries as the last drops descend.

He stills himself to hear if he has woken Deena. He can detect movement. Not a start, but a stop, an arrest, a bracing. Rule Number 8: "Check small things." Using Deena's boxers he mops up the mess made on the library books. There is also a small puddle next to Deena's leg. Crawling back to his side, he chucks the boxers deep under the bed.

In bed, his back to his wife, his heart beats like a leaky faucet. He wraps the sheet tight around his body. Every time he tries recalling the unadulterated version of the General's story, he sees himself driving to the restaurant's rear where the men are waiting for him. They shave the middle of his head so he looks like Curly from the Three Stooges. They pin the skin of his shaft to the head of his penis, cheering, Hide his Jewish, Hide his Jewish. They pull antlers off the front of a pickup and superglue them to his head.

It has been a day of unwieldy conversations, of unfocused and unconsummated aggression. If there is any hope of better results tomorrow, he must break this cycle at once and come up with the correct ending to this story. What would Colin Powell do? He can hear the General speak, the voice of the unemotional counselor, a soothing grouse oozing sensibleness, as if his lips are too cramped to hit the high notes of feeling. The General is steadiness. A man willing to put himself on the line, but only when asked to by others. He would not try to outfox the men at the picnic bench. What would Colin Powell do? He would not suffer the humiliation that would come with taking the burger. Colin Powell would rather suffer a different humiliation by returning to the base and eating in the officers' hall, and while eating his meatloaf with mashed potatoes and green beans he would feel satisfied, saying something to himself about not making waves and how the South is a sick cell in an otherwise healthy body and how patience is always the best course, justice, in the end, having its way.

Last week, before the Shenkenberg slight, this story about not making waves may have been worth sharing with Deena. Now, however, he knows: acquiescence only invites further abuse. Once sick cells hitch themselves to a body, they never go away for good. Remissions never last. Forty years of service has ended in a scapegoating. They have made this fierce warrior look like a dupe, and come Sunday night, Meiselman cannot allow himself to be the dupe, especially in front of his loved ones and the pink-haired woman.

Thursday

Beyond the black filling his head are the trilling pipes of a flushed toilet. Unsure of how much Deena heard of last night's unburdening, he keeps his lids sealed. Better to answer accusations barricaded behind an open newspaper. It must have been a dream, before pivoting to a puff piece on the front page about American soldiers in Iraq erecting plant nurseries.

The garage door cranking to a close is the next sound he hears. Separating his crusty eyelids, he discovers Deena's bed is made and the alarm is not due to go off for another seven minutes. He cannot recall his wife mentioning an early morning session or staff meeting.

Downstairs, a note taped to the coffee pot answers the mystery. "Off to gym. Home late. Father needs me. Don't wait up." No *Love, Deena*. No *Have a good day!*

A cryptic and troubling note. Lately, Deena has talked about returning to the gym, a "need to get back to it," although back to what is not clear. On long walks she does not pant. Weight gain is not an issue. Unlike his father, she does not suffer random bouts of lethargy. Like Meiselman, her lean frame is not designed to support cylindrical muscles. Additionally, the amount of exercise she does in a typical workday, snagging medicine balls and weights off the floor, supporting obese patients with as little as a hand against the small of the back, seems more than sufficient.

By writing "gym," is Deena not implying something ominous? After all, a gym is where Meiselman's chase of Deena, *née* Daisy, commenced. She and everyone else can think the essence of the relationship is fate, but is fate enough to sustain? By writing "Off to gym," does she not mean *Off to test whether fate has other plans for me?*

Does the note suggest that Deena will be incommunicado for the remainder of the day? Why else would she cram her plans from morning to night into a two-line note? Morning is no time for wantonness, meaning he can rule out the possibility of a morning tryst with the motorcycle maniac Randy.

Backing out of the driveway, he opens the car door, hangs his hand low to the ground, and snags the newspapers off the cement. Despite vowing to not turn his vehicle into a crap car full of empty bottles and crumpled receipts, detritus that causes a commotion anytime a passenger steps inside and a seat has to be cleared, Meiselman dumps the newspapers onto the passenger side floor. Turning off his street, he realizes he has forgotten to retrieve his parents' newspapers. He circles back to his house only to discover that they have already been collected. But by whom?

* * *

Meiselman turns into the library's lot with no recollection of having driven the streets of New Niles. The banter between the AM 670 newsman and the traffic chopper reporter is babble, and these are the first indications he is entering the zone, a state where the center of the mind narrows and the rubble, the non-essential, the (for now) superfluous concerns like Deena's letter, Frank's injury, and the continuing silence coming from Mrs. Woolf's lot are pushed to the outside in order to harbor central concerns like Shenkenberg and the pink-haired woman. In the zone, his mind is not open to intrusions. All he sees, at this time, is a checklist of today's tasks.

Each title and abstract is more incomprehensible than the next: "Political Order and the Specter of Antisocial Being in Shakespeare's Julius Caesar," by Gil, Daniel Juan; "The Weaponization of Empathy in Julius Caesar," by Gerard, Louis Richard; "Brutus's Erratic Ingenuity," by Tisdale, Sarah.

Not wanting to saddle the pink-haired woman with additional reading, and unsure of how he feels about the increasingly widespread perception that everything in the world is contrastable, he rules out easy-to-understand titles like "The Appropriation of Guilt in Shakespeare's *Caesar* and Ibsen's *A Doll House.*" His patience soon pays off. On page three of the search results, he locates a possibility: "Metellus Cimber: The Ultimate Cynic." The name in the paper's title, the abstract confirms, is a character in the play. He copies the title and abstract onto a separate file, deleting the name of the article's author. Three results later, another easy-to-understand title: "Julius Caesar: A Play for the Common Man." The paper, according to the abstract, contends the play's purpose is to warn of the chaos that ensues when leaders employ simple, straightforward language to relay political messages. The title and abstract of this paper are also copied onto the separate file. Needing to return to his desk before the other administrators arrive, especially if today is the day Ethel indeed returns, Meiselman copies down a third title and its abstract, even though it is utterly incomprehensible. He will have to sell topic number two hard, while keeping her away from topic number three.

Hitters say that when in the zone, the baseball looks the size of a grapefruit. They can see the stitching on the ball. The approach of a ninety-five-mile-an-hour fastball can be slowed and broken into distinct frames. Evidence he is operating in such a state mounts. While rifling through some papers on his desk, he comes across the proof for the Shenkenberg advertisement set to run in this week's *Chicago Jewish Chronicle* and, as out of thin air, a crafty solution to the formidable task of assembling a pool materializes.

As the phone rings, Meiselman pictures slovenly Barry Kranzler, a former classmate, scuttling downstairs in an open bathrobe to the basement office of the *Chicago Jewish Chronicle*, coffee sloshing over his mug's rim.

"Shying away from controversy is not how I would categorize it," Barry Kranzler answers Meiselman's opening salvo. "We did a piece on Shenkenberg last year. To mark the release of the hardcover edition. Besides, maintaining, not boosting, circulation is our primary objective here at the *Chronicle*. People peruse our periodical for wire articles on Israel, photographs of the President hosting Jews in the White House, and lists of all the classes at the JCC. A segment of the readership enjoys puff pieces about mothers becoming rabbis."

"My mother loved that article about the terminally ill woman in Schaumburg who became a rabbi, and she is no liberal," Meiselman concurs.

"Yes, our focus groups tell us even Orthodox women enjoy such articles. The men, not so much, but they aren't our core readership. They skim. More inclined to read the headlines. The focus groups, and this goes back to your initial proposition, tell us the most readers can stomach in terms of controversy is my weekly column, 'Kranzler's Korner with a K.' You're familiar, I assume? 'K because Kranzler is keeping the community kosher'? Generally provoking, occasionally uplifting. Last week, I wrote about the nursing home owner Skrumpnick ripping off Medicare by storing dead bodies in basement freezers. Women, according to focus groups, are quite taken with my column. They see me as a poor newspaperman, a *nebekh*, and, therefore, trustworthy. Men see me as bitter, and believe I operate with a score-settling agenda. Also, the ads. Women in the fifty-five-plus bracket read our publication for the ads, specifically the Germanic Kosher ad listing the weekly specials, the same one that's been running since the Jews came over on the Mayflower. One week, Germanic Kosher tried to modernize the font. Whoa, what an uproar! Yentas berating our customer service reps—"

Maybe because he is operating in the zone, or maybe because of the commitment to unleash his aggression, or maybe because of some combination of the two, Meiselman cuts off the editor and former classmate with a threat worthy of a Fruman, Shenkenberg, or Gershon. "Do I need to remind you that the New Niles Public Library is a loyal advertiser, as well? In my hand, in fact, is the half-page Shenkenberg ad for this week's issue. If you don't find the Shenkenberg event newsworthy, I can look for a more interested publication."

"Ack, ack, ack," Kranzler barks into Meiselman's ear. "After Ethel begged me to front page it, which, of course, was impossible given the rate. Although in deference to our history, I graciously bumped it up to page three. Plum, plum spot bordering a 'continued from page one' article."

Light resistance will not fold Meiselman.

"You provide coverage of the event, and we will place a half-page ad next week thanking everyone for a successful night," Meiselman proposes.

"Put in a full-pager and you've got a deal," Barry Kranzler counters.

"But sizeable. Two columns and a photo. And I'm not looking for a puff piece heaping praise on Shenkenberg. I want an article highlighting the controversy surrounding Shenkenberg's slandering of our dear Rabbi J-."

"I don't know about Shenkenberg and any controversy. Besides, as I told you, all controversy is reserved for my column, and next week's is already written. That retrograde Rabbi Margolis not accepting that lesbian couple's kid into the day school. This week, a personal reflection on my parents' transformation into rabid Republicans. If you see my father in shul, ask him about the 'domino effect,' or why he finds comfort in a leader who sees things in black and white."

"Gray, the argument can be made, is for ditherers and vacillators."

"You've caught the disease, too, Meiselman? Anyway, back to business. The piece will reflect the ad. Everyone came, everyone had fun. Inspired, inspiring, yada, yada, yada. I can use some leftover quotes from the piece we ran last year, in the event I don't manage to personally attend."

"No, Kranzler. The point is that the event is covered. I'm assembling a pool."

"I'll do my best. Got to run and take a call on the customer service line."

Meiselman dials Ethel with the news. Straight to voicemail. Possibly, at this very instant, she is ending a call or dialing Meiselman to update him on her whereabouts. Redials. Voicemail. Waits several seconds. Redials. Voicemail. Leaves a message. Uses the words "real coup."

Primed to strike minor tasks off the checklist, Meiselman sets out to perform a routine inspection of the troops. "To return the library to the boss in the condition it was received" is how he playfully puts it to Betsy Ross.

"Ethel's not coming in today," the secretary answers him. "Today is when she has the thing."

"She mentioned she might stop in before 'the thing.'"

"Is she in any state? And didn't 'the thing' start hours ago? They start those things at ungodly hours. Six, I think she said."

"Eight," he falsely corrects her. "It starts at eight. Prep at six."

"It's well past nine, and it's going to last hours," she says. Her jaw clicks from side to side, back molars grinding. "I'm on pins and needles. Why am I not there with her, I keep asking myself."

"Because she needs us here," Meiselman answers. "Which reminds me, any action on the letter?"

She stares at him across the desk with doleful eyes. Slowly, her eyes harden and narrow as if either she did not hear him right, or heard him all too well. Fists crashing the desk, she hoists herself from her chair and leans forward. Speaking in a raised whisper, she says, "That's really cold. Even for you. Let's not talk about the letter, please. Some respect for the situation would be nice. Can you manage that? 'Action on the letter.' Pshaw. You *are* unbelievable." Says the last bit as if she heard someone else make the point and now concurs with the evaluation.

Meiselman finds himself in a hole, fighting off bad pitches. Is he falling out of the zone or waiting for his pitch to hit?

Betsy Ross stumbles back into her chair and grabs both armrests, angling her face toward the ceiling, eyes closed, like a petrified flyer bracing for takeoff. After a couple of deep breathes, she says, "I'm a certified wreck."

An external force, one invested in his welfare, must be guiding Meiselman today. How else to explain the uncharacteristic, yet inspired decision to take the indecent approach of coming around to Betsy Ross's side of the desk and relaxing his hands on her shoulders. Lightly working his thumbs into her mushy back, careful to keep them away from her bra straps, he spouts claptrap about how Ethel would demand bravery and fortitude from them at such a time. Betsy Ross does not shrink or stiffen from his touch. She is loosening. The secretary reaches across her body and grabs the fingers of Meiselman's sheltering hand. She corrals his fingers into her palm and squeezes, offering an apology for snapping at him.

Having turned a possible humiliation into a resounding triumph, the walk back to his office should have the feel of a victory lap, but Betsy Ross's words are squatting in the front of his mind. 'Thing' intimates a medical procedure. But why the secrecy? What could be shameful about a bad back? Besides the back, Ethel is an emblem of strength, and even the back injury is not one of weakness, like when his father had to call Mr. Woolf to carry Meiselman down the stairs. Rather, the buckling back of an overworked stalwart.

The telephone is ringing, and the walls holding back the inconsequential start crumbling. Is it Deena apologizing for her early morning departure, or his mother sounding an alarm over an emerging crisis? Maybe it is the front of the library calling to inform him that Professor Westbound, today's Earth Day speaker, has arrived, or Ethel calling to explain the meaning of 'the thing.' Clearly, he is falling out of the zone. Some players end a hot streak and regress back to an average level of production. Others drop out of the zone only to begin a brutal slump.

* * *

"Paul Woolf here," the caller identifies himself in a wispy voice. "Your neighbor's son. Got a bit of a concern."

Siccing her son on him is a clever move. Fifteen years Meiselman's senior, the lone Woolf offspring is a man cool enough to threaten litigation in a non-threatening way. Back when Meiselman was a boy, whenever he would spot the visiting Paul out front smoking a cigarette, playing fetch with Spencer, Meiselman would grab his mitt and toss pop-ups to himself. Eventually, Paul would take notice, snuff his cigarette with a wet fingertip, and tuck the butt behind his ear. Across the front yard separating the Woolf and Meiselman houses—at that time it was either the Spiegelmans or the Days; both families occupied the house for no longer than five years—Paul would yell, "Hey, bro, let me chuck you some." Paul was no athlete. He threw the ball like a soldier lobbing a grenade, and expressed genuine astonishment with Meiselman's ball handling skills, even on the throws that sailed wide and high—"Ease up on the zippy throws"—or grounders that hopped into Meiselman's groin—"Nice scoop, bro." From a young age Meiselman was wary of men who displayed a dispassion for sports, but Paul overcame this bias by exuding a singular aura of manliness, one unparalleled to this day in Meiselman's life. Would Meiselman's father or brother ever stalk the front yard barefoot in cut off jean shorts, dirty blonde hair cinched in a ponytail, gold hoops through both ears, open white button-down, a gold medallion of a horse's head slapping a smooth, tanned chest? A locked-out Meiselman would sit huddled on the stoop, never considering hoisting himself through the kitchen window. Meiselman's family were unimpressed with his account of Paul calling him over that fall afternoon to give him a boost. "Lucky he didn't get shot," his father said. "Lucky you didn't get shot," his mother added. Unclear of what was acceptable for a boy to notice in another man, Meiselman kept certain details to himself, like Paul's blistering, red nose, or the aviator sunglasses precariously balanced on his head that lent him a paradoxical aura of relaxation and fast living. Why did Meiselman men not wear sunglasses? Freshman year of college, Meiselman finally satisfied a longing generated on the day of the boost, but the thick lenses and the clumsy exchange of his regular glasses for the prescription pair whenever entering and exiting buildings prevented him from approaching anything close to cool.

"Just spoke to your mother," Paul Woolf tells Meiselman. "Said she's tied up with errands, but mentioned you might be game for giving an old neighbor a hand. Here's the deal. Stuck here at the Arizona house, and I'm having trouble with my mother." Recent calls to his mother must be troubling Paul. Last week she may have mentioned plans to grow rice in her suburban backyard. The ditch, her son must assume, exists solely in his mother's deteriorating mind. To voice exasperation while still sounding sympathetic will be the challenge. He could question whether she should be living unsupervised, and explain how she has turned into a nighttime terror. Well-being, Meiselman reminds himself. It must be framed as concern for her well-being.

"Can't reach her," Paul continues. "It's happened before that she's knocked the phone off the receiver by accident while cleaning. If you'd knock on her door, I'd be mucho gracias."

"Gladly," Meiselman says. "But it will have to wait until dinnertime. I have a speaker in the next hour, and a meeting with a donor at four."

"If it's too much for you I can call cousin Eddie out in Schaumburg, but that's a hassle of a drive for a guy that just got a new knee. So what do you say, good man?"

"Isn't this what neighbors are for?" Meiselman answers.

"Like I said, bro. Whenever you get a chance. Thanks again, and good luck on your speech to the donors."

No, this is not what neighbors are for. Neighbors are for small levels of support, like the storage of an extra key, the collection of mail and newspapers, and the borrowing of an egg or cup of sugar. If one, however, will be out of town for more than three days, he should call the post office and the newspaper to request a hold. If one needs more than two eggs or two ingredients, he should put the recipe on hold and drive to the store. It is a slippery slope. Paul might call next week, concerned his mother is driving alone to an appointment in Waukegan. Soon Meiselman's duties will encompass grocery shopping, doing pickups from the pharmacy, and riding out to Cousin Eddie's family functions in Schaumburg. Deena says let the soup cool. Deena says you can freeze the cake. Deena rarely bakes for Meiselman. Is there even money to inherit?

If he has any chance of staying in the zone, he must continue with his day as planned, and not allow Paul's favor to sidetrack him. Cool Paul Woolf, after all, is not waiting next to the phone to hear of his mother's fate. Cool Paul Woolf probably hung up with Meiselman, jumped into his convertible, lowered his sunglasses, and drove down to the club to play a round.

This close to a book's ending, the reader's attention should be indivertible, yet Meiselman is barely following Shenkenberg's story. Paul's request *is* sidetracking him, and many mentions of Rabbi J- pass with Meiselman unable to establish disrepute. He is saddled with the creeping worry that news of his submission to Paul will come as a disappointment to his mother. Tell him to stop gallivanting and fly up from Arizona if he's so concerned, she might admonish him. As if you don't have enough in your bowl, with that event coming up. But if he were to refuse and give those same reasons to her, she might say, How could you say no? He was always so nice to you. Referred to you as his bro. Your own brother doesn't call you bro. What winning looks like, he will never seem to know.

Meiselman's obligation to Paul begins and ends with a knock on the door, which is executed in a musical, neighborly manner. But there is no response. He waits a civil amount of time before a second, louder rap. Then, the doorbell's coyote cry, which is met with a distant whimper from Sadie. The coyote cries again. Ear to the door, Meiselman hears nothing. He holds his fire for several beats before thumping the heart of the door with the edge of his fist, immediately following with two more rings. He steps off the stoop onto the unkempt front yard, still soft from the spring thaw, the grass's blades stringy and dry like angel hair pasta. Touring the perimeter of the house, there is no sign of the old lady, nor any indication the pit has been worked on since the day of the encounter. The hose has not been fished from the patty bed. Returning to the front yard, he leans over the low bushes abutting the living room bay window, careful not to press too hard against the unruly, shapeless foliage. The drapes are closed, but at the window's center, where the edges meet, a narrow opening allows Meiselman to see into the living room. The sun's glare is strong and dry rainwater clouds the windows, preventing him from seeing past the piano. Stepping forward, his midsection smashes the bushes. Another step and branches begin snapping. Damage already done, he pushes ahead, more branches breaking, buds fluttering to the ground, the tip of one branch lashing his neck right under the beard.

Standing on his toes and looking past the piano, he can see the top of Mrs. Woolf's head lolled against the couch's edge. He taps the glass with his fingernail, but there is no movement. Four testy slaps and Sadie slogs into view, one unsteady paw in front of the other, hips powering her forward, like one of Deena's patients. Is his neighbor still on the carpet from when he left her the other day?

His recently dredged memory of giving Cool Paul a boost through the kitchen window almost thirty years ago was no accident. On his dash to the side of his house, it occurs to him that the door is probably still unlocked from the other day, which it is, and this comes as a relief because who in his life could he have counted on to give him a boost? His mother wanted no part of this. Ethel and his father have bad backs. Deena and the pink-haired woman are too small to support him.

What greets him is a scene he never could have conjured. The upper half of Mrs. Woolf's body slouches forward, her head hanging to the side. Her good leg is flat out, while her fake leg twists outward, its toes pointing to the window. A bulge on the inner thigh of her shorts suggests that the prosthetic has dislodged from its stump. An arm wraps her chest, its thumb hooked into her shirt collar, stretching it and exposing a tan bra strap. The skin of her face is puffy and bumpy, as if someone sloppily stuffed it with soggy bread. The forehead and cheeks are greenish-blue, like one of those fancy, tropical flavored jellybeans Deena eats.

Is she clinging? The thought stirs Meiselman, because who has not fantasized about the feting that comes with saving a life. He moves the coffee table back and crouches down in front of her. Pressing two fingers against her neck, he perceives nothing, but would he know the throbbing of a pulse, especially a faint one? For a reference point, he wraps his other hand around his own neck, but, again, he feels nothing. Like with fever, are people incapable of performing self-evaluations? For all he knows, his fingers are not even on the right spot. The wrist, he knows, is another place to check. Finds on her a plump vein—or is it an artery? Maybe he feels something, maybe he does not. He cleans his hands on the couch cushion. Then he puts his ear to the old lady's breast, the flap of her shirt pocket tickling his lobe. He detects movement inside her body, but it seems more of a ceasing, than a pumping. Her eyes have not blinked since his arrival, and this is ultimately the clearest indication she is indeed dead.

Who has not imagined the feeling of piety that must come with running a hand over the eyes of the recently deceased? On the follow-through, he sees his too-tender touch has managed to close only one eye. He does feel pious, which encourages him to think of other ways to restore the woman's dignity. Mumbling the first five verses of the only Psalm he knows by heart, he sticks his fingers into her mouth and clicks her slightly detached dentures back into place. The gums are soft and dry like putty. Her lips are a leathery brown.

Under the guise of straightening her shirt, he cleans his fingers on its tails. It is when he reaches for her groin with the intention of reattaching the fake leg that he notices blood splashed on the thin strip of wood between the rug and couch. Droplets of blood dot the blue sky of her rug of that famous American painting of the farming couple. Blood slathers the tines of the farmer's pitchfork. A patch of his neighbor's hair is clumped with blood, its color and texture that of burnt tomato sauce.

His first impulse is to run. The authorities open any death investigation by seeking out the person who saw the deceased alive last. Coincidence is never an acceptable answer. The newspapers will plaster Meiselman's mugshot next to the most recent photograph of the victim, one taken at Uncle Eddie's Hawaii-themed post-surgery party, a *lei* around Mrs. Woolf's neck, her son the grocer planting a kiss on his mother's cheek. They will christen Meiselman the New Niles Neglecter.

Within minutes of calling 911, the police, paramedics, and technician arrive. Evans is the name of the officer tasked with talking to Meiselman in the house's foyer. Short and muscular, with dark eyes and a five-o'clock shadow, the antenna of his walkie digs the underside of his ribs. He has the habit of massaging his bicep while waiting for Meiselman to say something worth copying into his notepad. The joking of the other responders filters in from the living room, the technician jeering Evans's partner Morrison to stop peeking down the old lady's shirt.

Meiselman fiddles with the dish of peppermint candies, trying to calibrate a grieving tone.

"We don't want to be touching anything," Evans says. "Just start from the beginning."

Meaning the nighttime disturbances, or his mother's call two days ago about the ditch digging?

"Saw her outside earlier this week and she seemed intact. Physically, at least. Helped her move some hose. She was in good spirits."

"Unpleasant," Evans says. "Grim stuff. But let's focus on today."

It calms Meiselman to hear the officer is not interested in the history. So he opens with the call from Paul, emphasizing his closeness to the family by blabbing inconsequential stories about playing catch with the son when he was younger, letting out an anguished sigh and apologizing for not having dropped everything at once to come check on the lady who has been, in ways, like an "aunt" to him.

"Can't think like that," Evans says. "Between us"—he leans forward and knocks Meiselman's chest with the corner of his notepad—"I don't know what business a son has living across the country from an elderly mother."

"Paul, as I've been trying to describe him, is of a different mindset. He is very cool. The kind who doesn't anticipate calamity. But I agree. I could've moved to New York like my brother, but what prevented me, ultimately, was the question of who would look after my folks. They live next door."

"My mom lives in our basement."

"Seems pretty fresh." The technician's assessment carries in from the other room. "Faint smell, color."

Evans ducks his head into the room and instructs his colleagues to quiet down. Returning to Meiselman, he says, "Grim, grim stuff. How about we take this into the kitchen?"

The officer takes a step back and clicks his tongue, hanging his arm and snapping twice. Sadie, who since Meiselman's arrival has been heaped underneath the piano bench, trots into the foyer, slogging along with Evans and Meiselman into the kitchen. Locating a bag of dog food in the corner, Evans fills one of Sadie's bowls. He fills the second one with water.

"Unpleasant," Evans says. "You a dog owner?"

"I wish. Allergies."

Evans asks that they resume work on Meiselman's statement. The crinkling of the body bag breaks the silence, and the responders in the other room begin counting in unison. On three there's a loud grunt as they hoist the body onto the gurney. A smooth zippering follows. The gurney's wheels jangle and squeal.

"First body, I bet," Evans says.

What does it mean to be taken for a man who has never glimpsed death?

"This is one of the more gruesome ones. My first was also a senior. Laid back in his La-Z Boy, television blaring. WGN, I remember, because I joked—in the car—that it was probably a Cubs fan who'd finally had enough. The man was not ready. Half a glass of orange juice and a nibbled cookie on the table next to him. No dignity in death, my friend. Grim stuff. Seems the deceased took too much of a new medication. Happens more than you think. Caretaker goes away for a week assuming the person can watch over himself. A Holocaust-surviving rabbi, on top of it all."

The tone of the first responders in the other room shifts. They are discussing serious matters when Morrison calls Evans into the living room. This distresses Meiselman because maybe they've discovered something incongruous. Maybe a more combative Evans will return armed with questions meant to trip up Meiselman. Gone only a minute, Evans returns glum faced. The technician believes, he tells Meiselman, that sometime over the last several days, Mrs. Woolf took a fall and hit her head against the corner of the table, concussing herself. Then, she suffered a fatal heart attack sometime within the last twelve hours.

"Despite the gore, he wanted me to tell you, a painless, peaceful end."

The report puts Meiselman at ease. After all, how can he be blamed for unforeseen coincidences? In all honesty, he assumed that a ditch-digging woman could cleanly get up from the floor without assistance. He tells the officer what transpired after Paul's call, including his reading of Shenkenberg, the event on Sunday night, and his role as moderator. Evans looks bored. He stops writing and crouches to massage Sadie's belly. Meiselman skips to the 911 call, questioning the operator's terseness.

"Buddy," Evans interrupts Meiselman. "You got some…" He points to one of Meiselman's brown loafers, which has blood brushed across the small toe.

Bunching Deena's underwear like a handkerchief, Meiselman pulls it from his pants pocket and wipes at the blood. But the blood has dried and it is not coming off. He slowly pumps the inside of his mouth. His saliva builds up. When he can feel it sloshing, he parts his lips and lets fall a healthy gob onto an unsullied patch of the garment. The wet underwear does the job. Evans nods in satisfaction.

While Evans jots down some final notes, Meiselman wanders into the foyer, stopping at the silver dish in order to replenish his supply of peppermint candies.

What he has witnessed should give him the upper hand with Deena, so now is the time to confront and dismiss her note about staying away for the day, which may or may not connect to last night's moment of candor.

The new secretary muffles the phone before returning to inform him that Deena is unavailable and will not be for some time. He conveys urgency. The same muffling, the same answer.

"Tell her I just discovered a dead body."

More muffling. He is told she will take the call in her office.

Picking up the phone, Deena fires away in an exasperated whisper, "Would really appreciate it if you didn't freak out my coworkers."

"Mrs. Woolf," he says.

"Her, again. I don't want to talk about this, I don't think," she says. "No, I don't. Or Shenkenberg. We can talk about the note. That's something we can talk about if we must talk."

"What about it? I'm thrilled. You've been talking about getting back to the gym for some time. Listen—"

"Listen? I don't think I can right now. I'm not coming home tonight. I'm going to stay at my father's for the next night or two. You scared me last night. I shouldn't be scared in my own home."

This is the point when he is expected to apologize to Deena, to acknowledge his impropriety and say he will change. Foster new attitudes and dampen his less agreeable qualities. But only in the movies does a thirty-six-year-old man change. In real life, a man with his back against the wall can only double down.

"I'm not following. I discovered a dead body, Deena. Mrs. Woolf's dead body. This is what we should talk about. *It* was creepy. *It* was scary. Grim, grim stuff. Blood all over my shoes. Not to mention the guilt. We were witnessing her failing and did nothing. You tried to pass it off as harmless."

"Wait. Mrs. Woolf really died? This isn't you being you?"

"Yes, and I found her. And it wasn't some peaceful didn't-wake-up-from-sleep death. She had a terrible accident. Squid like pieces of cartilage and shards of bones spilled on the carpet and floor, Deena. Twitching in my arms as I tried to revive her. The technician said she was probably already dead. Brain's last spasms."

"That is awful. Did you really find her?" Silence. "Like that?" He lets the silence sink in. Finally, she says, "I'll come home tonight, I guess. That's it. That's all I can give, for now. Not even sure I can look at you. We still must discuss last night."

They have reached some type of understanding. Suddenly sick of the fibbing, he feels it is a moment ripe for a confession.

"Deena, I should tell you..."

"Can we do this later?"

"We could, but it's important. I—"

"Okay, fine, fine, just tell me. I have patients."

"I ate a considerable amount of the lasagna you made for dinner."

* * *

Sensitive to Deena's recent charge of creepiness, Meiselman abstains from lurking behind the History shelves today and arrives to the rendezvous spot early. The way she coolly tosses her bag onto the table, dropping open her mouth in an exhausted sigh before slumping into the chair and putting her forehead down against the edge of the table for a simulated banging confirms Meiselman's assumption that yesterday's exchange consolidated the relationship. She is in the same sweatshirt and torn jeans as the other times they met, but today the hair is combed through, meticulously parted, pink cleanly lined up against blonde.

Because nothing good can come from reading off the same paper, he reads the topic choices to her while pacing behind her seat. The pink-haired woman rejects the first topic as too narrow. "Besides," she says, "my professor takes the position that Brutus acted nobly."

He literally could not argue with that.

Despite his best effort to push topic two, it is topic number three, “Assuming the Moral Burden: Victimhood as Nihilism in Julius Caesar,” that animates the pink-haired woman. She begins writing before he can even finish reading her the abstract. Meiselman tries interjecting with another push for topic number two, and the pink-haired woman silences him with a finger up in the air, the polish of its nail black and shiny. Fresh for whom? Or routine maintenance as the weekend nears.

As if looking for guidance, she brainstorms aloud. She says, “Brutus revealing that Portia has committed suicide is a great example,” and he, knowing pushback is an effective way to establish credibility, comments, “Interesting, but what is the essence of Shakespeare’s message?” With each long stretch of silence, he grows anxious that his role as coach is starting to diminish, prompting him to throw out random comments like, “Keep it focused, you aren’t writing a novel,” or, “Clarity is key. This isn’t poetry.”

When finished setting down a thought, she jams the pen deep into her mouth, her molars grinding at the cap, a light squelching of saliva. Ready to put down a fresh idea, she pulls the pen from her mouth and holds it in front of her face perpendicular to the page, a strand of saliva thin as floss extending from the pen’s cap to her thin, glossy lips, tempting a pluck of it with his pinkie.

The utter assuredness in which the pink-haired woman operates has him speculating whether marks like the safety pin and pink hair are merely signs of eccentricity, a straight-lacer looking to imbue herself with spunk. Most women with nose jewelry, he has observed, have large noses, leading Meiselman to theorize that such piercings are executed with the design of disguising the nose’s deficiency. Ironically, the jewelry ends up drawing even greater attention to the imperfection. Is the pink-haired woman trying to hide a blemish or scar? The blondeness of her head hair is deep and rich, not a peroxide job done on a whim in a friend’s bathroom. The strands selected for pinkening, he sees now, were specially chosen for how they seductively fall into the space between her eye and temple. Also, possibly, for the way they wind her ear when she sweeps her hair back.

The pen is back in her mouth, and this time the incisor has a go at its cap, providing him with a solid view of her set. Gum recession and base yellowing are minimal for someone her age. Good money has been spent on straightening them. Whenever glimpsing Deena's silver-speckled molars and overlapping bottom row, he is reminded of how life with him is an upgrade over her meager upbringing.

The pink-haired woman slurps saliva off the cap and continues writing. Finished with another page of notes, she shakes a cramp out of her hand before turning to a clean sheet. He must prove his indispensability, at once, or he will lose any chance of forming a more permanent bond. Leaning in, head craned and peering into the notebook along with his mentee, he says, "You're all over the place."

She asks, "No good?" She proposes a new way of looking at the evidence she has compiled, and he follows with a steady nod, pleased at the uncertainty in her voice.

"Nailed it," he says.

She smiles, pleased that she has pleased him. She now reads back to him every jotted down idea. He slowly restates whatever she says, as if carefully considering its usefulness, before concluding with an emphatic "Yes, yes!" an act so convincing that eventually she drops the pen into her notebook and whines with pouted lips, "You should write this for me."

This playful outburst could not have come at a worse time. The dinky wheels of Anjali's wooden book cart wobble as she turns into the aisles behind them. Even if there are no more than a handful of history books to return to the shelves, Anjali, on her feet all day and still unable to shake the weight, pushes the cart as if it is a walker, arms stiff, plump backside swiveling like an amusement park pirate ship, head angled catatonically, as if drugged by whatever is being piped through the earmuff-sized yellow headphones on her head.

The pink-haired woman checks her watch. The pace of her writing quickens. At pauses, all she manages is a nibble with the front teeth. More regrettably, she has stopped conferring with Meiselman. All his initial assumptions about her have collapsed, creating greater urgency to pivot to the personal. You kids are wild with the piercings. In the early eighties, my mother got a second piercing and my father did not stop until she removed it. Like a street girl, no offense, he kept saying. Where do you get your hair colored? My wife found a few grays last week and is looking for a reputable establishment that will not foist on her foolishly unnatural colors like eggplant and copper.

Using the same pompous tone from before, he says, “Excuse me for prying, but community college? You’re such a sharp and spirited young woman.”

Staring into her notebook, she mumbles, “You think going to that retard N2C2 is my plan? I’ve already been accepted to NYU for the upcoming fall semester. That’s New York University in New York City.” She looks to him for acknowledgment. “Assuming I finish with an A average, which shouldn’t be difficult at that retard school.” She stabs the open notebook with her pen. “If I could just finish this stupid paper. It will be my downfall, I swear.”

Many questions answered. Like that she is a student at New Niles Community College and wears the NYU sweatshirt every day to remind her classmates she is not one of them. Yet new questions emerge, like why she did not attend a four-year college straight out of high school, or why she does not have her own copy of *Julius Caesar*? And what is she rehearsing for?

The prying must continue, so he says, "A year of community college before embarking on a four-year program is a fine way to cultivate healthy study habits and boost confidence."

"Confidence?" she asks, matter-of-factly. "That was—is—not my problem." She bats her eyelashes.

"If test-taking is the issue, you should know, we offer—"

"Please, the SATs were a breeze," she says, promptly plugging another avenue, tapping her pen against the desk's edge, demonstrating impatience with his obtuse line of questioning.

"An episode in high school," she blurts, "that my parents blew way out of proportion is why I go to that retard N2C2 instead of a real school like every other kid in the country my age, okay?"

Episode. A word intimating a shameful, anomalous occurrence, like a distressing scene of mania or disorder of abnegation. Unless she voluntarily elaborates, his progress will stall at banal imaginings of her sneaking pills from her parents' medicine cabinet, the ones her father pops for his creaky back, the same ones her mother pilfers for her dark moods. Or is it an unwillingness to eat meals at set times, nibbling apples, a water bottle dangling from her fingers as she moves through her day.

The definition of the word 'episode,' however, has undergone a recent transformation. It means something different to the pink-haired woman's generation. Episodes are no longer freestanding stories, where all tension is neatly resolved at their conclusion. One episode bleeds into the next, fitting into a grander narrative. A younger colleague of Deena's pressed her to watch an episode of that popular television show about the women lawyers who are acting silly all the time. She tried, he even tried, but the two of them were lost. Too much history had been missed, and they could not follow. The implication of this change in meaning is obvious. Stolidity, the ability to not allow an unfortunate incident to mark one's character, is no longer a virtue. The people of this generation want their episodes to define them, which is why people are willing to freely discuss personal shortcomings. Mothers boast to other mothers about seeking out specialists to designate their children as hyperactive and easily distracted. Everyone has become a specialist armed with studies and articles serving as sick notes for their inability to fulfill their obligations. This string-theory-crazed civilization has perforated the barriers between public and private. A life rife with hardships and tests is viewed as a life lived. Overcoming alcohol addiction and finding God in the process makes one godly, while born believers, people like Meiselman, possessors of self-control since infancy, are perceived as untested, soft, naïve. They are expected to act embarrassed by the privilege of living a life free of deprivation and degradation. What this means is that if Meiselman wants to learn more about the pink-haired woman, all he has to do is ask.

"Ah, an episode," Meiselman says, sounding as if he can relate, although he is not about to share details of his episode from the transition years, the one involving the photograph of his grandmother in her bathing suit. He does not need her poking fun about the obviousness of hiding it under a mattress. "Well, no wallowing has always been my rule," he continues. "Recognize the misbehavior, write it off as youthful indiscretion, and then dust off the knee patches and get that saddle back on the horse."

Flashing him those same arched eyebrows that accuse him of obtuseness, she says, "My saddle was never off. And it was hardly a youthful indiscretion. It was part of something profound."

Yes, 'profound.' How did Meiselman not incorporate this word into his ramble? This new generation freely picks and chooses whether an episode is profound or immaterial, and they never pick correctly.

Does she spot his skepticism? Why else would she follow "Trust me, its roots," with "Oh, forget it. You don't want to hear it." She relaxes her elbow on the back of her chair and stares across at him. "It's stupid," she says. "I hate talking about it."

He is not ready to point out that her episode has gone from 'profound' to 'stupid' in a matter of seconds. The reversal is an effort to get him to beg. Knowing how this generation believes in openness for openness's sake, he waits.

"Okay, so here it is." She exhales. "One night at dinner my mother's questions and comments wouldn't stop. 'Emily's parents must be shooting themselves for letting her take those art classes last summer.' 'Tilly's father, with the way he dotes on her, will end up slitting his wrists with her going so far from home.' 'Alexi's parents sending her to a state school is abuse, considering she got into two Ivies. They are drowning in money.' The noise became unbearable. I asked her if we could stop talking about my friends, but she kept on. So I muted myself for the rest of the meal. Got her pretty worked up. At breakfast the next morning, I still didn't want to speak, which only made her get noisier." Having told this story many times before, the pink-haired woman's tone is calm and matter-of-fact. She goes on to tell Meiselman how the silence had lasted six months, and how she'd contrived new vows and commitments along the way: veganism, a uniform of all white, a refusal to wash or cut her hair. The behavior terrorized her mother, a tiny woman who spends her days tutoring underprivileged children. But, then, as the pink-haired girl slowly started cracking, her mother turned militantly supportive of her daughter's vows. She stocked the refrigerator with vegan options. Left pads of paper around the house to help her daughter communicate. "She derived great pleasure from my vows," the pink-haired woman explains. "She's a masochist who liked making me her little sadist." The pink-haired woman puts her hand out in the direction of Meiselman's forearm. Without touching him, she adds, "That's my shrink's view."

"Oh, a Dr. Lin?" he asks.

"What? Who? No. Dr. Postman."

The doctor, according to the pink-haired woman's telling, theorized that her parents' subsequent decision to essentially retard their daughter's progress by keeping her at home and in treatment for a year when all of her friends were leaving town for university was an effort to feed the mother's masochism. She had a need to paint her daughter as unwell. She had a need for her to remain ill. Retarding her progress meant she could label her pink-haired daughter as fragile, and a constant source of worry. Periodically, the pink-haired woman recalls a forgotten twist or detail, and she puts out her hand in Meiselman's direction, her fingers fluttering above his forearm in excitement. He keeps his arm stiff.

"When they found out I was doing this play, my mother had my father call Dr. Postman to 'make sure I was up to the challenge.' As if I am making my Broadway debut, and not acting at some shitty playhouse in Rogers Park. What they are doing is setting themselves up for a letdown. Even if I give the performance of a lifetime, they will seize on the cardboard props and Fred's off-cue lighting and the squawking sound system and an audience filled with overly gracious friends and family and will say, 'That sure wasn't Broadway. Why does our daughter set her sights so low?' My mom, at least, will. Who knows where my dad is in all of this? Dr. Postman believes he used to play the role of sadist, but ceded the role to the children over time. Want to hear something else?" she asks excitedly, the tips of her fingers connecting with his arm. His intention is to act boldly as he did with Betsy Ross, but before he can lower his hand for a friendly pat, the pink-haired woman lifts her hand and runs it through her hair, their two hands passing without contact.

She continues to pepper this never-ending account of her 'episode' with the words 'sadistic' and 'masochistic,' words he, until now, had heard only in connection to gruesome dictators and sexual freaks, and that she can utter them with such casualness leaves him staring down into his lap abashed. So sophisticated at such a young age, while he is nearing his middle years unfledged. She has emerged from the mutism with an ability to prattle endlessly, a belief that every word is valuable and worth airing. Whereas, Meiselman, never having gone through such a transition, is ever vigilant of how others will receive his speech, worried his utterances will make him sound either like a know-it-all or a know-nothing. Whenever opening his mouth he agitates over who/whom, was/were, may/might. In most cases, he concludes that for the sake of his reputation he is better off staying quiet. He leaves the most mundane conversations thinking he said too much or too little, wishing he could take a phrase back or drop in a retroactive qualifier or two. Only Deena gets the unstilted, authentic Meiselman, and she does not seem to care for it.

If only he would have had his own episode. If only he had been more maniacal about achieving his few independent pursuits. If only he would have engineered a moment of defiance, and not allowed people to undo his wants with belittling comments.

"And what are you going to do about Shabbos?" his father had responded to Meiselman's desire to major in broadcast journalism. "Friday night and Saturday. Two games right there. Not to mention the holidays, which tend to fall out during the pennant races. What do they need you for?" Followed by that dismissive throw of the hand, like Meiselman was thinking childishly, or not thinking at all. He was not a child. He was eighteen years old and had shown aptitude. Would his transition years have played out differently had he not been cowed by his mother's argument to continue living at home, instead of renting an apartment in Rogers Park? Did she really think he was going to starve and walk around in dirty underwear?

In this relationship with the pink-haired woman, he is as much the mentee as the mentor. If so, does this not call for a change in strategy or, at least, tactics? Being aggressive is not only about an ability to stand up for oneself, a willingness to shout down others and sacrifice whatever stands in the way, but also a readiness to see opportunity, to grab the ram by the horns and wrestle it from the thicket. The pink-haired woman, a woman of this cocksure generation that holds up selfishness as a virtue, can be counted on to excuse his non-action with Mrs. Woolf. Now is the time to act aggressive, stick his neck out, literally, and torpedo his head of curls into the bosom of her overwhelming sweatshirt and confess his inability to unmoor from his mind the wretched image of dead Mrs. Woolf. Guts on the carpet. Crusty blood on my shoe. Then, the question of guilt. Obviously, he would have helped Mrs. Woolf off the floor had she been more explicit about her need for assistance. He is not a mind-reader. But the pink-haired woman will not give him an opening.

"Therapy is cool though," the pink-haired woman continues. "We discovered I was a late talker, apparently a sign of intelligence. Anyway, she—Dr. Postman—has turned this paper into a grand test of whether I can finally break free from this unhealthy dynamic. Personally, I think the test is whether I can finally take out this piercing," she says, flicking the safety pin. "My mother dry-heaved when she saw it. Removing it will ease her pain, which means a loss for her. Understand? Very complicated."

"The hair, at least, will grow out," Meiselman says.

"The hair?" she asks, petting the pink. "I like the hair. The hair stays."

"Well, I like the safety pin."

The pink-haired woman is startled to see the time. Shoving the notebook and play into her bag, she says, "At the playhouse they call me the diva, since I'm the lead and always late. I'm just overscheduled." The soft scrape of the chair pushing back on the carpet rattles Meiselman with panic. Her competence is clear. The paper will get done. Come fall, she will be off to New York University, and she will believe herself too sophisticated to step foot into the New Niles Public Library when she returns home for visits. Here she has provided him with an opportunity to leave behind another umbrella. Without a hint of creepiness, he can ask when the play opens. And even if she were to tell him the date, time, and location of the play, then, what? Would the shock of his presence—front center, a bouquet of pink tulips cradled in his arm—not cause the diva to stammer over her lines? What if opening night conflicts with the Shenkenberg event? She is supposed to come watch him.

The pink-haired woman stops at the end of the bookcase, throws her bag over her shoulder, and says, "Thanks for the help, mister."

He lunges from his seat and cries out to her in a loud whisper that gravels his voice like that of a dying man: "Yes, yes, I will."

* * *

Deena must be tiptoeing. She must assume he is frayed from discovering the old lady's corpse. How else to explain why he is stalled at the door rummaging his underwear-stuffed pants pocket for his house key?

Or she did not pardon last night's episode, did not deem it a spontaneous display of amorousness, and she is blockading herself from him. Removed from his episode-sharing reverie with the pink-haired woman, Meiselman now hears more clearly what Deena was saying on the phone earlier today. She locked the door because she wants a scene, one that will culminate in a confession and apology. That his eyes may have watered while he revealed his plan to acquire a child using his brother's seed he is willing to confess, but nothing more, and nothing about any utterances upon completion.

To postpone any discussion about last night, he must convince her that his discovery of the body is the greater trauma. Coat on, briefcase in hand, he will foggily amble into the kitchen and stumble into his chair at the breakfast table. Unmanageable chills will have him pulling his coat tight around his body. Too frazzled to hear whatever she is saying, he will mumble "sure" to every question. He will not have an appetite for dinner. He will not care to watch the White Sox. Will she need further proof that the discovery has rattled his core? For Deena to bring up what happened last night would be disproportionate, inconsiderate, cold. She will have the sense to wait until after the Shenkenberg event. Time will mute her anger. She may have difficulty recalling what she found troubling about his behavior. She may end up wondering why she did not find it loving.

How easily his confidence is stripped. It weakens when she does not reciprocate his boisterous hello from the foyer. It fully dissolves when she, at the breakfast table, head buried in an open newspaper—Homes—stays silent after he says upon entering the kitchen, "Grim news. I'm sure you saw the police tape across the front door? Unpleasant." The table is not set, and the lasagna is not warming in the oven. Clearly, Deena is laying claim to having endured the greater trauma. Now is not the time to take his seat across the table from her and present his case by unloading the gruesome details. It was like the farmer in the rug had stuck his pitchfork in our neighbor's temple. If he pulls the underwear from his pocket to show her the blood cleaned off his shoe, she may take it as a challenge to present physical proof of her own trauma, send her running upstairs to fish his by-now crusty boxers from underneath the bed. For the time being, he will subordinate his trauma and save the Mrs. Woolf card for later. Instead, he will try softening his wife's despondence through other methods, like crinkling the brown paper bag that holds the dessert treat he picked up on the way home.

But fidgeting with the bag does not manage to pique her curiosity. She straightens the newspaper with a shake of the wrists.

She prefers Israeli salad, so he dices the vegetables. She does not like her food too hot, so he takes the lasagna out of the microwave before the edges turn rubbery. She favors using a salad fork, even for the main course, so he acquiesces to this childish preference when setting the table. Even though they only drink pop on the weekends, he fills her glass with ice and diet pop, which succeeds in breaking her spell, if only to stand and dump the drink into the sink. Refilling the glass with water, she opens her mouth for the first time since his arrival and says, "Can't have caffeine. Want to sleep tonight. Deeply."

At dinner, his recap of the Earth Day event fails to elicit a response. She is playing with her food, scraping the cheese and sauce off each ribbon of pasta, stacking them on the rim of her plate. He mentions having recently read an article about the carbohydrate-free diet craze coming to an end, but she has nothing to add. He had planned on not showing much of an appetite at dinner, as would be expected of someone who saw a dead body earlier in the day, but both parties not eating is morose and will only stiffen her mood.

"Perfect ratio," he says, stuffed cheek, the next bite balanced on his fork. "My mother, if you want me to be honest, drenches it in sauce and skimps on the cheese. And she would never consider splurging for a foreign brand."

Finished scraping the noodles clean, Deena, using her fingers, weeds out the salad's diced red onions.

He has exhausted all other possible conversation topics. The mystery surrounding the letter Betsy Ross is drafting for Ethel is compelling, but he is not about to admit to his own wife that he is not in the know. Plus, he should refrain from mentioning the name Ethel. Now is certainly not the right time to tell his wife about the pink-haired woman. How and when to tell the wife about a budding, innocuous relationship with another woman is always tricky. Shenkenberg, she has made clear, is off-limits.

Deena has nothing to contribute. She mashes the tip of her thumb into a lasagna noodle and then holds the pasta up to the light over the table to examine the impression. Pulling another one from the stack, she crimps her fingers together, presses down and rolls them from side to side, as if taking fingerprints. Looking to flee or wanting to be found?

Finished eating, she does not clear her plate and glass. Yet, she informs him that she is off to watch television and, without a please or thank-you, asks to be brought "whatever is in that brown bag you brought home, as long as it's good."

Two full, smooth, ice-cream-parlor-grade scoops garnished with crushed walnuts he found in a cabinet are deposited into a bowl and brought to his wife in the family room, where she sits with her feet up, the oils from her soles further exfoliating the couch's brown hide. Chocolate ice cream is her favorite, yet she does not make a childish grab for the bowl. With a tilt of the head, she signals for him to set it down on the coffee table.

The woman on television works three jobs and is unable to bring home a living wage. Deena's eyes quickly moisten. If this were any other night, Meiselman might point out the woman's television that hangs in the background—newer, flatter, and larger than the one Deena is watching—and the cases of brand-name pop stacked in the corner of the kitchen, and the brand-name cereals assembled on top of the silver-door refrigerator. Too many teeth is this woman's problem. A second set of incisors descending from her upper gums push out her lip in a snarl. Her chin is bumpy from rampant teeth festering under the surface of the lower gums. The bumps have cost her jobs, so goes another claim. "They told me I'd scare the children," she tells the host, whose teeth are unnaturally white and straight. "The insurance don't recognize this as medical. Cosmetic, they say." The host puts his arm around the woman and, in a soothing hush, tells her he is going to fix this problem.

When the show goes to commercial, Meiselman nudges the bowl of ice cream to the edge of the coffee table. Deena points the remote at the television and turns up the volume. After apologizing for not being able to watch on account of work for the event, Meiselman returns to the kitchen, scatters his notebook and random papers across the breakfast room table, and opens Shenkenberg.

Meiselman does not manage to read more than a page before leaning back in his chair and putting his ear to the wall that divides the kitchen from the family room, hoping to hear evidence of his wife's enjoyment—a spoon clanking the bowl's bottom, a satisfactory moan. But all he hears is the doctor explaining how he will mend the woman. Gums will be incised. Teeth will be extracted. For six months after the surgery she will be an adult in braces.

At the next commercial, Meiselman is back in the family room to check on her progress. Melting is underway, the untouched scoops of ice cream glistening. Deena's self-control is impressive.

"No need to ration," he quips. "Bought an entire pint."

She grabs the bowl off the table and drops it into her lap.

"These shows are awfully eager to show how easily people can reverse misfortune and undo years of wretched living," he says.

"Let me watch," she says, returning the bowl to the coffee table without putting a dent in the scoops.

At one point, Meiselman shouts from his seat in the kitchen, "Bet your ice cream is all soup by now!"

A second later, he hears the spoon dinging the bottom of the bowl, too excessive to be a real spooning. More like a child mashing up food. She asks, "Why don't we get the movie channels?" Asks even though she knows the reason and has made her disagreement with it clear.

"We did the math and decided we do far better renting," he says, still seated, with no interest in carrying out this conversation face-to-face.

"*You* did the math. *You* decided," she answers.

When she inadvertently sins, she forgives herself by making Meiselman write checks to charity. When he sins against her, he is forgiven only if he agrees to up their standard of living. Just as he rips up the checks, he will make commitments he has no intention of fulfilling.

"Tomorrow I'll call the cable company, if you promise me to just enjoy the dessert treat tonight."

"And a DVD player. Other than your parents, we are probably the only people still without one."

"How many movies do you plan on watching?"

With a wall between them he is free to roll his eyes and mimic her. But what if she is rolling her eyes at him? What if she is mocking whatever he says? What if she is doing both at the same time?

"I want options."

The moment to play the Mrs. Woolf card has arrived, because at the next commercial break she will resume negotiations, and agreeing to a DVD player and pay channels will only encourage her to up her demands; new carpeting in the living room, a larger and flatter television in the family room, the stocking of brand cereals and pop, and a sleeker refrigerator. But how does he convincingly convey his trauma if he feels nothing? Encountering death was underwhelming, almost like a familiar feeling. Feels bad for Mrs. Woolf and Cool Paul, of course, he guesses, despite their differences and all that. Does he tell Deena that the smell of the rotting corpse is stuck in his nostrils? Like day-old socks or a blackened banana. Hours after the discovery, he can barely remember the sight, let alone the smell. Whiffing the bloody underwear in his pocket might stimulate a sharper simile, but he can expect a radical upping of demands if he is caught sniffing her drawers. A new house in a different suburb, one without a Meiselman within fifty miles. Sticking his head in the doorway to see whether it is safe to whiff, Meiselman spots the bowl still on the coffee table. They lock eyes. With his head he nods in the direction of the ice cream. She shrugs. He points at the bowl with his finger. She grabs it and holds it in front of her body. Slowly, she lifts the spoon and dips her face forward until the two meet. Lips glazed with ice cream, she inches out her tongue, her face souring the moment she tastes the drop hanging off her lip's peak.

"It doesn't have to mean we've reconciled. I just want you to enjoy."

She stares ahead at the television, eyes steely, and the intensity of her gaze tells him she is deliberating whether now is the time to unload. Her eyes close. She takes a deep breath. Bracing himself for the impending barrage, he retreats into the kitchen and stands stiffly against the wall.

"The ice cream you bought is sugar-free. I can't get it down. I'm sorry."

"For you. Out of consideration for you and your rule of not eating sugar past four, I bought diet."

"It's not a religious thing," she says. "If for once you are going to do something fun, do it right. Why does everything you do have to be...slightly off?"

The doctors are removing the braces and bandages, and Meiselman's curiosity prevents him from returning to his reading. The woman is brought a mirror. "I haven't seen this face since I was a little girl," she cries. The last shot is of her five-year-old boy hugging her leg and saying, "Mommy, you look like a princess."

Meiselman says to Deena, who is wiping the wet corners of her eyes, "You could at least give me a chance to rectify my mistakes, love."

"As much as you...disgust me sometimes, I didn't want to make you feel bad."

Minutes later, the television cuts off. Smells are too difficult to describe, so Meiselman determines to detail the horror of the lady's face. Skin the ashen white of winter's salted streets. Hair caked with blood like a clump of soggy leaves clogging a storm drain.

There are no sounds coming from the other room. Could Shenkenberg have had him so spellbound that he did not hear her exiting through the living room? Doubtful. Even with her featheriness, he would have heard the recoiling of a couch spring, or a footfall. Besides, there is the feeling of someone being nearby. At that moment, the couch creaks. Girding time.

He follows her from the corner of his eye as she enters the kitchen and takes position across the table from him, her hands gripping the chair's headrest, signaling that this will not be a conversation, but an address, most probably a harangue.

"I think you need to think about seeing that doctor again," she says.

He lifts his finger, pulls the notebook closer, and begins writing phony notes: "I still need to find instances of disrepute."

"No," Deena corrects herself. "I demand you go see that doctor."

Still writing, he answers his wife, "What, to be humiliated a third time? The number actually went down the second time. It's not going to happen. At least, not from me."

"Not that...goofball fertility specialist. The shrink you saw before we met. The one you talk about."

This is when having a beard is advantageous. After setting down his pen, he begins munching on his soul patch with his top teeth, a contemplative look that buys him much-needed time, because this is not an ultimatum he anticipated. "For what?" he finally asks.

"For whatever it was you were seeing her for, I guess."

"An unhealthy desire for solitude? We can agree I'm cured of that. And for what happened today, well, people are built to cope with such trauma. In fact, I recently read an article about the evolutionary advantages of squeamish—"

"Just...see her, please. Just make an appointment, and go. If you can't think of things to discuss, I'd be more than willing to accompany you and get the conversation rolling."

"If a week from now it's still festering, if images of the rotting corpse pop into my head at inopportune times, if I still cannot get my sandwich down, I will schedule an appointment. People have witnessed much worse and rebounded. Our soldiers witness worse on a daily basis. Interestingly, the officer at the scene—"

Releasing her hands from the chair, she winds one arm back as if she's about to slap him, but on the forward swing balls her splayed fingers, mid-arc, into a fist that pounds the table. He flinches. "This isn't about what happened today!" she barks. "This is about these last months, or...year, or however long it's been."

Knowing how people's claims of injustice tend to crumble into petty and childish-sounding annoyances when forced to move away from the general, he asks for specifics. "Something prior to this week? Because, admittedly, I've been a bit out of sorts lately with my mounting responsibilities for the Shenkenberg event."

"Okay, okay. Shenkenberg is a perfect example. Why would you call him, when your boss specifically directed you not to?"

"Because such a restriction severely hampers my ability to carry out my duties. Can't even begin thinking about stage layout if I don't know whether the speaker prefers to be standing or sitting. He's very, very short. If given the option, I'm sure he would rather not stand behind a lectern and risk the humiliation of trying to work the complicated mechanics of the microphone stand, especially after someone as tall as me just used it."

"Specifically, specifically, specifically," she says, the word petering out into a tired whisper, "instructed you not to call him directly. But you operate on your own frequency. And, yes, that is what I loved...love about you, that not everything you say and do is calculated to mesh with other people's views of the world. But this is also the problem. You take liberties without ever being aware you are taking them, without ever taking other people and their wants into account. Everything is about whether it's good for you or not good for you. And the crazy thing is that you don't seem to have a good sense of what is actually good for you. For me," she says, "see this doctor. Schedule the appointment. Talk to her about anything. If not..."

As she slogs upstairs, the halts between her feet thumping the stairs makes clear he has failed at conveying his trauma. Not one question about his state. Come morning, will her glumness persist, or will a night of sleep combined with his agreeing to her demand neutralize her mood, and cause her to revert to assaulting him with meaningless anniversaries? Her assessment of him as operating without calculations, of taking liberties, of being inconsiderate could not be more inaccurate. A lifetime spent sublimating. A lifetime spent measuring the decency of every action and word. Now that he is on the verge of a breakthrough, his wife asks him to keep his face into the wind. It is Deena's problem if she does not see where he is headed. Now is not the time to revamp his game plan and tinker with his mechanics. He has to stay the course, finish the so-called novel, and gear up for Sunday night when he will show everyone an unvarnished Meiselman.

Besides, even if he were to agree to Deena's unreasonable demand, calling Dr. Lin is not a matter of dialing a number and working with a receptionist to find a date and time. All calls go directly to the doctor. If she answers in the middle of a session—a practice that greatly annoyed him when he was under her care—how can he succinctly explain the reason behind his resurfacing? Will she assume a relapse has him once again stowing historical photographs of women in bathing suit under his mattress, as if he is not crafty enough to select a new hiding place—say, on top of the bookcases in the basement? If Dr. Lin refuses his request to reenter treatment, should he ask for a referral, whether she recommends a Dr. Postman? He does not even know how much an appointment with the doctor costs. All he knows is that his mother would make comments like, "We pay too much for you to spend the whole time staring at each other," and "A wife is a lot cheaper."

Although it may not be a total waste. They can work on removing from his mind the thought of dead Mrs. Woolf, and its accompanying guilt. Throughout their time together, Dr. Lin was constantly trying to assure him that nothing he said or did could disappoint her.

The doctor's phone number is long forgotten. In the phonebook, a handful of listings for Samantha Lin, two for a Lin, Dr. Samantha. If he accidently calls her private residence instead of her office, however, the doctor will never believe it was unintentional, and will want to spend the entire first session exploring the blunder. Coming up with a thought-provoking opening for their first session, and having additional material on standby, is crucial. This time he will not endure session after session of silence, the doctor throwing out dead-end questions about masturbation, homosexuality, and molestation. Tomorrow, he will have to head next door to his parents' house to look up the number in his mother's Rolodex.

Rabbi J-'s name does not appear in the novel's final pages, so Meiselman closes the book, satisfied he has read enough Shenkenberg, even if he never did locate any indicting passages.

In the living room, he turns to the game. Gload is waiting on deck, meaning Thomas is still out. The Hawk confirms this moments later. The trainer, fearing the cold might worsen the Big Hurt's hamstring, ordered the slugger to watch the game from the clubhouse. Meiselman sets the remote down on the coffee table next to Deena's bowl. An iceberg of the dessert treat floats in its soupy remains, the walnuts like circling driftwood. Wanting Deena to feel regret over rejecting his gesture, he leaves the bowl on the kitchen counter unwashed.

Meiselman is fading.

First date. Went to that World War II movie his parents had been hocking him to see. Spent the first hour of the movie debating whether he was expected to take her hand, a dilemma complicated by an inability to keep his palms dry. Deena had eventually put down her tub of popcorn and pulled Meiselman's hand into her lap. By the end of the movie, her head was resting against his shoulder, the curls of her hair tickling his nostrils. Ate at Dunkin Donuts. She laughed at him for ordering soup, calling him an old man, drilling her fingers into his dimples whenever he smiled. Talked endlessly about her mother. "'My little elf,' my father called her." Friends kept the refrigerator stocked with casseroles and pies for the first few months after her death, until, one day, the shelves were bare. Except for her milk and her father's beers, it would stay bare until Deena learned how to cook at age nine. Fetched him beers from age five. Done with that, thank the Lord, because he was a foolish drunk, she told Meiselman. "At the time I liked it, though. It proved to me how much he missed her."

One Saturday night, in the early stages of his wooing, when gestures rife with extravagance were executed to ensnare and not, as they are now, to recover lost ground, Deena cancelled plans for a movie and dinner on account of having to nurse her flu-stricken father. Meiselman, without telling his mother, pulled a Tupperware of chicken soup from the freezer, and on his way to her apartment stopped at Blockbuster, where he rented *Manhattan*. *Manhattan* because every time Meiselman came to pick up Deena for a movie, George would declare *Manhattan* the greatest he had ever seen, as if he could not understand bothering with any other movie. Could not stop laughing for weeks whenever he saw it. Not Meiselman. His excessive laughter that night was faked.

Soon Deena started expressing a desire to spend more time together on the weekends. He told her she could not be seen driving to his house after sundown on Friday. So she began staying over. Separate rooms, of course. Nervous all Shabbat about her father's ability to manage alone, Deena had Meiselman drive her to Albany Park the moment Shabbat ended.

One week, Deena said on the ride back to Albany Park, "It's fun watching you with your parents at Shabbat dinner. Everyone giving rundowns of their week. Your mother is so invested in you and your job. It's nice. Your dad is funnier than you make him out to be. Was it terrible that I didn't eat any of the orange chicken? Too sweet for me."

“The mistake was telling her you liked the stuffing,” Meiselman said. “Expect stuffing, from now on, every time you sit down at her table.”

“I cannot believe the leanness of this pork,” Deena’s father yelled to them when they entered the apartment. “You got to have some,” he said, holding up a shiny batter-dipped ball to Meiselman.

“He doesn’t eat it,” Deena said. “And I don’t think I’m going to eat it anymore either.”

Occasionally, Meiselman mentioned the Jewish education classes to Deena, but he did not push, because he understood she was still at the young age where the more she felt pushed, the more she’d resist. One night, she revealed she had attended one of the classes the previous day. “The rabbi was cool. Knows a ton of philosophy and has seen every movie.” This was all she was willing to share about the class, even after he pressed for more details, but, again, not pressing too hard because he wanted her to go back. The next week, Deena mentioned a friend. Molly.

Willie Nelson came to town, and Meiselman bought tickets for them and her father. During the intermission Meiselman took off for the bathroom and returned with pop, chocolate bars, and matching concert t-shirts. It was only once he got back to the seats and discovered Deena with her arms wrapped around her father’s waist that he decided the shirts would be for Deena and George. When the show resumed, Deena’s father closed his eyes, tilted his head up to the sky and fiddled his air guitar. Deena grabbed both of Meiselman’s hands, swayed her hips, and whispered into his ear, “You don’t know how kind you are, do you?” and kissed him on the lips. After he kissed her back, she shook her head as if he did not do it right. Collaring him with the crook of her elbow, she kissed him again, her tongue chafing his lips until he parted them. What did it say about her that she was willing to do such things in front of a parent? She pulled back, letting out a giggle. He smiled. Like forceps, her thumb and index finger came at his face and grabbed his dimples. His ability to amuse her had become the essence of the relationship, even though he never thought of humor as the linchpin of his charm. That she found him funny at his fussiest moments was slightly puzzling.

At a Friday night dinner—Deena not present—Meiselman asked his parents about procuring an engagement ring. Meiselman's father said to his wife across the table, "Mother wanted him to have her ring." 'Mother' meaning *his* mother. He turned to Meiselman and asked, "Sound good?"

Before Meiselman could answer, his mother broke in with, "Sounds dreadful. Why would he want your mother's dusty, discolored ring?" Facing Meiselman, she added, "We'll help you buy a ring as nice as the one your brother bought." Both Meiselman and his mother caught his father's eyes widening with dread. "As nice," his mother reiterated.

"A perfectly good ring, just sitting in a safe deposit box," his father burbled, cheeks full of chicken, head down, fork and knife dicing a chicken breast.

"She didn't leave a penny to your children. Gave it all to your brother's little *shgutzim*."

"Because she intended for the boys to have the jewelry."

"Money would have been fine, you should have told her. Could have gone and bought his own damn ring." She imposed a silence on the table that only she had the audacity to break. "I remember that ring. Hi-de-ous." Meiselman, unable to eat through this discussion, crossed his legs, curled forward and tapped the tines of his fork against his uneaten stuffing. "It was hideous then, it's more hideous now, I bet," his mother continued. She looked at Meiselman and said, "Your grandfather had the classiest, simplest taste. Looked like Steve McQueen. And your grandmother browbeat him into buying some gaudy yellow piece of crap. A lifetime of that. I see how Daisy dresses. In those little jeans and cute t-shirts. Never globs on the make-up. Doesn't fuss with her curls."

"Okay, okay," his father said. "I'll call my ring guy, and we'll go Sunday."

Why did it fall on Meiselman to normalize the mood? Fortunately, he had been sitting on an announcement for weeks.

"From now on Daisy wants to be called Deena," he said.

His father intensified his eating, stooping closer to the plate, sticking all the foods with his fork.

"Oh?" his mother asked.

"Yes, it's her Hebrew name."

"So, we won't call her Daisy anymore," his mother said.

At the end of the table, his father shrugged and said, "Daisy was kind of fun." Then Meiselman's mother shot him a look, forcing him to add, "But Deena is fine. Hey, whatever she wants. Whatever keeps her happy."

A postscript to the ring story:

Deena no longer wears her ring to work because it jabs and slices the bodies of her patients, although the compliments she gets on the ring's size fills him with pride, even if he did not contribute one cent to its purchase. Legally, his father is more connected to the ring than Meiselman.

A postscript to the postscript of this entire in-and-out-of-sleep story:

The practice of drilling his dimples was discontinued sometime in the past couple of years, proving that on a whim, people can decide they no longer find something charming.

Friday

"Dad gummit!"

The achy, clenched cry of White Sox announcer Ken "The Hawk" Harrelson wakes a recumbent Meiselman from his sofa-chair stupor. Keen on maximizing his misery, Meiselman moves to the couch, removes his purple button-down, and drapes it over his undershirted body before falling back to sleep. The announcer's Southern drawl—Georgia with a hint of South Carolina—is at its heaviest whenever uttering one of his trademark Hawkisms, which rouse Meiselman, who responds each time by adjusting himself into an even more miserable position.

"Stretch, stretch. You can put it on the board, yes!" And Meiselman moves to the floor, flattens his legs, and knocks his head back against the couch cushion.

"A duck snort to center puts runners on the corners." And Meiselman turns up the television's volume several bars. The irony. Finally able to sleep without fear of Mrs. Woolf's nighttime noises and he is busy manufacturing his own hellish disturbances. A question worth exploring if he ends up scheduling an appointment with...

"Come on, go foul, go foul, mercy!" and Meiselman flicks on the sleek ceiling fixture above the television, the one he and Deena rarely turn on because its bulbs' concentrated wattage turns the screen into a mirror.

"Can of corn, and we are scoreless after one." A replay of the game is airing, and all Meiselman can do to enhance his misery, at this point, is to put his shoes back on.

"Come on, stay fair," and Meiselman opens his eyes to a cement gray light dully penetrating the family room through the picture window above the couch. A third replay of the game is underway. In minutes, Deena's alarm will sound, so he musses his hair and brings his knees up to his body as if fighting the cold because it should be that when his wife comes downstairs and discovers light and sound mercilessly bombarding her husband's body she will feel remorse over not having sufficiently appreciated the magnitude of the trauma he endured yesterday. Is there no greater indication of a devastated mind, a life in disarray, than a man not sleeping in his own bed? The exception to the rules of not touching during a woman's period is when the husband is ill and his wife is required to care for him. Or does he have it backward, and it is when the wife is ailing and the husband's support is needed? One is permitted, one is forbidden. One is trusted to not become greedy, one is not...

The front door slams to a close, and he does not know whether Deena noticed his state of misery before leaving the house. But there is a note taped to the coffee maker: "No dinner tonight at your parents. Going to sleep early. You go. Call your doctor. Then we will talk." Today's note is unambiguous. You could have been strapped to a chair in front of the television with your eyelids taped open, and I still would not have engaged you because first you must call Dr. Lin. Meanwhile, the demand to tell his mother Deena will not be joining them for Friday night dinner is as challenging as calling the doctor. On Friday you are telling me this, he can already hear his mother answering. I would've made tongue had I known she wasn't coming.

Standing at the bottom of the staircase and looking up to the second floor, he knows it will require energy he simply does not have today, so he settles for performing his morning ablutions in the downstairs bathroom. Fondling his armpit hair, he catches a hint of something. Nothing overly offensive, but still he pumps three sprays of bathroom freshener into the air, extends his arms, and steps into its cloud. Follows this with an additional pump into the center of his purple button-down. He slimes his beard, neck, and face with liquid hand soap, lathers, and washes off with warm water. Wet hands comb his curls. Meiselman uses his lengthy pinky fingernail to scrape the plaque off his teeth, and then pops one of Mrs. Woolf's peppermint candies into his mouth. He is not a mind reader!

* * *

Meiselman easily locates the article selected by the pink-haired woman, and just as he begins reassessing his state, questioning whether the lethargy is lifting and giving way to a reentering of the zone, a steady clacking commandeers his attention. It sounds as though something is failing to catch, a problem with the air system above. He cannot squander his morning on maintenance issues, so he ignores the disturbance and plods ahead, highlighting the entire article and copying it onto a new, blank document.

Initially, the pink-haired woman rejected Meiselman's artful attempt at stashing another umbrella. "I can do my own papers fine, thank you," she responded in a deliciously dry voice that signaled she was not wholly outraged by the proposal. Inching toward her, he sowed her with doubt, suggesting her refusal was an act of self-sabotage. "Every day, every waking moment, we torpedo potential paths to redemption," he said, using a line culled from the rabbi's Pesach sermon weeks ago.

"You doing the paper for me? How does that make sense? It's weird."

"It makes plenty of sense. We are a library. This is what we do. What's the catch, what's the cost? you're asking. No catch, no cost." Unable to persuade her, he changed his approach. "Think of the paper as notes."

Stepping toward him, she reached out and pulled from the shelves a thin blue hardcover whose spine was sheared and dangling by its last threads. She examined its cover, *President William McKinley: Unfinished Business*. Opening the book, she dipped her face, eyes closed, and inhaled deeply. Lifting her head, she said, "Love that musty smell," before flipping to pages of black and white photographs. "Serious chin dimple on the dude," she said, studying a portrait of the former president. "What is it with eyebrows and presidents?" She is humming an unfamiliar tune as she studies more of the pictures. "Wife had a funky do." She abruptly slammed the book shut, the musty smell wafting toward Meiselman. "Not a paper," she said. "Notes." After handing him her notes, she rested the tips of her fingers on his forearm and said, "Good notes are so what I need."

The touching made him believe she was speaking euphemistically.

Rewriting the original article, *Assuming the Moral Burden: Victimhood as Nihilism in Julius Caesar* by Tad, George, into a more straightforward English, one that mirrors the wry, frank attitude of the pink-haired woman, is the challenge. For example, she would never write:

> *The scholar Brutus, a man deaf to his wife's implorations and inflictions, is unable to appreciate the pettiness of Cassius's denunciation of Caesar as a man too physically*

wretched to lead. Moreover, he is sympathetic to the transparently self-serving rationalization for the assassination introduced shortly thereafter. By offering dubious moral arguments, Cassius hopes to force the vacillating Brutus into a torturous state of moral uncertainty. The conspirators will use the dubiousness of the eventual verdict to recast themselves as the victims, the helpless souls forced to act against Caesar.

The Meiselman rewrite leaves the paragraph mostly unchanged, except "vacillating" becomes "dithering," "torturous" becomes "ungodly."

The clacking noise in the background is getting louder, dividing his attention and forcing him to work faster. It is not coming from the vents, but the hallway. Turning back to the monitor he becomes less certain and thinks maybe it is coming from beneath the floor.

Shaggy-brained and unable to carry thoughts to completion, Meiselman is forced to copy full paragraphs of the article without changing a word.

The tyrant argues to his victims that he was left with little choice. Undoubtedly, he did have a choice, yet in this framing, the aggressor turns victim. Simultaneously, the victim is tagged the aggressor. The tyrant will talk of a "forced hand" as if there was a true instance of violence perpetrated by the victim against the aggressor.

There is a problem of length. The article Meiselman is using for guidance is only five pages long. Meiselman, therefore, expands all passages cited in the article. He also incorporates the pink-haired woman's notes word-for-word:

Metellus Cimber, who has the clearest reason to kill Caesar, turns the assassination into joke. See recruitment of Cicero. Metellus Cimber is the ultimate cynic. Does not care about liberty or dictatorships. Exposes the dishonesty of the entire scheme. Not even present for the assassination.

Fortunately, Metellus Cimber does not have many lines, and it takes little effort to find the relevant dialogue concerning the recruitment of Cicero, which Meiselman tacks onto the end of the paragraph:

O, let us have him, for his silver hairs
Will purchase us a good opinion,
And buy men's voices to commend our deeds.
It shall be said his judgment ruled our hands.
Our youths and wildness shall no whit appear,
But all be buried in his gravity.

The sound is getting louder, suggesting an approach. Too light and too far apart to be heels. Besides, Ethel's stride is vicious. A sudden flash of movement out in the hallway sends Meiselman hunkering behind his desk. When he lifts his head back up for a peek, he identifies the umbrella swinging forward with Mitchell, a step behind. The underling plants himself in the doorway to Ethel's office, his back to Meiselman. Ethel's office lights are off and the boss is out, yet Mitchell stays rooted, even after Meiselman calls out to him. Just as Meiselman presses the knuckles of his fists down on the desk to lean forward and yell a little louder, Mitchell stabs his umbrella into the linoleum floor and pivots. In his other hand, a sky-blue, tulip-shaped mug.

"Thought I heard someone calling my name. You've snapped me from the throes of a most exciting, yet terrifying reverie," Mitchell teases. "A delight to see you here catching the worm by the scruff of its neck."

"Worm or no worm," Meiselman says to Mitchell, "I'm here at this time every morning. Eight-fifteen at the latest. Didn't you see my car in the lot?" Have the underlings not noticed? To think of all the wasted hours. Could have used the time to pursue a hobby, like tennis or golf. Could have engaged in Torah study. Although those black hatters at the yeshiva would have insisted on studying the Talmud, when the Prophets are what interest Meiselman. Meiselman points to the mug in Mitchell's hand. "The coffee you are drinking. That's me."

"This, my friend, is not the breakroom battery acid you all drink," Mitchell says, sinking his nose into his mug. "Apple-spice rooibos. Notes of cinnamon and clove. Sweet, savory balance. Let me know if you want to try some. A mutiny is afoot, you should know. I have June and Ada drinking my tea. Still working on Betsy. Jerry, as you probably know, doesn't touch caffeine. A religious insistence."

"Tea is too weak for my American blood," Meiselman says.

"Actually, rooibos is not a true tea—"

"Great Sox game last night." If forced to converse with Mitchell, better it is about baseball and not hot beverages. "Winning games without Frank is a good sign." Meiselman shuffles the pink-haired woman's notes on his desk and says, "Must get back to it. Filling in for Ethel."

"That's what they tell me," Mitchell answers. "Just got off the phone with her."

"You did?"

"Briefly. The medicine is making her loopy. Forgot why she was calling me."

Meiselman does not want to suggest the obvious, that she meant to call *him*, and not Mitchell. This encounter is turning meandering. Keeping his eyes buried in the pink-haired woman's notes, he hopes Mitchell will eventually take the hint. But the underling stands in the doorway staring, even after Meiselman lets out several loud sighs.

"Been meaning to tell you," Mitchell finally says. "Managing to do fine work without Ethel around."

"Don't think I haven't noticed," Meiselman answers, keeping his head down.

"Noticed what?" Mitchell asks.

"The fine work," Meiselman answers.

"Let's keep it up," Mitchell says.

After deciding to use the article's concluding sentence in full—"Any perception of arbitrariness undermines the institutions of justice used to redress narratives of victimization, turning the citizenry into the true victims."—Meiselman prints out the paper with the reworked title: "Julius Caesar: A Victim at Every Turn."

* * *

New Niles Village Hall faces the library from the opposite end of the football-field size parking lot. Built between the World Wars, the village's seat of government, with its red brick façade, gold cupola, and four white wooden columns girding the main entrance, is designed to emulate Independence Hall in Philadelphia. Meiselman has never visited Philadelphia, and only knows this detail as part of the spiel he delivers to distinguished library guests. Across the street from the well-landscaped and heavily flowered grounds of the two-story building, a one-screen movie theater decays at the corner. Plywood panels shutter the gilded gold entrance and ticket booth. Ivy climbs the walls' soot-stained bricks, like hands trying to pull the structure underground. Its marquee advertises leasing information.

This minor blight is quickly forgotten when one turns the corner and steps off the theater's mossy sidewalk and onto the red brick walkway of the recently consecrated Historic Street of New Niles. To mark its seventy-fifth anniversary, the village overlaid the facades of the detached shops on both sides of the street with crimson brick plating. In addition, the village compelled the storeowners to erect matching awnings. On the sidewalk, nursing trees are anchored to dirt plots, and parking meters gleam at the heads of diagonal spots, many of which are vacant. Cast iron, acorn-shaped streetlamps surely light the street in a custard yellow haze at night, although Meiselman has no way of knowing, since despite his position at the library and his family's history in the village, he rarely travels this revamped road with its twenty-mile-an-hour speed limit and dusty mom-and-pop shops like A1 Dry Cleaners and StationHarry's.

At the end of Historic Street of New Niles, before the road forks to the left, sits Cracowaia Bakery, a squat, flat-roofed structure. A sun-drained blue tablecloth lines its display window. Under a sagging string of bare bulbs, an array of plastic birthday cakes—yellowed frosting and chipped pink flowers—rest on cake stands that have pearls and naked baby angels beading the rims. Entering the narrow bakery, one is struck, literally, by a poorly positioned support beam. Handwritten advertisements for music lessons and tutoring and weathered campaign posters—Mayor Cardinal died in office when Meiselman was a boy—plaster the obstructing pillar, which blocks the meager sunlight coming through the door and its transom window. For light, the bakery relies on a low-hanging chandelier of wax-dripped electric tapers. Four tables of slightly different rectangular dimensions line the wall, their tabletops varying shades of brown. Only two of the tables have sugar dispensers. Around each table are four chairs taken from different sets. Some cushioned, others not. All sixteen seats are unoccupied, and it is a little before ten o'clock in the morning.

Ethel believes the bakery's disrepair and decrepitude are evidence of its charm, authenticity, and quality, similar to how young people shop at secondhand stores once reserved for immigrants and indigents.

Sitting cross-legged on a stool behind the display case is a black-haired, ponytailed woman holding a paperback up to her face. Her child-sized t-shirt exposes a stomach that stretches in a swirl around a diamond-plugged bellybutton. She glares at him over the top of the book before turning the page. On the book's cover a skyscraper burns and a tuxedoed super-agent, gun in hand, pulls a chesty blonde in a ball gown and pearls to safety. The book is not in English. A throat clearing or a knock on the display case glass will not push this worker into action.

The two-tiered display case is bare except for three sheets of baklava at the end closest to him, a stick of butter and carton of milk on the bottom shelf in the middle, and three frosted birthday cakes at the far end, one of them black with gold flowers, a male figure skater in a black tuxedo pitched into its middle.

The woman behind the counter whips her head to the side, yells in a foreign tongue, and is back to her reading by the time the response comes from the kitchen doorway. She is most probably a family member foisted on the baker Paprocki by an overseas relative. Presumably the baker saw her sourness and did not trust her to wait on customers, so he positioned her at the front like a shopkeeper's bell, or a junkyard dog.

Seconds later, a simpering, red-cheeked Stanislaw Paprocki emerges from the back wringing his hands. He covers Meiselman's hand in a two-handed shake, the salute of the innately warm. Meiselman's firm handshake falls limp to this two-handed grip.

The baker is the type of man who constantly fusses over his appearance; cordovan-dyed hair slicked back from a prominent widow's peak; a pencil-thin moustache dyed the same color breaking bald across his philtrum; modestly capped teeth. Skin-tenderizing oil glistens his face and makes him look no older than seventy. Despite working with flour, the baker has no qualms about wearing brown dress slacks and brown loafers of a reptilian skin. People like the baker, who are total in their fussiness, inevitably end up misfiring. For example, his weight is well below its set point, and his oval head pops like a hot air balloon from the buttoned up collar of his purple, silk shirt. Coloring only the center of his eyebrows, and not touching up the unruly, white ends that curl forward like breaking waves is another misfire.

Still locked in the handshake, the baker massages the top of Meiselman's hand with his thumb, a lack of recognition in his glassy eyes, which are roving, first up to the ceiling, and then over to the woman behind the counter. "A doll," Ethel proclaims whenever the baker's name is brought up. Meiselman reintroduces himself and states the reason for his visit.

"Yes, yes, but, of course," Stanislaw Paprocki says, releasing Meiselman's hand. "Sunday, Sunday, you say?" He pulls a folded handwritten calendar from his back pocket. "Where do I find the Sunday?" he sings, finger moving across the boxes, his thick accent a stumbling block to the mellifluousness he strives to achieve. Locating the box for this coming Sunday, he stabs at it. It is empty, and Meiselman's heart sinks. Messing up the food would be unpardonable, a far greater sin in the eyes of Ethel than not assembling a pool, or contacting Shenkenberg. The baker returns the calendar to his pants, claps his hands together and says, "Most excellent." Meiselman opens his mouth, ready to ask for some reassurance, but Paprocki spins him around by the elbow, escorts him to the table closest to the door and pulls a chair facing the entrance, but it wobbles, so he swaps it out for a different chair, which he deems sufficiently stable, even though it too wobbles.

"Everything will be perfect," Paprocki says, his palm cradling Meiselman's neck. "Relax, my friend." Speaking now in a whisper, his fingers manipulate the vertebrae at the top of Meiselman's spine. His other hand is brought in and soon he is giving a full massage. Meiselman's head lolls.

The type of support he has been searching for all week, as if the baker looked in his customer's face and saw a man splitting at the seams, everything turning shaky, a man who has seen things he should not have seen, a man dealing with matters beyond his scope, a man taking liberties he would not normally have taken. Paprocki's fingers dig deeper, and foreseeing how chills may give way to a blubbery breakdown, Meiselman stiffens and begins pulling his materials from his bag, strewing them across the table. Tightening his voice, Meiselman babbles details about the order for Sunday night, hoping his shift in tone will repel a particularly disburdening thumb knuckle to his lower back. He has come for a meeting with a student, he tries explaining, but the pleasure of this touching is muddling his thoughts. Paprocki cuts him off and says, "I go now and finish my work, yes?" which comes as mild disappointment to Meiselman since nobody, not even his wife, has worked on him like this in some time.

"Remind me just how many people I must bake for," Paprocki says.

The fear of failing Ethel must have triggered a particularly despairing look, because the baker's mercy comes fast, his face brightening maniacally, a cackle emerging from the back of his throat. “You think I am old man who remembers nothing?” he asks. Eager to escalate the hilarity, he drills his index finger into Meiselman’s dimple, and then when Meiselman pulls back, the baker’s finger drops and finds his stomach. Meiselman smiles at the baker, hoping this is the climax Paprocki is after, but this encourages the baker to bring in his middle finger to join the ribbing, and soon he is employing a scissoring motion against the taut skin of Meiselman’s stomach. It tickles Meiselman and forces him to fend off uncomfortable giggles by rotating away his body and munching the insides of his cheeks. The baker will not let up, and the scissors move across Meiselman’s body until they find an opening between the shirt buttons. The baker’s fingers enter and begin snipping at Meiselman’s two-day-old undershirt.

The touching of the baker Paprocki is seemingly unoffending, the hijinks of a man who relishes playing fun uncle to the world, a man who will not fold until Meiselman literally folds with a squirming giggle. Meiselman is prepared to give the man what he wants. They are, after all, depending on him for Sunday night. As Meiselman’s body buckles from a painfully, ticklish poke under the ribs, he notices the woman behind the counter is no longer shielding her face with the book, but watching, eager to see whether her boss’s latest victim will submit. Did the baker ever try his tickling shtick on her? She does not seem likely to crack.

For Ethel, for the library, he lets out a shriek, higher pitched and longer lasting than he would have liked, and the accompanying squirm is gawky, leaving him looking, no doubt, like a slobbering sissy who flails his arms as the schoolyard bully tickles his face with a feather plucked from a dead bird found next to the swings. Bored by the unremarkable way this touching has ended, or simply disappointed in witnessing another man easily folding, the woman behind the counter returns to her book. Paprocki smacks Meiselman’s back before retiring to the kitchen.

And what does Meiselman receive for enduring the teasing like a good nephew?

Treats, lots of treats.

"Kotek, Kotek," Paprocki croons from the kitchen, seconds later. It takes several more calls of her name before she puts the book face-down on the display case and heads to her boss. The conversation is heated and brief. Returning, she picks up the book before planting herself in front of the industrial coffee machine, the establishment's only untarnished object. Buttons click, levers turn, steam jets. Then, some dripping and knocking. All Meiselman can see from his seat is that this Kotek adeptly executes every step with her face buried in the book.

Why the sourness? he wants to ask her. We are not so different. I come from immigrants, too. His mother tells stories of Grandma Numi—PopPop's mother— peddling soap and sewing kits by horse and buggy across the American South while teaching herself optometry. Her husband—PopPop's father—never recovered from a horse kick to the head. Meiselman's father's side came from Lithuania. Sons of rabbis. Real estate.

Kotek is on her way to serve him, and not only has he never had coffee out of a glass coffee mug—shaped like a tulip, dainty handle on the side—but Meiselman has never had one of these fancy coffee drinks with the milk foam on top. Out of politeness, he refuses the offering, but, thankfully, she does not listen. Explain to me the science behind the separation's evenness, he wants to ask Kotek, but by the time he looks up she is back up on her stool with the book.

"Kotek, Kotek," the baker's voice calls out again.

This time when he returns from the back, she slides open the display case and begins dishing baklava onto a dinner plate, all while continuing to read. At one point, she is balancing a piece on the spatula, hanging it in midair as she finishes what must be an especially thrilling passage. If only Shenkenberg could have turned the reading of his book into a compulsion for Meiselman. Maybe Meiselman would have begged off his mother and her concern for his flooding lot. Maybe he would have suggested to Cool Paul that he call Cousin Eddie out in Schaumburg. Maybe Mrs. Woolf would still be alive.

Meiselman knows where this plate of baklava is headed. Ethel's preferred caterer wants him to taste the treyf fare for Sunday night, sign off on it. On Sunday, God tested Meiselman by placing Betsy Ross's chocolates in front of him, and he failed the test. God may still be deciding how the Shenkenberg event will unfold and has, in an act of compassion, dismissed the results of the first test, exacting minor punishment in the form of involving him in the fiasco of Mrs. Woolf's passing. The baklava headed his way is God's make-up test. Same test, but Meiselman now has the answers. Obviously, Meiselman does not believe God is directly involved in the affairs of the lowly servant Meiselman, but, maybe he has outsourced the matter to his lieutenant, the naked baby angel in charge of the American Midwest.

But how will Meiselman explain to this misanthropic immigrant that religious dietary restrictions prevent him from tasting the treats? Moreover, baklava is his absolute favorite. Looking over to the display case, he notes that the butter and milk are standard kosher brands. Besides, he can already see the tip of his tongue teasing the beads of honey on the pastry's surface. He can feel the honey-drenched bottom of the baklava pillowing his bottom lip, the phyllo dough crackling as he bites down, pistachio grounds rolling over his tongue and wedging between his teeth, the excessive honey burning his throat. None of his imaginings disappoint. Flakes of phyllo scatter the tabletop, and he uses his sticky fingertip to snatch them up. Then he licks the honey ringing his fingers, tongue flicking until all the stick is off. How can he not imagine the pleasure of licking it off a woman's body? With peanut butter, also a favorite, he does not have this desire, its dryness potentially fatiguing. Would Deena find such a request creepy? Should a man not be able to broach such a topic with his wife?

Does he honestly expect he will saunter into Dr. Lin's office armed with a newfound candidness? If this is the first issue raised, she will assume sexual dysfunction is the reason for his return. She will connect it to his and Deena's problem conceiving. Questions of homosexuality are always raised in these situations. In addition, it may be jarring to open with an issue of marital discord when the doctor does not even know that her former patient ultimately found his soulmate. At the time of his engagement, his mother wanted him to call Dr. Lin to share the good news, insisting the doctor would derive great professional satisfaction, but Meiselman did not see the point.

"He tells me to tell you, 'Fresh,'" Kotek says, disrupting his eating, dropping a new plate of cookies down on the table in front of him.

The still warm and soft *hamentaschen*, a pastry that until this very moment Meiselman thought was known only to Jews, are filled with honey-laced walnuts and a spice he cannot identify, and Meiselman becomes concerned about the food for the event, because how much honey and nuts can people eat? Also, on the plate are the more traditional *hamentaschen* flavors of poppyseed and prune. This gratuitous service is atypical in Meiselman's life, leading him to imagine the possibility of Cracowaia Bakery becoming his place. Instead of reading the papers at home, he might scarf his oatmeal, peck Deena on the forehead, and drive to the Historic Street of New Niles for baklava and fancy coffee before work. Make this his table. Oh, Kotek. Refill, please.

She is two minutes late, possibly stalled in her car, debating whether acceptance of the paper represents a step forward or backward. A future psychological assessment of this decision could go either way. If Meiselman's authorship of the paper goes undetected and the pink-haired women graduates, Dr. Postman will hail her patient for liberating herself from the stranglehold of her mother's masochism. Cheating is subjective, Dr. Postman will reassure her. Or the professor, with little analysis, will surmise the paper is not the work of a community college student, and while they may not publicly humiliate the pink-haired woman by caning her bottomless bottom in front of the N2C2 student body, the pink-haired woman might as well retire her New York University sweatshirt to a bottom drawer, a memento from a self-sabotaged life. Don't beat yourself up, Dr. Postman will attempt to calm her. The desire to regress is in all of us.

Is the charcoal suit and white silk blouse for him? Today she walks with poise, her ample breasts more pronounced without the sweatshirt. What about the chopsticks holding together a sloppily knotted bun, and the round wired-framed glasses that obscure the safety pin in the eyebrow? Are the alterations tied to the regrets mentioned during yesterday's conversation? Occasionally, Meiselman would come downstairs to find his mother dressed in a skirt suit, wearing more lipstick and blush than usual, essential cards, bills, and keys transferred to a flat purse. A downtown appointment was always the reason given. Generally, the dentist.

She swings a leather knapsack at her side. Reaching the table, she flings it onto a chair, her tongue simultaneously falling out of her mouth. Exhaustion? Disgust?

"I said we were meeting at a bakery, not a downtown restaurant," Meiselman quips, but she does not get the reference, forcing him to point. "Your suit."

"Job interview." This woman who hears every question as an invitation to share adds, "My mother insists I find a summer job to 'pay for school.' As if the two thousand dollars I make temping will make a dent in the thirty-thousand or whatever that NYU costs."

Meiselman considers taking the tack of presenting himself a bountiful man, like his brother and father, men who order excessive amounts of appetizers, never looking at the prices, men who have the gumption to order for others without asking. Some women find such boldness nurturing. Ethel is not this type of woman. Neither is Deena. His mother is certainly not this type. He is not ready to discover whether the pink-haired woman stands apart from the other women in his life.

"Let's get you something to drink," he says. "They treat me here like I'm the president," he says. Lowering his voice, he adds, "With the business I give them, they should."

He manages to get Kotek's attention on the first snap.

Ordering water would come as a disappointment, a bashfulness indicating they are barely more than acquaintances. Pop, especially flavored, like orange, would also be a letdown, because he is done thinking of her as vernal. Juice is fine as long as it is not apple. Diet pop would reinforce his new view of her as sophisticated. She orders an espresso and comments, "I haven't slept in days." At her age, he had never heard of espresso, and, other than knowing it is potent, he is still not entirely sure of what it is.

"Make that two," Meiselman says to Kotek. Turning to the pink-haired woman, he says, "This is not doing the trick," he says, lifting the drained glass, deflated white froth begriming its rim.

"Not much of a nut fan," she says, waving off his offer of baklava.

She snags a prune hamentaschen—very sophisticated choice—and nibbles at each corner until she reaches the filling. She sets it down and asks, "Don't they have anything chocolate around here?"

Is she a woman like Deena whose behavior constantly alternates between adult and child?

"Madame Ethel," the baker bellows from the kitchen entranceway. "Here in the time to taste a most wonderful treat." Paprocki approaches, plate held high over his shoulder, his free hand moving like a conductor waving a baton.

The pink-haired woman titters from the flamboyant greeting, not catching the baker's misidentification.

"You have outdone yourself, Stanislaw," Meiselman says.

"Now the man smiles like a little child." The baker dangles a crooked finger in front of the pink-haired woman's face and asks, "You also smile?" Her apprehensive face breaks into delight when he pokes the tip of her nose.

"*Widelac. Dwa,*" Paprocki barks at Kotek over his shoulder. Setting a platter of cheesecake down on the table, he says, "Only the best for Madame Ethel."

Kotek brings two forks to the table, but not another plate. Forced to share with the pink-haired woman, now is certainly not the time to fret over the cheesecake's kosherness. He is eager to get to the sharing, but the baker feels the need to explain the obvious. "This is a plain. This is a strawberry. This is a chocolate, chocolate swirl." The baker must have noticed the pink-haired woman lighting up at the mention of the word "chocolate," because he again dings the tip of her nose and says, "My Madame Ethel likes the chocolate, chocolate, yes?"

Properly holding a fork, which cannot be said of most adults, she breaks off a piece of chocolate, chocolate that is too big and when she brings it to her mouth the edges break off against the corner of her lips and trickle onto the plate. Chocolate, chocolate would not have been Meiselman's first choice.

"Shucks," he says. "Just the flavor I wanted."

"Sorry," she says, mouth stuffed, fingers covering her cheesecake-smeared lips. She turns the plate so Meiselman can take from the chocolate, chocolate. He uses the back of his fork to pick up her fallen crumbs.

The timing of his reach for a second bite is perfect, but just as the tines of their forks are about to collide and, hopefully, tangle, Stanislaw grabs hold of the pink-haired woman's wrist and redirects her to the strawberry. The baker points to the espresso, says, "Together," clenching his fist. After complying with the baker's request, she sets down her tiny cup, covers her stomach and says, "So good. This is, like, the greatest bakery ever. My mom buys the crap from the Jewel? Probably to punish herself, I swear."

"You treat me like czar, Stanislaw," Meiselman says.

"Sunday," Paprocki says, counting off with his fingers, "I bring the baklava, the hamentaschen, the cheesecake the plain, the cheesecake the chocolate, chocolate swirl, the cheesecake the strawberry." Then, his voice rising, he sticks a finger in the air and says, "For one thousand people."

By this point Meiselman is sure the man is teasing, but he is unprepared for the baker using the joke as a setup for the resumption of his silly uncle routine, this time for the benefit of the pink-haired woman, and he is caught off guard as the baker's finger plunges into his side, right above the hipbone, sending Meiselman sliding off his seat.

"You forget I am joke man?" The poking progresses into more scissoring across Meiselman's stomach. Meiselman restrains his laughter by keeping his lips sealed, bursts of air pumping from his nose. "See, now you smile," the baker says. "You are man who has beard to hide smile and sadness, but beard cannot hide smile from the baker Paprocki. Why you hide smile? You have nice smile for the girls. No, Madame Ethel?"

"Very nice," the pink-haired woman says.

"And the fruit, Stanislaw," Meiselman says, trying to gain control over his increasing need to giggle. "Don't forget the fruit."

"The fruit I wait to pick morning of party." The baker pulls his hands back from Meiselman and raises them over his head, as if picking fruit from a tree. He lets out a laugh and Meiselman thinks he is now safe to join the laughter around the table. Catching Meiselman off guard, Paprocki's hands dive and grab fistfuls of Meiselman's stomach.

Adding a woman to the equation brings out the worst in some men. Rav Fruman forbidding Meiselman to touch Deena, Shenkenberg asking Ethel not to have to deal with Meiselman. Meiselman was willing to giggle in front of Kotek for Ethel and the library. In front of the pink-haired woman, his mentee-slash-mentor, however, is asking too much.

"And the trayayayaya—" Meiselman is practically off his chair.

Regrettably, the pink-haired woman is enjoying the baker's tormenting. Earlier in the week he would have anticipated a juvenile laugh, crimped hand in front of the mouth bottling nervous squeals. But she has the laugh of a woman, the kind that takes over the entire face, nose scrunching, eyes moistening, upper lip lifting, exposing teeth and gums from molar to molar. The laugh's agreeableness encourages him to feed it further. What stops him is the uncertainty of whether she would ultimately find it endearing or foolish that a man in his mid-thirties can be made to look like a spasmodic child. All of this dodging of Paprocki's grapple has loosened the tails of his purple dress shirt and an untied shoelace slaps the floor. Meanwhile, the pink-haired woman's laugh is gaining strength. Even Kotek appears amused. Right at the moment when Meiselman is about to turn either spastic or impetuous, the sound of bells nimbly ringing the tune of "Three Blind Mice" diverts everyone's attention away from the proceedings and onto the pink-haired woman, who is trawling through her backpack.

Finger corking her ear, she takes the call away from the table. She stands in front of the door, her back to the two men. The baker disentangles his hands from Meiselman's ribcage and folds them in front of his body. Meiselman busies himself with his notebook, occasionally shaking his head in dissatisfaction, all the while trying to listen in on the pink-haired woman's conversation. She covers the receiver, looks over her shoulder at Meiselman and mouths "sorry," a loose, serpentine pink strand of hair slicing her eye. How could he ever have called her girl?

The moment the call ends, the baker's hands descend and attack Meiselman's stomach, but Meiselman is too preoccupied to feel the tickle. The pink-haired woman, attempting to atone for breaking up the gaiety, tries to restore the mood by forcing a smile, but, disingenuous, it fades fast. In a last-ditch effort, Stanislaw fingers move to Meiselman's underarms. Meiselman's armpits, however, are insensitive. He can stay calm as long as Paprocki does not go for Meiselman's nipples, or strip off his sock and run a finger up the bottom of his foot, or lap his tongue against the underside of his big toe. Stanislaw detaches and retreats.

The instant he and the pink-haired woman are left alone, Meiselman barricades them behind the Julius Caesar paper.

"This looks like a finished paper," she says, pulling back, snatching the paper from Meiselman's hand. "We said notes, I thought." She flips back to the first page, her balmy lips moving tenderly as she reads to herself. By the time she finishes rifling through the pages her attitude has shifted. "Whatever, right? Not really my tone, but I can change it around. This professor will not give a rat's ass. He's some burnt-out lawyer who teaches at N2C2 for kicks. Avoids paperwork at all costs. Does not even bring a briefcase or bag to class. Carries whatever book we are reading in the back

it in waves. Perhaps it is an unpleasant mix of otherwise-nice scents, residuals from his visit to the bakery clinging to his clothes, a blend of baklava, hamentaschen, pink-haired woman, and Kotek.

A lifetime of his senses flummoxing him. A perpetual squinter, glasses since the age of eight, Meiselman pleads with the optometrist every year to sharpen his prescription. Hot and cold are registered a millisecond later than most people. All dairy products smell, taste, and look off, regardless of the date stamped on the packaging.

Smells are especially puzzling. Spaghetti and meatballs he might giddily anticipate as soon as he steps into the house after work, only to be disappointed when he sits down to breaded trout, salt-free mashed potatoes, and steamed broccoli. Fortunately, nobody is sniffing out enemies anymore, or Meiselman would be rotating on a spit. Fortunately, nobody is using body odor trapped in genitalia hair to attract mates, because after lovemaking, he occasionally catches a whiff of Deena's odor and finds it unpleasant, striking fear in him that it means they are biologically incompatible. Might his faulty sense of smell be an evolutionary advantage, like how animals are able to wallow in their feces? Meiselman, unlike his mother, will never return from the Bahamas complaining how a musty smell in the room ruined the trip. Feces—human or animal—do not disturb him. On drives up to Wisconsin there is the joke of Meiselman lowering the windows and inhaling deeply as they pass fields of pasturing cows, while Deena plugs her nose and slaps at her husband's arm, pleading with him to raise the windows. Slight anosmia, symptomatic of his hay fever, is how his doctor diagnosed this handicap.

Taste is also a problem. The pleasures he must forgo on account of his ineffectual taste buds. Jeremy talks about an appetite for bitter ales, yet to Meiselman beer tastes like beer. Meat tastes like meat, yet everyone discusses cuts and gaminess and can ably answer the waiter when asked how they want it cooked. Wine tastes like wine, so what do other adults mean when they applaud a wine for its dryness? Why was Mitchell flabbergasted, yet impressed, by Ethel's decision to pair a light red with the salmon entrée at her holiday party last year? Does his father truly taste a difference between American and Israeli tomatoes?

Three months after they married, Meiselman and Deena had honeymooned in Israel, an additional wedding gift from his parents, who did not understand how Meiselman could have a wife who had never been. As the newlyweds loaded their plates at the Shabbat lunch buffet, the Russian waiter watching over the Viennese table sold Meiselman on a piece of flourless chocolate cake. "Like a dream," he said.

Cake without flour sounded novel.

One bite, one chew, and Meiselman could feel his body easing for the first time since the wedding. No, since the engagement, or maybe since the first time he saw Deena dancing.

"Extraordinary cake," he'd said to his young wife. Meiselman's seat faced the sea. Deena insisted on sitting cater corner from him. "And you know how fussy I am when it comes to chocolate cake."

"Good," she said, rubbing his back. This was before he became attuned to her sarcasm.

Using a fork and knife, Deena worked on a preposterously big salad—full leaves of lettuce, rounds of tomatoes the width of tennis balls, shavings of carrots the length of toothpicks all collected in a bowl the size of a satellite dish like the ones planted on the roofs of the Arab houses in Jerusalem. Choosing vegetables when the buffet offered duck and salmon seemed a waste to Meiselman.

After another bite of the cake, he leaned into his wife and said, "If you promise to keep a secret, I will tell you that this is even better than my mother's chocolate cake."

"Is it?"

"It is."

Deena stabbed a leaf of lettuce and used her knife to fold it into an edible-sized portion. "Your mother's cake," Deena said, the unraveling lettuce peeking out of her lips, Meiselman rotating his finger, instructing her to finish chewing. "Your mother's cake,"—several more chews of her salad, and a final swallow—"is too spongy."

Fearful that word of the flourless cake would spread through the dining room, and unable to imagine reaching some type of limit, Meiselman returned to the Viennese table and said to the waiter, "I don't want to wake up from this dream."

It was not a straight chocolate cake, and Meiselman was struggling to identify the dominant taste. The strain of trying to come up with its identity was lessening his enjoyment. He held the cake in his mouth hoping the taste would strengthen, but he could not control his teeth from grinding at the cake, his tongue from pushing it to the back of his mouth and down his throat. He wanted to have access to this taste for the rest of his life. He could not do this alone. It was, however, during Deena's sugar-free period.

"One bite is all I ask. One bite will not make you fat."

"Weight is not the issue. Weight, in fact, is barely mentioned in *The Rotterdam Report.*"

It was not about weight, it was not even about swallowing, she went on to tell him, launching into a speech he had heard many times, one about hormonal rage, yo-yoing brains, and toxins masking true emotional states.

Increasingly impatient, wanting to identify the taste so he could get back to enjoying the cake, he muttered in protest, "You use the word 'crave' as if my enjoyment of sweets is some type of addiction. Sugar for me is a small treat at the end of a day."

"For being a good boy and eating all of your vegetables?" she said, reaching an arm up to rub his back.

"Yes, I work hard, and my brain understands I deserve a treat," he answered stiffly, not allowing her to dismiss his concern with blithe comments and touching.

"Well, now I can be your treat at the end of the day," she said, reaching her hand underneath the table and running it up his thigh, appending her fingers to his belt buckle as Meiselman continued the face-off by pleading with her to at least smell the cake. Good naturedly, while tugging on his belt, she called him a sadist, the kind of man who would set a drink in front of an alcoholic. She slapped his crotch with the back of her hand and drilled a finger into his cheek dimple. He hammered the table with both fists, twice, and cried, "For me, your husband." A knock forceful enough that it caught the attention of the guests at the surrounding tables and impelled his wife to pull her hand from his pants so she could settle his rattling wine glass. She held out her hand to calm him down before dipping her head for a whiff.

"Tropical," she offered.

"Banana? You know how much I love banana." To make up for the violent outburst, he was looking to lighten the mood by turning it into a guessing game.

Trying to reach the cake's essence, she rubbed a piece between her fingers, crumbs breaking off and falling to the tablecloth until a white flake was all that remained. She held it up to the light, nodded her head, and then licked it for confirmation. The nodding intensified as she shoved crumb after crumb into her mouth.

"Coconut," she said, her mouth half full.

Taking another bite of the cake, he said, "I never would have guessed coconut, but you nailed it."

He was over the cake. What concerned him was the ease at which two bangs of his fists could erase four months of fundamentalist devotion. An indication that she would eventually tire of her newly adopted religious lifestyle? What also concerned him was the issue of whether he was establishing himself as a dictatorial husband, or "sadistic," as she framed it. Meanwhile, Deena had taken the fork from his hand and could not get the cake in her mouth fast enough. Soon, she abandoned the fork for her fingers. Eyes droopy, she ate with her elbows on the table, showy chewing, tongue falling out of her mouth after each swallow.

"The damage is done," Deena said at last. "It will take two weeks to cleanse my body. Dr. Gehani says in *The Rotterdam Report*—"

This was poor honeymoon conversation, so what choice did he have but to hook his foot around the leg of her chair, reel her in, drop his hand under the table and walk his two fingers under her skirt from knee to flab? She rubbed her hands clean of crumbs, put her hand on his shoulder, and opened her legs.

"Isn't coconut an endorphin?" he whispered into her ear.

"Is it an aphrodisiac, you mean?" She crossed her legs, sandwiching his hands between her inner thighs. She whispered, "Maybe, but it's also loaded with lauric acid, which Dr. Gehani says is the worst." Tugging his pant's belt loop, she said, "Let's go up to the room."

What happened after he and Deena returned to the room would make a perfect opening for Dr. Lin if he were not concerned about fixing it in the doctor's mind that vomiting is a problem for Deena. Though he would be curious to hear what the doctor makes of Deena silencing his worry for her wellbeing by stepping up to him and demanding a kiss, even though she had not brushed her teeth, or even rinsed her mouth as brown driblets from the heaved cake dotted her chin and a shred of sodden lettuce jammed an incisor.

Does he admit to the vomit taste in his new wife's mouth intensifying his desire and enhancing the lovemaking?

The allergist told him not to worry about his slight anosmia, yet, Meiselman worries. Coconut and feces are innocuous. But what if this acrid smell in the car is the result of a leaky valve, blown-out sparkplug, or overheated engine? Can one even drive with a blown sparkplug or leaky valve? In the event of an overheated engine, should the air conditioner be turned on full blast or off completely? That poisonous gasses are odorized to provide warning is the extent of Meiselman's blue-collar knowledge. If it is an odorized gas, might he soon lose consciousness and barrel into a street sign, hammering his head against the steering wheel, slight anosmia leading to severe amnesia? Deena will rush to the hospital. All will be forgiven and she will drop her demand he see Dr. Lin, and they will both have a reason to stay home from his parents' house tonight.

Shabbat starts in less than three hours. He can be home in five minutes. Deal with the car on Sunday. Still, a lot can happen in five minutes. Smoke can rise from the hood, the dials on the dashboard can swing, and the cabin can fill with the sound of pebbles bounding under the hood, forcing him to pull over and gamble on the kindness of passing New Niles motorists. Meiselman would never pull over for Meiselman. People, especially suburbanites, are suspicious of men with beards, believing they must have a religious bone to pick, a messianic axe to grind. People see a person in need and instinctively assume a con is afoot, which is reasonable in a time when fanatics shear lifelong beards and board planes with box cutters, and ladies dressed as nuns snatch babies from maternity wards.

It would be irresponsible to continue driving when there is a Mobil station up the road. A tow takes time, and if he rushes into the house right as Shabbat is starting, Deena will have to excuse his not calling Dr. Lin, and accept his promise to take care of it after the event. Hopefully by then she will lose interest in her demand. She will also have no choice but to pull herself together and join him for dinner at his parents' house. Yes, it is this second demand, he now believes, that is causing greater anxiety.

Before he calls a tow truck, is it not expected he perform an independent inspection? Expected by whom? It just is, so he parks his car in the back corner of the station's lot, next to the air hose, cloaked from any passing motorists or gas pumpers who risk witnessing his bumbling manhood, his inability to locate the hood's lever, his hesitancy to pull it once it is found out of fear there will be some irreparable consequence or that, once open, he will never get it shut. No fizzing, smoking, or bubbling. No overpowering odor. Simply a web of black metal. A brush of yellow discoloration on a pipe that connects to what he assumes is the car's motor catches his interest. Nose up to the pipe, he concludes there is an odor that may or may not be similar to the smell that has been harassing him since he left work.

If he had a phone he would be expected to update his wife regarding his delay, and Deena, always excited to find an area where her father's limited knowledge is of use, would tell him to hold off calling AAA.

The AAA dispatcher, who sounds as if she is speaking from a different part of the world, informs Meiselman that the wait should be no more than twenty-five minutes.

Did Meiselman not recently read an article about gas stations making a majority of their profits not from gas, but from groceries? A blue shopping basket in hand, he drifts down the store's aisles. Collapsible barbecue grills, sacks of wood-seasoned charcoal, grill brushes, thermometers, tongs, spatulas, mitts, lighter fluid, and barbecue sauces cram the shelves of half an aisle prompting the question: Why is he not doing more grilling? Does not every man derive gratification from feeding a fire? Every summer, one random

Sunday afternoon, his father would return home with a collapsible grill, legs as thin as the metal handles on Meiselman's shopping basket. In the living room, his father would sort through the newspapers, weeding out expendable sections. On the back patio Gershon would ball the pages of Cars, strategically placing them between briquettes. Over and over, Meiselman was ordered by his father to stand back. Up against the wall, he was ordered to watch from the other side of the patio door. Inevitably, his father had trouble whitening the coals. On account of just terrible wind, or no-good lighter fluid, or not being able to hear himself think because of the Woolf's yelping dog two houses over. Inevitably, his mother would have to finish the meat in the oven. The grill was left outside, its lid on the patio ground. Soon the grill's bowl collected rainwater. The first winds of fall tossed the grill onto its side. Winter snow buried it. The spring thaw revealed splotches of rust on the bowl's underside and legs. At some point, his mother would catch the landscaper outside and hand him a bill in exchange for clearing the grill from the patio. What could be the value in sharing this suddenly recalled memory with Dr. Lin? They can examine why Meiselman does not believe he has what it takes to become a consistent, confident griller like the men at Kiddush, men who discuss marinating strategies and wood placement, why he assumes that, like his father, he would fluster his way through a barbecue.

Sauntering down the store's empty aisles, which are bathed in a blinding white light and void of pestering clerks and other shoppers, Meiselman reflects on more questions about missed opportunities. Why has he limited himself to the same plain Jays potato chips his entire life? Why is he not walloping his senses with sweet treats and salty snacks on a daily basis, indulging his curiosity, seeing if the food scientists succeeded in making the corn chip taste like chili or pizza, the candy and gum like the fruits of an exotic island?

Having finished walking the three aisles, Meiselman loiters in front of the bulletproof glass that houses the clerk.

Pointing to a newspaper on the clerk's worktable, Meiselman says, "This Thomas injury is putting a big hurt on the Sox."

The clerk presses the intercom button and speaks into the microphone, his voice coming through in a static whoosh. "Not much of a baseball guy."

"If it wasn't drilled into you at a young age, you will never learn to love it. Like most things in life."

Button. "Too slow."

"To be honest—" a yawn delays his confession. To revive himself, he tugs on his beard hairs and slaps his cheek. "Sorry, tired. Yes, from a young age, and then still it tries one's patience. Can I tell you something I've never told anyone before?"

Button. "Yeah, I guess."

The clerk appears nervous.

"I, too, find it boring sometimes."

Button. "Yeah, more into action sports. If I'm watching, it means someone's going down. I don't watch anything I don't like. Life's too short, and I'm drowning." He tilts up a textbook to show Meiselman its cover. *Introduction to Medicinal Chemistry*.

The clerk buries his head in the textbook, refusing to engage Meiselman's next morsel of polite conversation. Left on his own, Meiselman's eyes drift to the rack of magazines on the wall behind the clerk.

The number of titles continues to drop. Many of the brand names, the ones that trade in photographs of accidental exposure—a breast falling out of an unbuttoned white blouse, a heavy wind hiking a dress—remain. The implausibility of the scenes in these magazines has always offended Meiselman. How can nurses effectively work in six-inch heels? If such an urge struck a judge in the middle of the trial would she not retire to the privacy of her chambers instead of diddling herself under the bench? Meiselman's wife does not own silk anything, and if she owned pearls she would not cavalierly toss them about or take them into the bathtub. The tameness of these brand-name publications is such that if a mother were to find one stashed under the mattress of her single, adult son, she would not be moved to put him under the care of a mental health professional.

The pioneers who publish the specialty magazines, on the other hand, cater to a readership with narrow and peculiar tastes, people who have dug deep to discover what unleashes them. Sure, Meiselman can have a good laugh over a magazine cover's headline trumpeting a hundred and twenty pages of "Pear-shaped Beauties and Watermelon Wonder Women," but he suppresses his snickers by reminding himself of the woman in the black and white bathing suit photo that, at one time, stirred him in a profound way, before he learned it was his grandmother, before it shifted from a peculiarity to a perversion. That the publisher of *XXXtreme Magazine* is still putting out new issues nearly two decades after Meiselman came across it for the first time heartens him.

The yeshiva dormitory had been emptied except for Meiselman, whose return to America from his year of post-high school study in Israel was now delayed on account of his parents helping settle Gershon into his first New York apartment. "You'll find it too depressing returning home to an empty house," his mother had said. "Your brother is now a big banker," his father had added. The book Meiselman was reading, *Bang the Drum Slowly*, could not stifle his midnight stirring. He was unable to muster his usual outrage over Wiggen's decision to keep Pearson's illness a secret from his teammates. When the clock struck one, Meiselman, eighteen and on his own, donned the black baseball cap he had purchased the day before in anticipation of the coming excursion and exited the dormitory into the cool Jerusalem evening. Located outside the Jaffa Gate, the store's sky-blue iron door was wedged between a Russian butcher shop selling forbidden meats and a grizzled Sephardi trading in pawned jewelry and contraband cigarettes.

The Arab proprietor sat on a stool in the corner, running prayer beads through his fingers, his other hand open to a nibbling cat. The magazines were displayed in plastic sleeves tacked to the walls, merchandise covering every inch from ceiling to floor. A ladder stood in a corner, but Meiselman was unsure of who would have to do the climbing, so he limited himself to eye-level product. Determined to finally settle on a choice before anyone spotted him inside the store, he selected a magazine with a black woman in an open leather vest on the cover. Black women were not his favorite, but leather was a preference, as was the color black. Besides, it seemed sensible to go for a double issue. The Arab shopkeeper insisted Meiselman wait for his change, arguing he was not a cabdriver and that five shekels was a lot for a student. While fishing coins from a clay ashtray, licking the tip of his finger before lifting each one, the storeowner told Meiselman he could get him whatever he needed. He mentioned German imports, which should have been the first clue.

Safe in the dormitory bathroom, Meiselman opened the magazine. The first set of pictures in the double issue of *XXXtreme Magazine* was not pleasing at all. Featured a black woman, heftier than the one on the cover, in black boots that reached the middle of cratered thighs. By leash, she led a scraggly man in leather briefs and a studded dog collar across an abandoned warehouse floor. In the next photograph, the woman was urinating into a dog bowl. The man, now on his haunches, ribcage pushing through his skin, had his tongue out and hands folded down at the wrists like a sitting dog. Meiselman skipped to the next set, which was even more vulgar. The same woman from the cover, although her vest was now gone. She, too, had to urinate. Right in the middle of a grocery store aisle. Introduced in the next photograph were three men in full astronaut uniforms, penises hanging out, black bands intricately tied around swelled testicles, sacs on the verge of bursting. In the reflection off the astronauts' visors the woman could be seen urinating, again, this time into a dog bowl.

The third set had promise. Two men, no collars, sat bare-bottomed on red stools at the counter of a '50s style diner. An anemic white waitress in a skin-tight white leather suit waited on the men. Her head and eyebrows were shaved. Three photographs later clothespins were clamped to her nipples, and she was urinating into Coca-Cola water glasses. In the set's last photograph, the waitress threatened the customers' roped testicles with the spiked heel of her boot. Luckily, Meiselman could find enough pleasing body parts and superfluities, like the wooden cross around her neck.

Afterward, he slid the magazine into a plastic grocery bag, trekked through the stone alleyways of the Jewish Quarter in his black baseball hat, and deposited the magazine into a garbage bin behind a playground.

Gracing the cover of the latest issue tucked into the rack on the wall behind the clerk is a boyish, Asian woman squeezed into a mustard-yellow rubber bodysuit. The readership's preferences have apparently changed. Do they favor a different color of urine, too? Clear urine and hefty black women properly reflected the fat Reagan years of the 80s, but with our boys fighting wars in the desert, the readership demands the darker urine of the dehydrated. Is any refinement of tastes the fruit of communal deliberations, or does the community rely on sages in the ranks to conjure new knots and forms of humiliation?

Since it was a photograph that originally brought him to the doctor, it may be worthwhile for him to introduce this memory of the magazine. Remember that issue of the photograph under my mattress, he will ask Dr. Lin after they greet one another. With a handshake or a hug? Surely nothing matching Ethel's stunning peck on the cheek when he came in for his library interview after not having seen each other for over a year. Caught off-guard, he botched it badly, feeding her too much of his furry cheek, his lips failing to make contact.

If the doctor asks him what he makes of this sudden memory, he may answer, How many men and women are we talking about? Am I crossing paths with these people?

Maybe the question we should be asking is whether you are the urinator or urinatee: the one tying the knots, or the one being pulled by the leash?

It's like, I want to be the urinator, and I'm standing in front of the urinal taking aim at a floundering fly at the bottom, but there is no splashguard, and the urine is spraying back at me.

And your mother?

Definitely the urinator.

But isn't she always presenting herself as the victim of great injustices, the one whom everyone is peeing on?

After twenty-two minutes, the tow truck arrives. Meiselman exits the gas station convenience store waving his arm over his head, but the driver shows no urgency exiting his truck. A pang of apprehension strikes Meiselman when he catches sight of the driver's face, but he cannot be certain about what he sees since he has never seen the man in his weekday clothes and, for a brief moment, he considers it may not be him but his nearly identical older brother, Marvin. Meiselman approaches, offering a warm smile. He says, "You don't say." Immediately, he spots his seatmate's marks of decay, the skin tag hanging off the eyelid, black and red specks on the whites of his eyeballs, the capillary-covered nose, swollen and bumpy like a plague sufferer, and, of course, the black fingernail.

The coincidence of them meeting like this does not seem to excite Ben Davis. Dressed in blue work pants and a tan polo with the logo of his employer stitched to the breast, he keeps his head in his clipboard and rifles through work orders while Meiselman tries bridging the silence with small talk. "Crede really got a hold of that one last night." Without warning or explanation, Ben Davis retreats into the truck, rests the clipboard on the steering wheel, and grabs a walkie-talkie from the visor. He turns his head to the open driver's side window and Meiselman, thinking he is wanted, steps toward the truck, at which point, the window powers to a close. Still on the walkie, Ben Davis goes from first beating his fist against the roof of the cab to pressing his palm against the windshield, as if testing its impenetrability.

In this fair-skinned community, the tanned skin and kinky black hair must have once lent young Ben Davis an air of beauty and invincibility. A boy destined to marry into a family of regard, a boy fated to sideline his schleppy parents and upbringing. His new father-in-law would set him up in an office and, with time, the tan would deepen from time spent on the golf course. Black hair would elegantly incorporate silver hairs. But Ben Davis never met the girl, and now he looks like a man left out for too long. Or left in.

It pains Meiselman to think his shul friend's reticence is out of embarrassment. Meiselman is a fellow White Sox fan, a family of South Siders, someone who respects blue-collar work. He is not like the other men in the shul, whose conversations focus on money and gluttonous hobbies. So when Ben Davis exits the truck for a second time, Meiselman says, "My savior," and concludes his brief summary of the problem by adding, "I'm a total dingbat when it comes to cars."

"You check under the hood?" Ben Davis asks.

"I did, I did. But, understand, to someone like me it's a jumble."

"That your car?"

"Yep, the jalopy over there. Gas-guzzler, tin lizzie. Bet you can't even find the parts anymore. Thought it was economical to drive the car into the ground. Don't tell me, I know, a recipe for disaster. Money is tight, always. I'm just a civil servant." Ben Davis leads them to the car. Meiselman, a step behind, says, "Amazing how you guys can diagnose a problem just from the sound of the motor."

Ben Davis licks the tip of his thumb and rubs at some stick on the driver side window. He runs his hand along the roof and examines his grimy palm before giving the front tire a kick, disgust covering his face.

"What kind of smell did you say it was?"

"To be honest, I don't know."

Ben Davis crouches and pulls at a tuft of weeds sprouting from a crack in the pavement. "You don't know?" he repeats, shooting a derisive sneer Meiselman's way. "Well, did it smell like something burning, like gas or rubber? Got to give me something. I'm not a magician. Rotten eggs, maybe?"

Rotten...rotting...

How foolish to think he could dismiss the discovery of the body as inopportune and isolated. Death's scent lingers and his clothes, unchanged from yesterday, must be saturated with the smell of Mrs. Woolf's rotten corpse. Or a more troubling possibility: the smell in the car is a memory of the smell from the house, which means he can expect this smell will hound him for the foreseeable future, periodically reminding him of the events and provoking unwarranted questions about his role in the neighbor's death, who never did explicitly ask for help. Exorcising from his mind any memory of the smell is a worthwhile goal if he ends up seeing Dr. Lin. Or it could just be his shoes, the first thing one should check whenever encountering a foul odor. Stealthily, he examines his soles. The treads are too worn down to trap crap. Or the smell is the result of not washing his body or changing his clothes—the same purple shirt all week. In other words, the smell is his own decomposition. Here, he thought, he was blessed with pleasing body odor, but that assessment was formed years ago. Maybe age has altered his constitution. Or the smell is tied to his current practice of stuffing his lunch into his coat pocket. Rotting carrot sticks, or a moldy peanut butter and jelly sandwich? Running his hand over his pockets, he feels a bulge underneath the coat in the front of his pants. Sliding his fingers into the front pants pocket, pushing to the side a peppermint sucker, the tips of his fingers brush the elastic band of Deena's underwear, the pair stained with the sopped bloods of Mrs. Woolf and Deena...

"Rotten eggs, exactly," Meiselman answers.

"Problem with your catcon, I bet."

Meiselman widens his eyes, trying to look as clueless as possible.

"Your catalytic converter."

"A cabbalistic convert?" Meiselman repeats, laughing.

"Feel like you aren't getting as much power as usual?"

"You bet. Not that I'm a revver. Never have been."

Ben Davis effortlessly pops the hood and makes his way to the front of the car. He directs Meiselman to take the driver's seat and step on the gas. Two men working on a car. "Not like a little girl," Ben Davis barks at him. Meiselman, wanting to prove he brings value to the partnership, flattens the pedal until the needle swings into the red and Ben Davis is waving and yelling, "Ease up. You crazy?" Meiselman is booted from his seat, the partnership dissolved. Ben Davis takes the seat and turns the air up all the way. Satisfied, he shuts it off and returns to the hood. He draws a flashlight from his back pocket and shines it down on the car's insides. Meiselman, anxious to renew the partnership, points to the yellow discoloration on the pipe. Ben Davis shakes his head, and then shoos him away. Meiselman steps back, but Ben Davis keeps flapping his hand until Meiselman is well out of his sightline. Knocking his flashlight against the metal, Ben Davis says, "Hoses and belts look damn good for such an old piece of shit. The originals, no?" before answering his own question, "Yep, sure are." Suddenly, something seizes Ben Davis's attention. The area of interest is close to the windshield, so he leans forward, shining his flashlight on the ledge underneath the wipers. He returns the flashlight to his pants and slams shut the hood. Repositioning himself to the side of the car, he lifts the wipers off the windshield and sweeps his fingers across the ledge, scooping up a glob of black gunk. Holding up his fingers to the stark setting sun, an eye closed as he examines the uncovered substance, short cackles of laughter pump from the man's throat, a different beast than the snort whenever they mock a ballplayer, or the Cubs, or Cubs fans. He reaches out his arm and sticks his gunk-covered fingers up to Meiselman's nose, and Meiselman falls back on his heels, bobbing and weaving because he does not need an explanation for the berry skins that coat the tow truck driver's middle and index fingers and make them look as if his hand got stuck in a blender. "Is this the smell?" Bed Davis badgers, not letting up until Meiselman has a whiff. "Park under a fruit tree, by any chance?"

"In fact, one hangs over my reserved spot at work. The shade—"

"Gave you the shit spot, huh? Had a pizza delivery job once where they made me park between two dumpsters. Every day it was something else on the windshield. Crushed pop bottles, ketchup packets, soiled diapers. Once, a big black garbage bag right on the hood."

"We don't keep the dumpsters in the administrators' lot. It's exclusive—"

"Not important. Probably got a clump of berries stuck between your hood and windshield sometime in the fall. Maybe froze, got nice and damp, and now with the warmer weather it's rotting and you're smelling it through the vent. Clean it with a rag, and you'll be good to go. Unless you can't stand to get your hands dirty and want me to do it. I'm required to offer, some bullshit full-service-something guarantee."

"These hands get plenty dirty," Meiselman mutters. "And bloody."

While Ben Davis finishes the paperwork, Meiselman debates tipping etiquette in regards to tow truck operators. The rule of thumb, for him, is to not tip for service that requires an expertise. That he sits next to Ben Davis in shul every week complicates the calculation. Better to be thought of as cheap, or patronizing?

After handing Meiselman the clipboard and pen, Ben Davis points to an X on the bottom of the page and says, "Be thankful they sent me and not some *ganev* who would have had you doing a thousand-dollar job," a comment suggesting he is angling for a tip, but when Meiselman reaches for his wallet, Ben Davis puts up his hand and says, "Eh, they pay me the same whether it's a ten-minute job or a tow that takes an hour. Thankfully there are enough boobs in the community who don't know a spark plug from a distributor cap. Most of the jobs end up being ten-minute ones. Bunch of boobs, all of you, I swear."

Not wanting a tip, Meiselman can respect. Wanting to be seen as a friend, an equal. It was Meiselman, after all, who in the name of equality, self-deprecated himself and assumed an air of ignorance.

Meiselman does not know the difference between a spark plug and a distribution cap, but does this make him a boob, superfluous tissue? The other remarks about an unwillingness to dirty his hands and being given the crap spot at work did not go unnoticed either. Ben Davis is not interested in walking away as an equal, so why should this be Meiselman's goal?

Wanting Ben Davis to think of it as charity, and not a tip, he takes out two crisp twenties, stuffs the two bills into the driver's palm, closes the man's beefy fingers over them and says, "How many boobs can there possibly be? I insist."

Ben Davis is fighting the temptation to surreptitiously unfurl his fingers and cast his eyes downward for a quick peek. He cannot resist for long. Lips move as he tallies the amount to himself before flatlining into an embarrassed grimace, his chin receding. Meiselman pats the man on the side of the shoulder and adds, "They can't pay you much," repeating something his father said to him in support of a suggestion that his son consider taking night classes in computer coding at N2C2. "And, actually, I think I would like you to clean up the berries." Meiselman offers the tow truck operator a peppermint candy before stepping into his car. He takes it. Through the windshield, Meiselman scrutinizes Ben Davis as he disinters the clumps of muck, pointing here and pointing there, making sure the mechanic gets every last skin.

Why is guilt plaguing Meiselman as he spies Ben Davis baby-wiping his hands in the cab of his truck? Because one Shabbat morning years ago Ben Davis happened to sit down next to one of the community's only Sox fans and blurted, "Sox lost a tough one"? Ben Davis could have asked, So you enjoy when a large black woman in black latex boots urinates in your face? And—guaranteed—Meiselman would not be sitting in his car right now feeling forty dollars was too high a cost for such a fleeting triumph, or wondering whether Ben Davis is the one who walked away triumphant, a man so thoroughly humiliated over the years that he has mastered the role of the schlepper, and uses it to extort his way through life. And the man was no help. Thanks to his efficiency, Meiselman is left with plenty of time before Shabbat to schedule an appointment with Dr. Lin. Or was it the task of telling his mother Deena will not be joining them that he was hoping to escape by turning the innocuous smell into something potentially catastrophic?

* * *

Paul Woolf's black Mercedes is parked in his dead mother's driveway. Meiselman is not about to offer condolences. He has no desire to revisit yesterday's scene.

Shortly after Meiselman moved out of his parents' house, the locks were changed. When Meiselman and Deena were handed the keys to their new home, his mother had insisted on keeping a spare. She has not reciprocated with a key of her own. "I'm almost always home," his mother has said. "If I get locked out, can't I just come and sit in your living room with a book until your father comes home?"

Cracking open the door and hustling her son inside, his mother murmurs, "You didn't come to pay your respects, did you? Jews don't do that before the funeral." Since Deena came into his life, his mother is always telling him what Jews do and do not do, as if he is the one new to the religious lifestyle.

Paul Woolf emerges from the kitchen, hand extended.

"No," Meiselman answers. "I came to get something."

He receives Paul Woolf, sidelining his mother.

"Thank you for your help yesterday," Paul Woolf says, twisting his wrist and forearm so his hand ends up on top of Meiselman's. In control of the handshake, he extends it at lulling rhythm, the two hands bobbing up and down.

Everything about Paul Woolf is cool and relaxed, the deep tan accentuated by a pink polo—collar popped—his rumpled tan pants, tan loafers, cropped white hair combed straight down, oceanic blue eyes, and the aviator sunglasses, which are folded in the palm of his free hand.

"I feel terrible," Meiselman responds. Stuck in this man's clutch, Meiselman adds, "Grim stuff. Unpleasant." The morose tone settling over the room affords him an opportunity to deal with demand number one. Swiveling his head back to his mother, he mournfully says, "Deena will not be joining us tonight." His mother's creasing forehead and sagging eyebrows tell Meiselman he is expected to provide a sufficient reason at once. "She has a 'thing,'" Meiselman explains.

She stares back at her son, the fingernail of her index finger digging at her thumb cuticle. Cool Paul releases Meiselman and excuses himself on account of the cookies and coffee waiting for him in the kitchen.

"Is it gynecological?" she whispers to him once her guest is out of the room.

"Not gynecological," Meiselman answers. "She's lethargic."

The crease in the center of his mother's forehead grows heavier, her eyes widen, and her lips pinch together as her despondency mutates into the rage he feared.

"Then tell her to nap!" she says. "Dinner is not for hours. Slaved the morning away making ribs, but then Paul tells me he doesn't eat red meat, so I stuffed a turkey. This, after defrosting two Tupperwares of soup and buying an extra head of lettuce. Ruined my manicure. I know the man's mother just died, and I'm not looking to throw a party, but none of this food freezes well. To have just the three of us sitting around the table is morose."

"Why only three? Four. I'm still coming," he says.

"And leave your wife at home? Absolutely not. You know—" Here it comes. A speech. The reason he suspected this demand of Deena's was the more challenging of the two. "Your father and I are perfectly happy eating alone," she continues. "We have you over here to make your lives easier. We know how hard the two of you work, but coming to me at the last second with a wishy-washy excuse is inconsiderate and ungrateful. She doesn't eat anything, Deena. This is too sweet, this is too sour, this is too spicy. There's no winning."

For his mother, he wants to answer, is why he drags Deena next door every Friday night. Knowing how easily collapsible she is, he is unwilling to ever test how she would respond to him telling her they would rather eat alone. So yes, every time she asks. A lifetime of tiptoeing around the truth. Now he sees and hears the victimization in her voice and face. In his mother's mind, in this instance, he and Deena have whipped theirs out, so-to-speak, and hosed her down.

"What will I do?" she asks.

She is asking his help in cleaning up the mess, and it is clear he been hearing her wrong all these years. She is not, as he always assumed, looking to draw everyone else into her eruptions. Rather, she wants to be soothed, and is looking to him as the panacea. Not his father. Not Gershon. Him. Meiselman. Because the other Meiselman men have repeatedly failed her. She sees him as sensitive and capable. Put on the spot to come through for his mother, to relieve her anguish, Meiselman easily triumphs, because this is what he, the perennial number two, has consistently done for her and everyone else. With ease he produces the name of the only person he knows that will not take offense to a last-second invite, a person that will not take offense if told he is being invited merely to take the place of a late cancellation, or is being invited simply because there is an excess of food. When Meiselman mentions the name to his mother, he expects a face. Instead, she says, "Why I didn't I think of that? God, am I glad you came over," as if already forgetting that her son was the source of the complication.

Having successfully executed task number one, Meiselman drifts into the kitchen to look up the number in his mother's rolodex. People—he and his father—touching her things—appointment book, pen, scissors, tape, rolodex—distresses his mother, who only foresees disarray and misplacement. Also, he is not interested in explaining why he needs the number. Fortunately, right at that moment, the telephone begins to ring.

"Hello?"

"Linda Meiselman, please."

Granted, he rarely speaks to the man on the phone, but how does his father not recognize his own son's voice? Meiselman stretches the cord of the phone around the counter and hands it to his mother.

Every distant relative, every doctor ever visited, every repairman that has worked on the house or any of its appliances has a card in the rolodex. Scotch tape binds the holes of many of the cards. LaValle, John, Gershon's high school math tutor. Meiselman flips forward. Lilly, Scott, a man from the village who acted when his mother called years ago to complain about Sadie's sidewalk droppings. The next card is Lewinson, Michael and Roberta, Ethel's parents. The card for Lin, Dr. Samantha, however, is missing. Flips through one more time until it is clear the card is gone. He checks the rolodex's rings for remnants. Not a trace of Dr. Lin remains.

Is there another place to get the number? He retreats upstairs to his former bedroom, but the second he opens its door and his eyes lock on the football field comforter covering his bed, he feels the overwhelming need to put his head on the pillow.

Mentioning that his old bedroom remains largely the same since leaving the house is a possibility, if he does ever contact Dr. Lin. The same school-bus-yellow carpeting and lime-green walls that eventually replaced the pinkish peach carpeting and walls. Underneath the football comforter the same Coca-Cola sheets he slept on until his wedding day. Tacked to the wall, at the head of his bed, the poster of Frank Thomas swinging a bat under a lightening charged sky, veins of electricity coursing his forearms, the barrel of the bat shattering as it connects with a flaming baseball. Perhaps his transition years would have played out slightly different had Meiselman been shrewder and tucked the bathing suit photograph into any of the hundreds of *Sports Illustrated* and *Newsweek* back issues stacked along the wall under the window. On the dresser, set in a straight row in front of a dried out stick of Old Spice, a can of Vidal Sassoon mousse, and a plastic dispenser of Walgreen's moisturizing lotion, is Meiselman's miniature batting helmet collection.

Bike rides with Ethel the summer before high school. Prior to setting out to meet his partner at Baskin Robbins, Meiselman had ditched his clunky bicycle helmet—a Gershon hand-me-down—behind the bushes at the front of the house. The store, as a summer promotion, dispensed the yogurt into miniature batting helmets. Meiselman set the goal of collecting one from every major league team. Ethel, however, frustrated the effort by insisting she receive her order in a standard cup. "I hate baseball," she responded to his appeals. Meiselman's mother confronted him at the door upon his return from one of these outings, scolding him for riding without a helmet. Not wanting to embarrass him in front of the girl, she did not stop her car to castigate him on the spot. "What's with you and helmets?" Ethel asked the next day. "You look like a penis." The frequency of their rides diminished over summer's last few weeks. Once the school year began, with Meiselman at the yeshiva and Ethel at the Jewish Academy, they ceased completely, with Meiselman having collected only thirteen helmets.

The doctor will throw out a slew of predictable theories to explain the bedroom's intactness. You want to remain a little boy. Your mother wants you to remain a little boy. You and your mother want you to remain her little boy. Your mother harbors the fantasy you will return home. You harbor the fantasy you will return home. You see these relics as infected, and you are scared of transferring the infection into your new home. The sight of them takes you back to times you don't care to revisit. It's as if you cannot commit to this new life with your wife. Is this the same reason you are failing to empower your sperm? If the doctor, for once, keeps them on topic, Meiselman will tell her how his mother implores Deena to help Meiselman clear out his bedroom, take whatever he wants next door, and box up the rest for Amvets.

What is it your mother wants Deena to see? the doctor may ask. The stamp or coin collections? The baseball cards are gone, sold off by Gershon. What could Deena care about his recorder or keyboard, instruments abandoned after a couple months of lessons? The weird cuts and colors of his old clothes will give her a good laugh, and she will not want him compromising the fun by explaining how elevated and born-again he felt going to school in his Michael Jackson leather jacket or Michael Jordan sweat suit or stone-washed jeans with the tag on the fly. On the rare occasion classmates noticed, it was to mock him for having a slightly dated or generic version. She will keep on laughing as she pulls his yearbook off the shelf, flipping to his senior profile. Pet peeve? It should have said: Pretty girls. But the yearbook committee had rejected this rare stab at sarcasm. So: "People who say, 'No problem' instead of 'You're welcome'."

Favorite quote: “If you are a minority of one, the truth is the truth.” - Gandhi, *Gandhi.*

All this agitating over how he will open the session, when the sensible move would be to start from where they left off. An unceremonious last session. Had he expected an exit interview, Dr. Lin offering maintenance tips, followed by a pin ceremony for a course completed, the doctor printing out a clean bill of health? To present to whom? Two weeks before, his mother had raved about him making “real strides” over the last year, and asked what he thought about terminating his relationship with the doctor. Although not enthused by the suggestion, he’d caved immediately with a steady nod, because talking about the doctor with her was as uncomfortable as discussing sexual matters, like his mother wanting to explore the sexual proclivities of a fallen politician. “How can someone think about sex that much?” Meiselman always shrugs. “The man has a wife, the man has kids.” Shrug. “Can it really be such a thing with men like they say? Always on the mind?” Shrug. Were these questions not more appropriate for his father?

At that last session, patient and doctor had stared at each other for some time until Meiselman opened his mouth to share a recently resurfaced memory. It was not revealed chronologically. He’d started with the car ride home from the bar mitzvah, Meiselman relaying to his mother what transpired earlier. A story about telling his mother a story, and this is what interested the doctor most about the story when he was done with its telling.

“But this only happened because you told your mother what the boys did to you,” Dr. Lin said, sweet rebuke infusing her voice. “Your story starts with you telling your mother about the trauma you suffered.” Ready to answer the doctor, she cut him off and said, “What were your expectations in telling her?”

“Was I asking her to protect me?”

“That sounds simplistic. Let’s think harder. Unfortunately, we’ve run out of time.”

She had not stood to shake hands or embrace. He’d let out a meek “thank you,” and she’d kept her eyes on him as he moved to the door. When he turned the door’s handle, he looked back at her one final time and she said, “Remember, you can always call to chat.”

What were his expectations in telling her about what the boys did to him? Answering this question feels crucial. And, suddenly, possible. He rises from the bed and steps to the desk in the opposite corner of his room, which sags from his father’s back issues of *Commentary* and the *Weekly Standard* and manila folders crammed with unread newspaper clippings. Next to the periodicals, a shoebox holds Meiselman’s paltry compact disc collection. He pulls Willie Nelson’s *Red Headed Stranger* and opens the jewel box. The doctor’s business card is in almost mint condition.

* * *

Sun sinking in the western sky, Meiselman stows the Willie Nelson disc in his car’s glove compartment before entering his house, where he discovers Deena waiting on the bottom step of the staircase, her head resting against the banister, keys clutched in her palm, and purse in her lap. A sleeveless pink summer dress flows regally, fully concealing the bottoms of her legs and feet. The straps of her white bra underneath are exposed. She has kinked her hair, its tendrils now jutting from her head like a rabbit-ear antenna. Pink blush blots her cheeks, and her lips glitz with sparkly pink lipstick. Whether she is leaving or has just arrived is unclear.

Is all this pink meant to mock him and his mentee-slash-mentor relationship? Meiselman sits next to her and throws his body back against the stairs. She scoots closer to the banister, away from him.

"Where are you off to?" he asks.

"Did you make the call?"

"Give me a second. Told my mom you'd be taking the night off. She's looking to round up another guest or two." The update does not mollify Deena. He pivots. "You know, I'm excited about seeing the doctor. So much to tell her, and a tune-up can never hurt."

She grips the keys tighter, her knuckles whitening. "Call."

"Where are you off to, so close to Shabbat?"

"Now."

"I will."

"I'm going to my father's."

There is some relief in the answer. But only some.

"And after that?"

"Just call."

Deena does not demand much from him. Every night, she sits on the couch reading the newspaper or a magazine or one of her helpful books, content with him watching the White Sox in peace, not pressing him about errands, or voicing anger over unpleasant exchanges and perceived slights. She is not his mother. In this relationship, she is not his father, either, because who could imagine his father sniping sarcastic comments across the breakfast table at his mother? Who can imagine his father ever reaching a breaking point and finally issuing a demand? Maybe they are a completely different dynamic. He, Meiselman. She, Deena. Her pinkness has her glowing. She looks more self-sufficient and desirable than ever. With ease, if it comes to that, she will find someone who will not treat her like a sponge. In addition to lacking bedside manners, he could not even manage to buy her the right ice cream. If only he could articulate this self-pity. She would be cruel to not immediately turn forgiving.

Calls to Dr. Lin were always made behind closed doors, out of his mother's earshot. Wanting Deena to hear, but not too well, he uses the phone in the kitchen. The doctor's mildly surprised, "Oh, hello," fills him with warmth and puts him on the verge of tears.

"I was wondering whether I could come in and see you next week," and then, as if his words to the doctor have fulfilled her one final obligation, transferring her husband to the care of a professional, she slams the front door shut, not once, but twice.

Saturday

The three-bedroom, two-story colonial is settling, and its aching floorboards jolt Meiselman awake. The sound strikes his heart like a sustained note of an out-of-tune piano. He fears the house is on the verge of collapse, its machinery on the brink of combustion. Before any decision to grab the wife and vital documents—passports, dowry—he attempts to verify the noise, to eliminate the possibility the disturbance is merely residue from a dream. Limbs stiffened, breathing halted, Meiselman thinks he hears something outside the bedroom, a shoe testing the hallway floor.

The pale and orange light from the streetlamps dies at the bedroom window. Across the room shadowy, blurry forms jut from the bedroom's darkness. A pack of rats scavenging for food? No, his tube of hand lotion, a stick of the chemical-free deodorant Deena demands he use, and a swan-shaped bottle of perfume, the same anniversary present his father gives his mother, a present Deena insists she loves but sprays only on nights they are spending at home.

Who is this intruder stepping down the upstairs hallway, and what does he want from Meiselman? Has the maniac motorcyclist Randy come to murder Meiselman so he can have his way with Deena on bedsheets soaked with the blood of the cuckolded husband? AB negative, universal receiver.

Here is the chance for Meiselman to finally unleash his aggressive capabilities, to assert his role as head of his household, to declare he is done taking it from everyone, done tempering his attitudes in favor of everyone else's diktats. The bedroom door will open and Meiselman, primed for the Jacobean tussle, will tear off his shirt like a mutating superhero. The metal of the bedside lamp is dense, but is there enough adrenaline to rip it from the wall? The cordless phone appears solid, but Meiselman recently read about the inferior quality of the Chinese plastic common in household items. The heels of his new dress shoes, which click the sidewalk like horse hooves, could leave a bloody nose. Grab the intruder by the throat and drive him against the wall. Roll the newspaper into a baton and jab him in the face. Poke him in the eyes until they bleed, and Deena is on the floor bawling, Enough, enough, you win.

Disrupted sleep on Friday nights is common for Meiselman. Prohibited from using electricity on the Sabbath, unable to listen to the radio, watch television, or even use a telephone, the detachment induces anxiety. What if there has been another attack, this time in Chicago? This is a dangerous world, and what if Meiselman is needed?

Nine-year-old Meiselman was alone with his parents on a Shabbat afternoon and the telephone had been ringing for half-an-hour without pause. Gershon, a lone wolf even at a young age, was out of the house. His mother paced the family room, scratching her brow. This was before they ripped up the room's shaggy orange carpeting.

"At what point are we allowed to answer the phone?" his mother asked. His father, barricaded behind an open newspaper on the couch, did not answer. Meiselman wanted to pace with his mother, but feared a collision. Finding it easier to mimic his father's disregard, Meiselman sorted his baseball cards on the family room floor. After an hour of ringing, Meiselman's mother sat down next to her husband on the couch, hands cupped around her eyes like blinders, fingertips massaging her temples, and asked, "Harvey, what do we do?"

"Probably a wrong number," his father answered, not bothering to lower the newspaper. "Or a prankster. A prankster with the wrong number."

"Harvey. Harvey. Harvey. Harvey. Harvey," she repeated, her rhythm parodying the ringing telephone, which finally forced her husband to fold down his newspaper and face her anxiety. "What if it's *pikuach nefesh*?" she asked.

"We are going to save a life? What, are we doctors all of the sudden?" Thinking he had resolved the matter, he reinforced the barricade. "Look at that," he said. "Rain all week, Pooch."

Finished sorting, Meiselman began counting the rings of the telephone. Twenty-four before it automatically hung up. Then it would immediately start ringing again. His mother moved from the couch to the floor, across from Meiselman, and picked up a stack of cards. Why was she studying the card of a player who held his bat by its middle, right under the barrel, as if he were using it as a weapon? Wanting to break the tension hanging over the room, Meiselman remarked, "This guy stinks."

"I can't hear over this ringing," she yelled back, setting the card down and straightening the pile before burying her head between her knees.

Meiselman looked over to his father, guiding him with his eyes toward his teetering mother. His father shrugged, but Meiselman insisted with widening eyes, finally forcing the man into action. He stepped to the phone's cradle, which hung on the wall behind the television. The far-sighted man peeled off his glasses and put his face to the telephone. "You'll answer it," he snapped at Meiselman. "You're not a bar-mitzvah yet."

"But aren't you and mommy responsible for all of my sins until I am bar-mitzvahed?"

"We'll manage."

The flick of a switch or the tearing of toilet paper on Shabbat would end in bolts of lightning, young Meiselman was convinced, and he reached for the phone with fear, because what if God was testing his family and his parents were failing?

"Wait!" His father grabbed his arm. "You must answer it with a *shinui*." A word Meiselman had heard, but whose meaning he had forgotten. He searched the room as if looking for a specific object. "You're the lefty, or is that your brother?" his father asked.

"I'm regular."

"Then with your left hand is how you need to answer it. But not with your hand, your elbow. Different than how you would normally answer it."

"Don't yell at him, Harvey," his mother, now at her husband's side, said. "Explain it."

"Knock it off the cradle with your elbow, left elbow, then, as it's falling, catch it with your left hand."

"It would be easier, I think, if I caught it with my right hand."

"But a *shinui*, you need the *shinui*."

"*Shinui* is the elbow, no?"

"Not *shinui* enough."

His father positioned Meiselman's bent left elbow directly underneath the cradle. Up and down he lifted it, demonstrating the desired motion. Then he showed him the movement of turning over his arm and opening his hand to catch the falling phone. When it came time to execute, however, young Meiselman could not straighten his arm in time and the phone crashed to the carpeting. Meiselman reached for the phone with his left hand.

"Wait," his father barked. "The *shinui* is still in effect. Get on your knees and put your ear to the receiver."

On all fours, Meiselman's hands dug into the plush orange carpeting, his ear dropping closer to the voice piping through the receiver.

"Is anyone there? This is Jeffery from New York. Harvey?"

Hands behind his back, Meiselman's father pushed Meiselman to the side, bent forward to a ninety degree angle and hollered at the telephone, "What's wrong with you, Jeffery? Some of us still follow the rules. Here, talk to your nephew."

His father pushed Meiselman back into position.

"Tell your father that Zeyde got very sick in the heart and that he's...*niftar*."

On the couch, his parents talked arrangements in low voices. In the background, replacing the constant ringing, the steady tone of a phone left off the hook. Steadily, his mother's voice rose until finally she was crying and yelling, "Nobody was good to him. Not you or your mother." Before storming upstairs she said, "He was a saint to put up with her all those years."

His father kneeled next to Meiselman and picked up the stack of White Sox cards. "Boy, this was a bad team. Not one guy that could hit the long ball. Goofy uniforms. What opponent would take seriously anyone wearing shorts? Minoso played that year. Was 50 years old." He threw a hand at Meiselman and said, "Enough with the cards. Enough with the *narishkayt*. Read a book."

Upstairs, more yelling. Only his mother's voice, always only his mother's voice. The funeral was the next day, and Meiselman's parents and Gershon rode in a limousine. Meiselman was left at home with Shaina Lipman, a girl with short dirty blonde hair parted down the middle. She wore socks up to her knees and chewed gum like it was cud. Meiselman asked her for some, and she ripped off a piece with her front teeth.

Parenthetically, this story was the first memory Meiselman shared with Dr. Lin, and a reanalysis is perhaps the perfect way to start again. Now, I see that it's my mother asking to be calmed, and I'm the one who steps up to the plate.

How long are Meiselman's eyes shut before a cawing noise has his head off the pillow for a second time tonight and he is crying to himself, How much strain can this thirty-six-year-old heart take?

The source of the unrest soon crystallizes. Last night, at his parents' dinner table, something noteworthy had occurred, and now he is drawing a blank, despite the instructions he'd repeated to himself, to remember. Was it a comment, an exchange, or general table conversation? Was he a participant or an observer? Did he want to remember so he could agitate over it later, or was he intending to execute a mulling that would lead to a theory or epiphany, a course of action or course correction?

Safe to assume it connects to a current tumult.

Hours ago, he thought his wife was out the door, yet here she is sleeping next to him on top of her made bed, still in her clothes from the night before. Pink skirt hiked, she is flashing thick thigh. The straps of her pink dress and white bra have fallen to her biceps. The immense amount of pink—she did not wash before bed—makes it look as if she is embedded in a fairy tale, possibly one where a desperate Meiselman slipped her a pill and lugged her comatose body up a flight of stairs and dumped her onto the bed. A corner of her lips is turned up as if she is smiling in her sleep, dreaming a fairy tale of her own, and even if he is not in her fairy tale, he is thankful she is home and sharing a bed with him. This still unclear turn of events must connect to what he wanted to remember from last night's dinner.

Not once had his mother ever followed through on a threat to stay home from a vacation or family function, so Meiselman was not wholly surprised to enter his parents' living room, dress shoes clacking the gleaming cherry red hardwood floors, to discover his wife sitting rigidly in the middle of the couch, legs crossed, hands clasped around the top knee, her rattling foot billowing her immense pink skirt. A white cardigan covered her skimpy dress and bra straps, thankfully. Next to her, depressing the cushions at the couch's end, sat the primary reason Meiselman was not surprised to see Deena: her flask-shaped father, George. When Meiselman had suggested to his mother she invite George, he'd done so knowing his wife would not trust her father to go to her in-laws unaccompanied and unsupervised.

Elbow monopolizing the armrest, George snapped through the pages of the *Weekly Standard*, which laid flat on his crotch. Respectful of how the Meiselman men treat their periodicals, Deena wheedled her father's fingers at the page's corner.

"My favorite son-in-law," the bitty-eyed George called out, extending his arm, and trying and failing to lift himself from the couch. The cavernous room, lowly lit, its white walls bare except for a painting of a whale over the couch, was without other people. With George around, his father would steer clear until dinner.

"When your mother called this afternoon to ask if I had plans, you know what I said? I said, 'Nothing I can't tape.'" His elbow jabbed Deena's side, until she finally grabbed a hold of it and returned it to his body. "Only had time for a shower, not a shave." His face bristled. Behind a range of tangled white curls at the front of his father-in-law's head, Meiselman's special kippa—white-knitted, reserved for the High Holidays—covered a jagged circle of baldness. "Thank you for the early birthday present," George said, picking at the chest of a silky, gray v-neck sweater. "Never owned anything from Nordstrom's before." This was not true. Whenever

Meiselman's mother extended an invitation to George, Deena bought him something from the store. "And thank you for letting me borrow a shirt. I think the one from Passover is still in the hamper." Indeed, he was wearing one of Meiselman's better shirts—light blue—picked up on recent father-and-son excursion to Brooks Brothers. "Sweaters are nice, I told your wife, but grandchildren are better." He laughed. Another elbow. Deena, this time, hooked her arm through his and pinned down his shoulder with her other hand. George wriggled his hips, sinking deeper into the couch. He stretched his legs past the coffee table and crossed them at the ankles. Black gum stamped the sneaker's rubber sole. Tipping the magazine back from his chest, he continued reading.

Meiselman glared at Deena for loaning out his clothes, and for shopping at stores they cannot afford. He struggled to interpret Deena's responding glare. Was she saying, Damn right you'll pay, or: No more fighting, please. Filled with an impulse to please Deena, he engaged George in friendly chatter. "So glad you could join us. You've never met Paul. Very cool guy."

A most perceptive observation came to Meiselman, and now in bed he wonders whether this is what he wanted to remember from last night, remember so he could share it with Dr. Lin at his appointment next Monday at four-thirty. Deena bought and lent her father these crisp clothes in an attempt to mask the man's disrepair, yet by failing to execute a full makeover, by neglecting the entire bottom half of his body, leaving the bleach-stained khakis with a tear at the pocket's edge, the white tube socks bunched at the ankles, and the blue Converse sneakers, soles smooth as ballet flats, his wife had spawned a clash that ended up drawing greater attention to her father's shabbiness. Perhaps an unconscious desire to humiliate the man, like her habit of pulling off George's pharmacy-bought bifocals in public in order to clean the smudged lenses? Maybe she grasps the futility of such a project and aims for small levels of respectability. Surprisingly, the man is diligent about his teeth, and his habit of flossing in public has ceased thanks to Deena's admonishments.

Meiselman cannot dislodge George's face from his mind, even though the next memory from the previous night is certainly not worthy of a serious mulling. Regardless, it plays as Meiselman moves a pillow between his legs, a rearrangement of his bedding that will hopefully put him back to sleep.

Deena had whacked her father George across the shoulder after he'd said at the table, "The only chicken soup I ever liked was Mother's. The rest, I find, are all salt." The comment, or possibly Deena's reaction, silenced the table, which was covered in a white linen tablecloth and set with the sky blue, gold-rimmed china, its matching cloth napkins, and the silverware his mother kept in a wooden chest. George, holding the soup bowl by its delicate handle and tilting it forward so he could draw the last drops, finally cracked the silence and said, "Still winning the war. That's good. Read that in one of your magazines."

This led to another brief silence before Cool Paul, who was sitting across the table from George, dropped his spoon into his empty bowl and said, "I don't know. It'd be a cakewalk, they told us. Now, all these kids are dying. And men. Guys with families. Women, too."

"What choice did we have?" his father glumly responded from the head of the table. A fast eater, he had finished his soup and had his chair pushed back from the table.

"We didn't have a choice," barked his mother, who was standing at the opposite end, bowl in hand, waiting for the others to finish so she could begin clearing, barked it as if maddened by the irresoluteness in her husband's voice. "You said that."

"I don't see how he gets reelected if gas prices stay high. And I like the guy," Meiselman offered, a comment culled from an article last week about early polling and gas prices. The numbers cited long-forgotten, he tosses off ballpark figures. "We are twenty percent above that right now."

"The newspapers hate him," his father said, throwing a dismissive wave his son's way. "Bottom line, he's the only one who understands the threat. I think that's the bottom line. The other guy sure doesn't. Buffoon. Wimp."

"To them, all of this terrorism stuff is a big joke," his mother added.

"Poll the guys I golf and do business with, and it's fifty-fifty," Paul said.

George leaned into Deena and asked. "Still talking about the war? Busy eating bread and missed it all."

Turning perky and breezy, his mother said, "Politics is probably the last thing on Paul's mind right now." She grabbed Paul and Deena's bowls and asked George about his ongoing health issues. Meiselman snatched the remaining bowls and followed his mother out of the dining room. "I'm listening, George," his mother yelled over her shoulder.

"Can't complain," George booms. "Complaining has never helped anything. Was over at Northwestern a couple of weeks ago. Thought I had polyps, but turned out to be nothing but fissures." Meiselman glared at Deena through the kitchen doorway, conveying the need for her to get her father under control. But she sat with her head bowed, ready to ride out this current embarrassment. At the end of the table, Meiselman's father nodded off. Cool Paul held himself solidly, feigning interest in George's update.

"They make you wait and wait in these waiting rooms," George continued. "People with lesions, eczemas, and rashes all around.

How do I know they aren't contagious? Then they bring you into the examination room to wait some more. Tried throwing around Daisy's name, but they had never heard of her. Other than the fissures, not much else. Wrist is better. Brace is off. The toothache comes and goes. Other than that, feeling good, can't complain."

Hoisting a carved turkey on a platter, his mother entered the dining room, Meiselman trailing, gravy boat in hand.

Meiselman's vivified father stood back from the table and fastidiously attended to the assemblage of his plate, directing Meiselman and his mother where to place the cranberries, turkey, stuffing, rack of ribs, and salad, voicing occasional concern about the mixing of sauces, juices, and dressings. He took a seat, draped a napkin across his lap and forked some stuffing. "Tremendous," he said, mouth full. He moved the food around his plate. "You know, George," he said, pointing at the dinner guest with his fork. Chewed some more until everyone was looking down the table at him. "Better a tear than a growth, no?"

George knocked his head from side to side. "Touché, as the kids say. Don't you say that, Daisy?"

"If you're still healing we can get you a pillow to sit on," his father added, winking at Meiselman, the flash of a sly grin, as if his son took pleasure in his ridicule of this man.

The despicable half-smile he gave his father in return, his decision to join in on the humiliation of this man, his wife's father, the future-grandfather of his children, must be what Meiselman wanted to remember. Right at the moment the light snort exited Meiselman's nostril he felt disgusted by his trashy behavior. Even before spotting the doleful look covering Deena's face. Doleful over her embarrassment of a father, or her unkind husband? Or both? Or did the cruelty of her father-in-law come as a disappointment? The memory of participating in this man's humiliation pains Meiselman, and hoping to snuff out this feeling he rolls over and mashes his face into the pillow, the cartilage of his nose cracking. Muffling an anguished groan into the cotton pillow cover, his trapped breath poaches the skin of his face as he gasps for air. Deeming the penance sufficient, he ends this facial flagellation.

Flushed from his mashing, Meiselman throws off his blanket. A cool breeze combs his body. The relief is momentary. What needed to be recalled from last night's dinner is still out there, and soon his heart rate is accelerating as he claws through his mind trying to remember. The bedding underneath scratches the back of his calves. Sweat trickles down the undersides of his knees. His warm buttocks are surely turning rashy. Open windows on a cool night are no longer sufficient. Someone turn on the air. Looking for relief, he moves to the floor, puts his back up against the side of the bed and draws his knees close to his body. He must replay every bland discussion until he arrives at the crucial moment.

Meanwhile, Deena has not adjusted her position all night, has not expelled anything louder than her usual nighttime, nasal hiss. She does not allow discord and disharmony to disrupt her sleep. "Nothing can keep me from sleep," she constantly boasts. Well, not nothing.

Did he fall back asleep? Suddenly his mind feels fresher and another memory from last night's dinner surfaces, one he is sure provides the answer of what it is he wanted to remember.

Turkey had jammed George's cheek like chewing tobacco, its juices glistening the cracks in his dried lips. "I wish," he said, "you wouldn't have gone through the trouble of cutting the dark meat off the polkie. Much prefer eating it off the bone." Another comment to silence the table, one Cool Paul smoothly broke by asking about the Himmelfarbs, the previous owners of Meiselman and Deena's home. The family had absconded to Minneapolis when the wife, a math professor of some regard, changed careers and accepted a corporate job.

Meiselman's mother spoke to Eleanor Himmelfarb just before Pesach. Meiselman had heard the update, and so had his father, who nodded off again as his wife told Paul how Jordy, the youngest, had joined the Marines. The parents were proud "even with their politics." The boy married his longtime girlfriend in a civil ceremony, in case there are benefits to be collected.

"Scary," Paul said. "Excuse me." He pulled the kippa off his head, folded it in half and handed it back to Meiselman. Directing his apology at Meiselman's mother, he explained, "It's getting in the way of my eating."

Paul asked about the older brother Joey. "Used to play ball with him. Good arm on the kid," he said, prompting Meiselman to turn and say, "With me. You used to play ball with me." "Sure," Paul answered, gripping Meiselman's shoulder. Deena looked across the table at Meiselman, one of the only times they would make eye contact all night.

Meiselman's mother leaned into Paul and dipped her head as if she were about to reveal something scandalous. She said, "I think he's a firefighter in North Dakota, South Dakota. Who knows? I don't want to ask too many questions. They can't be happy." Raised her eyebrows and sat back.

George turned to Deena and asked, "Why are we whispering?"

"Who's whispering? Not me," Meiselman's mother answered. She gave her standard spiel about the Himmelfarb boys not going to college despite having parents who are "big geniuses," a calamity recalled countless times, so definitely not the conversation worth remembering. Yet, Meiselman cannot stop the playback.

"It's strange," Paul said. "The uncles and cousins of mine who made it out of Europe all fought in World War II, and I had an uncle in Vietnam, but this country is fighting two wars and I don't know a soul over there. Not a kid or grandkid of anyone I know. Kind of amazing, no?"

"Oh, that's not true," Meiselman's mother said. "We know plenty of people. Don't we know people Harvey? Harvey? Harvey?"

His father shook off slumber and asked, "What?"

"The wars. We know people fighting, don't we?"

"The Himmelfarb boy," Meiselman's father answered.

"We said him already. Wake up and participate."

His parents stared at one another, struggling to come up with names.

"Pamela, my secretary? Her sister's kid is over in Afghanistan. It's no joke. George? What about that cousin of yours who was at the wedding?"

Deena, who had not uttered a word all dinner, answered, "He's been in and out of the Guard for fifteen years. Struggles every time he leaves and ends up reenlisting."

"You talking about Jared?" George asked. "Problem with the sauce." George taps the tines of his fork against the table. "Then had the solicitation arrest. Girl ended up being underage. Sure stepped in it. He's always stepping in it. Uncle Sam took him back. Wife took him back, too. Think he's over in Kuwait now."

Every time George opened his mouth, the conversation came to a standstill.

"Real nice family," Paul finally said. "The Himmelfarbs."

"Very nice," Meiselman's mother concurred. "I should call Eleanor and tell her about your mother. She just loved her. We all did. Hard to believe."

Meiselman's father and mother offered light reminiscences, mostly about Mrs. Woolf's projects over the years, like the rabbits and the fishery, and her sharp tongue and wit and boundless energy, and suddenly the chocolate cake's fudgy frosting felt oppressively heavy on Meiselman's tongue. The death of his neighbor, of Cool Paul's mother, was not a desirable discussion. When discussing a death, people inevitably ask about the cause and level of expectedness, and the last person to see the deceased alive. Everyone at the table would look to Meiselman to provide answers. Soon the cake was clogging his airway, forcing Meiselman to return the soggy mass back to the front of his mouth. Feeling he may retch if he tried forcing a swallow, he spit the half-chewed mess out into a paper dessert napkin, which he then surreptitiously chucked under the table in George's direction.

Before Meiselman could steer the conversation into more favorable territory, Paul mentioned unloading the house as quickly as possible, which meant tidying up the grounds by clearing the overgrown grass and weeds, and dredging and closing the pit in the backyard. Talk of the pit made Meiselman want to bolt. Thankfully, Paul jumped to the subject of packing his mother's papers and journals so they could be shipped to some no-name agricultural university in the south. His parents were trying to ascertain if the gesture was a solicited donation, but Meiselman was too terror-stricken to listen to the complicated answer. What if they find the hose? Focusing on Paul's open collar and sunglasses, which were on his person even at nighttime, it occurred to Meiselman that Cool Paul would not be doing any of the dredging. Toss it all, he would instruct. Nobody would link Meiselman to the pit. A calmer Meiselman rejoined the conversation. Paul was talking cremation, and a plan to round up friends and family for a sprinkling ceremony at the Hoover Dam.

Meiselman somberly asked, "Will the leg be cremated as well?"

"Of course. She very much considered it a part of her body."

"And what about the dog?" Meiselman's mother asked.

"Did he die, too?" George asked.

Writhing in discomfort on the floor next to his bed, hands clawing at his beard neckline, which suddenly feels pimply, Meiselman now realizes he has misinterpreted Cool Paul's sunglasses and open collar. As he knows from Gershon, it is the abandoners, the ones who depart to lead playboy lifestyles, who end up throwing money at all problems involving the folks back home. To ameliorate any guilt over their absence, they end up being the most vociferous about their devotion to their mothers. It is only a matter of time, therefore, until Cool Paul sees his mother's passing as an injustice, only a matter of time until he starts asking questions. Tomorrow morning, after lighting his morning cigar, Cool Paul will stroll the grounds of his mother's home, and a ripple in the pit's water will grab his attention. Laying down his cigar over the pit's edge, he will carefully roll up the sleeves of his button-down shirt, dip his hand into the water, and discover the hose. He will not call the police. He has a guy who is more thorough, more willing to work beyond the law's limits, a man who will have no qualms about strapping Meiselman to a chair in the basement, clamping laundry pins to his nipples, and dunking his face into a dog bowl of urine every time Meiselman tries explaining that the woman never explicitly asked for help. The handicapped are a proud people, Meiselman will argue to his tormenter. It's like seeing a blind person teetering at the light, head cocked to the barely audible clicking, stick swinging in front of the body. Asking if they need assistance is not a given.

Get rid of the hose and he can stop worrying that one day someone will question how he could leave an old lady on the floor. He peers over the mattress. Deena has managed to make it under the covers without his noticing. Any footfalls will have her crying tomorrow over the creepiness of his nomadic nighttime wandering, so he stays on all fours, palms padding the bedroom's baby-blue carpeting, the newest in the house thanks to some final pre-listing improvements by the Himmelfarbs. By the time Meiselman crosses the room's threshold onto the hallway's tattered bumblebee-yellow-and-black frieze carpeting, his shoulders ache, and he drops to his chest. Using his elbows and forearms, he army crawls down the hallway until he reaches the stairs, which he bumps down on his rear.

He settles for the trench coat, ideal since he will be handling water. His slippers are waiting for him on the doormat, but if Deena's return is a sign she is ready to turn the page, he wants to turn the page with her, so he grabs the slippers, marches into the kitchen, and deposits them in the kitchen's trashcan, leaving them on top so his wife can see he has put his childish peculiarities away for good.

Right when he feels calm for the first time all night, more cawing erupts in the distance. Attempts to isolate it prove useless. The caw of a siren, perhaps? Are the authorities surrounding his home, readying their battering rams? Through the front door's peephole, Meiselman expects to see police barricades cordoning off nosy neighbors, his mother in nightgown and slippers forcing herself through the police line, his father urging her at the elbow to return to bed, promising they will deal with the matter in the morning. All Meiselman sees is his front stoop bathed in near-blinding whiteness from the security light his mother installed after the attacks. Its motion sensor defective, the buzzing light inexplicitly thumps on and off all night.

Curled in front of the couch in the living room, a throw pillow tucked under his head, his trench coat blanketing his body, Meiselman plots his move to retrieve and dispose of the hose.

The orange streetlights and the linty skein of the nighttime sky provide sufficient light for his purposes. Through an aperture in the bushes, he enters the Woolf lot. Detritus from past experiments litters the grounds—spools of chicken wire and plastic sheeting, bags of plant feed, garden rocks, and fertilizer, tin drums, plastic buckets, forsaken planters packed with scorched earth, and rusty garden tools tee-peed against the side of the house. Plunging his hands into the paddy, grains of rice flitting through his fingers, Meiselman raises the sunken hose.

Tramping through the neighborhood, he wears the hose diagonally across his body like a messenger bag. As a boy, Fulham Park is where Meisleman spent hours playing one-on-one basketball against himself on the blacktop courts. Summers at the Fulham Park pool, he and Barry Kranzler stood on the air conditioners behind the ladies' locker room, peeking through tiny holes in the cement blocks. Only old ladies. The girls his age changed inside the stalls. Occasionally, he would run into Ethel and buy her ice cream with his snack money. The meager change would leave him with only enough money for one piece of Bazooka.

The sign at the park entrance states a closing time of 11:00 P.M with a warning that "violators" will be arrested. He is not a violator, is he? Meiselman trudges through the shared outfield toward the dumpsters at the far end of the park, the field's giant floodlights bathing the sky white. Weak cries in the distance pull him from his path, the cry becoming clearer as he drifts closer to the pond in the park's center. "Ad majorem Dei gloriam." The prayer is coming from the other side of a wall of corrugated aluminum, which blocks off the man-made body of water. A bent back sheet of aluminum allows him to peek inside. Congregating in a thicket of ferns on the pond's verdant banks is a group of current and former White Sox players. Mags and Crede. Ozzie, Karko, and Steve "Psycho" Lyons. The greats of the Meiselman era. Frank Thomas stands in the water and baptismally dunks the head of Lance "One Dog" Johnson. Squinting for a clearer look he realizes his mind is playing a trick on him, and it is not a group of ballplayers, but his mother and father, Rav Fruman and his beardless assistant, Mitchell and Ethel. The man standing in the water is not Frank Thomas, but Colin Powell, and he is dunking Betsy Ross. Someone is tapping Meiselman's shoulder, trying to get his attention, and Meiselman swats the hand away, but the tap turns into a nudge, and then a shove. Prepared to react physically, he turns to discover Dr. Lin sitting in a director's chair. She asks to meet his wife, but Meiselman cannot find her in the group. Dr. Lin pulls a bullhorn off the ground. Covering its mouthpiece, she whispers to Meiselman, "If you can't find her, then I'll be forced to give her role to her understudy." Panicked, he pulls himself through the wall's opening, but now the banks of the pond are bare except for a group of stiff-necked ducks arrayed like bowling pins. His shul seatmate Ben Davis grabs a duck by the neck and begins force-feeding it crushed duck shell...

This is all he can remember upon waking. But it is rich material. Perfect to use as his opening on Monday. The doctor was always harassing him for dreams, especially ones in which she featured. The eggs alone will take them through the session's first thirty minutes.

Yes, the park and pond are real, and so are the ducks, he will explain to the doctor, launching into a fertile memory. Exiting the house one day, he and his mother discovered a nest of eggs underneath the shrubs bordering the driveway. Concerned the eggs and mother duck carried diseases, his mother charged him with clearing them. Twelve years old and his mother was tasking him, and not his father or Gershon, with this yard work. Not wanting to touch the diseased eggs, Meiselman, using a rolled up newspaper, nudged the eggs off the nest and rolled them down the driveway. He prodded them down the sidewalk with the intention of returning them to the pond in Fulham Park. Inexplicable and capricious what happened next. At the park's entrance, where the street dead ends and the sign announces the park's closing time, Meiselman picked up an egg bare-handed, and winding up like a pitcher, threw it against the sign. One by one, he threw the rest of the eggs. Most of the throws fell short, the eggs spiking the street's pavement. Crouched over the shattered eggs, he expected to see chicks unfolding from the shards, but stringy yellow webbing was all he saw in the mess of shell fragments. Bloody brown spots flecked the yellow of one egg.

He can already hear the doctor's outrageous observations. She asked you, not your father, to clear the eggs, her eggs. Meiselman will try sharing a second egg-centric memory, a story he regrets never sharing with her, the story of his earliest recalled erection, which occurred at the egg hatchery in the Museum of Science and Industry. Incidentally, a story of humiliation.

But the doctor, tired of talking eggs, might try redirecting the conversation by asking him what comes to mind when he considers other elements from the dream.

Ben Davis force-feeding shell to the mother duck reminds me of an article I read about proposed legislation in Israel to ban *foie gras*...My love for Frank Thomas is much deeper than simple fandom...Last week, Rav Fruman, the top rabbi in Chicago, spit a gob of sudsy saliva onto my wife's bloody underwear. This was after sending me a threatening letter in regard...

Shenkenberg! Yes, Shenkenberg! This is what Meiselman had instructed himself to remember last night. Most definitely, Shenkenberg. With distractions waylaying him all week—squabbling Deena, enticing pink-haired woman, terrorizing neighbor, then decomposing neighbor—he has not paid sufficient attention to the impending encounter with his rival, which more than anything else in his life provides him with the opportunity to set a new course.

"The other day when I called, you said you were off to give a speech, I think," Paul had said to Meiselman, lifting his cup of caffeinated coffee by its handle, cooling it with a steady blow.

"Sunday night," Meiselman's father answered for his son. "The speech is Sunday night. But it's not only a speech. You're going to be interviewing Shenkenberg, right?"

He looked to Meiselman for confirmation, obvious pride in his voice. Meiselman had no interest in deflating his father and explaining that Paul was referring to Michael Westbound's Earth Day lecture.

"Yes, the debate is the main part of the event," Meiselman said. Turning to Paul, he said, "The writer Izzy Shenkenberg is coming to my library. Wrote a semi-popular book about a revered rabbi from our community. Called it fiction. All types of nonsense about the rabbi's hobbies and private life. I've had dealings with him and, between us, he's a bit of a schmuck, pardon my language."

"Whoa, whoa," his father interrupted. "He's a major, major writer. Highly regarded. He's won awards. Been published in the *New Yorker*. The *Times*, for crying out loud, reviews his books. He's a very big deal. It's a very big deal." Looking down the table at his wife, he added, "Went to the same high school, right, Pooch? Weren't they friends?"

Deena, who was in the process of moving her father's used tea bag from his crumpled napkin to the coaster, says, "My friend Molly won't stop with how much she loves the book, how hilarious it is." Even now, reflecting on this moment from last night, Meiselman is unsure whether his wife was trying to provoke him or team up with his father to bolster Meiselman in the eyes of Paul.

George, wanting to add to the conversation, sat open-mouthed, ready to wedge in a comment at any slight pause, but whenever he would start, Deena would squeeze the top of his leg and nod in the direction of whomever was in the middle of speaking. Sick of waiting, he turned to Meiselman's mother and said, "Did I ever tell you about the time I met Willie Nelson in a bathroom?"

“Expecting a good crowd?” Paul asked Meiselman.

George asked Meiselman’s mother for an ice cube and sugar-free sweetener.

“It’s a tremendous library,” his father answered. “Bigger and better than most university libraries, I bet. Last event we were at, not even such a famous writer, and hundreds of people showed up. Standing in the aisles. I’ve told him, ‘You’re putting together a nice resume with these events.’ Why not parlay what he is doing now into a real business. The *Journal* advertises speaking tours of financial planners teaming up with ex-generals or former athletes. Hundreds of dollars a ticket.” Then he turned to Meiselman and said, “You’d be really good at it. With your focus. You kidding me?”

“Harvey!” Meiselman’s mother, coming in from the kitchen with a bowl of ice cubes, yelled. “Enough.”

Even now, Meiselman does not know whether his mother’s reining in his father was a call for modesty, or whether she believed her husband was back to pestering her son about changing jobs.

“I just needed one,” George said, reaching to scoop a cube from the bowl barehanded, Deena’s intercepting hand a second too late. At that moment, her eyes locked on Meiselman with a smile suggesting embarrassment. Was it her way of saying that undesirable baggage accompanies her, too? He cannot remember his response, or whether he smiled back. He was not present in the moment. Shenkenberg and the anxiety of the remaining debate prep were monopolizing his thoughts.

* * *

Recent issues of *Interview*, pulled off the metal shelves in Periodicals before he’d left work yesterday, are stacked in front of Meiselman on the dining room table. The couple hours of disrupted sleep seems to have rid him of yesterday's lethargy, and he is determined to stay seated and working until he has honed a strategy and formulated challenging questions for the debate portion of the event or, at least, until the newspaper delivery van crawls down the street, which, judging from a glance out the dining room bay window—gray sky, dimming streetlights—will be in the coming hour.

The first interview he reads is with a singer whose music Deena enjoys. Whenever he is a passenger in his wife's car and they are listening to this singer, Meiselman feigns enthusiasm, reaching for the jewel box in the glove compartment so he can study the artist's picture because he still cannot decide whether he finds her attractive, what with her sizeable top shelf of teeth, overly wide mouth, and flat lips. No laugh is light with this woman. She reels you in when that jaw hinge cranks open, making you feel like you are the funniest person alive until the laugh suddenly turns homicidal, the jaw snapping shut, and the singer takes a bite out of your neck.

Interviewer: So, Alanis, I hear that you're off to Paris for a romantic getaway.

This interviewer's clubby tone is not some ploy to coax the singer into dropping her guard. Rather, the reporter is reluctant to jeopardize his access by asking uncomfortable questions. Instead, he offers questions that act as opportunities for the singer to surreptitiously boast. This is not the strategy Meiselman will take with Shenkenberg.

Interviewer: So, I was listening to your new album, So-Called Chaos, *and something that really blew my mind is that you put yourself out there on this record in a way you haven't before. You really take yourself to task for not living up to your own ideals.*

Ms. Morissette: Oh, yeah! I still engage the part of me that feels incredibly revelatory but also the part of me that can just laugh at myself. I can see what a hypocrite I am, how much I don't walk my talk with everything from environmental activism to social consciousness: There are times when I can live it very fiercely and others when I drop the ball entirely. Being in the public eye, the last thing I'd want to do is portray myself as being this perfect person that isn't even real. It's more inspiring if I portray myself as the very human person I am.

Years ago, Meiselman picked up on this awful trend of endeavoring idols branding themselves as "very human." Traces it back to those awful movies of the last decade where the heroes smoked dope, barely held onto menial jobs at printing shops, and spent their workdays dreaming of becoming rock and roll musicians despite showing only basic musical proficiency. Not exactly Robert Redford or Clint Eastwood. Does this mean Meiselman should cut Shenkenberg some slack for presenting Rabbi J- as a boozed up boxing enthusiast? Because maybe the writer has noticed the same trend, and his agenda is not to smash the idol of Rabbi J- into smithereens or melt it down in a fiery furnace, but to refashion the rabbi for this current generation by nicking up the body and chipping away at the idol's gold plating. See, I'm actually elevating Rabbi J- by highlighting his shortcomings, Shenkenberg may argue. Then, to prove the righteousness of his endeavor, he will proceed to bible-thump Meiselman with stories of Abraham pimping his wife out to Pharaoh and Jacob playing tricks on his boorish brother and blind father. He might toss the whole book of Genesis at his host when making this argument about imperfect idols. If Meiselman were truly convinced people desired "very human" idols, then he could ignore Shenkenberg's disparaging book and petulant behavior over the phone. But Meiselman knows how people say they want "very human," when all they will really accept is god-like. The newspapers may photograph the President hauling hay and driving a pickup truck, but they will never show him shoveling dung. When they ask the President to name a mistake from his first term, he is cautious to couch it with a boast. Didn't care enough. Cared too much. Too ambitious. Moses hit the rock and this all-too-human idol never became a Jesus or a Mohammed, and the number of Jews has been holding steady for thousands of years. In all of this theorizing there is a question for Shenkenberg, but because it is Shabbat and Meiselman cannot write it down, he folds down the page's corner and instructs himself to remember.

Interviewer: What does this record mean to you? Where does it figure in your oeuvre*?*

He has to stay away from words he cannot pronounce.

Soon the interviewer is back to asking Ms. Morissette about her upcoming trip, extending his fantasy of being a member of the singer's inner circle.

Interviewer: What are the romantic things that you want to do in Paris?

Ask Shenkenberg about what he looks forward to doing when he visits New Niles, and chances are Shenkenberg will take the predictable route of hailing New York City's superiority. He will claim he was able to become the writer he is today only after he moved away from his hometown, a town where everyone he knew looked and prayed the same. Oh, the horrors. He will twist the advantages of growing up in New Niles, an upper middle class neighborhood with negligible crime and graffiti-free streets, into retarding forces. Will use the word "provincial" to describe a Jewish high school with a graduation rate of a hundred percent. At the same time, he will trumpet the imperfections of his new town. Its dirtiness and overcrowding, its high cost of living, and streets filled with mumbling vagrants and scheming panhandlers will be presented as evidence he is living a "very human" existence, living on a more substantive plane, like how whenever Gershon and his wife visit, they insist on insulting Meiselman's mother by bringing cheeses, bagels, pickles, and desserts from what they insist are the best kosher establishments in the world, as if Meiselman and his parents live on some Jewish outpost. To add to the insult, they are continuously relaying instructions on how the food is to be preserved, prepared, and served. Or the writer will use the question to talk highfalutin nonsense like Ms. Morissette does in her response:

> *Morissette: Well, we just read* The Da Vinci Code, *so we're going to explore Paris and research what's fact and what's fiction in the book. We're also going to go to the Louvre and walk around the city, drinking cappuccinos—we'll just follow our noses. Also, I have this thing where I sit under the Eiffel Tower...Well, this is terrible to say, but I'm just going to say it anyway: Every time I've gone to Paris with a boyfriend I've sat under the Eiffel Tower and asked it to tell me what the fate of the relationship would be.*

Either way, a guarantee that Shenkenberg's answer will end up alienating the crowd, or make him look plain foolish. A second folded corner, a second question to remember.

Opening a different issue of *Interview*, Meiselman peruses an interview with the actress Christina Ricci. Round-faced and black-haired like Ethel. Also, like Ethel, the tendency to routinely drop too much weight. Once, Meiselman rented one of the actress's movies thinking it was about football. Turned out it was about a miserable family sitting around a dining room table spewing bottled up grievances at one another. The interview is boring. Story after boring story meant to underscore the very humanness of the actress. Christina once showed up to an audition with a black eye. Christina's mother was reluctant to allow her daughter to pursue acting. Christina struggles to navigate "the movie industry's rigid definition of beauty."

Next, he turns to an interview with an unfamiliar writer. The first question, "Have you always wanted to write?" is the question inevitably asked by an audience member at every author event Meiselman has ever hosted at the library. The answer can go only one of two ways. Yes, and then the audience has to hear about a precocious and preternaturally talented boy filling up notebooks with inane stories about space travel, patricide, and spying on an aunt using the toilet. No, and the writer tells of how they stumbled into it late in life, on a whim, while bored at work, also an account meant to emphasize his or her natural talent.

There is an interview with the actress Jennifer Connelly, whom Meiselman finds attractive. Like Deena, she is not afraid to leave a little hair on the brow.

Interviewer: Oscar Wilde believed that no man is truthful. Give him a mask, he said, and he will tell you the truth. Do you think we can be truthful to ourselves without masks?

Difficult but doable, if anyone is asking Meiselman. The profoundness of the question and the referencing of a canonical writer make it an ideal question.

Still in search of a question that will really bruise Shenkenberg, Meiselman opens the last unread issue of *Interview* and turns to a short exchange with a writer named ZZ Packer. Meiselman has never hosted her at the New Niles Public Library. Sure enough, straight off, she is asked if she always wanted to be a writer. No, she answers.

Interviewer: Your experiences show in your work, because you wear a lot of different skins in the collection. One thing your protagonists have in common though is that they're all estranged or ostracized, in some way, from those around them.

Ms. Packer: That's probably the most autobiographical part! (Laughs.) It's not as if I'm a hermit living alone, but in some ways I see a part of myself in those kinds of characters. Some of them are somehow shaken out of or feel distanced from their communities. And then there's the collection's title, which basically implies a distance and desire to be somewhere else—not just spatially, but somewhere else mentally and emotionally. When I see these characters struggling, I want to follow them and see what happens.

"Hermit" is a word that sticks out, because he recalls seeing the same word in Christina Ricci's interview.

Ricci: Well, I probably don't interact with the normal world as much as other people do because I'm sort of hermitlike anyway...I'm always afraid that I'll be yelled at in public.

Hermit. Hermitlike. Brings to mind another interview he came across yesterday when assessing whether this was the right periodical for his needs. With little effort, Meiselman finds the interview with Imad Rahman, a writer he has neither heard of, nor hosted at the library. "It just means that I'm a little more disconnected from my surroundings, and a little more connected to being disconnected."

Is Meiselman prepared to declare the emergence of a new trend? People needing to present themselves as estranged and ostracized, insisting they would feel more comfortable elsewhere, in a different town, in a different skin. True hermits, however, do not yap this willingly. It takes poking and prodding to get true hermits to come out of their shells and, usually, it is just for a slow crawl. Shenkenberg is certainly a type who, like Ricci, Packer, and Rahman, presents himself as disconnected from the community, and Meiselman knows there is an indicting, potentially undermining question to ask the writer about his boasts of severing ties with his past. Formulating the actual wording will have to wait, because in the distance he can hear the creaky squeal of car breaks as the newspaper delivery van slows in front of his parents' house. The van's beams poke through the morning fog, the delivery woman's arm hanging out the window, the sleeved newspapers clutched in her hand as she attempts an on-the-go drop. For the first time in days, Meiselman cannot wait to get his hands on the newspaper. Maybe it his usual Shabbat morning anxiety, his need to know nothing consequential has been missed during his period of disconnectedness, or, maybe it is a sign that after a week full of battling and falling out of routine, he is regaining his footing. After all, his wife is upstairs in bed, nobody knows anything of his last contact with the neighbor before her death, and in less than an hour he has produced four questions for the dialogue-slash-debate portion of the event, one of them potentially undermining.

✶ ✶ ✶

The moment his galoshes slap the cement, eyes fixing on the blue plastic bags at the foot of his driveway, the heart of the trench-coated Meiselman starts twitching; his strides lengthen, his arms swing for speed. All evidence points to the break in routine this week being more of a pause than a rupture. But then he spots his father's yet-to-be-retrieved newspapers from the corner of his eye and instead of changing course and cutting across his parents' front yard, he stays put, intent on discontinuing this seldom-acknowledged gesture. Seldom-acknowledged? Never-acknowledged gesture. Does his gesture even factor into his parents' pillow talk? Gershon is cleaning up in New York, Pooch. Just remember the one who was here, is here, and will be here, his mother answers. The ease with which Meiselman is able to abandon this chore may suggest an unleashing of his capabilities. A changing disposition, at the very least. Bad sign for Shenkenberg. Bad sign for anyone else who trifles with him from this point forward.

This may be an opportunity to further refine and augment routines that, over time, have become stale. So before he peels the blue plastic sleeve off the *Tribune*, he sets it down on the dewy grass with the other bagged newspapers and steps over to the bushes that separate his lot from the late Mrs. Woolf's. If his mother can speak fondly of her former nemesis and provide comfort to the lady's mourning son, Meiselman can embrace the old lady's desire to live in a neighborhood where children are not banished to basements and backyards, where adults sneak away from their homes, unseen, through garages, where the only people who walk the sidewalks are the help. Was this village not once a place where people relaxed in front of their houses and hooted banalities at passing neighbors? He does not know, but imagines it was. The old lady's ratty beach chair, whose uneven legs woke him and his wife on countless mornings, is behind a bush, folded and leaned up against the house's wall.

The forward and backward rock, what was one time a nighttime disturbance, now soothes him. Looking out from his new perch at the front of his house, he speculates over whether the crisp breeze penetrating the dress of his trench coat and the deep grayness enveloping the sky is weather- or time-related. A bird darts from rooftop to rooftop. Meiselman does not know birds or clouds or what their movements may mean.

Today's headlines are bland, the main one nothing but a puff piece. *Candidate's Best Tag: A Likeable Kind of Guy, Senator Battles Aloof, Remote Image.* An accompanying photograph of the senator bewilderedly staring down at a baby, an image that makes clear he will never become president. Right column, above the fold: *Jump in Mortgage Rates May Blunt Housing Boom.* A good headline to have memorized for Jeremy and the other men at the Kiddush. Left column, above the fold: *Insurgents' Escalation Taxing U.S. Capabilities.* Not interested in reading any more negative talk about the war, he flips over the newspaper for the headlines under the fold. Dominating the center is a puff picture from the tornado that hit south of the city; a family standing in front of a mound of wood, stuffed animals, photo albums, and a toilet. *President Ends Most Bans on Business with Libya.* This, the fruit of the labor, the return on the expended blood and treasure, they cram into the bottom left corner. On the opposite side of the page, in the lower right-hand corner, an obituary. *Esther 'Etta' Woolf, 86, Agriculturalist, Advisor to Six Presidents.*

A shortage of consequential events must have bumped his neighbor's obituary to the front page. Nevertheless, quite the achievement. One day, his children will see this newspaper framed and hanging in Meiselman's home office and ask about the lady who was the family's neighbor for over thirty-five years. After regaling them with stories of her ditch digging, he will proudly read to them the last line of the obituary's first paragraph. "A grief-stricken neighbor discovered her body late Thursday afternoon, and paramedics pronounced her dead at the scene." He, Meiselman, is the neighbor, he will explain to the children. He, Meiselman, the grief-stricken. He, Meiselman, was at the scene when she was pronounced dead. A recording of his actions, his emotions, his history, right here on the front page of the *Chicago Tribune*. He rereads the sentence several more times before launching into the rest of the obituary. "...sustainable agriculture...food security...land improvement...a member of President Clinton's World Food Summit delegation...a proponent of the Right to Food movement." Even with the excitement of his accomplishment, he cannot put off the White Sox recap any longer.

A White Sox winner. 4-3. *Crede Gets the Job Done Again*, the headline reads. More important than the win, however, is Frank rejoining the lineup. No signs of rust, either. Home run in the fourth. Walked twice. The slugger's return to the lineup coincides with Meiselman's return to routine? The slugger's hamstring heals at the same time Meiselman and Deena's relationship mends? Symbiotic. If Meiselman were to ever meet Frank Thomas, he would not pester him for an autograph. Instead, he will use his time to empathize with the White Sox all-time leader in home runs. That initial humiliation of not being drafted out of high school was the first of many humiliations. With every record broken, with every milestone reached, comes new slights from the media, the fans, the owners. Even Ben Davis makes the occasional comment about diminishing bat speed. Meiselman will tell Frank how he cannot imagine the pain of not being recognized as one of the game's all-time greats. You were born in the wrong era. Played in the wrong city, too. Chicago is not Milwaukee, but it's not New York or Boston either. It's not even Baltimore. Look at the love Ripken got just for showing up to work every day.

The screen door creaks open behind him. He quickly uncrosses his legs and slaps the newspaper down on his lap as if caught doing something untoward.

"Someone forgot to close the door," Deena, a towel wrapping her head, teases.

Unsure of the relationship's state, albeit pleased Deena is not attempting to finagle more concessions by dangling the threat of staying in bed all day, Meiselman laughs along. She keeps the door propped with her shoulder. Her makeup from last night washed off, she is pale-faced and frigid-lipped. She is wearing the robe with her name in Hebrew stitched to the pocket, a present his parents brought from Israel on a trip shortly after the engagement. Just his second time seeing her in it. Thought it was Amvetsed years ago. Whether it is intended as mocking or massaging is not clear. Now is probably not the time to probe, but he cannot resist, so he reaches behind, lifts the robe's flap and says, "Sexy robe." Down comes her hand, the edges of their fingers brushing. She says, "We have a ways to go until we can touch again." Is she speaking legalistically—she is a bleeder—or figuratively? She says, "Let me bring you your coffee."

"Better not. I've been thinking about cutting back." He has given this no thought, but it sounds repentant, as if acknowledging the need for changes in his day-to-day behavior. "Anyway, was about to come in. Wanted to lie down before shul. Been up for hours with this event, reviewing notes and last second details, trying to formulate new questions." He can tell she has stopped listening. He will not even bother showing her his appearance in today's newspaper. The last thing he needs is insufficient enthusiasm spoiling the excitement of this accomplishment.

"Well, I want to leave for shul together," she says, extending her hand and patting the back of his chair, her fingers fiddling the beach chair's plastic tube weaving. "Okay, Meisie?"

Maybe without enthusiasm or tenderness, but the name was uttered. What explains her rush back to normalcy?

* * *

Services started fifteen minutes ago, but no more than forty men are seated in the spacious sanctuary. Jeremy, Molly's husband, the pediatrician, Meiselman's new Kiddush friend, is loafing in the last row of the sanctuary reading from a folded *Tribune*. Meiselman nudges Jeremy's shoulder with the edge of his *siddur*. The man flinches and tries concealing the newspaper by tucking it inside his navy-blue suit jacket, but Meiselman snags it from his hand. He sets it on the seat next to Jeremy and slowly turns the pages until he is back on page one. But the obituary is not there. In its place, a puff piece: *Family and Friends Attempt to Cope with Storm Tragedy*. Jeremy is reading Friday's paper.

"Found it in the bathroom," Jeremy confirms.

Without the article in front of him, the boast sounds inconsequential, paltry, childish, especially since he was not even mentioned by name. He turns mumble-mouthed telling the story of the body's discovery and concludes by saying, "You probably don't see too many dead bodies, being a pediatrician."

"No, just in med school. But I've been in the paper a couple of times," Jeremy says. "Molly's parents announced our marriage in the *Times,* and last year the *Tribune* listed me as one of the city's top pediatricians in their rankings issue. A paid ad, basically. I'll show it to you when you come over later. You're coming to my birthday party, right?"

This is the first Meiselman is hearing of Jeremy's birthday party.

"We'll see," Meiselman says. "With the event, I'm quite busy. Need a nap."

"That's right. The writer dude. Molly is stoked. Been trying to get me to read that book. Outside of work, though, I only have a head for the newspaper and magazines. And riding. You into cycling, Meiselman?"

Meiselman mentions how much he adores the man's yellow tie. "Canary," Jeremy corrects him.

Still unsure of whether he left yesterday's encounter at the gas station with the upper hand, Meiselman feels it would be best to avoid Ben Davis. Besides, an upgrade is in order, something toward the front with the people who emphasize decorum, but locating a seat that is not a member's permanent spot is tricky. For some time, Meiselman has been eyeing an unoccupied seat in the third row, two in, next to Professor Benny Atlas. Walking up the aisle, he begins feeling guilty about spurning Ben Davis, so he stops in front of his former row and after getting the attention of his soon-to-be-former seatmate, who is not praying, but staring ahead, cheeks puffed with air, elbows back on the headrests of the adjoining chairs, finger bookmarking his spot in the *siddur*, Meiselman taps at his ear and points up the aisle. A thumbs-up from Ben Davis, and Meiselman is on his way. Professor Atlas is standing in the aisle, face grazing the pages of a scholarly book, glasses dangling from his fingers. The man's belongings are resting on the coveted seat. Meiselman stands patiently off to the side and when the professor looks over at him, Meiselman gestures that he is interested in the spot. Cramming his glasses onto his face, the professor points down at the seat. "Not going to work. That's for my stuff." With a nod of the head, he motions to a seat two rows back. "Next to Sofer and his boys."

Meiselman sways in his new seat, mouthing the words of the prayers, proving to those around him that he has no intention of importing the decorum-shattering ways of the back rows. Closing his eyes to heighten this show of deep concentration, Meiselman tries to attach the prayers' words to holy thoughts, but all he sees is the pink-haired woman's pink laced bun from yesterday, and when he manages to finally force the image from his mind it is replaced with one of his hands massaging Ethel's creaky back, his boss's neck lolling forward as he kneads her spine, Meiselman using methods picked up from the baker Paprocki.

Meiselman's thoughts finally transition to the exciting possibility of a party at Molly and Jeremy's house. The golf ball pearls Molly hangs around her neck suggest she is not a hostess who will put out grapes in a crystal bowl, pitch toothpicks into melon cubes, and call it a day. If fruit is served it will be dipped in chocolate, or pureed and used as filling.

Sensing someone is standing over him, he opens his eyes to discover Danny Sofer and three young boys clogging the row's entrance. Hovering, they wait for Meiselman to ask if he has taken their seats. The father confirms with an apologetic grimace, and the three boys—no older than five or six, although Meiselman is deficient at guessing the ages of children—push into the row, military action figures and baggies of cheerios clutched in their hands, sending Meiselman off to look for a new seat.

A fellow founding member like Lou Kipperman will be able to direct Meiselman to an open seat, hopefully, because this bouncing from row to row is turning into a humiliation. Meiselman looks like an out-of-towner, a guest, and not someone who got circumcised in this very hall, right near where the rabbi is sitting. Every time Meiselman points to what he thinks is a possibility, Lou Kipperman waves him off, the chunky green stone of his graduation ring flying in front of Meiselman's face. "Bill Robinson sits there, when he comes. You don't want to start with him. Len Ackerman's spot...obviously, he's not coming today, but I wouldn't. People talk, they point, 'You know what happened to the guy who used to sit there? You know where he's sitting now?' You don't need that." He scans the rows, flicking the underside of his white goatee with the back of his fingers. Finally, an idea strikes him, and he motions for Meiselman to follow. Headed down the aisle toward the back, the man pitches a promising possibility. "Not too much talking in this section. Get a nice full sound. Sufficient legroom. Can hear the rabbi perfectly. Over there, that aisle seat, right next to the Davis boy."

Fearing he appears aimless, Meiselman takes his old seat, and shakes Ben Davis's hand as he does every Shabbat morning, the man's callused palm scratching Meiselman's soft skin. Following the script is the lynchpin of the relationship, so he need not worry about who left yesterday's encounter with the upper hand or whether it may have upset the rapport. Meiselman, therefore, after opening his *siddur* and mumbling a prayer, sits back in his chair, opens his stance and says, "This Crede, boy."

"Look," Ben Davis replies. "I'm looking for some spirituality in my life, a connection kind of, so I'm going to *daven*."

Suddenly, they are not speaking at all. They are just standing, sitting, praying, and amen-ing with the rest of the congregation. When it comes time for the rabbi to deliver his sermon, Meiselman tilts his chin upward and listens closely, following the rabbi's opening question about why contact with a dead person makes one impure for seven days, whereas contact with a dead animal creates a state of impurity that lasts only until the following evening. This, according to the rabbi, whose every utterance comes out in a yell, is counterintuitive. How can a person, who has a soul and is created in God's image, be more defiling than a dirty animal?

Perhaps the rabbi read about Meiselman's encounter with Mrs. Woolf's body and is outraged over Meiselman coming to shul and spreading his defilement. Was Meiselman expected to immerse himself in the *mikveh* before reemerging in public? Not since the transition years has he accompanied his father for the annual pre-High Holidays dip. Started going when he was a boy. The steamy air of the changing room tightened his asthmatic lungs. The other men pranced naked, some of them with sweaty sidelocks unfurled, soggy beards and damp pubic hair on display. Only the Meiselman men insisted on tying towels around their waists before dropping their underwear. He managed to catch glimpses of his father and brother as they entered and exited the pool of water. Gershon, one year, was showing freshly sprouted hair. By the next year, his brother looked more and more like their father, filling Meiselman with feelings of inadequacy. Eventually, hairs took root around Meiselman. A contrast between Meiselman and the two other men in his family became apparent during his high school years. Theirs intimated a turtle frightfully peeking out of its shell, while his lolled like the unruly end of a garden hose. Does his ampleness resemble PopPop's?

Thoughts of the *mikveh* have distracted Meiselman, not only from following the rabbi's speech, but also from the numbness deadening his thigh on account of Ben Davis's crowding, which has forced Meiselman into a tightening leg cross like that of a little boy trying to hold back a pee. Needing to reverse the blood flow, Meiselman uncrosses and when lowering his leg he intentionally stomps the edge of his seatmate's foot. Ben Davis does not flinch, apologize, or narrow his stance. He plants his feet into the carpet and leans forward, not allowing the commotion to distract him.

Instead of getting worked up over this crowding, Meiselman's energy would be better spent on more pressing concerns, like whether or not Deena has absolved him for his supposed misbehavior this week, or whether he should hope for a large or small crowd this afternoon at Jeremy's party? A madhouse will allow him to sample all the desserts, and to discard after an unsatisfactory bite. Also, taking seconds or thirds will not look piggish. But a large gathering carries with it problems of careless cake-cutting, and guests using bare hands to serve themselves. Deep into the party he can expect foreign food littering dishes, and frosting-smeared plates strewn across the serving table. Additionally, at such large gatherings it inevitably becomes difficult to find a clean cup or fork.

"*Yasher koach, yasher koach*," the congregation mutters as the rabbi finishes.

By the time Meiselman enters the social hall, the men from his Kiddush group are assembled in a semicircle off to the side, each holding a bowl of steaming *cholent* balanced on top of a clear plastic cup filled with a brown alcoholic beverage. Ben Davis is camped in front of the herring platter, sticking salted fish with his used toothpick. Not wanting to miss out on the conversation, a plateless and cupless Meiselman joins the group. Jeremy and Scott are deep in conversation, ears practically nuzzling, as they try to hear one another over the clamor. Meiselman muscles his way into an aperture between Scott and Jeffery, a quiet guy with a cleft chin who wears a v-neck sweater under his suit jacket and always appears to be looking off into the distance. Jeffery does something in finance, and Meiselman engages him by asking what he thinks of the jump in mortgage rates he read about in this morning's newspaper. Jeffrey is not familiar with the story. "Could spell a premature end to the housing boom," Meiselman adds.

"Sure hope not," Jeffery says, "Just secured myself a sweet equity line with a super sweet teaser rate."

"Was telling Scott about my most recent acquisition," Jeremy yells across the circle to Jeffery and Meiselman. "A signed, game-worn Kobe jersey."

Jeffrey sticks up a thumb and says, "Sweet."

"Didn't know you were a sports fan, Jeremy," Meiselman says. "Sox or Cubs?"

"Yankees. Don't ask why. And in basketball it's the Lakers. Football, Cowboys."

"Your Yanks just took two out of three from my Sox."

"Don't follow the day-to-day. These days, for me, it's all about memorabilia. I'll show you the collection when you come over for the party. Remind me to show you my Shaquille O' Neal sneaker," Jeremy says. "Size 22."

"The size of a small baby from the Far East," Meiselman says, which gets smiles from everyone in the circle.

Jeremy reaches his arm across the circle, grabs Jeffrey by the lapel and runs his fingers down the edge of the jacket.

"Worsted?" he asks. Jeffrey confirms with a nod. "Sweet."

Deena and Meiselman walk the side streets of New Niles without uttering a word. Staring down at her striding feet, Deena chews her lower lip. The line of communication between them is apparently still frayed. Or, an even worse possibility, they have finally exhausted all possible conversation.

The birthday party is safe territory, although transmitting genuine excitement is crucial since she often accuses him of sounding insufficiently enthused about social engagements involving her contacts. How can he act excited about her coworkers' treyf dinner parties when Meiselman and Deena are relegated to munching on a garden salad of bitter, wilted lettuce, dismal carrot shavings, and uncut baby tomatoes that, when pierced, spray seeds onto his finest shirts? Yet, the possibility of mini pecan pies, flourless chocolate cake, and chocolate mousse served in champagne glasses does excite him, and he will also voice concern over the quality of the gift Deena has selected for Molly's husband. You never want to be the poor person in the relationship. You never want to be the much richer person, either. Let me contribute to the brainstorming. Beers, waters, cycling, sports memorabilia....

Beating him to the punch, she says, "Molly is having people over this afternoon." It spills from her mouth as if she has spent the walk thinking of how to tell him. "Just women, no spouses. Coffee and tea, I think. For what, I'm not really sure. So I will go." She pauses briefly before concluding, "Sorry to do this to you."

Calling her out on the apparent lie carries risks. Who readily admits to lying? She will blame him for forcing her hand, turning herself into the victim. She will proceed to tell him why she does not want him at the party, and he is not and never will be ready to hear such things.

"What are you sorry about?" Meiselman asks.

"That I'll be leaving you for the afternoon."

She is not ready to leave him for longer than an afternoon. The state of the relationship is solid enough.

Sunday

Despite repeatedly cautioning himself on the ride over against frittering away his morning feasting on the photograph of college-aged Ethel in a bathing suit and Betsy Ross's treyf chocolates, Meiselman's finger fidgets with excitement as he punches the access code. On his first attempt, the bulb flashes green, and he is through the door. Expected to execute the, so-to-speak, will of God tonight, he cannot afford to sully his spiritual mindset, so before throwing on the hallway lights, he steadies his breath. The fluorescents buzz to life, and the white walls and polished linoleum smolder, black skid marks and nail holes laid bare. Above, a ceiling tile is askew and off its rails. The intense luminosity makes him feel as if he is being watched, so he strides purposefully down the hallway, barely turning his head to see if the bowl of chocolates is on the secretary's desk. It is.

He hooks his coat on the back of his office door. At his desk, he empties the back issues of *Interview* from his briefcase and gets to work. The final tasks for the event, however, prove more tedious than immersing. Copying the questions formulated yesterday onto the fluorescent neon note cards takes mere minutes. Even coming up with the right phrasing for the indicting, potentially undermining, question takes no more than three. Editing Shenkenberg's introduction is temporarily diverting, Meiselman dragging his black Sharpie through lines and lines of the publisher-provided bio, blotting out mentions of best lists cracked by the writer's current and previous books. Lifts the Sharpie briefly to keep intact a passage acknowledging Shenkenberg as a finalist—not winner—of the Hirshhorn Prize. Sets the implement back down to strike a line noting Shenkenberg's win of something called the Copenhagen Prize. For every two accolades expunged, one is left untouched. The bio's last line, a mention of the writer's current city of residence—Brooklyn—where he lives alone, is kept. The essence of the joke Meiselman will use to open the event comes effortlessly. It will address the event's program card, which was printed last week and has Ethel Lewinson listed as Master of Ceremonies. A pithy quip about how he is obviously not Ethel, followed by a humble remark on the great honor of the library's director, his mentor, asking him to fill her elegant heels. He is having difficulty coming up with the joke's exact wording. A stroll through the hallway to stretch the legs and clear the mind may prove beneficial, even if he can predict where such drifting will lead.

Exiting his office, he manages to turn down the hallway without being lured into Ethel's office by the photograph on her desk. An unsullied spiritual mindset holding, he passes Betsy Ross's desk without taking a closer look at the chocolates in the bowl. Yet, right as his hand flattens against the brass plate of the swinging door leading out to the main floor, Meiselman can foresee how he will never make it to the auditorium to check whether maintenance has arranged the stage per his specifications.

Soon he is staring down at the empty bowl of chocolates on Betsy Ross's desk, and what he does not foresee is that upon dabbing the tip of his index finger against the thick dusting of chocolate powder covering the bowl's bottom and then cleaning it off with a lick, he will proceed to stuff his face into the bowl, the wiry hairs of his beard chin and moustache crunching against the ceramic, chocolate granules tickling and dissolving on the tip of his flicking tongue. When he comes up for air, he brushes the back of his hand across his mouth and beard. A plume of chocolate powder triggers a cough. Smeared chocolate sullies the bowl. Face back in the bowl, he laps at the chocolate until the bowl looks as if a considerate coworker has washed and returned it to her desk.

Save for a curly, dark beard hair pasted to the bowl's bottom. Using a wettish fingertip he slides it up the bowl's side, but every time he gets it to the lip, the hair slides back down into a puddle of his saliva. Reaching into his pocket for a handkerchief, he towels off his sodden beard hair only to realize he's pulled out the underwear stained with the bloods of Deena and Mrs. Woolf. He shrugs, then uses it to root out the hair and dry the bowl.

This slight descent into degeneracy animates Meiselman, like a soldier rubbing mud into the face before setting out for battle, or a ballplayer eyeblacking himself before the game. Upholding a standard of decency is a luxury for those who do not feel an imperative to win, for those who are content with becoming the collateral damage of life's winners. Meiselman, however, is certainly playing to win. And for the first time all week, he believes he can come out on top tonight. The difference a day makes. Yesterday was spent cowed before Deena, mistakenly believing that acquiescence—agreeing to see Dr. Lin, accepting Deena's lie about Molly and Jeremy's party without quarrel—would bring them closer to reconciliation.

Late in the afternoon, a feeble knock had drawn Meiselman to the front door. Head ducked into the upturned collar of her black trench coat, his wife brushed past him, mumbling something about not taking a key on account of the coat's shallow pockets. In front of the closet, she struggled to release her arms from the sleeves of her coat, struggled to get the corners of the hanger into the coat's armholes, and finally, standing on her toes, struggled to latch the hanger onto the rod. Just as she was ready to let the hanger and coat drop to the floor, Meiselman stepped in. She brushed past him, again. At the dining room entrance, she scratched at a drip of dried paint and told a tale about arriving to the party only to realize spouses were invited, too, and how she would have walked home to retrieve him had her feet not been burning from the new shoes. Was this staged entrance ginned up on the walk home, the result of overwhelming guilt? Or was this planned, soon after Deena came to the decision she would attend alone? Not wanting to lose any recovered ground, he told her he was happy having the time to reread Shenkenberg in preparation for the event, even though, in actuality, he'd spent his afternoon wandering the house, occasionally picking up various sections of the newspaper, only to promptly set them down out of boredom. Removing her new heels, his wife's body reduced to its diminutive state, she said, "Not your kind of party anyway."

With the beginnings of blisters blotching the arches of her feet, Deena stepped to the dining room table and set down a balled napkin. She said, "Brought you back a treat." Unclenching her hand, she dumped the gold paper napkin onto the table. Shoes in hand, she headed upstairs. He waited until he heard the bedroom door slam shut before unwrapping what turned out to be a chocolate truffle, whose shell was cracked and dented, its crumby entrails banded together in a mush that pasted the napkin's pulpy paper, damage resulting, no doubt, from Deena's tight clench on the walk home. While a child would never accept such a flawed treat, an adult is expected to shrug off such defects. Then there is his mother who, more than shrugging it off, shows an eagerness to act as a receptacle for the bad: the shattered meringue, the chicken wing turned bone crunching black on its third reheating, the scraps of burnt potato kugel, gummy onions stuck to the casserole. His father, on the other hand, has not once offered to take the bad. His mother's willingness to accept the bad is another possible opening for his session with Dr. Lin on Monday. He will tell the doctor he flushed the treat down the toilet.

Upstairs, he found Deena laid up with Shenkenberg.

"I'm loving the book," she said. "What time do Molly and I need to get there tomorrow night?"

"6:40 if you want seats."

"That popular, huh?"

"Smallish room." Then he added, "That might have been the best chocolate I've ever had."

"That was nothing. They had way better stuff."

"One can imagine," he answered.

"Molly is amazing," his wife said. "Right?"

Why was she asking for his endorsement? Meiselman, looking to get out of the inning, answered, "Yes, amazing."

Not better than Betsy Ross's chocolates, Meiselman assesses, licking at the residue trapped in his beard as he wheels to the end of Ethel's desk. He stands the photograph on the leather blotter and, using the heel of his hand, begins working on himself through his corduroy pants. The material scratches his unprotected skin, providing a kind of pleasure, but not nearly enough. He slides two fingers inside his zipper, hoping to uncover a complication like poor positioning or thigh-stuck sack or bent shaft. What shaft? Stalled at a vegetative state, droopy head conked out on the seat of Ethel's chair. Has this particular photograph finally lost its efficacy after so many Sundays? His entire hand now down his pants, he wheels back over to the collection of framed photographs clustered at the desk's end. Right away, he flips over photographs with nephews and nieces, even the two that include Ethel's tomboyishly skinny sister-in-law Ann, a woman Meiselman finds alluring because of a reddish beauty mark under one of her nostrils and the skimpy, army-green t-shirt she is wearing in both photos. Also turns over ones featuring

Lev, Ethel's younger brother, a stubby, prematurely balding kid who spent his teenage years at the gym drawing out untapped muscles. From the back row, Meiselman snatches a shot of Ethel and her mom taken at Ethel's bat-mitzvah. Knows the occasion from the zebra-print dress and short black leather gloves Ethel is wearing. Meiselman's mom had returned from the celebration questioning whether it was common for the bat-mitzvah girls in Meiselman's class to wear strapless gowns. A dress especially inappropriate for an Orthodox girl like Ethel, given her prematurely full "bosoms." She felt like calling the principal, she warned Meiselman's father. He cannot remember his father's response but imagines it involved a dismissive wave and an insult along the lines of, "They don't know appropriate from inappropriate. People like that are simply incapable of knowing." Then back to his newspaper. Without his mother, Meiselman would never have been aware of the dress's danger, even if it was clear that Ethel's development was rapid, and far beyond the other girls in the class. Embracing her maturation with self-assuredness, Ethel perched a bottle of deodorant on the top shelf of her locker and kept a tampon inched out of the front pocket of her knapsack. On the school bus, she confided in Meiselman secrets from her adult-seeming life, a story of a high school boy flirting with her in shul and ringing her up at home to set up a meeting at Fulham Park where he proceeded to stick his fingers inside her. How the tables had turned since Meiselman and Ethel shared that first kiss. Talk of this life always made him aware of his inadequate, smooth, and odorless body. If she were to lean in for a kiss, *he* would have been the one left defecating on the bathroom floor.

A new fantasy starts percolating. Why twelve-year-old Ethel is sitting on the edge of the very desk he is sitting at now, in the office she will one day occupy as an adult, why someone so young would wear black pumps, her feet loose in the shoes, is unclear. Shirtless, rib baring, mustard-yellow-glasses-wearing twelve-year-old Meiselman paws at her breasts over the top of the zebra-print dress, a version even skimpier than the one worn at the bat-mitzvah. Twelve-year-old Ethel flattens his hand against her collarbone and rotates his fingers so they dip into the top of her dress. Fearing she will soon end the dalliance with a laugh in his face, twelve-year-old Meiselman turns feisty. The dress, though, clings too tightly to the body, and he has trouble maneuvering, managing to shoehorn just two fingers into the dress's cup. Meanwhile, twelve-year-old Ethel flails for the dress's zipper, which runs down her spine. Finally, twelve-year-old Ethel, cheeky, even at a young age, says to twelve-year-old Meiselman, I'm not looking for a gentleman, just a little help. Twelve-year-old Meiselman obliges twelve-year-old Ethel, who stands with her leather-gloved palms flat on the edge of the desk. He deals delicately with a back he knows will one day be fragile, his fingers caressing the bumps of her spine. Head back, her permed curls sway.

Is there not something iniquitous, possibly unlawful, about a grown man imagining his twelve-year-old incarnation doing things to a twelve-year-old girl? Dampened by this sudden fear, he replaces twelve-year-old Ethel with her mother, who, like in the bat-mitzvah photograph, is wearing a fire-engine-red dress cut like a bathrobe straight down the middle, held closed by a thin gold belt, which hangs loosely off the waist. Flouncy black curls fall down each side of the woman's face, like a wig worn by a French king. He also replaces underage Meiselman with his current self.

Ethel's mother and Meiselman slide into the same positions that twelve-year-old Ethel and twelve-year-old Meiselman held, but Meiselman cannot maintain his tender approach with this older woman, and he reaches around to the front of her dress, sliding a hand inside and grabbing at a breast. She is not wearing a bra. Her agreeability with his aggressive turn comes as a surprise, as does the smallness of the breast, given the ampleness of her daughter. For what did my daughter give this up, Mother asks. To run away with some guy who makes his living playing basketball with kids after school? As the saying goes, A daughter's loss is a mother's gain. I've noticed you wear a tie now that you're the number one? Think we can make use of it? (Sometimes, Meiselman thinks he wants Deena to talk more, to direct him with vulgarities, but he fears the embarrassment once they are finished.) Not wanting to sully the tie, which was picked up on a recent father-and-son outing to Brooks Brothers, he pursues the spirit of her request by removing the thin gold belt that holds her dress closed. No, no. *Wanting* to sully the tie, which was picked up on a recent father-and-son outing to Brooks Brothers, he removes it and uses it to yoke Mother's neck. Too shamefaced to execute a suffocating yank, all he musters is a lazy tug. Some number one you are, Mother says. If you're not willing to dole it out, then maybe it means you like to be on the receiving end. All of the sudden, Meiselman is the one with his palms on the desk with his good tie around his naked waist. Not interested in seeing what comes next, afraid of what he might discover about himself, Meiselman is up from the desk, steadying himself with some deep breathing.

He has stalled his arousal. His spiritual mindset remains intact, his vigor safely stored for tonight's encounter. He may just be the one who can dole it out.

* * *

It takes one pitch, a called ball on an outside curve, for his father's reminiscing to commence.

"Nellie Fox, you know, the great Sox second baseman on the '59 team?"

"Yes, I know Nellie Fox," Meiselman answers. "He used the smallest glove he could find and removed all the padding so he'd have a better feel for the ball."

"That too. But bats the size of eggplants. Gave him better control. Sacrificed power, but boy, could he spray the ball. Kept a big chaw of tobacco in his cheek."

The next batter, Rolls, strikes out and, on the swinging third strike, the baserunner takes off for third and the catcher does not even challenge him, prompting a "tsk, tsk, tsk," from his father.

"Sherm Lollar. Couldn't run on him. Boy, was he good. Cannon for an arm. Could hit, too. Twenty-something homers in '59. Don't understand how a player like that never made the Hall. Because they don't value defense. That's why. Power is all that registers with people. Ahhh."

A single up the middle by Baldelli gives Tampa a 1-0 lead.

"Tampa, huh," Meiselman's father says. "Al Lopez, you know the great Sox manager of the '59 team?"

Before continuing, his father waits for his son to confirm he has heard of Al Lopez. Meiselman, seated in a rotating swivel chair next to the couch, can barely squeeze out a rote "Sure, sure," because Tampa is taking batting practice off the Sox pitcher Buehrle, and his father is stuck on stories from forty five years ago. Does his father harangue Gershon with scraps from the past? Whenever Meiselman drops in on a conversation between the two other Meiselman men, Gershon is regaling his father with stories of boardroom ambushes, or senior executives getting canned after decades of service. Perhaps Meiselman should feel flattered for his ability to put his father in a mood that has him recalling oddments from a glorious season when he was a young man in his mid-twenties, recently married, fresh out of law school, starting at the firm where he is now winding down his illustrious career, a time when his young wife was beginning graduate work in special education, a focus on autism, at the time a nascent area of study. Could his mother have been a pioneer in her field, like Mrs. Woolf, had she not abandoned her work to raise the Meiselman Boys?

Meiselman finally turns to his father, ready to indicate his familiarity with Al Lopez, when he notices there are no newspapers stacked at his feet today.

But his father, who has moved on, says to Meiselman, "Have I told you about the night the Sox clinched the pennant in '59? Mayor Daley, big, big Sox fan, set off the air raid sirens in the city. Height of the Cold War. Khrushchev and Eisenhower. You don't know, but we thought it could all be over, like *that*." His snap lacks smack. "Anyway, PopPop—" his father pauses to belt a few wheezy laughs. Every time he tries restarting, the laughter has him choking on his words, a choke that quickly morphs into a phlegmy cough. Out comes the handkerchief from his back pocket for a hack into the monogrammed cloth. "PopPop didn't know a thing about sports. He came running over with suitcases packed, trying to convince us we needed to go to Arnold Melman's shelter." He wags his finger at Meiselman. "Boxing was PopPop's thing. Loved boxing. The idea of two *shvartzes* beating the hell out of each other really excited him." The deep red in his father's face whenever he laughs that laugh has Meiselman fearing for the man's last gasp.

Sox have a runner on third with one out and Ordóñez at the plate. The Sox outfielder works the pitcher to a full count and then starts fouling off one ball after the next, an extended at bat that provides Meiselman with an opportunity to realign his father and focus him on the present and yesterday's 4-1 loss. His father has nothing to contribute and stays silent until Ordóñez's at-bat ends with a pop up to the shortstop, at which point he yells at the television, "Garbage! Swing looks slow. Guy is on the decline."

“Thirty years old,” Meiselman answers. “Guys these days are producing well into their late thirties.”

“Al Lopez was from Tampa,” his father says.

This unceasing sharing is wearying. Eight more innings of this will render Meiselman too lethargic to function. Meiselman stands from his chair and steps in front of his seated father. Stretching his arms heavenward, he screams, “Father!” Arms swooping down, momentum carrying his body into a forward bend, he tries touching his toes, but manages to reach only his shins. He holds the bend for several seconds before straightening, hands on his hips. He bends forward again, head lowering to the floor, exhaling as he feels the stretch in his hamstrings. This time when he stands, he thrusts out his pelvis, and his old man flinches as if his son is coming for him. His son’s movements clearly have him concerned. When Meiselman starts slowly stretching his neck from side to side, his father fully recoils into the couch’s crook and crosses his legs. Meiselman grabs an ankle and pulls up his leg behind his body. Deena has been preaching to him the importance of stretching, of increasing his flexibility, and she’s right. This loosening up has made him realize how tight he has been, as though he has been confined for the last week, year, years, an entire lifetime, in a veal crate. But he should ease up before he tears something, or before his father’s facial quivering works its way into a permanent tremor.

Moving to the television, Meiselman asks, “Remember Steve Lyons?” His father’s droopy-eyed stare will not silence him this time. “Steve ‘Psycho’ Lyons. Played for that overachieving 1990 team that finished in second place a year after they finished a million games out of first.” Meiselman, voice rising, paces the family room, coming to a stop in front of the decommissioned fireplace off to the side. He taps the plastic face of his framed graduation photo. A yellow poncho covers his gown, his mother, outside the shot, holds an umbrella over the maroon mortarboard covering his head.

"1990. Same year I graduated university. 'Psycho' set the tone for that surprising team. Once he dove head first into the first base bag, got up, called time, and trying to clean the dirt off his uniform ended up dropping his pants in front of the entire stadium. That's character, and it's what this year's squad lacks."

The man's lids are shut. His cheek is sliding off the hand that keeps his head propped. Is Meiselman such a poor storyteller? Or is his father generally not interested in what his son has to say because he believes his son lacks standing in the world? This will also change after tonight. Meiselman takes his seat and rotates his chair so he is facing his father. He puts a hand on his father's kneecap and gives his leg a shake to no effect. He says, "That was the season they introduced Turn Back the Clock Day. 50-cent tickets. Popcorn for a nickel. Turned off the scoreboard, organ, and PA system. You loved it. '90 was Frank's first year. Ventura and Sosa's, too, I think. No, I know. One hundred percent certain. The game they were no-hit but won 4-0 was that season. Thigpen saved 57 games. Same year I, your son, graduated, with honors from Loyola University. The summer of the maddening job search. Remember when I was offered a position with that traveling salesman who was selling an operating system for business computers? You persuaded me to not take the job, thinking it didn't sound concrete. You called the man a 'hobo.' 'What kind of businessman wears shorts, sandals and a t-shirt?' you asked." The patriarch's head is now back against the cushion, mouth agape. Otherwise, Meiselman would have told his father it was the same year his son grew a goatee, favored black t-shirts, and wore his sideburns long, prompting his father to constantly joke that he looked like Elvis. That year, near Christmas time, Meiselman asked out his red-haired coworker Ursula O' Brien. She said yes, and he took her to Johnny Rockets. She showed great annoyance at his unwillingness to order anything more than a milkshake, Meiselman too timid to explain his dietary restrictions.

Meiselman, troubled by his father's sleeping, announces the next scoring play loudly. Until recently, his father's dozing never troubled him the way it troubles his mother. Even when he was a boy and his parents were in their thirties, still wearing blue jeans and listening to music in the car, the rock and roll from the fifties and sixties, his mother would greet his father's spontaneous sleep with refrains like, "What are you so tired from?" and "Maybe you should go up to bed." Does it happen to the man at work, the judge recessing in order for Meiselman's father to collect himself? That it has been happening only at home all these years is a more distressing possibility. After Friday's encounter with his mother, Meiselman hears her complaints over his father's constant lethargy as frustration at being forced to navigate without a sidekick. So when he hears the *thunk* of the front door's retracting deadbolt, he swipes his father across the knee. His father's lips move. Through the narrow crack, he mutters, "Steve Lyons and his pants, huh? Big joke. Team hasn't made the Series since '59."

The front door slams shut, and there is a second *thunk* as the bolt slides back into place. Paper bags crumple, plastic bags crinkle, keys jangle, and, this time, when Meiselman turns back to his father to warn him of his mother's arrival, the man is alert, attuned to his wife's entrance.

He rests his hand on the armrest of Meiselman's chair and says, "Don't mention the newspapers."

"What newspapers?" Meiselman asks.

"Just nothing about newspapers."

His mother's approach is stealth, having recently switched to black, rubber-soled sneakers, and she is standing in the doorway, trench coat still on, purse hanging off her shoulder.

"Well, ready for tonight?" his mother asks. "Everyone is so excited. Susan Lipman is coming. Debbie Leiner, Rochelle Altman. I told Eleanor Miller about it. I just had to. She was going on and on about her son 'the professor.' You are going to have a huge crowd. I just hope Shenkenberg behaves himself. You make him sound so not nice. With a father like that..."

"Waitwaitwait," his father stammers in a severe tone, eyebrows plumped and ledged over his eyes, which are fiercely brown like a nocturnal animal. "What time do we need to be there exactly?"

"Need to be there" like Meiselman's work is a juvenile affair, a school play, their son playing the part of Wailing Wall Middle Section. "Ohh, Ohh, Ohh," went his only line, belted out as if he were Santa Claus, his interpretation of the teacher's direction to deliver the line with a godly moan that will successfully signal to the audience that Supplicant #1, Supplicant #2, and Supplicant #3 have entered a holy site. Barry Kranzler, he now remembers, was Wailing Wall Right Section. A sizeable boy even at age nine, his bellow drowned out Meiselman and Wailing Wall Left Section. "You looked so real," his mother praised him, following the event, as if her son were responsible for the costumes. "Very convincing," his father added before swiftly moving on to Ethel's lead performance as Hannah the Handmaiden. "So much poise for someone her age." "How she towers over all the other girls in the class," his mother added. "Looks like a college girl," his father continued.

Tonight has to be about breaking the status quo. If Meiselman tells his parents the actual start time of seven, he knows he can expect them to show by 6:45, at the latest, and he is not interested in having his parents witness him doing last minute schlep work like lugging chairs and tables, testing microphones, and taping down cables. Better to tell them 7:15, and when they show up at seven they will have to scrounge for seats alongside Deena and Molly. The thought of them abandoning hope of finding two together and wedging themselves into seats in the back rows, his father compelled into a crunching leg cross, his mother having to sit with her purse on her lap for the entire evening, tickles Meiselman.

"Waitwaitwait," his father says. "This is crazy. Can't you reserve seats for us?"

The thought of having a person on the inside strokes his father. It would take little effort to comply with his request, and he does not want to demean his status and give his father the impression that his son lacks pull. So Meiselman hems and haws and pulls a random receipt from his pocket and studies its blank back, stabbing his finger against the paper as if counting off names. After meticulously folding the paper in half and slipping it into his breast pocket, he says, "Two in the second row, off to the side, is doable. But I can hold them only until 7:00. Ethel hates noticeable gaps."

"Suresuresure, we can do that," his father says. "Right, Pooch?"

The satisfied smirk Meiselman has put on his father's face is quickly erased as Meiselman's mother steps forward to lord over him, arms akimbo. "Did you call the *Tribune*?"

"Working on it," he answers, steadying his hand in her direction.

"Tell them if they can't bother delivering it to our door, then goodbye." Turning to her son, she says, "So happy you thought to invite George the other night. Worked out perfectly. Eased Paul's mind. Just wish we had a funeral to go to. A Jew cremating his mother? Please, don't cremate us."

* * *

He will have to wing it. There is not enough time to compose elegant opening remarks. But when he sinks into his chair, the word "remiss" pops into his mind. The perfect word for the opening joke he has planned. Too good to chance to memory, he scribbles it into the margins of the folded sports section where he scribbled his other opening remarks.

"Can't say I'm surprised," Betsy Ross says, admitting herself into Meiselman's office without a knock. Hugging a manila envelope, she stands over his desk, cheeks puffed. Slowly she deflates. "I knew tonight would be a no-go. She's at her mother's house, as you know. Never a good sign. She was sucking on ice chips when we spoke. Could barely make out a word she was saying."

"Had the same feeling when I spoke to her on Friday," he lies.

Betsy Ross tosses the envelope onto the desk, and says, "Here it is," as if he has been anticipating its delivery.

"Ah, yes, the envelope," he says.

"And remember you have to meet Izzy at the front door in—" she turns her wrist. "Now."

She comes around his desk and hustles him from his chair, helping him get his arms through the sleeves of his blue blazer, picking lint off the shoulders and a loose thread off his purple shirt and turning him around so she can straighten his even purpler tie. She places her hand on his back, gives him a couple of pats and says, "Good luck." Meiselman snags the envelope and scurries out of the office. When he reaches the middle of the hallway, Betsy Ross calls after him. "You're going to do fine," and the warmth in her voice has him breaking out in chills, until he is reminded of the well-wisher's character. Ethel is sick, and Betsy Ross is angling.

The queue posts and ropes in front of Circulation have been dismantled for the evening's reception. Paprocki and his crew of men in buzz cuts and black muscle shirts mount trumpet-shaped glass vases, ostrich-necked flowers sticking out, onto tables draped in gold linen. Cutting across the floor, Meiselman pinches together the envelope's metal clasps. While his fingers enter the mouth of the envelope, it occurs to him that without Ethel in attendance he must edit the first line of his opening remarks. Rewriting the line in his head, he is mugged by a fear that saying, It would be remiss of me not to, is incorrect. I would be remiss not to, sounds better. Plays over both versions in his head and each one sounds right until it sounds completely wrong. The last thing he wants is to come across as ignorant. Up and back he goes until suddenly he is standing outside the main entrance, tossing off a two-fingered salute to Head of Library Security Fyodor "Fred" Galitsky.

Forty-five minutes from the start of the event and the parking lot is unfilled, except for a New Niles police squad car off to the side cordoning off the employee lot, an officer leaning against the car's hood, chomping on an apple and talking on his phone, pink flares blazing at his feet. The fear of a Rav Fruman-led protest, now, certainly, seems dramatic, possibly delusional. The only threat to arriving attendees is navigating the poorly lit parking lot made darker by the comingling grays of twilight, asphalt, and a raggedy blanket of fog.

"Everything excellent, thank you," Fred says, not diverting his straight-ahead stare. He proceeds to tell Meiselman about his brother-in-law taking him sailing on Lake Michigan earlier in the day. "Crap sailboat," Fred continues. "Sit on one side, not a minute, sail swings across, duck and move to other side of crap sailboat. Sit not another minute, sail, swing, duck." Fred rambles on about boat motors, the state's byzantine fishing regulations, how his sister-in-law suns herself to excess, and how his wife approaches wine coolers as if they were non-alcoholic.

It would be remiss of me not to now sounds correct.

Now Fred is talking about his wife, who does nails for a living. "But her boss is greasy, shit man—"

But, I would be remiss not to sounds more correct.

Two car doors slam in the distance.

"But," Meiselman answers Fred's complaint about how poorly suburban women tip, "something was pulling you to this great country."

"Yes, wife's bitch sister."

In matching tan trench coats, New Niles Public Library tote bags clutched in their hands, an elderly couple Meiselman recognizes as semi-regulars emerge from the parking lot's depths, looking both ways before crossing the car-free fire lane. The wife stops in front of Meiselman to ask if they have come to the right place for the Shenkenberg lecture. Meiselman directs them through the double doors and the husky, bow-legged husband hooks arms with his wife so she can help him step onto the sidewalk.

It would be remiss of...

A white taxicab with mint-green racing stripes bounces into the parking lot, turns right, and creeps down the carpool lane before stopping in front of the idling Meiselman and Fred. Its headlights illuminate the misty air, and exhaust pumps from the double-pipe muffler in the car's rear. Meiselman spots his nemesis in the back seat, waiting for the driver to hand him his change.

Maybe his incessantly benefit-of-the-doubt-giving wife, along with everyone else, should stop questioning Meiselman's perceptivity, his ability to size up shameless bullies like Shenkenberg. Maybe they should not have dismissed Meiselman's groaning over the writer's phone conduct. Because the first thing the writer does when exiting the cab, even before the men shake, is hand Meiselman a receipt, while remarking, "This is your department, from what I gather." Then, pointing to a folded-open cell phone, says, "I got to take this," turning his back on his host.

On the other hand, maybe Meiselman should pity Shenkenberg, whose appearance is more abject and wretched than anticipated. Entropy is underway for the writer. Black hair once kinked into a puckish fro has thinned, the pate now filled with fuzzy underbrush and glimmering patches of scalp. The sides of his hair are shorn, like old Velcro. Bushy eyebrows threaten a merge, and eye bags that at one time were dark and brooding now have a purplish tint, as if he suffers from a deficiency. His charcoal wool overcoat is faded, as if dragged through chalk dust. Underneath the coat is a blue pinstriped blazer with buttons hanging by their last threads. Below the belt: baggy blue jeans and brown work boots, tongues loose and slumping forward, a uniform meant to suggest a life of mucking and scrabbling.

Maybe Shenkenberg is, in fact, decent, because when he snaps the phone closed, he moves toward Meiselman, apologizing over and over for his "rudeness" before engaging the host in a vigorous handshake, a clutch neither crushing nor limp. Then he pats Meiselman on the side of the arm, sincere regret in his voice over how long it has been since the two men have seen each other.

"Your graduation," Meiselman answers. "'86. You won a scholarship prize for English literature, appropriately. Shira Aaronson was valedictorian and Donald Schey delivered the class speech. Talked about the sex lives of rodents."

"Is that so? Who knows, who cares? God. High school was a long time ago. That I survived is the best thing I can say about it."

As Meiselman escorts the guest through the doors, the writer pauses in the vestibule to allow his host to enter first, and this has Meiselman reconsidering whether he should excuse the man's behavior on the phone as uncharacteristic, a momentary lapse. If so, should he not avoid the word "remiss" altogether and redact any mention of a controversy?

Escorting Shenkenberg to the holding area, an alcove in the back of Classics with a circular coffee table and two brown, leather guest chairs, Meiselman hurries his pace, hoping to avoid Paprocki, because the last thing he needs is for the baker to start his tickling shenanigans for the benefit of Shenkenberg, who shuffles several paces behind, knees bent, head down, hands in the pockets of his coat, which lifts off his hunched back like a cape. There is no sign of Kotek.

Meiselman offers his guest a complimentary water bottle and gestures for him to take the seat with its back to the narrow atrium window. Rather than sit in the opposing chair, Meiselman places himself in the tight space between the back of Shenkenberg's chair and the window. Shenkenberg slumps into the chair, cracks open the water, and chugs until he has drained three-quarters of the bottle. He wipes his mouth with the back of his hand and begins massaging his shins, throwing back his head and muttering, "Bone spurs." Or did he say, "Lone wolves." How could one know with the words coming out in a tepid grumble? Next he says, "Tough couple of weeks," or is he still talking about the shins and said, "Rough tumble in the weeds"? The man's tone projects gloom, and this may be an opportunity for Meiselman to brush off any anger over the call by teasing Shenkenberg about detecting his level of stress over the phone. He is even willing to dismiss the slander against Rabbi J-, adopt the charitable theory hypothesized the other morning that Shenkenberg's goal is merely a rebranding of the great rabbi for a generation demanding "very human" idols.

Maybe Meiselman's initial assessment was dead-on and Shenkenberg is, in fact, a boorish disregarder, because what subsequently comes out of the writer's mouth is surely meant to agitate and cripple his host. "Flew in early this morning and went straight to the house," he says. "Was with her for almost three hours." The condescension is clear. Veiled ribbing over Meiselman not having spent a second at Ethel's side. Shenkenberg is now speaking louder, drawing out the words, enunciating each syllable, constantly looking over his shoulder at Meiselman, who keeps his back to the writer and stares out the window even though it is a wall of glare, and he is left staring back at his own crumpling face.

"Based on what I saw today," Shenkenberg continues, "I don't see how she makes it to New York for the operation, procedure, whatever she's calling it."

"Procedure," Meiselman clarifies, even though this is the first he is hearing about a trip to New York.

"Operation," Shenkenberg counters. "'Procedure' is her tenacity talking. You hear how she talks. 'Minor this,' 'minor that.'" As if Meiselman needs further inducement to scrap his plans to go soft on Shenkenberg, the writer crosses his legs, folds his body forward and drumming the bottom of the water bottle against the edge of the table, beating out a church-bell rhythm for a story intended to cut, says, "Her eyes were closed for a good ten minutes when I first got there, but then she suddenly squeezed out a request for me to read from my book." Shenkenberg polishes off the bottle of water. "When I got to the end of the chapter, Ethel's parched lips curved into that smirk of hers. You know it, right? She said, 'Better save your voice for tonight, Izzy. Go.' Kissed her on the forehead. Skin tasted cold, chalky."

A light snort tags the end of his story, as if he knows Meiselman has never had a taste. At once, Meiselman must extricate himself from this conversation, return to his office and examine the contents of the envelope, which, hopefully, explain why Ethel is back home sucking on ice chips with plans to fly to New York. Also, maybe, the envelope contains her justification for keeping everything hidden from him. Could not afford to have you distracted at this crucial moment for the library. You are my anchor, my safety pin. Meiselman fingers the edges of the envelope. More a packet than a letter. Her will? To my number two I leave my collection of framed photographs. Or guidance for running the library? Ego-stroking is ultimately what motivates a worker like

Betsy Ross. Don't let Mitchell's cool demeanor fool you. He's angling like everyone else. Can Meiselman expect revelations? Don't think I never took you seriously in that way.

Water bottle to his lips, face skyward, Shenkenberg milks the bottle's last drops, and Meiselman contemplates occupying himself with some drinking of his own, buy him time as he ponders a new plan of attack, because Shenkenberg has made Meiselman feel as if he does not even register with Ethel, as if his history with her, his oldest friend, is insignificant. Before events, however, he tries drying out. A need striking in the middle of an event risks turning into an incapacitating obsession. Putting his face to the window, he shields his eyes and looks out into the tight atrium. Green ivy climbs the four walls of the library. The budding branches of a slender winter-stripped tree that grows from a circular patch in the middle poke the library's second story windows. Weeds, twigs, and refuse—crushed pop cans, empty chip bags, wads of soiled leaves—begrime the asphalt walkway ringing the tree. Monday morning he will send a memo to the village requesting a decluttering of the grounds. "Eyesore" is the word he will use.

Meiselman says, "I knew you were friends with the guys in my class; Reuben Fishman, Larry Schneider, Todd—"

"'Friends' is a stretch. Whatever, sorry to interrupt. Your point?"

"Well, I never realized how close you were with Ethel."

"Tara, the Japanese girl I was with for four years too many?" Says it as if everyone is expected to know about his relationships. In this case, it happens that Meiselman knew about the relationship through Ethel. How she raved about Tara. "Tara," Shenkenberg continues, "ran the computers for one of the Northwestern libraries when Ethel was doing her PhD. One day, the two of them made the connection and the three of us formed a gang. Ultimately, Tara tired of me, and to the loser goes the spoils."

To sell the spontaneity of the memory he is about to deliver, Meiselman rips three cackles, and then says, "Just remembering the time with the Tabasco sauce." Shenkenberg is silent. "School cafeteria?" he asks, turning his back on the atrium and now facing Shenkenberg's back. The goal in recalling this episode is not to foster comity, but to break the status quo between the men. He continues, "You guzzled down an entire bottle." Stepping around Shenkenberg's chair so he can get a better look at his face, he spots the writer's teeth nibbling the water bottle's plastic ring. Should he not pity a man whose parents can disregard such overlapping and yellowing? Meiselman continues, "As you were just about to hurl—"

"Let's not talk about this—"

"Waitwaitwait. Reuben, Larry, and Todd escorted you to the Russians'—"

"Please—"

"Pasted the poor kids," Meiselman says. "Turning wistful, he adds, "How you guys terrorized those recent immigrants. Would run through their hallway spraying deodorant. Must say that I never had it in me. Witnessing all that cruelty actually hurt my insides, which is maybe why I never got along with guys like Todd and Rueben—"

"Jesus, give it a rest, man." His voice is edgy and low. "I don't particularly enjoy thinking about me then. It causes me physical pain. Actual physical pain. How can I ever make that right?"

Meiselman, despite telling himself that the goal of bringing up the memory was not to foster comity, eases the reins and says, "I understand. I don't care much to think of myself then either, but it's unavoidable.

"Inescapable," Shenkenberg concurs.

"Even if you think you are a different person now..."

"...you know, deep down, you possess..."

Shenkenberg does not finish his thought. Sadism is the word on his lips, though masochism is how Meiselman would end his own sentence. Despite the discrepancy, there is no denying the comity fostered.

“Can I have time to myself?” Shenkenberg asks. “Need to get into the role, so to speak.”

Pulling the note cards from his jacket’s inner pocket, Meiselman explains that he, too, needs time to review the questions for the debate portion of the event.

“Debate?” Shenkenberg asks. “Go easy on me,” he says, followed by a snort and tittering laugh that suggest he is not terrified in the least.

“Dialogue,” Meiselman says.

“It will be fun.”

Exiting Classics with the manila envelope tucked under his arm, Meiselman hurries past the arriving attendees making their way in to the Lansky auditorium, or the Slide, as it is affectionately called by the library staff because of the room’s narrowness and steepness, and the illusion created when the seats are folded up and showing their metal-sheeted bottoms.

Meiselman does not feel bad about kicking a college-aged foursome out of the front row of reserved seating, ignoring sighs and complaints about having arrived well before everyone else. Two older women, who look like they could be sisters, wearing matching elastic-waisted blue jeans and similarly styled turtlenecks, one pink, the other black, take their eviction without fuss. Sliding into the aisle, coats draped over their forearms, they identify a pair of seats near the top. Anticipating the trudge up the stairway, its steepness burdensome like a stalled escalator, the one in pink grabs the elbow of the one in black and snipes at her to take hold of the banister.

Behind them, Meiselman announces, "Stadium style seating. Not a bad seat in the house."

He now has the task of filling the first two rows with people of stature. Spotting Mitchell and his wife, Roslyn, in the fifth row, Meiselman motions for them to move down to the reserved seats at the end of the second row, stage left. The two older ladies have not progressed far, and Meiselman benevolently redirects them to the vacated seats.

"Good to see you, mate," Mitchell says, looking like a tycoon in a three-piece burgundy suit, its vest tight around the belly, the chain of a gold pocket watch dangling from pocket to button.

"Looking rather dapper," Meiselman says to the underling.

"Dress the part, my friend," Mitchell says. "You say that, don't you?"

His wife has long, dry, graying hair and the skin, body, and teeth of someone who eats only vegetables and roots. Turquoise everything. Sleeveless dress, stone necklace, dangling earrings. Her brown, overstrapped sandals are forgettable.

Meiselman leans forward to kiss Roslyn on the cheek, but catching her off-guard, he misfires and dabbles the corner of her salmon colored lips. Does his scratching beard hair repulse or charge these casually-kissed women?

"Hello, everyone," the descending Betsy Ross says, Ada and June several steps behind. After the underlings exchange kisses with Mitchell and Roslyn, Betsy Ross whacks Meiselman across the shoulder and says, "We saw each other already." But he has not seen Ada and June. Numbers has not arrived.

Meiselman seats the underlings together at the end of the row.

To fill the reserved section, Meiselman wrangles benefactors Mr. and Mrs. Tanner and Dr. Ana Mukerji and her husband, Dr. Sin Yang. Self-aware of their eminence, Village Clerk Danny Sparks and

Trustees Jill Thomas, Tania Spalding, and Scotty Giulokowsky move to the front without invitation or prodding. Several librarians approach to ask if there are reserved seats for them. Meiselman tells them there are not, and they trudge back from where they came. Still no sign of his parents or Deena and Molly, but counting off the remaining seats in the reserved area, he is not worried about overcapacity or, even worse, noticeable gaps. Right then, someone sidles up to him and asks, "Where would you like me, sir?"

The meeting at the bakery was not goodbye. Here she stands in front of him in the same pinstripe charcoal suit and white silk blouse from the other day, albeit with some slight modifications. She has ditched the eyeglasses and chopsticks in the hair, and has tightened the bun. Instead of black flats, she is wearing black heels that expose the full tops of her feet up to her toe stubs. Assimilating his never-uttered critiques, she has unfastened the second button of her shirt and now hangs a silver chain from her neck, although the pendant dips inside. Disappointingly, the safety pin has been removed from the eyebrow, as have a majority of the earrings that once crowded her rims. The diamond sticking the inner lobe remains. Her hair is darker—honey gold—subduing the pink strands. What is responsible for this curtailing? He escorts the erstwhile pink-haired woman to a first row aisle seat, stage right, one that will provide her with a direct view of Meiselman when the two men are seated for the debate portion of the event.

Having identified Meiselman as the man in charge, audience members queue in front of the stage waiting for him to finish with the pink-haired woman so they can bombard him with complaints about the room being too cold or too warm, or certain to become too warm once the auditorium fills. Concern after concern summarily dismissed with feigned interest and deliberation until he reaches his parents, who are hanging in the back of the line.

"Everything is so nice," his mother says. "Did you turn up the microphones? Last time we couldn't hear a thing."

"Meet Shenkenberg yet?" his father asks from the side of his mouth. Meiselman nods. Father winks. "Get an autograph if you can," he says, plunging a copy of the paperback into his son's hands. "For one of my guys."

Meiselman directs them to two seats in the second row, left of center, out of his direct sightline because he fears his mother trying to catch his attention mid-event, motioning for him to speak louder or slower. It has happened.

A final check of the microphones, followed by an issuance of orders to the underlings, Betsy Ross tasked with announcing four minutes from now that attendees should begin finding their seats, at which point, Ada will dim the lights. "Game time," Meiselman mutters under his breath, and he is up the stairs, two at a time, off to retrieve Shenkenberg from the holding area.

Cutting back across the main floor, Meiselman inches the pages out of the envelope. A Post-it note stuck to the top of the page reads "Welcoming Remarks." Underneath, at the top of the first page, in bold, the typed words "START HERE: Ethel Lewinson, Director of the New Niles Public Library, and the organizer of this momentous event, deeply regrets she cannot be with us tonight, but she has asked me to deliver the following welcoming remarks." Post-it notes are attached to the tops of other pages. "Questions." "Closing Remarks." Head down, Meiselman collides with one of Paprocki's muscle men, who is hauling a milk crate of coffee cups and coasters, jolting an already-jolted Meiselman. Did all his talk of controversy make Ethel fear he would strike a belligerent, ungracious tone if left to deliver his own remarks? Otherwise, why would she ask him to stand up in front of his wife and parents, the underling administrators and librarians, the pink-haired woman and Molly, the members of his community and the library regulars, and, most importantly, in front of Shenkenberg, as some kind of puppet, a mouthpiece, as if his title were Library Spokesman, Ambassador to the Director. Loyalty is the only compliment ever paid to an ambassador, who is never seen as part of the brain trust.

Shenkenberg is pacing the floor of Classics, beating the spine of his book against his palm, grumbling to himself as if reviewing talking points. Upon noticing Meiselman, he itches his bristly bangs, and then sticks a finger in his mouth to floss his front teeth with his fingernail. He looks up at Meiselman and says, "If not now, when?"

The lights dim. Claps and hoots accompany Meiselman and Shenkenberg as they descend the auditorium steps, all eyes trained on the guest, except for the audience members who incorrectly assume the celebrity writer is the one with the fuller head of hair, the bookish beard, and the better teeth. Standing off to the side, waiting for Betsy Ross to finish delivering instructions to the audience, Meiselman shuffles the manila envelope and the sports section with his opening remarks chicken scratched into the margins. Whichever one is on top feels like the wrong decision. Surely, nothing but adulatory words fills Ethel's remarks. Does Shenkenberg deserve praise after the way he treated him earlier in the holding area, not to mention his behavior on the phone last week? And the purported slandering of Rabbi J-, of course. Maybe Shenkenberg is irrelevant. Maybe he is collateral damage in this stepping out party Meiselman plans on holding tonight. This is about the chase for a new, aggressive posture, the opportunity to feel like the number one for one night, meaning he must read his own words. Yet uncertainty remains regarding the word "remiss." No closer to a decision, his train of thought discombobulated, his palms turn clammy and a dry sweat tickles his forehead. If he were not agitating over which opening remarks to deliver, his anxiety would surely attach itself to another concern, like the question of

Deena's whereabouts, or why the pink-haired woman is sitting with her legs crossed, her foot devilishly rocking, heel of her shoe off the foot, her middle finger scratching her temple. Put your feet up on the chair, he wants to scream at her. Sit on your hands. Play childish and misanthropic. Because this ladylike you is making my heart skitter.

High school and college kids and twentysomethings hogging the rows directly behind the reserved section, part of what is definitely a record crowd of two-hundred plus, stand and whoop and squawk, clapping the covers of Shenkenberg's book, as Meiselman shows the writer to one of the two navy wingback chairs on the stage. Familiar faces from Meiselman's shul and the broader community, couples from Rogers Park, Lincolnwood, and Lakeview, and the seniors who come to every reading, lecture, concert, and class and who would probably attend children's events if permitted, comprise the rest of the cheering crowd, although no sign of Deena or Molly. Leaning forward to grab one of the water bottles off the round table that separates the two men, Shenkenberg raises a gracious hand and the applause intensifies, as he surely knew it would.

Meanwhile, Meiselman steps to the podium and sets down Sports and the manila envelope side-by-side, eyes darting back and forth between his two options. Mouthpiece, or man who is not afraid to mouth off? Hunched over, he squints, straining to read his microscopic writing, the correct usage of "remiss" continuing to flummox him.

Leaning into the microphone and clearing his throat several times, which succeeds in finally quieting the crowd, Meiselman says, "Dr. Ethel Lewinson, Director of the New Niles Public Library and the organizer of this momentous event, deeply regrets...."

Once Meiselman modulates his voice, inflecting it with the sassy, snippy tone Ethel intended when penning the remarks, the same tone she uses to regale administrators with anecdotes about mouthing off to Trustees or silencing lippy patrons, the chosen course feels right. "It was not even worth asking Izzy, I thought..." gets Meiselman his first breezy chuckle from the crowd. There is a pose to be mimicked, as well. Hulked back, head listing, hands gripping the lectern's sides, a bent knee behind the podium, toes digging the floor. Irreverence, for this gum-chewing generation, establishes stature. With the cadence and posture down, Meiselman has the audience in a continuous state of merriment as he delivers Ethel's remarks. He draws rumbles of laughter for moderately humorous lines like, "As people know, I am ever eager to place library business ahead of my personal life," even though few people in the audience know Ethel or anything about her personal life. Hiccups of laughter pop from the audience midway through a mildly funny anecdote and cascade into full-throttle laughter after Meiselman nails the punch line: "...Izzy saying it would be an honor to return to the scene of the crime, to where this nonsense began." The warm, collective laughter, the sporadic yuks, cackles, and coughing fits, intensify as Meiselman reads Ethel quoting Shenkenberg, like, the writer's putdown of a reviewer- "...the imagination of a dried carob..."—and the title of his first story collection—*They Shaved My Face with a Blade*. This is a crowd that wants to laugh, and how can Meiselman not feel responsible for the cheerfulness that has taken over the auditorium? Yes, they are Ethel's words, but his ebullient delivery, the way he pauses after each quip and cues the laughter with a tilt of the head, has brought his boss's words to life. The audience is unaware of the masking—Meiselman in the name of Ethel, occasionally, in the name of Shenkenberg. By this point, they see him, Meiselman, as funny and magnetizing.

Anticipating Ethel's pivot to serious matters, Meiselman pauses to straighten his gait and harden his demeanor. After several mournful strokes of his beard, he tightens his voice for Ethel's analysis of Shenkenberg's importance as a writer and the significance of his novel. "...ultimately, uncovering the uneasy particulars of Rabbi J-'s solitary, mysterious existence away from the high school where he has taught for close to fifty years, does not undermine or obfuscate, for Ely, the rabbi's message, which is in line with Ely's realization that sunlight may be the best disinfectant, but, at times, it forces us to obsess over immaterial stains." The turn to weightier matters has not dimmed the audience's rapture. In place of mirth, heads nod as they plead for insight. Using the occasional wag or stab of the finger to drive home a point, Meiselman, once more, is delivering with aplomb. Even the men, who tend to be stubborn in the face of speechifying, seem smitten by Ethel's words as read by Meiselman. Meiselman is the provocateur. Meiselman is the penetrator. Even his father, whom Meiselman thought would be in a deep slumber by now, has his head lolled and a finger up in the air, his posture when assessing any deep argument. The pink-haired woman, fingers rapping her knee, keeps a steady focus on Meiselman. Still no sign of Deena, or her friend Molly, but the lights over the stage are hot and blinding making it difficult to see past the fifth row.

Six months ago, at the last major public event, Meiselman was insufficiently pleased with the thank-you Ethel delivered as part of her opening remarks. A string of banalities—"hard-working," "obsessive devotion," "doesn't know when to quit"—failed to capture his indispensability. Deena disagreed. It did not paint him as a mere assistant, a man with little autonomy, she insisted. The private acknowledgments are appreciated, but the time has come for the private to turn public. All will be forgiven if the thank-you he reads to the crowd tonight in Ethel's name stands above the many other thank-yous he is about to read. He will no longer care about Shenkenberg's dismissive behavior on the phone, or whether he defamed the great, late Rabbi J- in some barely read book, a controversy that, as it appears now, has hardly registered with the wider public. Such a public approbation would crown this ongoing ascendency of Meiselman, who is, surely, by this point, being mistaken by many as the number one.

Half-heartedly rambling through thank-yous to benefactors, village officials, and librarians, Meiselman considers whether lowering his eyes and feigning embarrassment and humility is the right pose when reading Ethel's words of praise for him. Or better to deliver it with swagger, looking all of them—especially his father—straight in the eye? He arrives at the more particular thank-yous for the administrative staff, Ada, June, and Jerry, all thanked for "keeping the lights on, the books and periodicals on the shelves and, most importantly, freeing me from any added aggravation." This gets a laugh, and following Mitchell's lead everyone directs a round of applause Ada and June's way. Then, in Ethel's name, Meiselman proclaims Betsy Ross "our indomitable office manager...last one in, last one out...a paragon of sangfroid...my right hand, left hand and, at times, the horns on my head," earning him, in the name of Ethel, another laugh. Without prodding, the secretary stands and takes a bow, drawing additional laughter.

"And, finally, Meiselman." That she sets him apart from the underlings is promising. "You," he reads. What tenderness in this one word. His throat catches. His eyeballs dry in anticipation of the flood that will surely follow. Before continuing, he exhales into the microphone, not once, but twice. "You," he repeats, "know how important you are to the library and me."

Displeasing in its brevity. But should he be chagrined? Does its vagueness not intimate a close relationship between the number one and two? Does it not allude to a shared understanding? Mightily satisfying, upon closer reflection.

His contentment is reflected in the warmth in which he proceeds to deliver Shenkenberg's unredacted publisher-provided biography. A liberated Meiselman is a more generous Meiselman. He can feel his chest thumping, as if Ethel's words tore open his sternum and, for the first time in his life, his core is aglow. Meiselman executes a two-handed shake with Shenkenberg at the lectern, holding the writer's hand and refusing to let go through the applause. Upon release, each man puts a hand on the other's shoulder.

"What an honor, what a great honor to be speaking here at the New Niles Public Library," Shenkenberg begins. "Thank you for that introduction. A fairly good reading of my work, I must say." He, too, must be confused as to who authored the words Meiselman read in the name of Ethel, because he follows his praise with a nod in Meiselman's direction. "So sorry Ethel could not be with us tonight," Shenkenberg continues. "An eternal friend and a relentless peddler of my works," and even after Meiselman reminds himself that he is the setter of this festive mood, it stings to realize that the crowd is as eager to laugh for the writer as they were for him.

Shenkenberg's bravado is on display as he opens his novel, bends back its spine, and launches into his reading without explanation.

Chapter 13; Or A Polish Holiday

Rabbi Michael stood our group of fifteen in front of the brick building, its chimney towering over us. Icy shards whipped our faces. I waited for someone to suggest we continue inside. "Do we know the country that supplied the bricks?" Bertha Borestein asked, a pen and notepad in her hands, as if she were taking names, as if she were the first reporter on the scene.

Does this man who has performed countless readings not hear how his voice lulls? Uses the same bassy, glum tone as the poets who come to read for the National Poetry Month event, bouncing from word to word in a singsong rhythm, momentum and energy building as the sentence advances, only to dwindle to a morose thud at the period.

Rabbi Michael silenced her with a finger to the lips. "We will have plenty of time for recriminations." He bowed his head and closed his eyes. A moment of silence passed and Frank, adjusting his professorially round glasses with a crushing grip of the lens, said, "Rabbi, I'd like to say a Psalm." Rabbi Michael sighed and answered, "Over the next four days we will have ample opportunity to say Psalms. The only response to this, for us, is silence."

Soon everyone's eyes were shut, and I could finally itch my backside and soothe the hemorrhoids that had been raging since hour five of the flight. Such immense pleasure at such a dark place.

Rabbi Michael instructed the group to "turn a hundred and eighty degrees and face the rolling field that, at one time, was manicured by the prisoners of this death camp." A majority of the group were senior citizens, and many had difficulty maintaining their balance on the turn. Some appeared disappointed at the ordinariness of the snow-splattered field, the weather denying them the clear contrast between manicured and death. Others seemed unsure of whether they had even turned to the right spot.

"Yes," Rabbi Michael began. "In the past, a lush field. But a good fertilizer blood does not make. And as we look past the fence surrounding this field, surrounding this camp of death, we see a group of high-rise luxury condominiums, and I ask,

'What did the countrymen of the inmates, sitting in their salons, feasting on sausages and sauerkraut, sipping absinthe and chugging beer, see when they looked out the window?'" A dense fog prevented us from seeing past the camp's fence.

We moved inside to the damp and poorly lit crematorium. Red brick ovens were in the center of the room, their steel doors open, the handles of stretchers protruding. The same style of ovens they had at Gio's, the pizza place I waitered the summer after high school. A memory of Ray, the manager, a balding man with a cycloptic tuft of hair well below his hairline, pulling me aside one day and commenting, "All this time and I didn't know you were Jewish." Then, a joke he thought I'd appreciate, one about fitting an inordinate amount of Jews into the ashtray of a German automobile. And I laughed. Out of politeness, out of deference, out of discomfort, I laughed. Close-mouthed, but still. May have even knocked back my head. May have even said, "That's good." The rest of the summer I waited for another joke, an opportunity to tell Ray what we Jews do not find humorous. But that was the only Jewish joke he knew, or the only one he thought I'd appreciate, and the chance at redemption never came.

The audience is laughing harder for Shenkenberg than they were for Meiselman reading Ethel, and the uplift Ethel's thank-you provided, one that sufficiently plumped Meiselman and had him inclined to continue playing the role of library spokesman, had him willing to scrap his questions in favor of the ones provided by Ethel, is evaporating. Dissatisfaction brews. Yes, he wants to answer Ethel. I do know how important I am to you and the library. But they do not, and I need them to know; my mother and father, the pink-haired woman and Shenkenberg, the underlings and members of the community, and, especially, Deena and her new best friend

Molly, wherever they are. Hunks of homage were heaped on the dull librarians and dime-a-dozen administrators. Shenkenberg, who, it should be stated, bears no responsibility for Ethel's slight humiliation, got an entire pie to himself. Maybe Meiselman should be thankful that, at least, he was acknowledged, unlike Mitchell, whose omission was surely accidental, a case of out of sight, out of mind. Poor, poor Mitchell. Meiselman's goals greatly reduced, he is no longer looking to challenge Shenkenberg. Hogging the hub from the writer, he now realizes, is no longer realistic. Squeezing himself onto the stage and having the spotlight pass over him on its way to Shenkenberg would be enough to put tonight in the win column.

Passing notes from the stage during events is an effective way of parading one's authority. Couriering Ethel's messages, when she hosts, is his job. Sometimes the notes are for him and say things like, "Told you he'd be a rock star. I'm a genius. Check the food." Tonight, it can help make up ground lost by Ethel's vague, *pareve* acknowledgment. Seeing how Betsy Ross has been angling, and knowing her as someone always eager to parade, Meiselman beckons her to the stage with a two-finger flap. Catching his signal, she makes a small show exiting her row. Meanwhile, Meiselman leans forward from his chair, a folded paper fastened between his knuckles. Shenkenberg continues unperturbed, even if Meiselman can feel most of the eyes in the audience watching the note passing hands. After receiving the message from Betsy Ross, the photographer scampers in a crouch down the aisle in front of the stage. Kneeling in front of the pink-haired woman, whose pen is perfectly placed between her front teeth, a pocket notebook balanced on her knee, he snaps away. Knowing she is being photographed, the pink-haired woman furrows her brow and curls her tongue over her top teeth. The photographer looks back to Meiselman, who approves with a wink.

Most of the candles running along the exhibit's protective railing had extinguished prematurely. Rabbi Michael, who had authorized himself to stand on the other side of the railing, pointed out stains of black ash on the ovens' inner walls, insisting that if we looked closely we could see the handprint of a child. "Disgraceful," Bertha Borestein commented. To me, the stain resembled the Pillsbury Doughboy. Rabbi Michael pointed out a partition in the corner of the room where the camp commandant had his personal bathtub, an ideal spot because of the heat generated from the burning bodies. Gas showers and ovens is something I heard about over and over as a child. It had, sadly, become banal. Seeing this bathtub in the same room where they burned bodies, however, hit me in the gut, and I could feel the juices in my stomach climbing my throat.

Panic attacks had become common since the breakup with Jenn, symptomatic of an overall breaking down. I anticipated the dry sweat across the brow and clammy palms that usually followed the reflux. Soon, I'd feel the need to shed my clothes and bolt from the room. The obsession fueling this nervous outbreak focused on something my father said when I told him of the planned trip to Poland. Sitting at his desk in a yellow-pitted undershirt tucked into gray slacks, he didn't bother looking up from the homework assignments he was grading. "What do you need to go there for? Your mother took me there in '92, and a neo-Nazi youth stole my wallet from our hotel room. You know what it was like being transported from camp to camp while trying to get in touch with my bank?"

Because he never dealt directly with Shenkenberg prior to the event, he does not even know how much time was allotted for the reading, but he assumes no more than twenty minutes. Boredom and distractions have skewed his sense of time. Nevertheless, he passes a note—"5 minutes!!! Thanks!!!"—to Shenkenberg. The writer makes a public show of stopping his reading to examine the note. He crumples it into his palm and stuffs it into his back pocket. He reads for another minute before putting the book down and whispering into the microphone, "The powers-that-be have asked me to wrap things up, but is everyone okay with me going an extra few minutes?" A "yep" from the front and a "please" from the back, morph into a howl of "Yes! Yes!" followed by a round of applause. Shenkenberg leers across the stage at Meiselman for final approval and Meiselman can see the triumphant glint in the man's eyes. In a look of playful deliberation, Meiselman's top row of teeth munch on his soul patch as he knocks his head from side to side, and this garners a few giggles that cascade into a loud approval when Meiselman lights up with a grin and throws his hand at Shenkenberg.

Stuffed, again, although thanks to his quick thinking, he narrowly avoided another humiliation at the hands of Shenkenberg. A razor-thin victory, but a win is a win. Maybe it is time to accept that fate is his master, that he is not captain of his soul but rather an overmatched man. He should ignore unimaginative dreams of overcoming. Get out now with his tail between his legs. Better than getting out with no tail at all. If it renders him a defeatist, so be it. Or does he take one more stab at the dialogue-slash-debate and read the questions penned yesterday morning?

In minutes, Shenkenberg will conclude his reading, so Meiselman must resolve this latest fork in the road. Pulling the neon index cards from his blazer's inside pocket, Meiselman expects to encounter inadequacy, mediocrity, and shallowness, thereby settling the dilemma. The questions, however, are surprisingly probing and professional. Why should he be surprised? (For the record, he will tell Dr. Lin tomorrow morning, my parents never told me to dream. They preached practicality. Did we ever analyze the time I expressed a desire to become a broadcaster?)

The prolonged ovation at the conclusion of Shenkenberg's reading settles the matter. The neon index cards are tucked away. In their place, Ethel's questions now rest on the thigh of his crossed leg. Shenkenberg takes his seat as the crowd settles down and waits for the host Meiselman to continue. Hoping to inject tension into the proceedings, his squinty-eye stare bores into the writer for an uncomfortable length of time. Oddly, or perhaps not oddly, simply a case of great minds thinking alike, Ethel's opening question, like Meiselman's intended opening question, focuses on Shenkenberg's homecoming, asking the writer how it feels to "be back."

Shenkenberg parts his knees and stoops. He relaxes both forearms across his thighs, hands dangling in the space between his legs, the microphone lolling in his hand. Several strong whooshes of air expel from his nostrils before answering.

A visit to New Niles, he tells the audience, is more than anything, for him, a chance to visit Hubs, the rib joint across the street from the shul his family attended when he was a boy. He tells a story to explain his answer, one that he fills with low, creaky pauses of "and, uh," as if pained by the effort to regurgitate this reminiscence. "Every Shabbat morning, Father forced me to sit through hours of prayers. And, uh. Father would snap at me to stop daydreaming and start praying or I could forget that *cholent* at Kiddush. Don't tell me you don't smell it! Oh, I smelled something, but it wasn't beans and potatoes boiling away in a slow-cooker downstairs in the social hall. It was the smell of barbecue wafting in from across the street and wringing my adolescent innards. And, uh. Some of the best ribs I've ever eaten. Saturday morning, right when they open, is the time to go."

Then Shenkenberg tells of a second mandatory stop when returning home, one also centering on an eagerness to eat treyf. An old Jewish lady with an Old World accent who lived in the apartment above him in East Rogers Park, his last Chicago address before moving to New York. And, uh. A running joke about him not having a woman to cook for him. And, uh. A frying pan of paella left on his doorstep every Sunday night. And, uh. The clams and shrimp decoratively nestled into the rice.

Every mention of treyf meats and seafood leaves Meiselman feeling the castrating crush of his tight leg cross and the full bend of scoliotic stoop. Do these stories leave any question that he is less worldly, less experienced than the man across from him? This is supposed to be a debate, a conversation, and instead he is like a fifth wheel in a conversation about mortgage refinancing, beers, cycling, and child-rearing. But is this not the writer's purpose for talking treyf in front of this primarily Jewish crowd of kosher keepers? To make Meiselman and his coreligionists feel inexperienced, unworldly? People like Shenkenberg see men—and women—of religious rectitude as possessing prim hearts and genteel imaginations. Tethered to ritual, to routine, practiced at shutting out temptation, how can the religious man—and woman—understand anything about dark urges? Sheltered squares. Trapped in desiccating cocoons. The boys—and girls—who fail to sprout. Shenkenberg, meanwhile, the beautiful butterfly tasting from this and that. How many times has Shenkenberg used the word "liberated" in this answer, which thankfully comes to a close?

Ethel deserves credit for not shying away from the Rabbi J- controversy, even if the mention is oblique, and its language of "ruffled a few feathers in narrow quarters" paints the scandalmongers as a crazed minority. The question Meiselman asks in Ethel's name highlights Shenkenberg's "audacity to thinly fictionalize the life of a man revered by so many."

"Overall reception?" Shenkenberg responds, repeating part of the question Meiselman asked in the name of Ethel. "First, let me correct a misconception. I'd set out to write a book about a man and his father. The first scene I put down is the one of Ely walking in on his father using his wife's razor to cut his inner thighs. Out of that came the scene of Ely walking in on a tipsy Rabbi J—in his undershirt and boxers, a near-empty bottle of Manischewitz on the side table. This sequence kept on repeating itself. Father. Rabbi J-. Father. Rabbi J-. What did the proximity of these two men and their stories mean?" Shenkenberg is speaking explosively. Gone are the "and uhs." He has straightened his back, and he is practically off his chair. "It's not enough for him to kill his own father. Liberation, for him, means killing any potential fathers, too."

Who is asking to hear Meiselman's musings on fatherhood? Or is it childhood Shenkenberg is pondering?

Shenkenberg breaks to ask Meiselman if that's a good answer to the question, then apologizes for the digression before continuing without waiting for Meiselman's blessing.

"The crudities are what I anticipated they'd be up in arms over, the sex stuff. Ely lusting after the Russian teenager in the Krakow cemetery." Meiselman now wishes he had given the book a more careful reading. "Yes, I am surprised 'the narrow people in narrow quarters' took greater issue with the scenes of Ely and Rabbi J-watching old Mohammed Ali fights and episodes of *Murder She Wrote*. But I'm also not surprised."

Who is asking to hear a story from Meiselman's time as a student of Rabbi J-? Granted, a rather pitiful memory.

Senior year of high school, the signs for Spring Review went up. Meiselman put his usual personal prayer on hold—I ask that you give the White Sox an opportunity to fairly compete by keeping the team healthy, not allowing injuries to linger, and instilling wisdom and judiciousness in the manager and coaches, and fairness in the umpires—to ask God's help in arranging for Ethel to be his Spring Review date. It should be that when I enter the Lewinson house it is without embarrassment over past episodes, and while impressing Mr. Lewinson with small talk about post high school plans, Ethel will come down the stairs in a gown similar to the one she wore at her bat-mitzvah. God should forgive me for introducing such impure thoughts into my prayers. Let it not jeopardize my request. I cannot force it from my mind. See, I tried and failed. Oh, it's just getting dirtier. Out, out. Provide me with the profoundly American experience of having a girl slide a boutonniere through the slit of my tuxedo collar. Allow me to cuff her wrist with a white corsage. Ethel does not do pink, as God knows. Of course you know. You are God.

A week passed and God had still not infused Meiselman with the courage needed to ask Ethel. One day, Rabbi J-, who had not spoken directly to Meiselman all year, asked him to stay after the bell.

"This is a girl, who is causing you this disturbance?" Rabbi J- asked. What else in Meiselman's mind had the rabbi seen? "She is one of the girls who sits on the bench outside the room?" Meiselman nodded. "Then, like two spies we will walk past the benches and you will show me her."

Rabbi J- gripped Meiselman's flexed bicep, and they shuffled down the hallway. Reaching the water fountain at the end, Rabbi J- whispered, "The one in all the black? Maybe now I will examine her eyes?" On the return to the classroom, the two spies stopped in front of Ethel, who looked up from her notebook and smiled back at the rabbi. Why, on the day of her evaluation, did she have to wear the necklace with the skull?

Back in the classroom, sandwiching Meiselman's hand, Rabbi J- announced his findings. "The whites of her eyes are clear, but it is white all around. So this is good and this is not good. This is sign of strength and this is sign of weakness."

"No, Rebbe. She is the strongest."

Plucking a wrapper-free sucker from the pocket of his suit vest and handing it to Meiselman, Rabbi J- asked, "You like sour?" Then he patted Meiselman's leg and said, "Maybe if you read for us from the *gemara* tomorrow it will help clean the mind?"

He never ended up asking Meiselman to read from the *gemara*, but later that week, Ethel suggested to Meiselman that they go to Spring Review together, since neither of them had a date. She told him to beep his horn, since her father still spoke weirdly about what happened in the bathroom when they were kids. "And we aren't going to do any of that flower crap," she added.

"We tell ourselves we're searching, but we're scared to go down the dark alleys," Shenkenberg says, still wrapping up his answer about the controversy. "This is what haunts me on a daily basis."

Who is asking to hear what haunts Meiselman on a daily basis?

She in the first row, whose black-nailed fingers wag in the air with the other sprung hands the moment Meiselman opens the floor to questions. That's who. But he is resistant to call on her, because what if her aim is to humiliate him in public? Speaking of hidden lives, she might say, perhaps the audience is interested in hearing about a creepy library administrator who spends his time at work stalking young women, touching them accidentally, and looking to trade favors. And yet is it not possible that, finally, after thirty-six years, God has taken notice of his suffering servant in New Niles and set a scheme in motion last week, one that put the pink-haired woman in Meiselman's path, all for the purpose of this moment that will have her asking a question that will work in Meiselman's favor, a question that will lead to his liberation? So after Shenkenberg answers someone else's question about whether he always wanted to be a writer, Meiselman calls on "the young woman in the suit with the bunned hair. Please stand."

The pink-haired woman drones—not surprisingly—drawing on personal anecdotes about memoirs stacked on her mother's nightstand and a great uncle who wrote a book about bringing baseball to the sub-Sahara. Her necklace's pendent is outside her shirt, clutched in her fist, and she jerks it up and back along the chain as she speaks. A hand out in Meiselman's direction, she clarifies that the question is for the "moderator" and not the "guest." Were you hoping a plagiarized paper would have me stuck in New Niles for the rest of my life like you, he fears she is about to ask, until he realizes from her silence that the question had been delivered during his brief reverie; an ebullient "thank you both" is delivered before sitting down.

Indeed, she is his liberator. You've made it to the stage, is the pink-haired woman's message. The light shines on you the same as it does for Shenkenberg, while the rest of us sit cramped in narrow seats on the other side, faceless in the dark. Now is the time for you to earn your bread. Show everyone else what you've shown me this week. Not wanting to betray that he has been caught off guard, he works off the assumption she is asking about memoir proliferation, particularly those focusing on themes of overcoming. Grabbing the neon index cards of questions prepared for Shenkenberg, which moments ago he had tucked between the armrest and cushion, he places them against his knee, on top of Ethel's pages. After a quick perusal of the second card, he knocks back his head and glances into the blinding stage lights above, as if the ideas he is about to impart are extemporaneous.

"Oscar Wilde believed that no man is truthful," Meiselman starts. "'Give him a mask,' he said, 'and he will tell you the truth.' But what about the truths we tell ourselves? Do we need masks for this? What do we make of our guest writer's decision to mask his own name, but not Rabbi J-'s?" He lowers his eyes to read the next card before lifting them again to the lights. "Writers see themselves as members of a truth commission tasked with exposing the 'very human' qualities of people, but for what purpose?" Unable to riff on this argument he turns to the final index card, the one with the indicting, potentially undermining, question. "Which connects to a recently noticed trend of people, especially artists, presenting themselves as hermits, estranged, ostracized, constantly insisting they would feel more comfortable elsewhere. Meanwhile, everyone, for the most part, stays put. How many people are bold enough to sever ties, move off to the UP, and start from scratch? Incidentally, this, I believe, connects to what is at the heart of the controversy surrounding the book. The book's critics are not angry with the book, but are bothered—even jealous—by the ease at which the author disowns his past, without inward or outward conflict." Careful to exude dispassion, he looks Shenkenberg in the eye and triggers his finger at him. "You, they feel, flaunt your disconnect. You relish in disowning, discrediting past affiliations, tribal and familial, presenting them as lighthearted horrors. You make disengaging seem easy, exhilarating. But, when it comes down to it, is there anyone more connected than you? Read your books. Holocaust this, rabbis that, Israel, shul, shofars, shiksas." Fearful he is red in the face and spouting more than speaking, Meiselman smiles and goes for earnest. "Look at your readership? People who work daily to maintain the status quo. Status quo, for the record, is not necessarily a pejorative. Status quo, some would argue, keeps upheaval at bay."

The silence of the crowd is palpable. Has this rant left him underwater? But before he can degrade his speech as rambling, stilted, and another angry misfire, Shenkenberg, his former nemesis, says into the microphone, "Ethel said this would be a light, friendly chat. Nothing light about that. Possibly unfriendly," tagging it with a laugh to show it is said in jest. Then, he lets out a groan and tilts his head back, the buttery yellow lights above splattering his face as he contemplates an answer. Dropping his head, he goes back to massaging his shin. He brings the microphone to his lips and calmly says, "Essentially, our moderator is accusing me of having my cake and eating it too. A fair point. Every single one of us—unless we grow up in a truly closed society—works at some point in life to become our own rebbe. Some fail with nothing more than a weak attempt to show for it. Some succeed effortlessly. Most, however, stay engaged in the struggle until the day they die. Do I think my success means I'm better, freer, less encumbered, and that I operate with a greater self-awareness than people still tethered and tied to a world of rules and rituals? More often than not, I do. But that doesn't mean it's a fair assessment. And it—eating ribs and shellfish—doesn't mean I'm free, either." Shenkenberg wriggles to the edge of his seat, puts forward a leg in the direction of the pink-haired woman and stares directly at her. "Thinking it is without qualms or downright pain, as the moderator suggests, maybe says something about his fantasy of the situation," he says. "Only a sociopath embraces the position of rebbe with ease, without mourning over the killed fathers. The book is titled *The Sad Rebbe*." Finally, turning to Meiselman, he says, "'Very human,' I like that. Might steal it."

Without missing a beat, Meiselman responds, "Please, it would be an honor," and Shenkenberg's snort is followed by a solid chuckle from the audience. Then, when Meiselman suggests to the guest that they take another question, Shenkenberg snappily says, "You sure you don't have any more questions for me? I'm rather enjoying this hot stoving." And they all laugh again. These exchanges are not Meiselman merely generating a festive mood by reading Ethel's words. Unadulterated Meiselman is feeding this merriment. The crowd's laughter is appreciation for the high-minded repartee between the men on the stage. Shenkenberg and Meiselman mesh. The audience sees them as operating on the same plane. The audience sees them as operating on the same plane! This is why the pink-haired woman's head bobbed in discernment as

Meiselman gave his answer. Did he not see his father knock his mother on the shoulder and give her a wild-eyed shake of the head as if saying, Who knew he knew about such things? If Meiselman could find Deena anywhere in the crowd, he likes to think he would have seen her whispering to Molly, Oh, yes, despite what I've told you about his fastidiousness and creepy nighttime assaults, the man is no jackass. He has many provocative theories.

Do you not wish you could sustain this feeling forever, Dr. Lin may ask, if he chooses to open tomorrow's session with this triumphant episode? He does, he does. To accomplish this, he must treat Shenkenberg as a co-panelist for the rest of the evening. So when Shenkenberg responds to an audience member's question with the rhetorical, "Does satisfying this curiosity make my protagonist a bad person? Your girlfriend's diary is lying open on the bed. Do you not read it?" Meiselman answers, "I'm married," and it comes out sounding wry and gets a solid laugh from the audience. "Definitely don't want to read it then," Shenkenberg responds, getting a bigger laugh that explodes when Meiselman slips in a "touché."

This high-quality banter continues when a kippa-wearing college kid with a neat side part and goatee asks, "Why do you think so many young Jewish writers still write about the Holocaust? Is it not a beating off of the proverbial dead horse?"

Shenkenberg answers, "First, I am not that young. Second, I did it for the press. If a writer features the Holocaust in his or her book, it's a guarantee people will debate the book's merits and pass judgment even without having read it. And it will fall into either one of two categories. Genius, or anti-Semitic. Take Primo Levi. Find me five people here who have read a Primo Levi book, but everyone loves the guy."

Shenkenberg eyes Meiselman as if cuing his co-panelist.

"Or Elie Wiesel," Meiselman says. "Night, Day, Morning, Dinner. Read one of them in high school, and I can't tell you a thing about it, yet, when asked, I feel compelled to say it's a masterpiece."

With every question and answer, Meiselman thinks of ways to insert theories that until now have drummed the inside of his mind, just awaiting recipients: I read once that every person harbors the fantasy of either writing a book, opening a restaurant, or designing a building. And: Jewish humor trades in anti-Semitic stereotypes. The Jew as miser, wimp, brainy.

Yet, sadly, gone are the days of Lincoln-Douglas when people could endure the exchange of profundities for hours on end. As much as Meiselman never wants this to stop, since at the next event Ethel will be back on the stage, and he will be the one running up the aisles passing notes, nobody asking what he thinks of the state of Jewish fiction, or what role Jewish writers have in bringing peace to the Middle East, the audience will turn resentful if he and Shenkenberg go on much longer. Free food is, by now, all that is on the minds of audience members.

Meanwhile, Ethel has "Closing Remarks" for him to read, most probably a crowing over the library's accomplishments under her stewardship, a semi-technical ramble aimed at the village higher-ups that guarantees to drain the excitement Meiselman and Shenkenberg generated. He will be forced to speak over throat clearings and coughs and the rustling of coats and bags as attendees prepare to charge the aisles. So after Shenkenberg answers a question about influences, Meiselman abstains from sharing a Colin Powell anecdote and, instead, returns to the podium to lead everyone in a round of deafening applause that is surely meant for them, the team of Meiselman and Shenkenberg.

Another fork in the road. Ethel, in her closing remarks, is asking Meiselman to introduce Mitchell to say a few words. From the corner of his eye, he spots Mitchell's wife straightening her husband's tie and dusting off the shoulders of his suit jacket. Meiselman is not sure how much of an appetite the crowd has for listening to Mitchell's outlandish plans for the library's digital future, but he cannot think of any other option but to comply. Besides, he is anxious to bring the evening to a close so he can go out and receive 'atta boys' and back slaps from the underlings and attendees and, of course, his parents, and Deena, if she is here.

Upon hearing his name, Mitchell stands and approaches the stage, pulling remarks from his jacket's inner pocket. Meiselman, buoyed by his victory tonight, settles on a two-handed shake for the underling, but Mitchell thwarts the effort and comes at the Events and Programs Coordinator with arms out wide for a bearish hug that ends with a mussing of Meiselman's curls. Meiselman stands slightly back, so he can rush Mitchell off if he goes on for too long.

"Let us have a round of applause for tonight's moderator extraordinaire," Mitchell says from the lectern, his British accent thicker than ever. "Ethel will certainly be proud and thrilled to hear how glorious an evening this turned out to be, a genuine celebration of a fine author, a fine book, and suburban Chicago's largest library. She will not, however, be surprised." Looking back at Meiselman he says, "Your supreme work ethic and obsessive devotion are no secret to the people who work with you."

Is this how respect sounds?

"As only a handful of you know," Mitchell continues, "for the last year, our dear director Ethel Lewinson has been saddled with considerable health issues. Despite its greatest efforts, the enormous, superior strength of this illness has failed to subdue or conquer her. With the pressing work of securing funds for the library's expansion, not to mention the day-to-day responsibilities of bolstering our various collections and planning original and prolific programming like tonight's event, resistance was her only option. But in the coming years, the library will face considerable challenges, like reengineering our innovative computer databases, which are already the envy of libraries across the country. And as we move to the future, the library's mission," Mitchell says, "must be safeguarded. Quote: 'As a springboard for personal growth and to raise the level of civilization, New Niles Public Library promotes discovery, enrichment, and the exchange of ideas through a broad spectrum of materials, technologies, and experiences. It resists abridgment of free expression and free access to ideas, and/or denying or abridging a person's right to use the library because of origin, age, background, or views. The library reflects the pride the community takes in itself.' End quote. We must continue promoting these values. We cannot become solely a space for fast, free internet.

"Because of her recent poor health, Ethel, at this time, lacks the necessary energy to work on the expansion. Therefore, several weeks ago, she submitted her resignation to the Village of New Niles, effective tomorrow morning. Finding a replacement, a person equipped with the industriousness and passion needed to lead our library into this challenging, yet exciting age, was not a particularly laborious task."

In hindsight, Meiselman's agitation over the tepid tribute earlier suddenly seems overblown. Shielding his gloat over the news Mitchell is about to share with the crowd is proving difficult. He can feel the sink in his cheeks as the underling prepares to announce him as Ethel's replacement, and he is suddenly fearful that he will be caught smiling, a rather indecent look, especially given the horrific news about Ethel. Oh, God, yes. His concern is definitely for Ethel's health.

"I, Mitchell Eliot, have humbly and graciously accepted her offer to lead our library into the future..."

Meiselman's core empties. What one feels in that brief moment when he thinks the wallet has gone missing. But the wallet is not right there in the back pocket. Relief does not come. Instead, a numbness spreads to his extremities. Then, horrible pressure on his anus, like he has to shit. Fighting it off with a tight clench, the fibrous muscles around his mouth begin twitching. His face is buckling, and he cannot blink away the tears blurring his eyes.

The first cry leaks out of him, the squeak of a small rodent. Eyes cinched, he buries his face in his hands to fight back what he knows is coming. Here he figured his spilling at Deena's bedside the other night was hitting a nadir, the kind that sets someone on a course correction. Now there will be no triumphant march into Dr. Lin's office tomorrow. Instead she will hear of increasingly frequent breakdowns, first private, and then public. He can expect some hippie claptrap about men not needing to hide emotions. She will ask if his father is a crier. Inside and outside the man does not shed a tear. Leaves the emoting to the wife. Or the doctor will linger on his use of the term 'breaking down.' You use it figuratively, but what about literally? Have you been keeping up with your teeth? Your hair, especially the crown, does not have the bounce I remember. On your medical form you checked the box "other" and noted an inability to impregnate the wife.

From the quiet in the room—Mitchell has paused his remarks—he can tell his swallowed sobs and muted weeps have stunned everyone into silence. He dares not lift his head. An arm wraps the back of his body, a hand gripping his shoulder. The new director, the new number one, reels him in for a side hug. From his pants pocket, Meiselman pulls out something and dabs at his eyes before giving his nose a solid blow. Looks down: again, Deena's underwear. Mitchell whispers his concern into Meiselman's ear. He says, "She was afraid you would take it this hard, given the relationship and everything."

"Sorry, this is all just too much." Meiselman is now almost right in front of the microphone, and his gusty breathing as he works to compose himself carries through the room. "Poor Ethel," Meiselman says, his lips grazing the microphone's mesh head. "Not only a boss." He looks over to the underlings and says, "She's like a mother, sister, and daughter to us. Dare I say, a rebbe?" The underlings, especially Betsy Ross, assent with mournful nodding. "Seeing her as fragile is tough. Steady and resolute in her beliefs. Willing to stand up to oppressors. Can tell you stories from when we were children. But this is not a time for eulogies. This is a celebration, and no better way to celebrate her than by continuing this great evening." As if poking fun at his outburst, he clears his throat, smiles broadly, and asks, "Were we in the middle of something?" which gets a warm laugh, but it rings disingenuous, as if everyone in the auditorium has been tasked with bucking up poor Meiselman.

Throughout all of this, Shenkenberg has been staring into his lap, twisting the cap of his water bottle, restlessly rocking his foot, doing his best to appear disengaged, to show the attendees that the maneuverings and drama of this small village do not interest or concern him in the slightest. Does not even bother clapping along with the rest of the crowd as Mitchell continues delivering his prepared remarks, which are rife with campaign speak utterances about "children being the future of New Niles," "a shining library on the flat lands of suburban Chicago," and "if we could handle Y2K, we can tackle any challenge." Meiselman does not have the luxury of appearing bored and detached.

Mitchell invites everyone to the reception, and when he says into the microphone, "Betsy, please," the lights go up, and the applause is thunderous. The new director acknowledges the ovation with a hoist of his umbrella, which fuels the crowd. He points the umbrella's tip at various sections of the audience, mouthing thank-yous to various supporters. The weird habits of successful people are heralded as signs of genius and eccentricity, while the eccentricities of life's losers are summarily dismissed as creepy.

Assuming his loved ones will stay behind to check on his state, Meiselman tarries, carrying out janitorial tasks like turning off the sound system, chucking Shenkenberg's empty water bottle, and cleaning "Reserved" signs off the floor and chairs. But the room empties completely, except for a burly, bearded fellow in the top row huddled behind a laptop screen, his cramped fingers feverishly typing. Slogging up the staircase, Meiselman soon identifies the man, who constantly pauses to wipe his oily lenses across the front of his salmon pink polo.

"Holy cow! What a scoop! Am I glad I showed up," Barry Kranzler says to Meiselman, without looking up from the screen. "Ethel resigning! A new director! I'm going to need a quote."

"Now?"

"Hey, you wanted to assemble a pool."

"Okay. As Events and Programs Coordinator...No. We here, um. We here at the library...Wait."

"Nothing profound. Filler for a puff piece. Something sappy."

"Ethel Lewinson, a boss who stirred her workers to dream different—"

"Something Jewish, please. Actually, could use that in the version I sell the *New Niles Village Voice*. The Jewish angle for my paper. How about," Barry Kranzler's fingers flutter over the keyboard before he sets them down, bellowing, "The diverse Jewish community of New Niles, who are great supporters of the library, should not expect any changes to the dynamic, Jewish-related programming they've come to expect and appreciate over the years. Sign off on that, will you?"

Sick of other people putting words in his mouth, Meiselman is inclined to decline, tell Kranzler he will get back to him when he drafts something profound, perhaps a pun that insinuates his reservations about the choice. But Barry Kranzler will not wait. He will approach Mitchell or Ada, Betsy Ross or June, and it will be an underling, and not Meiselman, who has the thrill of spotting his or her name in print, so he nods.

Outside the auditorium, the baker Paprocki has outdone himself. The elegance of the reception far surpasses Meiselman's expectations. Transformed into a banquet hall, the main floor is bathed in a dim, gold light, glittery gold streamers hanging low across the ceiling, gold linen covering the serving tables. Waiters and waitresses in tight black t-shirts and silky black pants clear soiled plates and glasses from small cocktail tables. On the food tables, halved and hollowed pineapples are repurposed as serving bowls for other tropical fruits. Cheesecakes rest on crystal cake trays of varying heights. Baklava crams lacquered blocks of wood. Someone—not Meiselman—decided on using ceramic plates, proper silverware, and wine glasses.

A receiving line of trustees and patrons wait to bestow good wishes on the new director and his wife. There is guffawing, shoulder slapping, rigorous handshaking. The other attendees crowd the tables, fressing. Meiselman stands alone, everyone steering clear of him and his grief.

"The baklava sure looks good." It is his mother's voice. She is advancing behind him. "Are you sure we can't eat it?" she asks her husband, to no response.

His father pulls at Meiselman's elbow and murmurs into his son's ear, "What does all this shuffling mean for you? Need me to call my guy—"

"Everything was delightful," his mother deposits into his other ear. When he turns around, he catches her shooting her husband a scolding glance.

His father says, "My only question is whether, after so much time off, you would need to take a licensing exam to get back in the game."

"Did you know that about Ethel?" his mother asks. "I suspected something. Ran into her mother a couple months back at Germanic and she mentioned the back troubles, and I remember how it usually means it's in the bones—"

"If this guy becomes president, taxes are going to go through the roof and there will be a real need for scrupulous, yet creative accountants—"

"You should really call—"

"You should really write—"

"It's the nice thing to do—"

"Don't take the chance—"

Which voice does he engage? They are the parents of a grown man who cried in front of a roomful of people, and they have not a word of comfort to provide. They are not speaking to his grief because they cannot speak to his grief. For this you have a wife, his mother would probably answer, if he ever voiced this frustration. And she would be right, and it is why he has someone like Dr. Lin, too. But where is his wife in this crucial moment of need? Giggling it up with her new best friend Molly? Tickling herself with the thought that her husband is ripe for further ultimatums?

Choosing not to engage either one, he nods along to the hectoring.

"Did I tell you about the son of my proctologist, Dr. LaFleur—"

"Such an independent-minded girl. One wonders if that isn't part of the problem. Never married, not religious—"

"Really, it's not a question of if, it's a question of when a man will have to—"

“Her father, I don’t feel bad for him. Such an animal. You may not remember, but once when you were a boy—”

“You’re going to want to stop playing around and start a family. With day school, orthodontia, dermatology, nice vacations—”

“What do you know about nice vacations—”

A hand grips Meiselman’s side. “Don’t forget the pearls, Meisie,” Deena says in that tone, her hair nuzzling the shoulder of his sport jacket. “I expect a fat pearl necklace.”

The arrival of Deena silences his parents, each stepping forward to kiss the daughter-in-law on the cheek. As the parents broach the stressful topics of the night, Deena is quick to squash the talk with assurances that there is nothing to worry about. “He’s good,” she says about her husband, not necessarily a vote of confidence in him, but a reminder that they shouldn’t parent in front of her. From the way Deena is rubbing his back, working the heel of her hand into the space between his blades, he believes she is showing mercy and allowing the petty problems from this past week to slide, for the meantime. He is not about to remind her they still cannot touch. Surely she has chosen to disregard.

Her hand falls away the moment they separate from his parents. She does not offer encouragement or sympathy. She does not try bucking him up through other means. What comes out of her mouth is a command. “Take her to meet Shenkenberg.” He spots Molly waiting in the wings. Only once they start walking does she say “thank you” before dropping back so she is in stride with her friend.

They find the author holding a plate with a fork impaled into a half-eaten piece of chocolate cheesecake. The pink-haired woman is standing next to him, nibbling the lip of an empty juice glass.

“Ah, so you’ve met,” Meiselman says to them.

“Oh, yes,” Shenkenberg responds.

“Although we keep getting interrupted. Mr. Important here,” the pink-haired woman says, poking Shenkenberg in the chest.

“Just trying to sell books, girl,” the writer says, putting his hand on the pink-haired woman’s shoulder, carefully lifting a cheesecake-smeared index finger so as not to sully her suit.

Meiselman makes the introductions, and Molly and Shenkenberg begin talking. Apparently, Molly thinks of herself as a writer. At first, the threesome of Meiselman, Deena, and the pink-haired woman listen in. But they cannot keep up with the shop talk—point of view, authorial decisions—and soon break away.

Introducing the pink-haired woman to his wife ends up being less fraught than he would have imagined. “One of our eager beavers here at the library,” he explains to Deena. “Although, we’ll be losing her. Off to NYU in New York.”

“Your husband is a godsend,” the pink-haired woman says to Deena, and from there she is soon on automatic, sharing with Deena her home and school situations, peppering her account with those words from the other day. She tells his wife about the paper, and the afternoons spent upstairs, and he does not know whether he should be glad or fearful that Deena is probably teeming with jealousy, but when he looks over to his wife he spots nothing but boredom in her face. She knocks back her drained glass of seltzer, an ice cube sliding into her mouth where it clinks against her teeth before she blows it back into the glass. She engages the young woman with a polite smile before taking the ice cube back into her mouth. Seconds later, the munching of ice is competing with the tale of the pink-haired woman’s “episode.” On the other side of Meiselman, Molly, hand on her hips, pecks her head like a clucking chicken, as she digests the writer’s words, the fingers of her other hand pinching and wriggling her pearl earring. Deena makes brief eye contact with Meiselman before turning back to the pink-haired woman and saying, “Geez, sounds rough.”

Standing between these twosomes, Meiselman loses the thread of both conversations. More pressing concerns enter his mind. Informing the foursome he has library business to attend to, he excuses himself. Only the pink-haired woman reacts to his withdrawal. She points to Shenkenberg and says, "If the two of us are gone by the time you get back, then *ciao*, and thanks for everything."

Disappointing, but not surprising. Like all young people in this country—except for the brave men and women serving—the pink-haired woman flits from opportunity to opportunity, everything quid pro quo. She was never ripe for instruction. Having seen nothing, she thinks she knows everything. Give Meiselman your tired, poor, and hungry. Give him Kotek?

On his way to the back offices, Meiselman passes Betsy Ross and Ada, who lean against the circulation desk sampling cheesecake off each other's plates. The secretary gives a thumbs-up and rubs her busting stomach. Ada gives him a smile that may be interpreted as sad.

The moment the door to the administrative offices swings closed behind him, he feels himself entering the zone, as if he knew this day would come and had been preparing for it all along. In Ethel's office, he finds the photograph on the desk where he left it this morning. The clasps on the frame's back rotate smoothly. The photograph of Ethel and her mom at her bat-mitzvah sticks to the glass, but he peels it off without harming the image. It fits perfectly into the back pocket of his pants. The frame is too bulky for any pocket, so he stashes it under his blazer, using a forearm to secure it against his body. In the break room, he kicks the overflowing can several times, balled paper towels and granola bar wrappers tumbling to the ground. Using a clean paper towel as a glove, he removes several more layers of peels and balled aluminum foil. Ceremoniously, he sets down the frame in the can and covers it with the removed trash. Before dealing with the photograph, he returns to the office to filch something from his briefcase, because now is the time to finally recover some ground.

How paranoid his mother's discovery has made him? He cannot risk bringing the photograph home. Betsy Ross and Ada are no longer using Circulation as a table, and Meiselman manages the ten-foot walk to the staircase without being noticed. The library's second floor is dark except for the yellow streetlights filtering in through the windows and the emergency exit signs at the far ends of the open floor. Eyes adjusting to the scant light, he skitters across the carpeted floor and through the aisles of Kids Area's low bookcases. Reaching the rendezvous spot behind History, he immediately spots a thick tome that is sufficient for his purposes. *For Good and for Evil: Theodore Roosevelt's "The Man with the Muck-rake."* The book's threadbare binding, its yellowed tape peeling off the spine, makes it particularly ideal. As suspected, the most recent return date stamped into the inner cover is February 28, 1991. Even if a patron were to peruse this book, is there a chance he or she would make it past page three hundred? He stashes the photograph in the later chapters, but before the index, and then misplaces the book by returning it to the shelf that starts with the Zs.

Most of the attendees have left and the main floor's standard lighting has returned, exposing soiled tables and cheesecake-smeared carpeting. Fyodor "Fred" Galitsky, always anxious to make a couple extra dollars, uncoils the vacuum cleaner's cord. Meiselman steps to the circle of Molly, Deena, and his parents.

"I agree," Meiselman's mother is saying.

"They should never have let him speak," his father adds.

"And the worst part is," Molly is saying, but before Meiselman can hear what the worst part is, Deena engages him and says, "We were just discussing the Klopman controversy?"

“Is that the thing with the Jesus symphony?”

“No,” they all seem to correct him simultaneously.

“The movie,” his mother answers.

Not in any mood to engage himself in another controversy, he pulls the Willie Nelson disc from his pants, holds it up to Deena, and says, “Was clearing out my office and look what I found.”

“Why were you clearing out your office?” his mother asks.

“That’s our CD,” Deena answers. Is that giddiness or forlornness in her voice? Definitely not a trace of sarcasm.

“Wait, he’s clearing out his office?” his father asks his mother.

“Willie Nelson? I swear, you two are so queer,” Molly teases. “Mine and Jeremy’s disc is—”

“Haven’t heard this in ages,” Deena says, staring down at the case’s cover. A smile breaks across her face as she adds, “Remember how you—”

“Waitwaitwait,” his father says, grabbing Meiselman’s elbow, turning them away from the group, saying to him in a hushed voice loud enough for everyone to hear, as if he needs them to know he is acting fatherly. “Does this shuffling mean—”

“Cleaning up. Not clearing out. Something I do before I speak. Clears the mind of its clutter so I could have that laser focus you all just witnessed.” He says, “You two need to get your hearing checked. You can’t hear past yourself.” Deena and Molly laugh at the outrageousness of someone speaking like this to his parents, and in this moment, liberated Meiselman can see how it will unfold with Dr. Lin tomorrow.

In the waiting room, he will flip aimlessly through a back issue of *Newsweek*, leg fidgeting as he anticipates the doctor’s greeting. When she welcomes him without a word, holding the door open for him in the same manner she did week after week so many years ago, it will come as a letdown.

The office will have undergone a thorough remodeling, a white shag rug now covering most of the wood floor, tiny-framed black and white photographs of fallen, desiccated leaves hanging on the white walls. Despite years of regret over never having tested the efficacy of lying down for a session, he will sit properly, wanting the doctor to think he remains mildly skeptical of the process. Though, this time, he will avoid childishly tucking his hands under his thighs. A strand of lustrous gray at the front of her otherwise black head of hair will be the only noticeable difference in how the doctor looks. Behind her, the white wooden blinds will stayed closed, as always, and she will sit with her legs up on a black ottoman, folded bifocals clutched in her hand.

Wanting to show the doctor he returns from his hiatus a changed man, now verbose and uninhibited, Meiselman will open the session right away by saying, "Endured a significant trauma this past week," looking her straight in the eyes because during their prior union she occasionally wanted to explore why he spent the entire session staring down into his lap, once asking if this was an issue he had when facing men. She pointed out that he was, in fact, looking down at his penis.

"You are not a mind reader," the doctor will agree. "She never did explicitly ask for your help." Still, she will find the story edifying, utilizing the next pause to recall Meiselman's initial reason for coming to her during the transition years.

"Not nudes," Meiselman will have to correct the doctor's recollection of the photographs. "And I didn't know she was my grandmother. For me, it was all about the bathing suit, the pinup pose."

"Your mind, on some level, must have noticed the resemblance?"

Dr. Lin will ask if the dead neighbor bears a likeness to his grandmother and, if so, whether it has anything to do with his mother's objection to the woman.

"My mother, come to think of it, despises most elderly ladies. She hated another neighbor, Mrs. Schulhof. Accused her of beating her husband."

The doctor will use the next silence to accuse Meiselman of avoiding the episode they were discussing before they took their multi-year break.

"We were," she will tell him, "trying to understand your expectations in sharing with your mother this terrible story of suffering abuse at the hands of your classmates, you being the butt of their practical joke."

The doctor will review how they had already established the foolishness of the plan his mother came up with after he relayed to her the story, the arrangement in no way sparing Meiselman of further humiliations.

"It's like she was not speaking to my grief," he said to the doctor. "As if she were addressing only her anxiety of the situation."

The doctor, forever eager to hollow out bedrocks, will salute this analysis, even using her signature line, "Now you're cooking with gas." To show they are on the verge of a breakthrough, she will put her legs down and sit forward. "Quite a burden for a young boy to always have to come up with the right words."

Meiselman will come to his mother's defense.

"We've always shared this language of feeding each other our dismay. I knew how to get a reaction, the right reaction. More than my father. He didn't want to hear from her."

Months from now, he will feel the drain of sitting in near-silence for forty-five minutes each week.

“Maybe I’m reluctant to progress,” he will finally say to the doctor. “I disagree,” she will answer, before tallying his achievements, turning minor triumphs into major ones, like his new routine of stopping at Cracowaia before work for a post-breakfast snack. “Testing your palette with not-kosher delicacies like brioche, cannolis, whoopee pies, moon pies, and bear claws. Without religious reservations or guilt, I should add.” “Some religious reservations,” he will correct her. The tallying will continue: befriending the waitress—who would have guessed Kotek is studying criminology? His willingness to arrive to work a little before nine, without concern of how he is viewed by his fellow administrators. “Some concern,” he will correct her again; being less dogmatic about catching every inning of every White Sox game, and showing an enthusiasm to watch Deena’s shows, will also be counted as victories. Would he spend his nights watching waifish, pale women competing for arbitrary titles if the White Sox were making a late-season push? Doubtful. The doctor will even applaud him for his breakdown at Ethel’s memorial, one so severe he could not continue, forcing him to ask Mitchell to finish reading his prepared remarks.

The doctor will challenge Meiselman to ask his father for the deed to the house, and to express a readiness to assume the mortgage payments. It will represent, in her mind, a major step toward liberation. But every time he envisions this moment, he will tell the doctor that he hears that classic Islamic proverb. Or is it a fortune cookie quote, or something he read in the newspaper in connection to the two wars, or a theory produced around the time when he had the misunderstanding with Shenkenberg? Whatever its origin, its truth is undeniable. Every story that begins in humiliation must end in humiliation.

Dr. Lin will insist this is false, arguing that one can always work past the shame of earlier episodes and chart a different course. "Nothing is final in life. Everything can be undone."

"Like the saying, 'Streaks are made to be broken'?"

"The saying, I believe, is 'Streaks are meant to be broken.'"

Even better.

This is more or less how it will unfold.

Acknowledgments

I am grateful to my parents for their endless love, support, and encouragement.

Thank you to my brothers, Yossi and Ezra, for a lifetime of closeness, and for teaching me where to find the funny.

Thank you to my grandmother, Naomi Landes, for our honest conversations about literature and life.

Thank you Aharon and Richard for your deep friendships, encouragement, and guidance.

Thank you Aaron Hamburger. You are a great friend, and the persistence and honesty you bring to everything you do continuously inspires me.

Many thanks to some amazing teachers and mentors, who gave so much of their time to me through years: Joseph Skibell, Jane Bernstein, Allen Hoffman, Jaime Manrique, Binnie Kirshenbaum, Sam Lipsyte.

Thank you to the David Berg Foundation.

Thank you Shaindy Rudoff z"l. Your spirit still inspires me.

Thank you Dr. Samuel Weiss z"l for helping me get to this point.

Thank you Caitlin Hamilton Summie for helping me get this book into the hands of readers.

My profound gratitude to Jerry Brennan. For years, I fantasized about how my publishing journey might look, and I never imagined it would include such a fine editor, caring publisher, and decent person like you. You've made this a much better book.

Dalia, you're always encouraging me to sit and write. Never for what it may amount to, but for what it means to me in the moment.

Hadar and Yishai, I love you, but maybe wait a few years to read this book!

About the Book

Meiselman has had enough. After a life spent playing by the rules, this lonely thirty-six-year-old man—"number two" at a suburban Chicago public library, in charge of events and programs, and in no control whatsoever over his fantasies about his domineering boss—is looking to come out on top, at last. What seems like an ordinary week in 2004 will prove to be a golden opportunity (at least in his mind) to reverse a lifetime of petty humiliations. And no one—not his newly observant wife, not the Holocaust-survivor neighbor who regularly disturbs his sleep with her late-night gardening, and certainly not the former-schoolmate-turned-renowned-author who's returning to the library for a triumphant literary homecoming—will stand in his way.

About the Author

Avner Landes earned an M.F.A. from Columbia University, and has over a dozen ghostwritten titles to his credit. He lives near Tel Aviv with his wife and two children. This is his debut novel.

About Tortoise Books

Slow and steady wins in the end, even in publishing. Tortoise Books is dedicated to finding and promoting quality authors who haven't yet found a niche in the marketplace—writers producing memorable and engaging works that will stand the test of time.

Learn more at www.tortoisebooks.com, find us on Facebook, or follow us on Twitter @TortoiseBooks.

CPSIA information can be obtained
at www.ICGtesting.com
Printed in the USA
JSHW032043160121
10866JS00002B/2

9 781948 954143